# AFTERMATH OF A MURDER

V K McGivney

Printed and bound in Great Britain by Clays Ltd, St Ives plc

Authors Reach
www.authorsreach.co.uk

Cover design by Corinna Edwards-Colledge

ISBN: 978-0-9957883-5-0

With thanks to Corinna, Jill, Maggie, Rashmi and Todd
for all their help and encouragement.

# Chapter 1

The doorbell chimed minutes after Karen Armstrong had settled herself on the patio to enjoy the late afternoon sun. She rose reluctantly from her garden chair and went into the house. When she opened the door she was alarmed to find two uniformed police officers, one male, one female, standing on the front step.

She stared at them as they held up their ID badges. The man was tall and had a prominent Adam's apple. His colleague was short and rather stocky. They both looked very young. Youthfulness in others was something she had started to notice after passing her fortieth birthday.

The policewoman stepped forward, her expression grave. 'Mrs Armstrong?'

'Yes?' Karen nervously pushed her fair hair back behind her ears

'I'm sorry. I'm afraid we have some distressing news.'

Karen was instantly seized with panic. 'Has something happened to one of the children?'

The policewoman looked uncomfortable. 'May we come in?'

She led them rapidly into the living room. '*Tell* me. Is it one of the children?'

The male officer cleared his throat. 'No, it's your husband.'

'Howard?' Karen put a hand to her throat. 'Has something happened to him?'

He coughed. 'I'm afraid there's been an incident.'

'An incident?' she repeated faintly

'Please sit down Mrs Armstrong,' the policewoman said gently.

'I don't want to sit down. What *kind* of an incident? Is Howard alright?'

The policeman shuffled his feet. 'I'm afraid not. He's been…wounded …shot.'

Karen gasped. 'Shot?' She felt the blood drain from her face.

'I'm afraid so.'

'Shot?' she repeated, wondering if this wasn't some kind of ghoulish joke.

He fixed his gaze somewhere above her head. 'According to witnesses, he was coming out of the main door of Bartholomew Court when someone drew up on a motorbike and …shot him.'

'No!' Karen felt the ground sway beneath her feet. She clutched the back of a chair for support. 'That's not possible.'

'I'm sorry, Mrs Armstrong.'

'Oh God!' Karen staggered over to the sofa and collapsed on to it.

The policewoman gazed at her sympathetically. 'Can I get you a glass of water or something?'

'Is he… Is he…dead?' Karen had a horrific vision of her husband lying in a pool of blood on the pavement outside his office.

'No, but he is badly injured. He's been taken to St Catherine's for emergency surgery.'

'I must go to him.' She started to get up from the sofa.

The policewoman put out a restraining hand. 'We'll take you there in a moment. You said you have children?'

Karen made a supreme effort to steady her voice. 'Yes.'

'Are they at home?'

'No.' She tried to collect her thoughts. 'Erica's having a sleepover at a friend's; Simon's at school camp and Poppy's staying with her godmother.' She felt vaguely guilty, although it was extremely rare that all three were away from home at the same time.

'Do you want to contact them before we go to the hospital?'

'Yes, no...I don't know...' Tears started to pour down her cheeks. She rose shakily to her feet, aware that her legs were trembling. 'No, not yet. Not till I know how Howard is.'

'We'll take you to the hospital now.'

Karen grabbed her bag and keys and followed them out to the police car.

'When ...When did it happen?' she asked tremulously as they drove through streets busy with peak-time evening traffic.

'About half past four,' the policewoman answered from the front passenger seat. 'We don't know much yet, Mrs Armstrong. The road's been closed and the front of the building has been sealed off as a crime scene. There'll be forensic and ballistic tests. Everybody who was in the area at the time is being questioned.'

'But who..?' Karen croaked, dabbing at her eyes. 'Do you know who--?'

'Who did it? Not yet.' The policeman steered the car carefully round a corner and stopped at a red light. 'Apparently the perpetrator was wearing a crash helmet and a visor.'

Through the fog that had enveloped her mind, Karen tried to make sense of what was happening. 'How is it possible?' she whispered. 'How could something like this happen in broad daylight?'

'It looks like a professional job,' the policewoman said grimly. 'Your husband seems to have been specifically targeted.'

'Targeted?' Karen repeated. 'Why? Who would target Howard?' Her voice tailed off, and she slumped helplessly back in the seat.

\* \* \*

At the hospital they were informed that Howard had undergone emergency surgery and was in the Intensive Care Unit. Karen was led through a labyrinth of corridors to a waiting area. Too stressed to sit, she paced restlessly up and down a dimly-lit passage, flattening herself against the wall whenever hospital porters hurried past, pushing trolleys bearing white-faced patients on stretchers. It felt chilly. She was still wearing her flimsy sundress and wished she had put on a cardigan.

A woman appeared beside her and laid a gentle hand on her arm. 'Mrs. Armstrong? I'm sorry, but I need to take some details about your husband.'

Karen accompanied her back to the waiting area and was still answering her questions when a group of grave-faced medical staff emerged from the Intensive Care Unit.

After a muttered conversation with the police officers, a man in a white hospital coat approached her. 'Mrs Armstrong? I'm very sorry. We did all we could, but one of the bullets had penetrated...'

Karen didn't hear any more. Her legs gave way and she tried to suppress a wave of nausea. She was half carried to a chair and given a glass of water. When she looked up, she found that she was surrounded by a group of people, a doctor, several nurses and the policewoman. They were gazing at her anxiously and speaking in low voices. Someone felt her pulse; a nurse with a kind face.

'Is there anyone we can call?' the policewoman asked her. 'A relative? A friend or neighbour?'

Karen barely registered the question which seemed to come from a great distance.

'How am I going to tell the children?' she whispered. 'How can I tell them their father's dead? He was only fifty one.' It struck her forcibly that her husband of fifteen years would now never be any older than fifty one. She started to shiver violently and someone draped a blanket round her shoulders. Someone else took the glass of water away and thrust a cup of hot tea into her hand. 'Drink this, dear, it'll make you feel better.'

The policewoman sat down beside her. 'You've had a terrible shock, Mrs Armstrong. You shouldn't be alone at a time like this. Are there any relatives or friends we can call?'

'My sister, Joan.'

'Do you have her number?'

In her dazed state, Karen couldn't remember Joan's number. 'I'll have to look it up.' She rummaged in her bag for her mobile, went shakily through her contacts, then gave the number to the policewoman who rang it on her own phone.

A few moments later she laid a gentle hand on Karen's arm. 'Your sister said she'll come immediately. Before she arrives, perhaps you would like to see your husband.'

'Oh...' Karen had never seen a dead body before and she was seized with panic at the prospect. 'Yes, I suppose so.'

'As next of kin, you'll need to formally identify him,' the policewoman continued.

'You'll also need to give permission for a hospital post-mortem examination so that the cause of the death can be confirmed.'

'What will happen to Howard?'

'Don't you worry, dear,' said the nurse with the kind face. 'Your husband will be taken care of. His body will be laid out and kept in the hospital mortuary. After the post-mortem, you can arrange for the funeral directors or the family to collect him. A doctor will give you a medical certificate showing the cause of death. You'll need one of these before the death can be registered.'

Karen gazed at her uncomprehendingly. It was too much to take in.

'Now, if you don't mind waiting here, there are some things we need to do. Then we'll take you to see him.' Accompanied by another woman, the nurse returned to the Intensive Care Unit and closed the door.

After a while they came out again. 'You can go in now, dear.'

Karen took a deep breath and rose trembling to her feet.

The kind-faced nurse led her inside. 'Take your time, dear. Come out when you're ready.'

Karen slowly entered the room.

Howard was lying on a bed surrounded by monitors and other pieces of medical equipment. He was covered with a sheet that had been pulled back so that only his head was visible.

Karen trembled with shock as she gazed down at him. The face she was looking at didn't resemble Howard's. It was stone white and strangely smooth. Without its habitual frown and tension lines, it looked astonishingly youthful. The pale lips were slightly apart, as though Howard had been about to say something before death had overtaken him. The slack mouth gave him a slightly foolish expression. She was relieved that his eyes were shut and weren't staring sightlessly up at her. She stooped and tentatively touched his cheek. It felt clammy and she recoiled with horror.

She slumped on to a chair that had been placed beside the bed and gazed at the white face on the pillow, overcome with a wave of violent emotions – anguish, fear, despair, and finally guilt; guilt that at the time when her husband had been fighting for his life, she had been sitting in the garden enjoying the sun and fantasising about a more exciting life: a life away from Moxton; a life without Howard.

She felt a sudden compulsion to admit the truth to him as well as to herself. 'I'm sorry,' she whispered, glancing upwards in case Howard's spirit was hovering somewhere above the body it had recently left. 'I'm not sure if I really loved you. But I did try to be a good wife to you.'

It was true. She had tried to be a good wife because she felt grateful to him. Howard had taken charge of her life and had relieved her of the burden of asserting herself and fighting for a place in an adult world in which she felt uncomfortable. But now he had gone leaving her a widow - a widow and a single parent. The realisation filled her with a sudden and irrational rage. How would she manage?

It was another cruel abandonment, like when her mother had died when she was only eleven years old. '*Why* did you let this happen, Howard?' She hissed, clenching her fists convulsively. '*Why?*'

But her anger dissipated as quickly as it had arrived, and she was again consumed with guilt that instead of grieving, she was agonising about whether she would be able to cope on her own. Hot tears stung her eyes. She bent and forced herself to kiss Howard's cold cheek, then hurriedly left the room. Numbly, she signed some papers that a nurse handed to her, then followed the two police officers back through the labyrinth of corridors to the hospital main entrance.

'We'll stay with you till your sister arrives,' the policewoman said gently when they reached the door.

'No.' Karen made an effort to steady her voice. 'You've been very kind but I'd like to be on my own now if you don't mind.'

The policewoman hesitated. 'Are you sure you're alright, Mrs Armstrong? You've had a terrible shock.'

'Absolutely sure.' Karen saw her sister hurrying towards them.

'There's Joan now.'

The policewoman put a hand on her arm. 'A Family Liaison Officer will be assigned to you. Whoever it is will try to support you as much as possible.' She smiled apologetically. 'And when you're up to it, some detectives will need to ask you some questions about your husband. I'm sure you understand.'

Before Karen could answer, Joan arrived at the entrance and the two of them fell weeping into each other's arms.

# Chapter 2

When the police returned, there were again two of them, a man and a woman, but this time they weren't in uniform. They told Karen they were members of an enquiry team set up specifically to investigate Howard's murder.

The woman, a detective inspector (Karen didn't catch her name), was about forty and had an air of brisk authority. After expressing her condolences, she introduced her companion - a man with a middle-aged face and prematurely white hair - as Detective Constable Harrison. 'DC Harrison is your Family Liaison Officer. He will be your main point of contact with the Senior Investigating Officer and the team.'

The liaison officer smiled at Karen. He had very bright blue eyes and there was a small lump on his forehead, some kind of cyst that her eyes kept straying irresistibly towards.

He handed her a large envelope. 'This is an information pack, Mrs Armstrong. It has details on all the areas you may need to know about: the inquest, how the criminal justice system works and how to handle the media, as well as a list of relevant support agencies. And here's my number.' He handed her a card. 'You can contact me at any time with any questions or problems you have. I'm here to help. But my main role is to be a link between you and the enquiry team, to gather information that could assist the investigation, and to keep you updated on its progress.'

Karen found the man's words hard to take in. She stared blankly at the envelope and card then passed them to Joan who was sitting protectively next to her on the sofa.

'We would like to ask you a few questions, Mrs Armstrong,' DI Something-or-Other said gently, taking a notebook from a pocket. She glanced at the door. 'Are your children at home?'

'No,' Karen faltered, 'I--'

'A family friend is looking after them for a few days,' interjected Joan. 'As you can imagine, they're extremely distressed, we all are, and we thought it best that they were not here when you come to ask questions.'

The detective nodded. 'Of course. We don't want to upset you any further, Mrs Armstrong, but we do need to find out as much as we can if we're to find the person who shot your husband. Do you feel up to answering questions?'

'Yes.'

'Did your husband have any enemies?'

'Enemies?' Karen murmured, bemused. She twisted her hands nervously in her lap. 'I don't think so. Howard hated any kind of confrontation.' She recalled how, after any domestic argument, he would retreat into a lengthy and oppressive silence that could last for days.

'You're not aware of any arguments or grudges... any threats, personal or professional, that someone may have made to your husband?'

'No,' Karen said wonderingly. One didn't expect to encounter threats in a sleepy market town like Moxton. 'But I don't know if he'd had any arguments at work. You'd have to ask his partner, Geoff Murray, about that.'

'It's an avenue we're already exploring, Mrs Armstrong. Did your husband have any worries or problems that you were aware of?'

Karen tugged a strand of her hair. 'I don't think so.'

'Any financial problems?'

'No, at least none that I knew about. Howard is...was... fairly well-off.'

'I see.' The detective glanced briefly round the expensively- furnished sitting room.

Karen followed her gaze. She had always disliked the heavy leather armchairs, the mahogany cabinet, the dark landscape paintings in ornate gilt frames. Everything in the room had the imprint of Howard's taste rather than her own.

'What was your husband's mood recently?' the detective continued. 'Did he seem preoccupied?'

'No more than usual. Howard was very...private, quiet, even when he was at home.'

'Was that a recent development?'

'No. He was always like that.'

'Did your husband mention any disturbing communications he had received in the weeks before he died - phone calls, letters, emails?'

'No.'

'Did he mention any problems he was experiencing in relation to his work?'

Karen reflected for a moment. 'No. Howard never discussed work with me. He did such long hours that he needed a break from it by the time he got home, which was usually quite late.'

The detective exchanged a glance with DC Harrison.

'How often did your husband work late, Mrs Armstrong?'

'Virtually every day. His workload had increased because of the recession, businesses in trouble, that sort of thing.'

The detective consulted her notes. 'But last Friday evening, Mr Armstrong left his office at about half past four. Was he coming home early that day?'

Karen shook her head. 'No, Howard never came home that early. He rarely got here before seven thirty.'

'So where would he have been going at half past four on Friday?'

'I've no idea. To see a client perhaps?'

The detective was observing her closely through pale and rather protuberant grey eyes. 'We've spoken to his secretary and apparently your husband had no scheduled meetings late on Friday afternoon. Neither she nor his other colleagues knew where he was going at that time.'

'Well I don't know where he was going either,' Karen snapped, surprising herself at this departure from her habitual timidity. 'Howard was the founder and a director of the company. He didn't need to tell people where he was going every time he left the office.' She wished they would go away; stop plaguing her with questions. Joan gave her arm a reassuring squeeze.

'Of course not,' DC Harrison interjected quietly. 'Please don't upset yourself, Mrs Armstrong. DI Parker and I want to do all we can to find out who could have shot your husband. If we knew where he was going yesterday afternoon, it might give us an important lead.'

'I gather your husband's car wasn't in the company car park on

Friday,' the woman Karen now knew to be DI Parker, continued.

'That's right. Howard usually walked to work. He only took the car when he had to visit clients.'

'So wherever he was going he would have been on foot?'

'I suppose so.' Karen couldn't remember Howard ever taking a bus.

'Which implies it must have been quite near?'

'I don't know. Possibly.'

DI Parker was regarding her intently. 'I'm sorry, Mrs Armstrong, but I have to ask you this. Was your husband faithful…as far as you know?'

Karen blinked. 'What?'

Joan grabbed her hand protectively.

'Was there another woman?'

Karen gave an incredulous laugh. 'Howard? Good heavens no! He wasn't like that. He was so wrapped up in his work, he wouldn't have had time, even if he'd had the inclination.'

'But you said he almost always came home late.'

'Yes, but not because of *that*. I'm sure of it. I would have known.'

The detective smiled grimly. 'The wife is usually the last to know these things, Mrs Armstrong. It's just possible that a jealous husband or boyfriend-- '

'No, it's out of the question.' Karen declared resolutely. But she was unable to suppress a flicker of doubt. After Poppy, their youngest, was born, Howard had displayed little inclination for sex with her.

'Howard was a decent man,' Joan declared. 'Anything like that would have been totally out of character.'

'So would you say yours was a happy marriage, Mrs Armstrong?' asked the detective after a brief pause.

In the silence that followed, Karen became conscious of

the ticking of the clock on the mantelpiece. 'Happy?' she murmured, wondering how to define her marriage. She stared at the clock - an ugly, ornate one that Howard had bought during their honeymoon in Switzerland. The row of colourful birthday cards marking Poppy's recent sixth birthday looked incongruous beside it. 'We rubbed along, like most married couples, I suppose.'

'I'm sorry to ask this,' the detective persevered, 'but did you and your husband have any arguments recently?'

Karen was startled by the question. 'Yes, occasionally. Don't all married couples?' Tears started trickling down her face and she turned instinctively to her sister. After their widowed mother had died, Joan, her elder by six years, had watched over her with a fierce protectiveness.

Joan put an arm around her. 'Why are you asking such insensitive questions?' she demanded sharply.

'Because we need as much information about the victim as possible,' DC Harrison responded gently.

'Shouldn't you be getting on with finding the person who killed Howard rather than harassing his widow?'

DI Parker ignored Joan's outburst. 'We know how difficult this must be for you, Mrs Armstrong, and I assure you we don't want to cause you any further distress. These questions are just a routine part of the investigation. Your husband's recent demeanour; his state of mind, could be of relevance. Would you like to have a break now? Have a glass of water?'

Karen shook her head.

'What progress have you made in finding the person who shot him?' Joan persisted.

'It's still very early in the enquiry, Mrs er... We haven't yet found the motorbike the perpetrator used but we've identified the firearm used from the bullet casings, and we're now looking for the murder weapon. We hope to identify a possible suspect after CCTV footage has been examined. However, one thing we have to consider is whether the Mr Armstrong was the intended target.'

'You mean it could have been someone else?' Joan asked in astonishment.

'It's possible. There are three enterprises in Bartholomew Court. As well as *Armstrong and Murray Accountants*, there's *Barkers Insurance Services* and *Duttons Estate Agents*. For all we know, the perpetrator may have mistaken Mr Armstrong for an employee of one of the other companies.'

Joan's face had turned pink with anger. 'So why aren't you looking into that instead of harassing my sister?'

'Because in a murder investigation we have to follow *all* lines of enquiry,' DI Parker said patiently. 'We are, of course, considering the possibility that the target could have been someone connected with *Barkers* or *Duttons*. But assuming Mr Armstrong was the intended victim, I would be grateful, Mrs Armstrong, if you would give us your consent to examine phone messages, emails, letters, documents - anything that could give us a clue as to why someone might have wanted him... out of the way.'

'I suppose so.' Karen muttered wearily.

'We already have Mr Armstrong's smart phone and iPad,' continued DI Parker. 'They were in the briefcase he was carrying when he left the building. We also have his keys.' She took a plastic container out of her bag, extracted a bunch of keys and held them up for Karen's inspection. 'We've established that some of these are for Bartholomew Court. I assume these are for the house?' She indicated three keys on the bunch.

Karen stared at them. 'Yes, two of those are his door keys and that small one's for the shed padlock.'

'What about this one?' DI Parker selected an even smaller key.

Karen peered at it. 'I don't recognise that one. It looks as though it could be for a drawer.'

'It doesn't fit any of the drawers in Mr Armstrong's office or the safe. Did your husband work from home at all?'

'Yes, he has…' She *must* get used to using the past tense. 'He had an office upstairs.'

'Do you mind if we take a look?'

Karen reluctantly conducted them up to Howard's study. She had always disliked this room. The children had never been allowed in there and she herself only entered it in order to dust and vacuum, which Howard had insisted on her doing daily.

She glanced round the room as she ushered them inside. Behind the door stood the filing cabinet in which Howard kept personal papers, bank accounts and household documents. In the recesses on either side of the window, bookshelves extended from the ceiling to the floor. On them books were arranged in strict alphabetical order. None of them was tilted or placed horizontally on top of others. A shaft of sunlight, alive with whirling motes of dust, created a gleaming rectangle of light on the polished surface of the overlarge wooden desk in front of the window.

The desk provided evidence of Howard's obsessive tidiness. On one side of the computer and printer, six ballpoint pens were neatly lined up in front of a metal basket containing a pile of documents, their edges firmly paperclipped together. On the other side of the computer, an anglepoise lamp, a photo of the children, an A4 diary and a telephone were arranged in a diagonal line. Howard had felt uncomfortable if any of them had been nudged out of position and would immediately push them back to maintain the symmetry.

DI Parker was still holding Howard's bunch of keys. She removed the small key from the key ring and handed it to DC Harrison. 'Could we try this in the desk drawers or in the cabinet?' she asked Karen, 'just so we can eliminate it?'

'Yes, but I don't think Howard locked any of the desk drawers.'

DC Harrison tried the key in the filing cabinet and the desk drawers but it didn't fit any of them. Shaking his head, he handed it back to DI Parker who replaced it in the plastic container.

'We'll hang on to this one until we can identify it, if you don't mind.' The woman detective left the rest of the keys on the desk then gestured at the diary. 'May we take a look?'

Karen nodded.

The detective picked up the diary and opened it at the page dated the previous Friday. 'Hm,' she murmured, showing it to DC Harrison, 'interesting!'

As they scrutinised the page, Karen leaned between them to see what they were reading. Under a reference to a morning meeting with his partner, Geoff, and a reminder to himself to ring a plumber, Howard had written two letters surrounded by a pencilled circle, PP. After it were three letters, DEP.

DI Parker looked enquiringly at Karen. 'Do you know what the letters PP signify, Mrs Armstrong?'

'I have no idea. Something to do with Howard's work I

imagine.'

The detective flipped rapidly through the rest of the pages. 'Here it is again - PP - and again here. It must mean something significant, don't you think, especially as the letters are circled?'

'I don't know. Perhaps it's a client's initials. You could check with Howard's partner, Geoff.'

'We will.' DI Parker closed the diary. 'With your permission, we'll take this with us and compare it with the entries in your husband's computerised diary in his office.' She pointed at the phone on the desk. 'Business line?'

'Yes.'

'May I check?' Without waiting for an answer, DI Parker picked up the receiver and tapped in four digits. The only messages left since Friday were faltering messages of condolence from Howard's colleagues and business clients. Any previous ones had been erased.

DI Parker put the receiver down. 'May we look in the desk drawers?'

'What exactly are you looking for?' Karen asked.

'We won't know till we find it,' DI Parker replied enigmatically. 'It could be a letter, an address, unusual credit card receipts, anything that might provide a clue to what happened to your husband.'

Karen watched dubiously as the detective searched the desk drawers and extracted a number of folders and documents, some of which she put to one side. 'I must ask your permission to take the PC and some of these papers away for examination.'

Karen stared at her. 'Do you have to?'

'They could be relevant to the investigation. Do you use the PC yourself?'

'No.' The truth was that Karen rarely used a computer these days. It was another thing she had always left to Howard or to the children. Although she had her own laptop, it usually remained on top of the wardrobe.

'We'll make a note of everything we remove and return it all in due course.' The detective continued. She took out a notebook and wrote something in it. 'May we look in the filing cabinet?'

Karen glanced at Joan who was hovering anxiously in the study doorway. 'The stuff in there's private – personal papers, bank accounts, things like that. Now that Howard's...not here, I will need to go through them to check my financial position.' The prospect of going through the documents in the cabinet terrified her. Joan had already suggested that she should investigate whether Howard had made a Will or had a life insurance policy (he had never mentioned either), but she hadn't yet found the courage to look.

DI Parker nodded. 'I understand. But we will need to examine the documents at some point in case they prove pertinent to the enquiry. As Mr Armstrong was an accountant, it's possible there could be a financial issue that has a bearing on the perpetrator's motive.'

'For example, DEP might refer to deposits your husband made,' DC Harrison suggested. 'Do you have a joint account, Mrs Armstrong?'

Karen blushed. 'No. Howard took care of all the finances. He gave me a regular allowance, of course, for the house and children.' She realised this must sound odd, but she had never pressed Howard for a joint account as it was clear he liked to have complete control over domestic finances. He didn't even like her having a credit card in case she got "carried away", so she had stopped using one. However, the allowance he gave her for the children and household expenses was generous and, without telling him, she had opened a savings account with the money she had left over every month. She knew he would have been furious if he had found out.

After she had signed a form, the two officers carried Howard's computer, his diary and a bundle of documents downstairs. When she opened the front door for them, she saw a large crowd of people, some holding cameras, waiting in the road and on the pavement outside the house. Reporters and photographers had started arriving the morning after Howard died. A number of them now swarmed around the two officers as they walked to the police car. Karen shrank back in the doorway, relieved that the children weren't there.

A small group of neighbours stood watching on the opposite pavement. They stared at her curiously and several of them waved. She was touched to see that some bunches of flowers had been placed outside the gate and half-smiled at the irony. Howard hadn't liked flowers and never wanted any in the house because he thought they made it look "messy". The stricture even applied to the garden which he kept strictly functional, with a rather patchy lawn, some nondescript shrubs and a small vegetable patch. It was only after much persuasion on the children's part that he had allowed some of their playthings – a Wendy house, a small trampoline – to be placed in an underused shady area near the side fence.

DC Harrison strode back up the path and stood facing her. 'I'm afraid your husband's murder has caused a bit of a media sensation, Mrs Armstrong,' he said gravely. 'It's probably the most dramatic thing that's happened in Moxton for decades. As you can see, reporters are sniffing around. We've asked them not to bother you and you don't have to speak to them, but be prepared for them pestering callers or your neighbours with questions. You know what media folk are like. At some point you may wish to discuss with me how to handle publicity about the case.'

Karen shuddered at the thought of intrusive publicity. Joan had already shown her some of the headlines: *Accountant Gunned Down in Broad Daylight. Why was Howard Armstrong Killed?*

There had also been items on the TV news, showing police, some wearing protective forensic clothing, milling about outside Bartholomew Court, the lower part of which had been covered in some sort of tent. The road the building was in had also been temporarily sealed off.

'The brouhaha shouldn't last long,' DC Harrison told her reassuringly. 'Just until the next story catches their attention. But we have to be careful. Media reporting can compromise an investigation and any trial resulting from it.'

DI Parker joined them on the doorstep. 'Thank you for your cooperation, Mrs Armstrong. We realise what a very difficult time this is for you. DC Harrison will be your main point of contact from now on, but I or another member of the team may come and ask more questions as the enquiry proceeds. In the meantime, please let DC Harrison know at once if there's anything you can think of, anything at all, that could help the investigation, however trivial it may seem. It could be a remark your husband may have made, his reaction to a phone call or a letter, or if you remember him appearing worried or disturbed in the last few weeks.'

DC Harrison gazed at her with an expression of sympathy. 'If you have any questions or need help with anything, Mrs Armstrong, you can ring me any time. Leave a message if necessary.'

As the two officers returned to their car, they were again surrounded by a mob of reporters.

Karen hastily shut the door.

# Chapter 3

Karen returned to the sitting-room and stood staring distractedly out of the window. The woman detective's question was nagging at her mind: *would you say yours was a happy marriage?*

If she was honest with herself, it hadn't been particularly happy. She wasn't in love with Howard when he asked her to marry him but she had been flattered by his proposal. Ten years older than her, he had already set up his own accountancy business and had an air of authority and easy charm she had found difficult to resist. He was also attractive - tall with thick dark hair and deep-set brown eyes, and always impeccably turned-out. She couldn't understand what he could possibly see in her. She had never attracted much male attention before.

Several years into the marriage, a voice deep inside her told her she had made a terrible mistake. Howard was irascible and obsessively tidy and, after Poppy was born, he became increasingly withdrawn. When he returned from work in the evening, he would eat his meal then immediately retire to his study. In bed he would lie as far away from her as possible, as though she had some kind of contagious disease. At weekends and during the summer evenings, he would spend long periods in the garden shed, cutting himself off from her and the children by locking the door. If she complained about his absenting himself from the family, he would retort that he worked extremely hard to maintain them all and she should understand his need for his own personal space. After a while she came to the conclusion that it was *her* fault he had become so distant; maybe she didn't satisfy him either sexually or intellectually.

During the years they were married, they seldom socialised, except for infrequent meals with Joan and her husband, Greg, Howard's partner Geoff and Celia, his wife, and her friend Mo and husband, Tony. She recalled how, on these occasions, Howard would invariably undergo an abrupt, chameleon change of personality. Reserved and morose at home, he would miraculously turn into the life and soul of the party, cracking jokes, relating witty anecdotes and laughing heartily at the wisecracks of others. She rarely mentioned his customary moodiness to anyone else since even Joan found it hard to believe there was such a contrast between his public and private personas.

She wondered what she was going to do, now that Howard had gone. Liberated from his exacting household standards, should she look for a job? After spending so many years at home, the idea frightened her. Once, after Poppy had started pre-school, she had plucked up courage to visit the local Job Centre. It had been a humiliating experience. The man behind the desk told her that the only part-time local jobs available for someone in her position were cleaning or stacking shelves in supermarkets. She was too old, he implied, to start a new career. *Too old?* She went to the mantelpiece and peered closely at her face: not pretty – she had never been that, and there were definite creases between her brows, but there were only a few lines round her eyes and no grey yet in her hair.

'Are you OK, Karen?' Joan's reflection appeared next to hers. 'I hope they didn't upset you.'

'They were only doing their job.' Karen turned away from the mirror and surveyed her sister. She had often wondered at the lack of family resemblance. Whereas she was tall and thin with straight, shoulder-length fair hair, Joan was short and stocky and her curly dark hair was already liberally streaked with grey. 'What about your job, Joanie?' she asked. 'Are you sure they don't mind you taking time off at such short notice?

'Perfectly sure. The community centre's fairly quiet at the moment.'

'Well what about Greg? Doesn't he mind you spending so much time here? '

'No,' Joan declared firmly. 'He quite understands.'

Karen could believe this. Unlike Howard, Joan's husband was a meek man who danced willingly to his wife's tune.

Joan scrutinised her. 'You look pale, Karen. I think you could do with some fresh air.' She opened the patio doors leading to the garden. 'Why don't you sit outside for a while? It'll make you feel better.'

Karen gratefully followed her suggestion. The shock and mixed emotions of the last few days had left her feeling exhausted. She sank on to a garden chair and closed her eyes, savouring the warmth of the sun on her face and the sound of the insects buzzing and droning in the hedges separating the garden from its neighbours. On such a lovely day, the horror of what had happened seemed unreal, like one of those elusive nightmares you can't quite remember when you wake up.

A cloud momentarily obscured the sun and she shivered as an image of Howard's inert body on the hospital bed suddenly insinuated itself into her mind.

'Karen!' Joan's voice startled her. 'You have a visitor.'

Geoff Murray, Howard's business partner, stepped hesitantly on to the patio. Bald and overweight, he had always seemed considerably older than Howard although he was about the same age. His heavily puckered forehead lent his face an expression of habitual anxiety.

Karen rose to greet him. She was fond of Geoff (though less so of his wife Celia). He had been Best Man at their wedding and was Simon's godfather.

'Karen, my dear.' Perspiring, his face furrowed with distress, Geoff lumbered towards her with outstretched arms and enveloped her in a bear hug. 'What can I say? Such a terrible thing … dreadful shock...I still can't believe it. None of us can...We're all completely *devastated*. Celia sends her deepest condolences …She would have come but she… um...had an important meeting; couldn't get out of it.'

As Karen extricated herself from his embrace, he grabbed one of her hands and held it in a tight grip. 'Why would anyone do something so...so barbaric? It's totally… inexplicable...' His voice was thick with emotion and tears glistened in his eyes.

'Yes,' she whispered. 'It is.'

'I can't begin to imagine how you must be feeling...' he swallowed hard, '...but I want you to know I --'

'Thank you, Geoff,' she said quickly. Tears had started cascading down her cheeks as they invariably did whenever anyone expressed sympathy. She retrieved her hand, mopped her eyes and took a deep breath. 'Please sit down.'

She resumed her seat and he lowered himself carefully on to a metal chair beside her and sat twisting his hands anxiously in his lap. 'How are you, Karen? How are the children? '

'The children are staying with my friend Mo for a few days. I haven't been in a state to look after them, you see, and I didn't want them here when the police came round.' She turned away from him and gazed down at the small rectangle of lawn. It had turned a scrubby brown after several weeks without rain. 'Erica and Simon are absolutely devastated. We haven't told Poppy, she's too young to understand.'

'Of course, of course,' he murmured.

'I call them every day and Joan's been wonderful. She's taken care of everything. I couldn't have managed without her.'

He looked at her, shamefaced. 'I'm sorry I didn't come earlier. It seemed too much of an intrusion, so soon after -- '

'It's OK, Geoff.' She gave him a tremulous smile. 'I got your phone message. It would have been too soon for visitors. And the police keep coming round asking questions about Howard.'

He nodded. 'It must be extremely difficult for you.'

'It is. A detective came round this morning with the family liaison officer. They took Howard's PC and all the papers from his desk... a whole boxful of them.'

'Well I'm glad they're being thorough. Let's hope they find the bas... whoever did it, soon.' He gazed at her searchingly. 'Karen, do you have any idea--?

'Who shot him? None at all. It still doesn't seem

possible. I sometimes can't believe it's happened.'

Geoff mopped his glistening brow with a handkerchief. 'Had Howard quarrelled with anyone?'

'Not to my knowledge, but then, he was always very ... that is, he never told me much about...' Karen paused, feeling that to hint that there were problems in the marriage so soon after Howard's death might seem like gross disloyalty. 'Could he have had an argument with one of his clients?'

Geoff shook his head. 'The police asked me the same question. I told them I wasn't aware of any bad feeling. Though, in the current economic climate, many of the individuals and companies we work with are experiencing financial difficulty, so it's possible there may have been an occasional misunderstanding. But Howard was totally...scrupulous; very precise. As you know, he could sometimes be a bit, um, unyielding, but always reasonable. He wouldn't have spoken or acted in any way that might be construed as...confrontational... Oh thank you.' Geoff turned to Joan who had joined them on the patio and was offering him a cup of coffee. 'Very kind.'

Joan put a tray with milk and sugar down on the garden table. 'Call me if you need anything, Karen.'

Karen watched as Geoff added milk then three lumps of sugar to his coffee.

'What about the funeral?' he asked. 'Do you have any idea when it might be?'

'I can't do anything about that yet. The investigation's ongoing and Howard's body can't be released until after the inquest.'

'That must be difficult for you.'

'Yes it is.' Karen watched two magpies alight on the vegetable patch at the bottom of the garden. *What was that old rhyme? Two for joy? Joy? That was a laugh!* She turned back to Geoff, searching for something to say. 'Howard very rarely talked about his work at *Armstrong and Murray*. I know next to nothing about it.'

'Oh?' Geoff stirred his coffee vigorously. 'Maybe he thought it would bore you.'

'No!' she said with some asperity. 'It was because he thought I was stupid!'

'Surely not.' Geoff shifted uncomfortably on the garden chair which was far too small for his bulk.

'Whenever I asked him about his work, he said I wouldn't understand. I know I don't have degrees or diplomas and stuff, but I would have *tried* to understand.'

Geoff gave an embarrassed laugh. 'He was probably just trying to spare you. As you know, accountancy isn't the sexiest subject in the world.'

'Maybe not, but he could have shared something about his working life.'

'Hm.' Geoff cleared his throat. 'I suppose I don't say much about work at home either.'

'Geoff, do the letters PP mean anything to you?' Karen asked after a brief silence.

He looked surprised. 'PP? No, why?'

'The police looked in Howard's diary, the one he kept on his desk here. They found he'd written the letters PP on the day he died and on some other days as well. I thought it might have something to do with his work.'

'PP? Doesn't ring any bells. An acronym perhaps?'

'Do you have any clients with those initials?'

He reflected. 'Well, we look after the company *Polytechnicals*, but Howard wasn't involved with them. Then there's *Planning for Parenthood*, but we won't be doing their accounts till their annual audit, so there wouldn't have been any reason for Howard to be in contact with them. Who else...?' he scratched his head. '...We have Mr Passmore, the restaurant owner, but his initial is R, R for Rolf. There are probably other Ps on our books. I'd have to check.'

Karen twirled a strand of her hair round her index finger. 'Could Howard have been working with anyone privately, outside the firm?'

Geoff frowned. 'I suppose it's possible, but I hope not. It's something we agreed we wouldn't do when we established the business. But as you know, Howard sat on the board of several charities. He was very generous with his time. '

Karen resisted commenting that this quality had not been very evident in relation to the children and herself. 'Do you have any idea where Howard was going when he left the office last Friday?' she asked.

'No. I had a meeting with a client at the time so didn't see him leave the office. I assumed he had gone home.'

'Home?' Karen gave an incredulous laugh 'At half past four? That would have been a first! I can't remember the last time Howard got home before half past seven.'

'Eh?' Geoff who had been in the process of raising his cup to his lips, held it suspended in the air in surprise. 'Howard often left the office early. Jennifer - you know his secretary, of course - she said he very occasionally scheduled a meeting with a client after five, but most days he liked to keep his diary clear after four thirty. We assumed it was because he wanted to spend time with you and the family.'

Karen stared at him open-mouthed. 'You mean Howard

*wasn't* working late every evening?'

'Well,' Geoff's face had turned a slight pink, 'I'm sure he had a good reason to leave the office early. He could have gone to a charity board meeting, though admittedly that would have been unusual on a Friday afternoon. And very occasionally, we socialised with clients in the evenings. Howard and I had regular meetings of course, but we didn't check up on each other's schedules. We didn't need to.'

'I know that, Geoff. I'm sure there's a perfectly good explanation.' Although Karen managed to keep her voice steady, her thoughts were in turmoil. Why had Howard claimed he had to work late every night? The police must have noticed the discrepancy between her assertion that he never came home before seven thirty and his colleagues' testimony that he frequently left the office before five. For the second time that day she wondered whether what the detective had suggested was true: maybe there *had* been another woman in Howard's life; a woman with the initials PP. She felt a sudden surge of anger and resentment. All those evenings when he came home late, leaving her to have supper with the children on her own then get them to bed, he might have been with someone else...

Something of what she was feeling must have showed on her face as Geoff hastily swallowed the rest of his coffee and put down his cup. 'Must go, Karen my love. If there's anything Celia and I can do to help...anything at all...please don't hesitate...' He eased himself stiffly off the garden chair. 'Such a terrible, terrible business,' he murmured as she accompanied him to the door.'

After he had left, Karen went upstairs and searched through the pockets of Howard's suits hanging in the wardrobe. Apart from a few coins, they were empty. She peered and sniffed at the collars of his jackets and shirts to see if she could detect any signs of another woman - a smudge of lipstick; an unfamiliar perfume. Again nothing. But Howard had always been exceedingly particular about the state of his clothes and she knew that if he had been seeing someone else, he would have been very adept at covering his tracks.

# Chapter 4

A few days after the murder, the police held a press conference about the case, part of which was shown on television news channels. Karen watched as the senior investigating officer, Detective Chief Inspector Evans, responded cautiously to reporters' persistent questioning.

'After investigating the other two companies in the building, we believe Mr Armstrong probably was the intended victim.'

'Witnesses say they saw a tall person on a Honda motorbike, wearing leathers and a visor. The perpetrator appeared to be young.'

'No, we haven't yet discovered a motive.'

'We are pursuing all relevant avenues of enquiry and following a number of leads.'

'We would still like to hear from anybody who was in the vicinity of Moxton High Street around four-thirty pm last Friday.'

Karen wondered why it was taking so long to identify the culprit. Not many people were gunned down in broad daylight in a sleepy place like Moxton, were they? The white-haired liaison officer, DC Harrison, had visited her several times but had given no indication that the police were any nearer to discovering either the perpetrator or the motive.

Flowers and messages of sympathy had begun to arrive at the house, and a trickle of visitors, some of them Howard's colleagues whom Karen barely knew, called to offer their condolences, striving with obvious embarrassment to find appropriate words. The visits were discreetly managed by Joan who made sure that no-one stayed too long.

Not all reactions to Howard's murder were sympathetic and Karen was devastated to receive several obscene texts and phone calls. When she reported this to the family liaison officer he told her the police would investigate. He advised her to change her phone numbers. 'This kind of thing happens all too often to people who are in the public eye. It's an unpleasant feature of modern life.'

The children returned home at the end of the week. Karen had called them every day, endeavouring to keep her voice calm and reassuring when the two eldest tearfully plied her with questions. She didn't know how they were coping with the shock of their father's death, and worried that she lacked the skills to console them.

Erica and Simon had reacted in different ways when she and Joan told them, as gently as they could, what had happened. Thirteen- year-old Erica had been distraught; she had shouted and screamed and it had taken a considerable time to calm her down. Of the three of them, she had been closest to her father.

Simon, two years younger, had gone bright red. He insisted on her repeating the details, after which he had run up to his room and slammed the door.

Poppy hadn't yet been told and her siblings had been instructed to say only that Daddy had had an accident and had been taken to hospital. Karen intended to tell her the truth when she judged the time was right. She had also decided that the children's normal routines should be disrupted as little as possible. They still had five weeks' holiday before the new school year started, and she hoped that when they returned to their classes, they wouldn't be pestered by pupils curious to discover details about Howard's murder. She wondered whether she should enquire about the possibility of counselling for them. Howard used to accuse her of being over- protective towards the children, of mollycoddling them. It was one of the few subjects on which she had the courage to argue with him. 'You can't be overprotective of your own children,' she would counter fiercely and sometimes tearfully. 'They're the most precious things we have.'

'They need to be toughened up,' was his invariable response.

'Especially Simon, he's far too sensitive.'

Poppy accosted her as soon as the children came through the front door. 'Why did a bad man kill my daddy?' she demanded, gazing at Karen with huge, accusing eyes.

'We didn't tell her, Mum,' blurted Simon on seeing Karen's shocked expression. 'She heard Auntie Mo speaking to you on the phone.'

Karen's friend Maureen, who had followed the children into the hall, looked sheepish. 'I'm terribly sorry Karen. I didn't know she was listening.'

'It's OK, Mo. It's not your fault.' She kissed Poppy who was tugging insistently at her skirt. Her lips were trembling. 'Mummy, *why* did a bad man kill my daddy?'

'We don't know yet, darling,' she answered helplessly.

Erica pushed past Poppy and clutched Karen's hand.

'Dad didn't do anything bad, Mum, did he?' Uncharacteristically, for she had inherited Howard's obsessive neatness as well as his intensity, she let her jacket and backpack fall in an untidy heap on the floor.

Karen kissed the top of her head. 'No, of course not.'

'Have the police found the man who did it yet?'

'Not yet, but these enquiries can take a long time.' Karen gazed anxiously down at her two daughters, so physically different from each other. Whereas Erica was brown-eyed and dark-haired like her father, Poppy's amber eyes and auburn hair must have been inherited from some distant ancestor. Simon was unlike either of them. Pale and skinny, with fair hair and grey eyes, he was the only one who resembled her.

Erica's eyes filled with tears. 'But--'

'Come along children,' Joan interjected swiftly, 'there's chicken salad for lunch and I've made a fruit crumble for after.' Practical as ever, she swept the three of them off to the kitchen, leaving Karen and Maureen in the hall.

'Do you want to stay for lunch, Mo?' Karen asked. She and Mo had been friends ever since they met in the school playground on the day Erica and Gemma, Mo's daughter, had started in the reception class. She had been touched by Mo's evident distress when she heard about Howard.

Mo seemed eager to get away. 'Thanks, but I must get back.'

Karen took hold of her hand. 'It was so good of you to look after the children for me, Mo. It can't have been easy in the circumstances. I'm really grateful. I couldn't handle their distress. You've been such a good friend.'

Mo blushed. Petite and with almost white blonde hair, she had a fresh-faced, youthful prettiness that Karen had always envied. 'It was only for a few days. Albert was a great help. There's nothing like a puppy to distract unhappy children.' Her face crumpled. 'I still can't believe that it's happened...that Howard's dead.' She quickly turned away and blew her nose. 'Have you heard how the investigation's progressing?'

Karen sighed. 'Not yet. It's like the whole thing's a complete mystery. No-one seems to know why he was shot, or if they do, they're not telling me.'

Simon reappeared in the hall. 'Aren't you coming to eat with us, Mum?'

Karen gave him a hug. 'Of course I am, sweetheart. I'm just saying goodbye to Auntie Mo.' She worried about Simon. He had a permanently anxious expression and a nervous habit of tugging his right earlobe. There had been a tension between him and Howard that had long concerned her. Although Simon had always tried to please his father, he never seemed to succeed.

When she joined them at the table, Karen found Joan distracting the children with details of the afterschool activities being planned at the community centre where she worked. Karen felt a surge of affection for her sister and wondered how she would have managed without her. While she had been lying on her bed or sofa, trying to come to terms with what had happened, Joan had cleaned the house from top to bottom, done the laundry, replenished food supplies and stocked the fridge. She had also helped Karen plan the eventual funeral and draw up a list of people to be invited. It was a relatively small list as Karen had few relatives and Howard's own family was virtually non-existent. He had always refused to be drawn on the circumstances of his childhood. All she knew was that he had been brought up in foster homes.

As she pushed her food around her plate, she reflected on her new situation. With Joan's encouragement, she had finally got round to looking in the filing cabinet and had come across a large envelope entitled *family documents*. Inside it she had found a life insurance policy of which she was the named beneficiary, and a Will stating that the bulk of Howard's assets would come to her after his death. Certain sums of money had also been set aside for the children's education. The document, which had been witnessed by two of Howard's colleagues, was dated eighteen months before. She recalled a visit Howard had received around that time, from a solicitor acquaintance who specialised in wills and probate. When she had taken coffee to them in Howard's study, she heard the man urging him to make provision for his family as '*it's never too early*'. Howard had muttered a non-committal response and had never mentioned that he had acted on this advice.

DC Harrison had already advised her on various matters she would need to sort out. He told her that once she had the death certificate, she should inform the Land Registry, banks, insurance companies, the local council, utility companies and other agencies of Howard's death, and make sure that documents and services were transferred into her name. She found this all very confusing, but realised that from now on she would have to start taking charge of the family finances herself. One of the other things she would do, she resolved as she toyed with her food, would be to replace the furniture in the sitting room, and change Howard's Volvo for a smaller car. She pulled herself up short. How could she be thinking about removing traces of Howard so soon after his death?

Simon's voice broke into her reverie. 'Mum, you're not eating.'

She looked down at her untouched meal. 'I'm not very hungry, darling.'

Joan frowned. 'Try to eat something, Karen.' She appealed to the children. 'We don't want your mother wasting away, do we?'

Karen reluctantly put a forkful of food in her mouth.

After lunch, she was surprised to receive another visit from DC Harrison. Joan shooed the children into the garden as she ushered him into the living room.

He sat down heavily on one of the leather armchairs.

'Has something happened?' she asked, trying hard not to stare at the cyst on his forehead. She wished he would have removed. 'Have you found out who shot my husband?'

'We're making some progress but murder enquiries have to be very thorough. DCI Evans, the Senior Investigating Officer, has decided that there is going to be a reconstruction of the attack on your husband.'

'Oh,' she said faintly, unsure what that meant.

He smiled reassuringly. 'We often stage reconstructions of serious crimes; it's a useful part of an investigation strategy. It could jog the public's memory. Some witnesses may have seen the motorbike before or after the perpetrator shot your husband, and any details they give could help the investigation.'

'When will it be?' she asked.

'On Friday afternoon, like the original incident.'

'Oh.' She looked away and twiddled a strand of her hair.

He gazed at her for a moment. 'How are you doing, Mrs Armstrong?'

'As well as can be expected, I suppose.'

'And the children?'

'They're totally devastated of course. My friend Mo who they've been staying with, said that Erica never stops crying and Simon's been having terrible nightmares about being chased by a man with a gun.'

'Oh dear, poor kids. It must be very difficult for you, for all of you.'

'It is. Are *you* married, Mr...Detective Harrison?

'Martin,' he said. 'Please call me Martin. Yes I am married.'

'Do you have any children...Martin?' She felt awkward using his Christian name; the informality seemed premature.

'Just one.' He smiled. 'He works in London.'

'Do you often do this?'

He looked puzzled. 'Do what?'

'Liaise with families after a murder?'

'I volunteered for FLO - Family Liaison Officer - training a couple of year ago. I wanted to be more involved with the people I was coming into contact with during policing, especially those who have experienced traumatic events - not just a murder; it could be a case of a missing person, or something like a house fire.' He cleared his throat. 'There's something I need to ask you, Mrs Armstrong—'

'You can call me Karen,' she said timidly.

'Karen, what can you tell me about *Sherwood Enterprises?*' He was watching her closely as he waited for a response. His eyes were so blue that the pupils were hardly visible. Those eyes were wasted on a man, she thought.

'Sherwood what?'

'*Sherwood Enterprises.* It's a company.'

'I've never heard of it.'

'Are you sure?'

'Perfectly sure,' she replied, bewildered. 'Why are you asking?'

'Because we found the name in some of your husband's papers.'

'Well that's not surprising, is it? Howard was an accountant. He worked with a lot of different companies.'

'*Sherwood Enterprises* is not a client of *Armstrong and Murray.*'

'It's not?' She felt uncomfortable under his steady gaze. 'Maybe my husband had dealings with other companies besides those he worked with.'

'Karen, did you know about your husband's offshore account?'

'Offshore account?' she echoed, 'you must be mistaken.' All she knew about offshore accounts was that very rich individuals and large corporations opened them to avoid paying tax.

'There's no mistake. You *weren't* aware that Mr Armstrong opened an account in the Cayman Islands in 2008?'

'What?' She twisted her fingers together nervously. 'No, I had absolutely no idea.'

'Or that he had set up a company called *Sherwood Enterprises* in order to do so?'

'No.' Karen was stunned. 'Are you sure?'

'Yes.' He continued to scrutinise her, making her feel uneasy and oddly guilty.

'What kind of company?' she asked to break the uncomfortable silence.

'One that ostensibly markets second-hand children's

clothing to developing countries; the kind of stuff that's collected door-to door by charities.'

Karen suppressed a hysterical giggle. Howard, an extremely fastidious dresser, wouldn't tolerate an item of second-hand clothing in the house. 'That's impossible!'

'I'm afraid it's a fact. You weren't aware that he was involved in such an enterprise?'

'No, I don't believe it. Howard never mentioned a company dealing in second-hand clothes to me.'

'Maybe not, but we've found evidence that suggests something wasn't quite above board.'

Karen felt a flurry of anxiety. 'Was it something illegal?'

He coughed. 'There are some ... discrepancies in the business your husband set up.'

'What kind of discrepancies?' By now Karen was distinctly alarmed. She dug her nails into her palms.

'Just... matters that need to be cleared up. There's a considerable sum of money in the offshore account.'

She stared at him aghast. 'How much?'

'A *very* large amount, Karen, far more than one might expect to accrue from such a business. So it would assist the investigation if we knew who else was involved in *Sherwood Enterprises*.'

'I'm afraid I can't help you. I know nothing about it.' As Karen spoke, she had a sudden jolt of memory. At the time when she and Howard met, he had been living in a Sherwood Road or Sherwood Crescent, something like that. Before she could mention this, Martin Harrison asked her another question.

'Do you know someone called Gerald Manning, Karen?'

'No, why?'

He gazed thoughtfully round the room before replying.

'Just a name that's come up in connection with something. And now, would it be possible to take a look at any financial documents your husband kept here, just to check on a few things?'

'Yes,' she said reluctantly.

He rose from his chair. 'May I look in the filing cabinet, the one in the office upstairs?'

She accompanied him up to Howard's study and watched while he opened the cabinet. He searched through it and extracted various papers which he scrutinised. He held on to some of them and replaced others. 'I'll have to take some of these to be examined if you don't mind.'

She nodded assent.

Eventually he shut the cabinet and straightened up with an air of disappointment. Karen wasn't surprised. She suspected that Howard wouldn't have left anything secret or confidential where someone else could find it. He had been far too careful. But what exactly had he been doing with an offshore account?

'How many bank accounts did your husband have?'

'I'm afraid I don't know. Howard did all the financial stuff online. I told you my sister rang his bank to see if his current account could be transferred to me, but they refused because it isn't a joint account. Like you said, they need a copy of the death certificate and other documents, but we're still waiting for the inquest.'

'Yes, of course.' Martin followed her back downstairs, 'That's all for now, Karen. But if you do remember your husband mentioning *Sherwood Enterprises* or Gerald Manning, please let us know. And don't forget, I'm here to help if you have any queries. I can come round any time.'

'Thank you,' she said, although she was beginning to

wish he wouldn't come round quite so often.

After Martin had left the house, the children came bounding in from the garden, followed by Joan. Erica accosted her immediately, her expression accusing. 'What did that man want?'

Standing behind their sister, Simon and Poppy gazed at Karen expectantly.

'Just to ask a few more questions, darling.'

'Why's it taking so long,' Erica demanded. 'Why haven't they found the man who killed Dad?'

'I've no idea, sweetheart. I suppose it's a difficult case to solve. Go upstairs or back outside for a minute. I need a word with Auntie Joan.'

'Has something happened?' Joan asked after the children had returned to the garden. 'You look shell-shocked. What did that detective want?'

'He says Howard had opened an offshore account.'

'What?'

'And that he started a company called *Sherwood Enterprises* that sells second-hand children's clothing to charities, or from charities, or something.'

Joan stared at her. 'Howard? Second-hand clothes? You must be joking.'

'Ludicrous isn't it? But he said they've got evidence.'

'And you didn't know?'

'I had absolutely no idea.' Karen gazed at her. 'But if it's true, why wouldn't Howard have mentioned it?'

Joan frowned. 'It sounds very out of character. Was the detective sure?'

'Yes. He said they'd found details on Howard's computer. Is it illegal to have an offshore account, Joan?'

Joan looked worried, 'I don't think so, unless it involves

some kind of fraud, like money laundering, but Howard wouldn't have been involved in anything like that.'

'Wouldn't he?' Karen clenched and unclenched her fists. 'Howard never told me anything about his financial affairs. I've no idea what he might have been up to.'

Joan patted her shoulder reassuringly. 'I'm sure he wasn't up to anything. That company, whatever it's called, was probably one Howard was working with.'

'DC Harrison said it wasn't.'

'What does he know?' Joan snorted. 'Why don't you ring Geoff? He'll be able to tell you.'

'Yes, I will. I'll do it now.'

The phone rang a number of times before it was answered.

'I'm sorry,' Geoff responded without any kind of a greeting. 'I'm too busy to talk now.'

She was surprised at his curt tone. 'I only need a minute, Geoff. I've just had a police officer here asking questions.'

'Oh?'

'He told me that Howard had opened an offshore account in the name of a company called *Sherwood Enterprises*. Do you know anything about it?'

'No!' he replied sharply. 'I don't.'

'I thought it might be a company you were doing accounts for.'

'I can assure you, Karen, *Sherwood Enterprises* has nothing whatsoever to do with *Armstrong and Murray*. We've had detectives here too, asking about it, and it's completely disrupted our routine. I know it's not your fault, Karen, it's a terrible time for you and the family, but I've got to keep the company ticking over, you understand? It doesn't help having the police here all the time, going through the files. I have our reputation to think of.'

'I'm sorry, Geoff,' she stammered, 'but I just thought I'd ask. I've never heard of *Sherwood Enterprises*. I have no idea what Howard was up to.'

'Neither have I, Karen. Neither have I! I'm sorry but I have a meeting.' He abruptly ended the call.

There had to be a simple explanation, Karen told herself as she replaced the phone. After all, Howard had been an accountant who worked with all sorts of companies. However the fact that he hadn't mentioned setting up a second-hand clothes business made her deeply uneasy. The way Martin Harrison had questioned her suggested that there had been something very suspicious about the enterprise.

That evening, the phone in the study upstairs suddenly rang.

Joan glanced up from her knitting. 'Aren't you going to answer that?'

Karen sighed. 'It's probably someone else Howard worked with. I don't think I can bear to hear any more expressions of sympathy.'

The ringing stopped but started again a few minutes later. Afraid that it might wake the children, she ran upstairs and picked up the receiver. 'Yes?'

There was a brief silence then a man's impatient voice. 'Is Howard there?'

'No, he's not. I'm his wife --'

'Can you tell me where he is?'

Karen thought she could detect an Australian accent. 'Who is this?'

'One of his business associates, Gerry.'

'Gerry?'

'Gerry Manning. I need to speak to Howard, urgently.'

*Where had she heard that name before?* 'I'm afraid you can't.'

'Why not?' the man barked.

'Because he's...he's dead.'

There was a loud exclamation at the other end of the phone.

'Dead?'

'I'm afraid so. You didn't know?'

'No.' He sounded stunned. 'I've only just arrived in the UK. How? When did it happen?'

'The Friday before last.'

He uttered a grunt of surprise. 'Was he ill?'

'No. He was... he was ...murdered... shot.' She still found it difficult to say the words. 'It was on the news.'

She heard the man gasp. 'Did you say he was murdered?'

'Yes.'

'Good God! I had no idea. I'm totally...' His voice tailed away.

He seemed at a loss for words.

'I'm sorry,' Karen found herself saying, although she didn't know what she had to be sorry for.

'Who?' he asked abruptly. 'Who did it?'

'We don't know yet. The police are still investigating...' She didn't continue the sentence as the man abruptly rang off.

'Who was that, Mum?' Erica was standing at the study door in her pyjamas.

'Just someone who wanted to speak to Dad. He hadn't heard about what happened. I'm afraid it gave him a shock. Go back to bed, Erica.'

As she was descending the stairs, she suddenly remembered. Martin Harrison had asked her if she knew a Gerald

Manning when he had dropped the bombshell about Howard's offshore account.

She called him early the next morning.

'Gerald Manning!' Martin sounded excited. 'Where was he was ringing from?'

'I don't know. He said that he'd been out of the country and had only just arrived.'

'Did you check caller ID, or look for the number after you put the phone down?'

'No.' Karen felt embarrassed that this hadn't occurred to her. 'Never mind. Has anyone called on that line since?'

'No.'

'Well you could ring 1471 and let me know if there's a number. If not we'll see if we can trace the call.'

'Yes, I'll try.' She wondered why he was so interested in the man who had phoned. 'Who *is* Gerald Manning, Martin?'

'Someone connected with your husband; someone we'd like to get in contact with.'

'Why? Do you think he's a suspect?'

'Not necessarily. But we'd like to check him out.'

She rang him back a few minutes later. 'I just dialled 1471 but the number was unavailable.'

'OK, I'll get someone on to it.'

# Chapter 5

'Mum! There's someone in the garden.'

Roused abruptly from sleep, Karen sat up and switched on the bedside light. Simon was standing by the bed. 'What's the matter?' She glanced at her alarm clock. It was just after 3 am.

'There's someone in the garden,' he repeated.

'How do you know?'

'I heard a noise, something banging.'

She felt a prickle of fear. 'I'll come and look.' She jumped out of bed, switched on the hall light and hurried into Simon's room. It was at the back of the house and the window overlooked the garden. She peered through it and in the light afforded by the nearly full moon, she caught sight of a man walking past the shed. He disappeared through the gate leading to a narrow alley where people left their rubbish to be collected. She waited for a while then, as the figure didn't reappear, switched on the light.

'Is it a burglar, Mum?' Simon asked nervously.

'I don't know, darling, but whoever it was, he's gone now.'

'Are you going to call the police?'

Karen hesitated. She peered out of the window again but nothing moved in the garden. 'I'll call them first thing in the morning. There's no need to disturb Auntie Joan or the girls.'

'But what if he comes back...?'

'He won't. As we've switched some lights on, he'll know that we've been disturbed. You can come into my bed if you like. And Simon, please don't say anything to Poppy and Erica. It'll be our secret.'

After checking to make sure that the girls hadn't woken up, she returned to her room. Simon lay down beside her. He quickly fell asleep but she lay anxiously awake for the rest of the night.

\* \* \*

'Why on earth didn't you wake me?' scolded Joan as they were clearing up the breakfast things.

'I didn't like to disturb you, and I asked Simon not to mention what he saw to the girls.'

'Why didn't you ring the police?'

'Because whoever it was had gone. I must have disturbed him when I put the hall light on. And I didn't want the police trampling over the garden with flashlights, waking the neighbours. I rang them at eight this morning and left a message for Martin Harrison.'

Joan pursed her lips disapprovingly. 'You should have rung them immediately. They might have caught him.'

'I don't think so. Anyway, it was probably only an opportunistic intruder.'

'Well I'm not going home today if you're in danger of being burgled.'

'I won't hear of it.' Karen endeavoured to sound serene as she put the last of the mugs in the cupboard. 'We'll be perfectly OK, Joanie. You've done quite enough for us already.'

Martin Harrison rang back later that morning. 'Why didn't you call us?' he asked after she told him what had happened.

'He'd already gone and I didn't want the girls disturbed.'

He clicked his tongue. 'Unwise! Is the house secure? Is there a security light at the back?'

It struck her now that the light hadn't come on. 'Yes there is, but when I looked out of the window, it wasn't on. Maybe it's broken.'

'I'll come over and take a look. If it is broken, we'll arrange for you to get a new one as soon as possible. Don't worry, Karen, we'll make sure you and the family are protected.'

'Why, do you think we're in danger?' she asked in alarm. 'Do you think the man who attacked Howard might have come back?'

'That's extremely unlikely. Our assumption is that what happened to your husband was the result of a personal grudge, revenge, possibly for some business-related matter. I'll come round as soon as possible and check out the garden.'

\* \* \*

Karen felt abandoned when Joan returned to her own home that afternoon. She was soon distracted, however, by Martin's arrival. He was accompanied by a young, uniformed policeman.

The children stood on the patio and watched the two of

them as they walked across the back lawn. 'What are they doing?' Erica asked anxiously.

Karen gave Simon a warning look. 'Just checking something for the investigation. Nothing to worry about, darling.' As her daughter seemed unconvinced, she added, 'why don't you all go inside and make some cupcakes? We can have them for tea later.'

Making cupcakes was Erica's latest favourite thing. She agreed to the suggestion enthusiastically and returned to the kitchen, followed by Simon and Poppy.

Martin and the youthful policeman walked slowly up and down scrutinising the rectangle of rusty grass. They then did a quick survey of the alley outside the back gate. After completing their inspection, they joined Karen outside the kitchen door.

'The lawn's too dry for footprints to show up clearly,' Martin told her. 'Though there are some in the alley round the bins. But if you've had a refuse collection recently, it might be difficult to separate your guy's prints from the others.' He gazed up at the security light fixed to a bracket on the back wall of the house. 'Looks like that wire's broken, most likely been cut.'

Karen stared at him in alarm.

'Do you have a ladder?'

'There's a stepladder in the shed.' She hurriedly fetched the key from its hook by the back door and accompanied by the two men, went down to the shed, an ugly brick construction next to the vegetable patch at the bottom of the garden. Although she had wanted to have it demolished, Howard had refused. He said it was useful for storage.

'Oh!' she exclaimed as she bent to insert the key into the lock. 'The padlock's broken!'

Martin peered over her shoulder. 'What's in there?'

'Tools, garden stuff, decorating materials, kids' bikes, that sort of thing.' She pushed open the door and gasped. 'Oh my God!'

The articles stored in the shed were now lying in a chaotic heap on the floor. Garden tools and plant pots lay strewn amongst seed trays and tins of paint. The formerly neatly ordered shelves had been swept clean of their contents.

She groaned in dismay.

The youthful policeman whistled. 'Bloody 'ell!'

Karen made to enter the shed but Martin put a hand on her arm, restraining her. 'Don't touch anything. Was there anything of value in there?'

'I don't think so.' She peered at the jumble of objects. 'The kids' bikes and the lawnmower are still there, and I can see Howard's power drill by that bucket. 'Why would anyone break into the shed?'

Martin frowned. 'Might have thought there was something worth taking in there. It could just have been a routine break-in. It's not necessarily connected with what happened to your husband.'

Karen felt relieved. She preferred to think that the intruder was a burglar; it was less frightening.

'We need to check for prints. I'll get someone to come over later. Then you can see if anything's missing.' Martin made a quick phone call on his mobile. 'Now, we'd better take a look at that security light, if we can find your ladder.'

She peered inside. 'It's usually just behind the door, but it's not there.'

'Maybe took the ladder to reach a window. In which

case, it may be in the garden somewhere.'

Karen was perplexed. 'But if he only wanted a ladder, why would he trash everything in the shed?'

'It's quite common,' Martin said grimly. 'Some burglars deliberately make a mess, just for the hell of it.'

They found the stepladder lying in the narrow space between the garage and the garden wall. The young policeman placed it against the back wall then climbed up and inspected the security light. 'Yep,' he called down to them. 'Wire's been cut.' He clambered down and stooped to pick up some secateurs that were lying on the ground. 'Probably used these. Must have got them from the shed.'

Martin frowned. 'I'll arrange to get that light fixed for you, Karen.'

She was overcome with anxiety. 'What will I do if he comes back?'

'If you hear someone outside at night, don't wait for the morning. Ring us at once. In the meantime we'll check the locks and bolts on your front and back doors. Have you got locks on the windows?'

'Yes, Howard did that when he renewed the house insurance.'

'Good.'

Karen followed Martin and his colleague as they tried the door locks.

'They seem secure enough,' Martin said as they were about to leave, 'but make sure you put the security chains on inside at night. And remember, don't touch anything in the shed until someone's been over to check for prints.'

After Karen had closed the front door, Poppy, her face and hands smeared with flour, appeared in the hall. 'Have those mans gone, Mummy?'

'Yes, darling. Have you finished the cupcakes?'

'Yes they're in the oven and when they're cooked, we're going to put icing on, and Smarties and Hundreds and Thousands.'

'Wonderful! I hope there'll be enough for me.'

As Poppy trotted back into the kitchen, Simon, his face characteristically creased with anxiety, joined Karen in the hall. 'What did the policemen say, Mum?' he whispered.

She put an arm round him. Simon always seemed to need her reassurance more than the girls. 'Someone broke into the shed. But there's nothing to worry about.'

'What?' Sharp-eared Erica had overheard. She bounded away from the oven and through the kitchen door. 'Did you say someone broke into the shed?'

Karen sighed. 'Yes, that's why the police came.'

'Who was it?'

'We don't know, probably just an intruder looking to see what he could find. I don't think he took anything.'

'What about my bike?' Simon asked worriedly.' He wiped his hands on his trousers and made to rush out the back door but Karen stopped him.

'No, Simon, we can't touch anything in the shed yet because the police are sending someone to check for fingerprints. Don't worry. Your bike's still there. I saw it.'

'What are you talking about?' Poppy had joined them in the hall.

'Nothing, darling.' Karen gave the older two children a warning glance. 'Are you going to put the Smarties on the cakes?'

'Yes, Erica says I can do it. Come and watch, Mummy.' Poppy trotted back into the kitchen.

'Do you think the burglar will come back?' Erica asked

Karen anxiously.

'I don't think so, and the detective said the police will come straight away if we hear anyone in the garden. Now let me see those cakes.'

\* \* \*

After an officer had arrived and checked the contents of the shed for fingerprints, Karen started to clean up the mess the intruder had made. Simon helped her at first but soon got bored and returned to the house to play computer games.

She dragged garden equipment and tools to one side to make a passage through, then lifted the tins of paint and placed them against the back wall. In this part of the shed, there was a rickety wooden table which Howard had used for occasional DIY activities, and an old canvas chair that was now lying on its side. As she bent to pick it up, she glimpsed something under the table. Crouching down, she saw that it was a metal box, the kind used to store valuables and important documents. Grunting with effort, she pulled it out. The box was heavy and locked. She looked around for the key but it wasn't on the shelves or hanging on any of the hooks on the walls. She hurried back to the house and searched the drawers of Howard's desk, but the key wasn't there either. Nor was it in any of the pockets of his clothes. It occurred to her that the key to the box might be the small one that the detectives hadn't been able to identify. Maybe she should ring Martin Harrison and tell him about the box. But what if its contents revealed yet more disconcerting details about Howard?

On reflection, she decided not to call Martin, at least not yet.

# Chapter 6

After the inquest had returned the expected verdict of unlawful killing, Howard's funeral finally took place.

Karen spent an inordinate amount of time deciding what she was going to wear, unsure of what would be appropriate for a new widow. In the end she chose a plain navy skirt and jacket. She pinned back her hair and put on the diamond earrings Howard had given her after they became engaged. The period of her engagement had been the happiest time she had ever spent with him.

When Karen's car arrived at the crematorium, she saw Martin and DI Parker standing a few yards away from the door. Martin had told her that they would be coming and asked her to let them know whether any uninvited or suspicious individuals turned up. There were also some news reporters loitering outside, though fewer than the mob that had waited outside the house after Howard had been shot. As Martin had predicted, media interest in the murder had waned after other incidents claimed its attention.

There weren't many mourners apart from the immediate family, just a few neighbours and mutual friends and a small number of Howard's colleagues and business associates.

Karen sat in the front row between Erica and Simon,

gazing numbly at the coffin that bore the remains of her husband of fifteen years. She hadn't been sure whether the two older children should attend the cremation, fearing that they might find it too distressing. But both were adamant that they wanted to be there. She considered Poppy too young, and had left her at the house of one of her school friends.

It was a simple service. After reading from the gospels, the female vicar described Howard, whom she had never met, as an exemplary husband and father and a man of many talents. Geoff then stood up and gave a fulsome eulogy. He had kissed Karen when they met outside the crematorium, and seemed to have forgotten his recent brusqueness on the phone.

Karen had chosen two pieces of music she knew Howard had liked, Bach's first Cello Suite and Pachelbel's Canon, and the mourners spent a few minutes in silent meditation while these were played. Afterwards the coffin slid slowly out of sight behind deep purple curtains. At this point Erica started to sob loudly and Simon, sitting on Karen's other side, gave a cry of anguish. She clasped their hands tightly, tears cascading down her own cheeks. She didn't weep from grief or because she missed Howard; she wept for the unfulfilled promise and emptiness of a passionless marriage, for the violent and untimely manner of her husband's passing, and for the pain the children were feeling at the loss of their father.

After the ceremony, she stood at the door, accepting the sympathy of the mourners, little groups of whom lingered on the path outside the crematorium before making their way to a local function room where refreshments were being served.

\* \* \*

'Such a sad occasion, Karen,' murmured Geoff's wife, Celia. She was holding a wine glass in one hand and a plate piled with canapés in the other.

Celia was tiny and round. She had a round head with short, severely cut grey hair, and a completely round body with short legs. From a distance she resembled one of those wobbly toys that always rights itself when you try to push it over. Celia was a local councillor and sat on numerous worthy committees. She had a brisk, forbidding manner and never failed to make Karen feel judged, and in some obscure way, found wanting.

'So what are you going to do now?' Celia demanded. She selected a canapé from her plate and bit into it.

'Do?' Karen stared down at her, bemused. 'Well, the children and I will be going home as soon as everyone has left.'

'No, I mean, what are you going to do now that...' Celia's voice dropped to a whisper, '... now that Howard has gone. You'll be making big changes in your life I expect.'

'Oh I don't know about that, Celia... it's much too soon.'

'Are you going to buy a bigger house?'

Karen was perplexed. 'A bigger house? No, why should I?'

'Well, you'll be a wealthy woman soon, won't you?'

'Wealthy?' Karen repeated wonderingly. The idea had never occurred to her.

Celia's eyes were cold grey pebbles behind her glasses. 'Didn't I hear that Howard had amassed a fortune in an offshore account?'

Karen's heart sank. 'I don't...I didn't know anything about that. Howard never mentioned it.'

'Oh?' Celia fixed her with a hard, disbelieving stare. 'How odd. I suppose you know that the police have been investigating the company because of Howard's moonlighting activities? It's been very unpleasant for Geoff.'

A wave of hot anger surged through Karen's veins. She took a deep breath and drew herself up to her full height so that she towered over Celia. 'Unpleasant for *Geoff*? Perhaps you've forgotten that my husband has been murdered, Celia, and our three children have been left without a father? None of this has been particularly *pleasant* for us.' Trembling with indignation, she marched away, marvelling, not for the first time, that Geoff, the most amiable of men, had married such a disagreeable woman.

Joan, who had been circulating among the mourners offering them platters of food, appeared beside her. 'Are you OK, Karen?'

'No, I'm not OK.' Karen's indignation had given way to tearfulness. 'I've just been speaking to Celia Murray.'

'Oh her!' Joan, who shared Karen's dislike of Celia Murray, pursed her lips.

'She said Howard's offshore account has been causing problems for Geoff and the firm.'

'Why bring that up at the funeral?' Joan muttered angrily. 'As if you don't have enough on your plate.'

'She thinks I knew about the account. But I had absolutely no idea.'

'I know.' Joan patted her on the shoulder. 'Take no notice. She's the original Poison Dwarf.'

Karen dabbed at her eyes. 'Geoff obviously thinks I knew about it too although I assured him that Howard never told me anything. And Joan, I've been meaning to mention it. After someone broke into the shed, I found a metal box in there... a sort of strong box. It must have been Howard's.'

'Oh? What was in it?'

'I don't know. It was locked and I couldn't find the key.'

'Have you told that detective?'

'Martin, the liaison officer? No, not yet.'

Joan put an arm round her. 'You'd better tell the police as soon as possible, just in case. There could be something in there that could help the investigation.'

'I'll report it in a day or two,' Karen said without conviction. 'I just want to get today over with first.'

\* \* \*

Martin Harrison rang the day after the funeral. 'How are you, Karen? Yesterday must have been a terrible ordeal.'

'It was. I'm relieved it's over particularly for the children's sake. They were very upset when we came home.'

'It must have been incredibly difficult for all of you.'

Feeling the familiar tears prick her eyelids, Karen quickly changed the subject. 'By the way,' she said casually, 'when I was clearing up the shed, I found a metal box, a kind of strong box. It must have belonged to my husband.'

'Oh?' Martin sounded surprised. 'How did we miss that?'

'It was under the DIY table, right at the back. I only saw it because I bent to pick something up. It's quite heavy.'

'What's in it?'

'I don't know. It's locked and I can't find the key. I think it might be that little one, the key you couldn't identify.'

'May I come and take a look?'

He arrived less than an hour later and carried the box from where Karen had placed it, in the cupboard under the stairs, into the kitchen. He put it on the kitchen table then took a small key from his pocket and tried it in the lock. It fitted. He opened the box and with a grunt of surprise, extracted a laptop.

Karen gaped at it. 'Why would Howard put a laptop in a locked box?'

'That's fairly obvious: to stop someone finding it and, I assume, seeing what's on it.'

A tremor of alarm went through her. What would Howard be trying to hide? 'Do you think this is what the intruder was looking for?'

'Maybe.'

Karen's anxiety increased. 'If he *was* looking for it, he might come back.'

Martin ran a hand through his white hair. 'You haven't had any further disturbances, I take it?'

'No, thank goodness.'

'Well ring us immediately if you do, and someone will come round straight away. Try not to worry, Karen. You should be safe now that the security light's mended and you've installed a burglar alarm. I'll take the laptop to the station for analysis. It was under a table in the shed, you say?'

'Yes, right at the back. Howard had a sort of cubby hole there.'

'Mmm.' Martin gazed at her thoughtfully. 'Did your husband spend much time in the shed?'

'He used to shut himself in there at weekends and

sometimes in the evenings. He said it was to get some peace, away from the children's noise.'

'What did he do in there?'

'Bits of DIY, stuff like that.'

'Can you show me exactly where you found the box?'

'Mummy I want a drink.' Poppy had appeared at the kitchen door and was staring curiously at Martin.

Karen poured her a glass of milk and put some biscuits on a plate. 'Take these to the living room and share them with Erica and Simon. I'm just going to show Mr Harrison the shed. I'll be back in a minute.'

'Why have you got white hair?' Poppy asked Martin. 'Are you very old?'

He laughed. 'Extremely old by your standards, young lady.'

'Why have you got a lump on your face?' Poppy continued.

'Poppy!' Karen remonstrated, with difficulty suppressing a giggle. 'Don't be rude!'

'Because there wasn't enough room inside my head for my brain,'

Martin replied solemnly. 'So it started to poke out.'

Poppy seemed to accept this explanation and returned to the living room carrying the milk and biscuits.

Karen accompanied Martin down to the shed.

'It's a lot tidier than the last time I saw it,' he commented with a smile.

He examined the area she had described as Howard's "cubbyhole" and knelt down to peer under the DIY table. 'You didn't find anything else your husband may have left lying about?'

'No, but I wasn't looking for anything else. And

64

Howard wasn't the kind of person who left things lying about.'

'OK.' Martin glanced round the shed. 'There's a heck of a lot of stuff in here. It's easy to see how one wouldn't notice the box.'

'There's something I need to speak to you about, Karen,' he murmured awkwardly when he had finished his inspection.

'Yes?' Karen shut and locked the shed door behind them.

'We've been checking your husband's emails and the messages on his phone, and...'

'And?' she prompted.

'The investigating team has been tracing the senders and recipients.' He coughed and looked away from her. 'There's someone Mr Armstrong had an exchange of messages with over a period of time: a person who doesn't appear to be a client or business associate.'

'Oh? Who's that?'

'A woman called Maureen Field.'

'Mo?' Karen exclaimed, stunned. 'You know her?'

'Yes, she's a friend, Poppy's godmother. Her daughter Gemma is in the same class as Erica. She was at the funeral.'

He nodded. 'I see.'

Suspicion spread like a stain through her mind. 'What kind of messages were they?'

'Mainly just confirmations ... of ... um...times of meetings.'

'Meetings?'

'Rendezvous if you like.' Martin looked uncomfortable. 'We know that the lady lives in Gladstone Avenue, within easy walking distance of Bartholomew Court.'

Karen felt the blood rush to her face. She realised the implication of what he was saying. Could Howard have been going to see Mo on the afternoon when he was shot? And on all those days when he was supposedly working late? Her legs started to tremble and she leant against the shed wall to steady herself.

'We're checking all of Mr Armstrong's contacts as a matter of course,' she heard Martin mutter hastily. 'There is a Mr Field, I gather?'

'Yes, Tony's an architect; he has an office in London.'

'And you didn't know about the...meetings with Mrs Field?'

'No I didn't.' She tried to prevent her voice from trembling. 'I'm sorry, Karen, I had to mention it.'

'Yes,' she whispered. 'I know.' It had started to rain, gentle easeful rain, and she held her burning face up to it as she accompanied Martin back up the garden.

'I'll be in touch,' he told her as he left the house carrying the laptop.

Her mind was racing as she closed the door. When the woman detective had asked whether Howard had been seeing another woman, she had dismissed the idea as absurd. But Mo, her closest friend? Surely not. It wasn't possible. Or was it? She sank on to a kitchen chair and buried her face in her hands. If it was true, how could they have managed an affair? After a minute of furious thought, she worked it out for herself. Tony rarely got home before seven thirty in the evening. Two afternoons a week Gemma and Erica stayed after school to do music and drama. On another afternoon, Gemma went straight from school to a gymnastics training session in town. Howard could easily have called round on those days. But what about the school holidays? With a start she remembered that at the time Howard was shot, Gemma had been on a two-week camping trip.

She shouldn't be that surprised, she thought bitterly. They would have made a good pair - Mo, petite and doll-like, youthfully pretty; Howard, tall, good-looking, self-possessed, very unlike quiet, bespectacled Tony. She tried to imagine the two of them in bed together. What had it been like? When Howard had made love to her, it wasn't anything like the passionate grappling she had imagined love-making would be: it was a brisk, emotionless affair on his part that invariably left her disappointed and dissatisfied. Had he displayed more feeling when he made love to Mo?

She recalled Mo's explosion of grief when she had been informed of Howard's murder. It had seemed understandable at the time - a good friend's expression of grief for her and the children. She realised now that Mo's loud wails were too heartbroken to have been other than an expression of her own sense of loss. What was it the woman detective had said? *The wife is always the last to know.* The double betrayal pierced her guts like a blade.

# Chapter 7

After spending several days in a state of shock and rage, Karen decided that the start of the new school year, when the children were at school, would be the best time to confront Mo. It wasn't an easy action for her to take. Naturally timid, she usually went out of her way to avoid confrontations, but this was something she felt she had to do.

After dropping Poppy off at the school gates, she walked purposefully round to Mo's house. As soon as Mo opened the door, she could see from her face - bereft of its habitual welcoming smile - that she had guessed the reason for the visit. The police must already have called.

'Come in, Karen,' Mo said quietly. Dressed in a white T-shirt and blue dungarees, she looked infuriatingly pretty as usual, more like a teenager than a woman in her thirties.

'You were seeing Howard,' Karen blurted before the door was even shut.

Mo avoided her eye. 'Yes, I was. Come in.'

Albert, Mo's black poodle, yapped and bumped round Karen's legs as she followed Mo into her gleaming, state-of-the-art kitchen; a place where the two of them had enjoyed many cosy conversations in the past.

'How long?' Karen demanded, pushing the puppy away.

Mo hesitated. 'About a year, maybe a little bit longer.'

She opened the back door to let Albert out, then motioned Karen to sit down.

Stunned, Karen remained standing. 'A *year*? And all that time you were pretending to be my friend?'

'I wasn't pretending, Karen, I *was* your friend. I never stopped being your friend.'

Karen snorted derisively. 'Didn't you? When exactly did it start, you and Howard?'

Mo's face flushed pink. 'It was after that time you came to dinner here. We sat and had drinks in the garden, re-member?'

Karen remembered the occasion only too well. Howard had arrived home in a filthy mood and had snapped at her before they left the house - *why is the house so untidy? Why are you wearing that boring grey dress? Why isn't Poppy in bed yet? Why is the babysitter late?*

For her, the evening had been ruined before it even started, whereas he underwent his customary personality transformation as soon as they got to Mo's - laughing, ex-changing witticisms, complimenting Mo on her clothes, her hair, her cooking, the way she had arranged the table. Mo had lapped it up, gazing at him admiringly, while she, Karen, remained sunk in misery, knowing that as soon as they left the house to go home, Howard would revert to his normal persona and criticise her for her lack of convivi-ality, for any remarks she had made that he took exception to, for leaving too much on her plate, for spilling her wine on the tablecloth.

'Yes, I remember that evening,' she said bitterly. 'So how did it start?'

'Howard rang me the next morning to thank me, and he asked if he could come round that afternoon. I said yes, and it sort of took off from there.'

Karen held on to the back of a chair to steady herself. 'How often did he come round after that?'

Mo flushed. 'On the afternoons when Gemma was doing afterschool activities.'

'Was he coming to see you the day he was killed?'

'Yes.' For the first time Mo looked shamefaced.

'Do the police know that?'

'They do now. A detective called round yesterday.'

'Why didn't you tell them before? It would have saved them a lot of trouble.'

'That's what the detective said, but nobody asked me at the time. Nobody knew about Howard and me, and anyway, it was irrelevant. It had nothing to do with the murder.'

'How do you know it was irrelevant?' Karen asked, flabbergasted. 'Someone must have been aware of Howard's movements otherwise he wouldn't have been targeted at that particular time.'

'The attack on Howard had nothing to do with Tony, if that's what you're getting at. He was still at work.' Mo sounded flustered. 'Anyway, Tony didn't... he doesn't know about me and Howard.'

'Well he'll find out soon enough now, won't he?' Karen was surprised to hear the venom in her own voice. 'The police are bound to want to question him.'

The silence that followed was broken only by the sound of Albert yapping frantically at the garden door.

'I know how this must seem, Karen,' Mo said eventually. There was a look of defiance in her large, baby blue eyes. 'But I knew that you and Howard weren't happy--'

'What?' Karen interjected sharply. 'I don't remember

ever telling you that.'

'No? Well maybe... maybe it was Howard who--'

'*Howard* told you we weren't happy?'

Mo squirmed under her scrutiny. 'No, well yes, he said...he said you weren't interested in him sexually--'

'You mean he implied I was frigid?' Karen forbore to mention that it had been Howard who had withdrawn from marital sex, not her.

'Yes, in a manner of speaking.'

'I'm surprised you fell for that line, Mo. I suppose he told you I didn't understand him as well. But of course you understood him, didn't you? And, unlike me, *you* were interested in him sexually.'

Mo's face was crimson. 'There's no need to be like that, Karen. You're blowing this up out of all proportion.'

'Out of *proportion*?' Karen found it hard to control herself. 'You were having it off with my husband for a year, all the time pretending to be my friend, and you tell me I'm blowing it out of proportion?'

Mo took refuge behind the kitchen table. 'Well, there's no point in going on about it. It's not as though it can continue, is it? And remember I've always been there for you, Karen. I'm Poppy's godmother and I've helped you out with the children. I looked after them for you after Howard died, didn't I?'

'Do you think that compensates for what you've done?'

'What *have* I done? It was only an affair. It didn't mean anything.'

'*Only an affair*?' Karen shouted. 'You betrayed me when I thought you were a friend.'

'Don't be so melodramatic, Karen!' Mo snapped irritably.

71

'*Melodramatic*?' A surge of fury coursed through Karen's veins. She lunged at Mo across the table, giving her a hard push so that she staggered and fell back against the wall. 'You disgust me, Mo. I never want to speak to you again.'

She left the house, slamming the door behind her. When she got home she sank on to a chair, laid her head on the table and sobbed. It was the most she had cried since the day Howard had died.

\* \* \*

'Oh the bitch... the two-faced bitch!' Joan exclaimed when Karen rang and told her tearfully what had happened. 'Mo of all people. How could she do that to you?'

'I don't know.' Karen tried to compose her voice. 'She's the last person I would have suspected. '

'You poor love, finding that out after all you've been through. I've a good mind to go round and tell her exactly what I think of her.'

'Don't bother. When the police question Tony, he'll find out what she's been up to and then--'

'The shit will hit the fan! Serve her bloody well right. But I'm really surprised that Howard let himself be tempted by a pretty face. Mo must have given him the come-on.'

'She said Howard made the first move.'

'And you believe that?' As ever, Joan was reluctant to think badly of Howard.

'Yes, as a matter of fact I do.'

After the call ended, Karen stood at the patio door and watched the rain lashing down on the lawn. What else had Howard been hiding from her? she wondered. Why had she allowed him to dominate her and dictate their life to such an extent? She knew the answer of course. She had been too timid, too over-awed by his stronger personality. She had been dependent on him and grateful to him. Now she felt that she loathed him. The final years of their life together had been a sham.

Gazing out at the garden, she began to redesign it in her mind. She would get rid of that ugly shed and install a summer house; plant flower borders round the edges of the grass; bring the children's trampoline and Wendy house closer to the back door. She might even get a pet for the children – all things Howard had absolutely refused to contemplate. She would rearrange the house and replace the heavy leather armchairs in the sitting room with softer, fabric-covered ones. But, she realised, it wasn't enough to change the furniture and restructure the garden. She need-ed to change and restructure her life. She had to find a pro-ject or an occupation. But what? She shuddered at the thought of another humiliating and fruitless visit to the Job Centre.

At three o'clock she went to pick Poppy up from school. Her mood lightened when she spotted the little girl amongst the explosion of squealing children that erupted out of the classroom door. She swept Poppy up in her arms. 'How was school, pet?'

'I got a sticker,' Poppy announced proudly, showing her a gold star stuck to her dress.

'That's wonderful! What's it for?'

'The teacher said I was a good listener!'

Erica and Simon returned from high school about a half an hour after Karen and Poppy got home. Erica burst into the house and ran straight upstairs, all the while yelling into her mobile phone, probably to a school friend she had seen only minutes before.

Simon trailed through the front door behind her, his face a picture of misery.

'Are you OK, Simon?' Karen asked anxiously. 'How was school today?'

'It was...it was ...' His eyes filled with tears.

She crouched down and hugged him. 'What's the matter, darling? Has something happened?'

He swallowed hard. 'Some boys kept running after me. They were laughing at me because of what happened to Dad. One of them said Dad must have done something bad and that's why he was murdered.'

'Oh Simon, I'm sorry, that must have been awful.' Karen was dismayed. She had contacted the heads of both schools and had been assured that the teachers would monitor the three of them for any signs of distress. 'What are their names? I'll ring the school.'

'No Mum. Please don't say anything.' Simon tugged worriedly at his earlobe. 'If they know I've dobbed them up, they'll try and get me after school.'

'I'll make sure they don't,' Karen said angrily. 'I'm not letting you be picked on just because of what happened to your dad.'

'No Mum, please.' The boy's face was a picture of anguish.

'OK, you needn't give me their names.' Karen was aware that Simon was a prime target for bullying and resolved to ring the school as soon as he was out of earshot. She stroked his hair. 'What happened to your dad is bound to attract stupid comments from ignorant people who don't understand how terrible it's been for us. We have to be strong and try to rise above it.'

He gazed at her tearfully. 'It's hard.'

'I know it is, darling. Now, why don't we have some of that chocolate cake? The one Auntie Joan made before she left.'

Simon's face lit up and he followed her eagerly into the kitchen. She cut him and Poppy large slices of cake before going upstairs to Erica's room where she found her daughter sprawled on the bed, still chattering on her mobile phone.

'Erica?'

With a look of annoyance, Erica removed the phone from her ear.

'What is it, Mum?'

'Stop talking on the phone. I want to speak to you.'

'I'll call you back in a minute, Lisa.' Erica switched off the mobile and hurled angrily it to the foot of the bed. 'What do you want?'

'I want to know how you got on at school today. What was it like?'

'Is that all?' Erica snapped. 'Boring, like it always is.'

'I mean, did anyone ask about your dad?'

'Yes. Some girls did, and lots of the kids kept staring at me and whispering. '

'Did it upset you?'

'Of course it upset me!'

'It'll blow over, darling. People will stare at you for a while because of what's happened. But they'll soon forget about it.' Karen remembered how she had become an object of curiosity at school after her mother had died.

'Yeah, whatever. Can I speak to Lisa again now?' Erica muttered impatiently. She reached down the bed to pick up her phone.

Karen sighed. Had it been unwise to let the children return to school so soon after their father had died? Erica had become increasingly moody and rebellious recently. She wondered how much this was due to grief and how much to normal teenage angst.

\* \* \*

The following afternoon, Erica burst through the front door, her face set in a ferocious expression. 'Gemma says you've quarrelled with Auntie Mo,' she shouted accusingly. 'Is it true?'

Karen stiffened. She had been expecting something like this.

'Yes, I'm afraid it is.'

'Why?'

'It's... just something between adults, darling.'

'But Auntie Mo's your friend.'

'She *was* my friend.'

'What happened then?'

Karen hesitated. 'What exactly did Gemma tell you?'

'She said you went round to the house and were nasty to Auntie Mo. Why?'

Karen felt a rush of indignation. 'That's not true, Erica. I wasn't "nasty" to Mo. I found out that she had done something I thought was...wrong, so I went to speak to her about it, that's all.'

'What? What did she do that was wrong?'

'I'm sorry, darling, I can't tell you. You wouldn't understand.'

'Yes I would!' Erica's face turned crimson. 'Tell me.'

'No, as I said, it's something between adults.'

'You're always telling *us* to sort things out when we quarrel... to make up.'

'I'm afraid this is different, darling. It's complicated. But it doesn't mean that you and Gemma can't still be friends.'

'Gemma doesn't want to be my friend any more, and it's all because of you. I hate you!' Erica ran upstairs and slammed her bedroom door.

Poppy came out of the sitting room and gazed at her questioningly. 'Why's Erica shouting? What's happening?'

'Nothing's happening, darling. Tea's ready. It's on the kitchen table.'

After Poppy had trotted into the kitchen, Karen turned to Simon who had been listening silently to the exchange with Erica. 'Did you have any trouble from those boys again?'

'No, but that was only because Mrs Maxwell was hanging about in the playground at break-time, and she was standing at the gates when I went to catch the bus. Did you say something to her, Mum?'

'I asked the head to make sure it didn't happen again.'

Simon's lip quivered, 'But they'll think I dobbed them up.'

'You didn't tell me their names, so you can't have dobbed them up, can you? And the head said you must tell her at once if you have any more problems.'

'But--'

'Don't worry, Simon. She said she'll make sure no-one bothers you. Now, could you ask Erica to come down for tea?'

Simon reluctantly climbed the stairs and called down a few seconds later. 'Mum, Erica's locked her door. She won't come out.'

Karen went up herself and knocked on Erica's door. 'Come on Erica, tea's ready.

'I don't want any tea!'

Karen sighed. 'OK, if that's your choice. But you'll be hungry later.'

There was no answer.

# Chapter 8

Karen found resuming a semblance of normal life was difficult after the children had gone back to school. Her few friends rarely called her and when she met acquaintances in the street, they either pretended not to see her or crossed to the other side of the road as if she had some kind of contagious disease they might catch. When she went to collect Poppy in the afternoons, the other mothers turned away from her and formed impenetrable small groups. She felt very alone.

She was surprised, therefore, to be approached at the school gates one morning, by a woman aged about thirty with thick chestnut coloured hair fastened on top of her head with metal combs. She was wearing a short red cotton skirt, a denim jacket and dizzyingly high heels.

'Hi!' The woman extended her hand. 'I'm Juliet Morgan. My son Joe's in the same class as your daughter.'

Karen shook her hand. 'Karen Armstrong.'

'Yes I know. I'm really sorry about your husband. You must be going through an incredibly tough time.'

'Thanks.'

'I think you're very brave, going out and about so soon after what's happened.'

'That's nice of you.' Karen gazed defiantly at two

women surreptitiously watching them nearby. 'But what else can I do?'

Juliet followed her gaze. 'I guess some people can be a bit... insensitive.'

Tears sprang to Karen's eyes. She brushed them away. 'I suppose they're embarrassed.'

Juliet smiled sympathetically. 'It's a common reaction when something terrible's happened to someone else; it upsets one's sense of security. Look, would you like to come and have coffee with me some time? I work three days a week but I'm at home on the other mornings.'

Karen was surprised and pleased. 'Yes I'd love to. Thank you.'

'Shall we say Friday? I live in Shaftesbury Road, the messy house on the corner. You can't miss it. It's the one with all the scooters and bikes in the front garden. There isn't room for them inside.'

Karen's pleasure at the unexpected invitation was short-lived, for not long after she had returned home, Martin came to the door. She had begun to associate his visits with horrifying revelations about Howard. Ominously, this time he was accompanied by DI Parker, the severe-looking woman detective who had questioned her a few days after Howard had died. The detective's presence filled Karen with a sense of foreboding. She led them quickly into the living room.

'Has something happened?'

'There has been an important development in the case.' DI Parker's face was expressionless.

'Does that mean you have a suspect?'

'The investigating team is still following up witness reports after the crime reconstruction, but we now have a new line of enquiry.'

Karen wasn't sure whether she should ask what this was. She perched nervously on the edge of the sofa and looked enquiringly at Martin. 'Are you any closer to finding the person who shot my husband?'

'We're following certain leads,' he answered cautiously, 'but we're somewhat under-staffed at the moment. How are the children, Karen? Have they settled back at school?'

Startled by the change of subject, she took a moment to answer. 'The older two have been having a few problems - people pointing at them, whispering, that kind of thing. But Poppy seems OK. She still asks about her daddy, but she's only six and doesn't really understand what's happened.'

Martin nodded sympathetically. 'It must be very difficult --'

'Oh it's gone!' Karen exclaimed. She had noticed that the lump on his forehead had been replaced by a small, puckered red line.

He stared at her in surprise. 'What's gone?'

'The cyst on your forehead.' She blushed with shame at her tactlessness.

He gave an embarrassed bark of laughter. 'Oh that! I had it removed at my wife's insistence.'

'Mrs Armstrong?' Evidently keen to return to the purpose of the visit, DI Parker fixed Karen with an unblinking gaze. 'We have some more questions for you, if you don't mind.'

'Yes?' Karen tugged nervously at a strand of her hair.

'We've checked the hard disk on your husband's laptop, the one you found in your shed,' Martin said quietly.

She felt a stab of anxiety.

'There's no easy way to put this, Karen,' he continued, 'but I'm afraid we found... stuff on it.'

'Stuff?' Alarm bells started ringing in Karen's mind. 'What kind of stuff?'

He ran a finger round the inside of his collar. 'Images.'

'What kind of images?' She dug her nails into her palms, fearing the response.

He hesitated for a second. 'Images of children and of people abusing them.'

She felt the blood drain from her face.

Martin shifted uncomfortably on the armchair. 'I'm afraid there's a lot of them, Karen, a very large number.'

She gaped at him, transfixed with horror.

DI Parker leaned forward in her chair, watching her intently. 'Your husband was a member of a child pornography ring, Mrs Armstrong.'

'No!' Karen leapt to her feet. 'That can't be true!'

The two officers regarded her in silence.

'It's *not* true, is it?' she whispered, gazing beseechingly at Martin.

He shifted uncomfortably in his armchair. 'I'm afraid there's no mistake, Karen.'

Trembling with shock and disbelief, Karen collapsed back on to the sofa. It was a moment before she managed to recover her voice. 'Are you certain Howard knew about the images?' she croaked, clasping her fingers together so tightly that they hurt. 'Just because they were on the laptop doesn't mean that he--'

'I'm afraid it does,' DI Parker said grimly. 'There's no doubt that he was involved. It's a large paedophile ring and highly dispersed. They use a code - PP. If you remember, there were a number of references to PP in your husband's diary.'

Karen nodded dumbly.

'PP stands for *Pied Piper*. It's a very slick operation. Some members of the group entice and groom poor children in Asian countries, and others traffic them round Europe.'

Karen attempted to fight off a wave of nausea. 'No! Howard could never be involved in something like that.'

'Unfortunately, he had a very strong connection with the operation,' DI Parker declared. 'The images date from 2008, when he set up the bogus charity.'

'What bogus charity?'

The two detectives exchanged a glance.

'Karen,' Martin said gently, 'I told you about the enterprise Mr Armstrong used to open his offshore account in the Cayman Islands - collection of second-hand clothing for children in developing countries. Your husband was actually engaged in the third stage of the paedophile ring's activities – selling pornographic images of the trafficked children. He was funnelling funds from this into his offshore account, passing them off as profits to be reinvested in the charity. It was cyber fraud: a form of money laundering.'

'Oh God.' Karen covered her face with her hands.

'An international investigation, headed by police in the Netherlands, has been investigating the ring in Indonesia. Gerald Manning, the man you spoke to on the phone, is one of the key figures, but there are many others. The investigating team hasn't yet identified all of those working at the European end. The *Pied Piper* online stuff is encrypted and well disguised. Members use what is called the Dark Net.'

'*Dark Net*,' Karen repeated. 'What's that?'

'Information circulated on the internet that's hidden or inaccessible to most people,' replied DI Parker. 'It's sometimes called Deepnet. It's used by criminals – drug-dealers, paedophiles, extreme fetishists.' She gave Karen a searching look. 'You had no idea? No inkling of what was going on?'

'Good God, no!' Karen stuttered. 'Absolutely none.'

Martin cleared his throat. 'Your own children, Karen; could your husband have ...um --?'

'No!' she almost screamed. Her stomach had started turning somersaults. She jumped up abruptly, ran to the small cloakroom in the hall and vomited violently into the hand basin.

When she eventually emerged, she felt cold but her face was damp with perspiration.

She found Martin waiting in the hall. He looked concerned. 'Are you OK, Karen?'

'No I'm...I'm--'

'Come and sit down.' He took her gently by the arm and led her back to the living room where DI Parker was now standing by the window. 'I'll get you some water.'

Karen collapsed on to the sofa and covered her face with her hands.

Martin brought a glass of water from the kitchen and handed it to her. 'I'm sorry, Karen. This must have come as a terrible shock. Would you like me to contact your sister?'

'No.' She felt a surge of hostility towards him and the stony-faced woman detective. 'No. I just want to be on my own.'

DI Parker sat down opposite her. Her expression had softened. 'I'm really sorry we've had to cause you further distress, Mrs Armstrong, but this obviously has an important bearing on the investigation.'

Karen gulped down some water without responding.

The detective produced a notebook and pen. 'If you feel sufficiently recovered, I'd be grateful if you could answer just a few more questions. Did Mr Armstrong always keep the laptop in the shed?'

Karen wiped her forehead with the back of her hand. 'I don't know.' She wished they would leave her alone.

'Did you ever see your husband use the laptop?'

'I didn't even know he *had* that laptop. The first time I saw it was when Martin...DC Harrison, opened the box.'

DI Parker looked thoughtful. 'You told DC Harrison that your husband used to spend time in the shed. How often did he go there?'

'Sometimes at weekends, sometimes in the evenings after he'd eaten. He used to do bits of DIY in there.'

'Did anyone ever visit your husband and spend time with him in the shed, or in his study?'

'No...yes... occasionally some business associates came to see him. But he always took them up to his study, never to the shed.'

DI Parker scribbled a note in her book. 'Do you remember their names?'

'No!' Karen jumped up abruptly and shrieked, 'that's enough! No more questions. Go away and leave me alone.'

The detectives gazed at her in consternation before also rising to their feet.

Martin took a step towards her. 'Are you sure you don't want me to call your sister, Karen?'

'Perfectly sure. I just want to be on my own.' She felt calmer after diverting some of her sense of shock into anger towards the two of them.

'I would advise you not to tell anyone about what's on the laptop,' DI Parker warned as they walked through the hall. 'It could compromise the enquiry.'

Karen gave a bitter laugh. 'You've just informed me that my husband was engaged in child pornography. I'm hardly likely to shout that from the rooftops, am I?'

'Of course not,' the detective said gently. 'But please be circumspect, Mrs Armstrong. It doesn't take long for gossip and rumours to spread. If anything gets out about your husband's involvement in this kind of thing, it will be all over the tabloids within twenty four hours. I'm sure you'd want to avoid that.'

Martin lingered on the front doorstep. 'I realise this is an extremely delicate matter, Karen,' he ventured awkwardly, 'but if you're concerned about your own children--'

'Please,' she begged before he could go any further. 'I can't bear to think about that.'

He nodded. 'I understand, but there are specialist agencies and helplines that deal with situations like this. I can give you a list if you like --'

'Thank you, no!' She shut the door with a bang and went slowly upstairs.

She lay on the bed, shivering. Of all the terrible things she had discovered about Howard, this was the worst; worse than his offshore account and bogus charity, worse than the affair with Mo. The man she had been married to for fifteen years; the man she had respected, though perhaps not loved, had turned out to be a monster, not just a cheat and a fraudster, but also a paedophile.

Unbearable questions raced through her mind. How

could she not have known? How could she have shared a bed with a man who was sexually interested in children? Had their marriage been a front, a way of disguising his real urges? Could it have been a marriage of convenience on both sides; on his, because his sexual urges were focused in a forbidden direction; on hers, because she craved security? Had they forged an unspoken mutual bargain? The idea filled her with shame and disgust.

It made sense to her now why Howard would have been attracted to Mo. Tiny, fresh-faced and invariably dressed in dungarees or very short skirts, Mo, though a little over thirty, could still pass for a teenager.

Had there been signs during the fifteen years they were married, any indications she could have missed? After some reflection she recalled with a start that the three charities Howard had assisted, ostensibly out of altruism, had all been involved with *children*. A chill ran down her spine when she remembered that some years before, he had visited an orphanage in Indonesia for a charity of which he was a trustee. Had he gone on the trip in order to groom vulnerable children for the paedophile ring? With a shudder she tried to block horrendous visions of Howard with small Asian children. Now, with a cry of anguish, she was forced to confront an even more horrifying possibility - one she had refused to contemplate earlier. What if Howard had abused his *own* children? If he had and she had failed to notice their distress, wouldn't that mean she was a terrible mother?

She took a deep breath in an attempt to calm herself. So far as she could recall, neither of the girls had shown any signs of stress or discomfort in Howard's company, although there had been occasional tension between him and

Simon. How could she find out whether he had done anything to them without divulging her reason for asking? The children had been in a very vulnerable state since Howard had died. Erica was likely to fall into a rage at the slightest provocation, and both Simon and Poppy had become anxious and clingy, perhaps fearing that she would disappear as abruptly as their father had.

Who could she turn to for advice? Could she bear to keep the information to herself as the detective had advised? If Howard's membership of a child porn ring ever became public, how could they go on living in Moxton? She could already imagine people whispering, *there's no way she couldn't have known...*

Desperate to escape from her unbearable thoughts, she took a sleeping pill and eventually drifted off to sleep.

She was woken abruptly by the bedside phone.

An accusing female voice: 'Is that Mrs Armstrong? Poppy's still here. All the other children have been collected.'

'Oh God!' She glanced at her watch. It was after three thirty. She had slept for nearly four hours. 'I'm so sorry, 'she stammered. 'I wasn't feeling well, I'll come straight away.'

She jumped up, wincing at the jangling headache induced by the rude awakening, pulled on her shoes and hurried to the school.

# Chapter 9

She decided to speak to Erica after school that evening and waited for the right opportunity. It came when Erica was in the kitchen, busily making cupcakes to take to school the following day.

Karen hovered awkwardly beside her as she sieved flour into a mixing bowl. She was dreading the response to the question she was going to ask. Erica had always adored her father and she was still sulking about the quarrel with Mo.

She took a deep breath. 'Erica?'

'Yeah, what?' Without looking up, Erica carefully cracked open some eggs and dropped the contents into another bowl.

'I'm afraid I have to ask you a rather difficult question, darling,' Karen stumbled, 'and I want you to answer me as honestly as you can.'

'What?' Erica repeated impatiently.

'You know that the police need to look into every possibility while they carry out their investigation?'

'Yeah, so?' Erica switched on an electric whisk and started to beat the eggs.

'Erica,' Karen spoke loudly to make herself heard over the whirr of the whisk. 'Did your father ever...touch you?'

Erica switched off the whisk. 'What do you mean?'

'Did Dad ever....touch you...in an... inappropriate manner?'

Erica gaped at her for a moment, then, as understanding dawned, her face tightened into an expression of fury. 'What are you suggesting?'

'I'm not suggesting anything, darling, I'm just asking.'

'If you mean what I think you mean, no of course he didn't!' Erica was incandescent with rage. 'How could you even think something like that?'

'I'm sorry, Erica, but I had to ask.'

'*Why*? Why did you have to ask something like that?'

'The police were here again this morning. Because it's a murder investigation, they have to examine the case from every possible angle, however unpleasant, and that includes intimate family relationships, I'm afraid.'

'But they *can't* have suggested that Dad...That's gross! It's disgusting!' Erica's dark eyes burned with fury. She dropped the whisk on the kitchen table and bits of egg mixture spattered over its surface. 'How could you have let them suggest something like that?' She ran out of the kitchen, tore upstairs and slammed her bedroom door.

A few moments later, Simon entered the kitchen. 'What's going on, Mum? I heard Erica crying. Have you had another row?'

'No, we didn't have a row, darling. I asked her a question and she was upset by it.'

'What question?'

Karen hesitated, fearful of provoking another angry scene, although she knew that Simon was far less volatile than Erica. 'It's just... oh dear; it's so hard to do this.'

'Do what, Mum?'

'Ask questions about your dad.'

Simon looked so worried that she felt overwhelmed with protective love for him. 'You see, darling, the police are investigating everything, including family relationships, and they asked...' She swallowed hard before continuing. 'Simon, did Dad ever touch you...inappropriately? Did he ever do anything to you that you didn't like?'

Simon gazed at her uncomprehendingly. 'What do you mean?'

'I mean,' she swallowed again. 'Did he ever...touch you in an unpleasant way, or hurt you?' She felt ill-equipped to ask such questions. Maybe she should have asked for advice first. She wished now that she hadn't been so rude to Martin when he had told her there were specialist agencies that could help with such delicate matters.

Simon stared at her with his innocent wide grey eyes. 'No,' he said finally. 'Dad hardly ever touched me.'

That was true, she thought. Howard and Simon had never been very close. She couldn't recall Howard ever cuddling their second child, even when he was a baby or toddler.

Simon peered at the unfinished cake preparation on the table. 'If Erica's not coming down, can I finish making the cakes?'

'Yes, that's a good idea.' She felt a surge of relief that he hadn't displayed any signs of discomfiture at what she was asking and hadn't even seemed to understand the implication.

But what about Poppy? How could she possibly ask a six-year- old whether her daddy had interfered with her? It was the kind of question best left to an experienced child psychologist or one of the specialist police officers she had heard about, who used dolls as gentle prompts with small victims of paedophilia. She decided not to say anything to Poppy until she had received advice on how to go about it. Maybe she *would* call one of those helplines Martin had suggested.

She rang Joan. 'Joan, something's happened? Can you come round later, after the children have gone to bed?'

\* \* \*

'No!' Joan sank, chalk-faced, on to a kitchen chair. 'I don't believe it.'

Karen took a gulp from the large glass of red wine she had poured before her sister arrived. 'There's no mistake. The police examined the laptop and found hundreds of disgusting images on it.' She shuddered. 'Howard was selling them on the internet.'

'Jesus Christ!' Joan looked shell-shocked. Karen had rarely seen her so lost for words. 'Howard?' she stuttered eventually. 'It can't be true.'

'I'm afraid it is.' Karen twisted a strand of hair nervously between her fingers. She repeated what the detectives had told her about the way in which the paedophile ring worked. 'Apparently the set-up is already being investigated by a Dutch police force. They identified some of the people operating in Asia, but they've only just started to follow up the European connection.'

Joan shook her head wonderingly. 'It doesn't make sense.

Howard was... I mean he always seemed... such a good man, decent.'

Karen snorted. 'Good? Decent? Everything I've learnt about him since he died suggests he was anything but good and decent.'

Joan removed her glasses and mopped her eyes with a tissue. 'Do you *really* believe he was involved in this kind of thing?'

'Yes,' Karen said miserably, 'I'm afraid I do. The police say there's no doubt about it.'

Joan stood up, walked over to the window and gazed silently into the darkness outside. After a while she sat down again. 'I still can't believe it. Were there any signs? Did you ever suspect--?'

'Of course not.' Karen took another large gulp of wine. 'But after the detectives told me about it, something occurred to me. Do you remember those charities Howard assisted on a voluntary basis, the ones he was so smug about? They were all charities to do with helping disadvantaged children.'

Joan gasped in dismay. 'And you think he may have got involved with them for...' (she whispered the words) '...*pornographic* purposes?'

'Possibly, but that's not the worst bit for me.' Karen hesitated. She knew how much Joan, who had no children of her own, doted on her own three. 'I felt I had to ask Erica and Simon whether Howard...you know...did anything to *them*--'

'No!' Joan cried, appalled. 'Surely he wouldn't have interfered with his own children.'

Karen gave a bitter laugh. 'There's nothing I wouldn't believe about Howard now. It was such a difficult question to ask them. Of course I couldn't tell them what their father had been up to. I just said that the police needed to examine every aspect of family life for the investigation. From the way Erica and Simon reacted, I don't think

Howard interfered with them, thank God, but I don't have a clue how to bring the subject up with Poppy. She's so little.'

'Not *Poppy!*' Joan's face was almost grey with shock. 'Surely he wouldn't have touched *Poppy.*'

'How can I be sure?' Karen shivered and hugged her cardigan tight round her body. 'I need to find a way to approach the subject without alarming or upsetting her. Martin told me there are specialist helplines you can ring for advice.'

Joan replaced her glasses on her nose and attempted to compose herself. 'That sounds like a sensible idea. But if you believe Howard didn't touch Erica or Simon, the chances are he won't have interfered with Poppy either.'

'I'm praying that he didn't.' Karen clasped her hands tightly together. 'The woman detective told me I mustn't tell anyone about this in case it jeopardises the enquiry. But I would go mad if I had to keep it to myself. Anyway, who could I tell apart from you? I don't want anyone else to know; it's too awful.' Her face crumpled. 'It's like the sky's fallen in on me, Joan. It's like a curse, Howard's curse. What else can happen to me now? I thought the affair with Mo was bad enough, but this...' She started to weep convulsively.

Joan stood up and put an arm round her shoulders. 'You poor love. What a bastard! If someone hadn't already beaten me to it, I'd feel like murdering Howard myself!' She waited until Karen's sobs had abated, then fished in her bag and handed her a pack of tissues.

'Do the police believe the shooting was connected with Howard's membership of the pornography ring?' she asked after a short silence.

'Yes, I think so.' Karen hiccupped and dabbed at her eyes. 'But now I know what kind of man he was, I don't care who killed him. I'm *glad* they did it!'

Joan sat down again. 'What a terrible thing to find out after you've been married to someone for...how long was it?'

'Fifteen years.' Karen blew her nose before adding, falteringly, 'I've never mentioned it before, Joanie, but I wasn't really happy with Howard.'

'You weren't?' Joan exclaimed, astonished.

'No, especially during the last few years. After Poppy was born, Howard became very withdrawn, distant, from all of us. We hardly ever...I mean, he wouldn't touch me... you know, in bed.'

Joan gasped with surprise.

'I didn't mind that too much,' Karen added hastily, 'but he was always angry, criticising me and putting me down. I used to dread him coming home in the evenings.'

'Karen, why didn't you say?'

'I didn't like to, you were always so impressed by him, and so was Mo.'

Joan snorted contemptuously. 'Well now we know why that was, don't we? But you could have told *me* for goodness sake.'

'I didn't think you'd believe me, Joanie. Howard was totally affable and charming when other people were around. Besides, I thought it was *my* fault he was so unpleasant to me; I thought I wasn't good enough for him.'

'That's nonsense.'

Karen gazed beseechingly at her sister. 'You don't think I'm to blame for what he did, do you? Because I didn't satisfy him; didn't give him what he wanted?'

'Good God no.' Joan squeezed her hand. 'You mustn't think that for a moment. The man was obviously evil through and through, though I must say he hid it extremely well. What Howard got up to, had absolutely *nothing* to do with you.'

'How can we stay in Moxton, if any of this gets out?' Karen wailed despairingly. 'We'll have to find somewhere else to live.'

'Why? You're not responsible for what your husband did.'

'You know what people are like, Joan. They'll be whispering, pointing. It'll be like with that offshore account. The police thought I must have known about it, and so did Celia Murray.'

'The Poison Dwarf? She thinks badly of everyone.'

'And what if the children are victimised? You know how cruel kids can be. Simon's already been bullied since Howard died. His teachers stepped in and it seems to have stopped for the moment. But I don't know how he'll cope if the other kids got wind of the fact that his dad was a ...paedophile.'

'Now you're leaping ahead,' Joan said firmly. 'Don't beat yourself up about what may never happen.'

'But if the police want to go through all of Howard's accounts again, Geoff's bound to find out why, and he'll tell Celia, then she'll tell everyone else. Oh God! I can't bear it.' Karen poured herself another large glass of wine and took a gulp from it.

Joan, a teetotaller, regarded her disapprovingly. She was now sufficiently composed to have recovered her elder sister mode. 'Calm down, Karen. You don't know that that's going to happen. And hitting the bottle won't help. You must think about the children. You need to stay in one piece for their sake.'

It had become chilly in the kitchen and Karen shivered. 'There's another thing. What if this affects our livelihood?'

'What do you mean? How could it?'

'Well, if some of Howard's money was obtained through criminal activity, then maybe we won't be entitled to anything. If the police decide to confiscate all his assets, what will we live on?'

'You needn't worry about that,' Joan assured her. 'It should be easy enough to separate Howard's offshore account from his legitimate earnings. And you'll still have the life insurance.'

'But that could take ages to come through. The insurance company won't pay out if someone has died in suspicious circumstances. They have to wait for the result of the investigation. And I still can't get access to Howard's bank account.'

Joan patted her on the arm. 'You know we'll help out financially while you're waiting for things to be sorted.'

Karen managed a weak smile. 'Thanks, Joanie. I may take you up on that but I've still got savings and Child Benefit.' A wave of fury towards Howard washed over her. She rose unsteadily to her feet and grasped the back of the chair for support. 'I want you to witness something.' By now her voice was slightly slurred. She opened the kitchen cupboard above the sink and took out a ceramic pot.

Joan stared at it. 'What's in there?'

'Howard's ashes. I hid them because I thought the children would be upset if they saw them. Come with me.' She wobbled unsteadily out of the kitchen.

Joan followed her into the small cloakroom in the hall

and watched, stunned, as Karen raised the toilet lid and emptied the contents of the pot into the bowl.

'Goodbye Howard!' Karen hissed as she pressed the flush button.

'Good fucking riddance!' She started to laugh hysterically. 'Karen!' Joan remonstrated, 'you'll wake the children up.' The laughter turned into sobs as Karen began to cry again.

# Chapter 10

After taking a sleeping pill, Karen fell into a heavy slumber. She woke to the sound of Poppy happily chattering away to herself in the room next to hers, and for a fleeting moment she believed everything was normal again. Within seconds, however, the memory of what had happened struck her like a sledgehammer and she was plunged back into revulsion and despair.

Her head throbbed painfully as she dressed, and when she bent to put on her shoes, the room revolved around her in a violent spinning motion. She cursed herself for having drunk so much the night before.

She went down to the kitchen where Erica and Simon were squabbling over a cereal packet. Their voices drilled painfully into her skull.

'Mummy!' Poppy, still in her nightdress, pulled urgently at her skirt. 'Don't forget it's dressing-up day at school and I'm going as a pirate.'

Karen *had* forgotten. She fought off nausea as she wearily improvised a costume. She dressed her daughter in baggy pyjama bottoms, wellington boots and an old black waistcoat she found in a cupboard, completing the effect with a plastic eye patch left over from the previous Halloween, and a cardboard sword that Simon swiftly created for his sister.

After delivering the pirate to school, she started to re-move all remaining traces of Howard. Ignoring her throb-bing head, she pulled his expensive clothes and shoes out of the wardrobe and stuffed them into bin bags. Her initial intention had been to take them to a charity shop, but she now considered that anything worn by Howard must inev-itably be tainted with the imprint of his evil. The thought of tossing his immaculate suits and shirts on to a reeking pile of household rubbish at the local refuse tip appealed to her. It would be a kind of poetic justice.

She was carrying the bags downstairs when someone rang at the door. She rushed to open it, hoping it would be Martin. She wanted to apologise for her previous abrupt-ness and ask for details of the child protection helplines he had mentioned. But the person standing on the doorstep wasn't Martin; it was someone who bore no resemblance to him, or indeed to any of the men one normally encoun-tered in Moxton. Tall and aged about fifty, he had a crag-gy, lined face and greying fair hair scraped back in a skimpy pony tail. He was wearing a cream linen suit and an open-necked white shirt that revealed an ostentatious gold chain nestling on top of a tuft of grey chest hair. A matching gold earring dangled from one earlobe. He was considerably more tanned than one would have expected after a British summer.

'Mrs Armstrong?' The man extended his hand and smiled, displaying a row of unnaturally white and even teeth.

'Yes?' Karen took his hand with a sense of apprehension. There was something in his manner that she instinctively distrusted.

He held on to her hand longer than necessary. 'Gerry Manning. We recently spoke on the phone.' His voice had a distinctive Australian twang.

She stifled a gasp and with some difficulty, extricated her hand.

'I'm an associate of your husband, your *late* husband. As I'm visiting the area for a few days, I thought I'd call to offer my sincere condolences. I was devastated to hear the news. It's unbelievable. It must have been a terrible shock.'

'Yes, it was,' she murmured, rubbing her aching temples.

Manning's face was a mask of concern. 'I'm very sorry for your loss. Do you know who did it? Do the police have any suspects?'

'I believe they're following a number of leads,' she replied cautiously, trying to hide her mounting fear. Could this be the man who had murdered Howard?

He nodded grimly. 'The sooner they catch the perpetrator the better. Howard was a very good friend of mine.'

'Was he?' She couldn't help injecting a note of sarcasm into her voice.

'Yes indeed.' Manning took a step towards her as though expecting to be invited into the house, but she barred his way.

'How did you know my husband, Mr...Manley?'

'Manning. We were business associates. We met a few years ago.'

'Oh? When was that exactly?'

'I believe we first met when he visited an orphanage in Indonesia.'

'Really? He never mentioned you.'

'Didn't he?' Manning gave a forced laugh. 'That's

probably because we didn't meet very often. I live abroad'

'You do? Where?'

'Thailand.'

'Oh.' Karen suppressed a shudder. She remembered reading that Thailand was notorious for sex tourism.

Manning bared his cosmetically-enhanced teeth in another ingratiating smile. 'Howard was a dark horse. He never told me he had such an attractive wife.'

She recoiled with a distaste he displayed no sign of noticing. Instead, he leant forward and clutched one of her hands again. 'Now that I'm here, I wonder if you could do me a very big favour, Mrs A.'

'Mrs *Armstrong*,' she retorted curtly, rapidly withdrawing her hand. 'What kind of favour?'

'Well, Howard, your husband--'

'I'm perfectly aware who Howard was.'

'Of course.' He gave an apologetic cough. 'As I was about to say, Howard and I, and our other associates, were engaged in a little enterprise together, and--'

'What kind of enterprise?'

'We were involved in charitable work...' he blinked rapidly, '... helping disadvantaged children in the Third World.'

'Really?' Karen pretended to be astonished. 'That's strange. Howard never said anything about that to me.'

Manning uttered a bark of false laughter. 'Well that was Howard for you; always hiding his light under a bushel. Of course it wasn't his main line of business, just a charitable sideline, probably too insignificant to mention. He did the admin for us here in this country, while we did the donkey work overseas, at the chalk face as it were. But now...' he assumed a grief-stricken expression, '...now that Howard has sadly left us, we need to access the data he compiled.'

'What data?'

'The accounts, Mrs A, the accounts! Howard did the figures. And if we don't have them, it will be impossible for us to continue our valuable work.'

Karen shook her head as though mystified. 'I'm afraid I don't know anything about figures, Mr M. Howard never spoke to me about his charitable work.'

An expression of relief flickered across Manning's tanned face. 'He was far too modest. But I happen to know that he had entered all the accounts on a laptop which he kept at his home, and which he used uniquely for our enterprise. It would be enormously helpful, Mrs A, if you could let me have the laptop so that I can transfer the files to our database.'

Karen suppressed a start of alarm. Was Manning the intruder who had broken into the shed? 'I can't do that. The police took all Howard's computers away after he was shot.'

'I assume those would be his work and personal computers?' Manning suggested smoothly. 'Howard told me that he deliberately kept *this* laptop separate and concealed in a safe place at home.'

'Oh?' She feigned surprise. 'Why would he do that?'

'To avoid confusing it with his principal work and so that it couldn't be used for any other purpose. So my thinking is that the laptop could still be here, in a cupboard or drawer perhaps, or somewhere else in the house. If you could find it for me, you would be doing vulnerable children in the Third World a great service.'

Karen pretended to reflect. 'I don't recall seeing any laptops in a cupboard, Mr M, but if you give me your phone number, I'll let you know if I find one.'

He shook his head. 'Time is of the essence, Mrs A. Why don't you take a look round the house now?'

'No,' she said firmly, 'I'm too busy. But maybe the detectives leading the murder enquiry can help you. I'll give you their number.'

Manning produced another rictus grin. 'There's no need to waste the police's valuable time. If you could just see if you could locate that laptop—'

'I'm sorry, I must go.' Karen took a step backwards, but before she could close the door, he planted a large foot against it.

'I must emphasise, Mrs A, that this is *extremely* important. I'm sure you wouldn't want to deprive destitute children of our invaluable assistance.' He thrust his face close to hers. 'You wouldn't be deliberately keeping that laptop from me, would you? That would be very regrettable.'

Within the depths of her timid being Karen found a reservoir of angry courage. 'Take your foot away from my door!' she shouted. 'Go away or I'll call the police.'

Manning stepped back and quickly rearranged his features into a contrite expression. 'Didn't mean to offend, Mrs A. But I would be extremely grateful if you could help. I'll call back another time, in case you happen to find the laptop.'

Karen slammed the door and stood trembling behind it until she heard his footsteps recede. Then she picked up the phone and called Martin.

He sounded excited. 'We'll send a car immediately, see if we can pick him up.'

'He'll be gone by now.' After so long maintaining a

semblance of composure, Karen was almost sobbing with tension. 'He frightens me, Martin. He said he's going to come back.'

'Don't worry, Karen, I'll organise a patrol car to watch the house. He's not after you. He's just fishing. He's hoping the laptop may still be where your husband hid it. Do you think he suspects we already have it?'

'I told him the police took all of Howard's computers, but he seemed sure nobody would have found the laptop.'

'He didn't give you a phone number by any chance?'

'No, I asked him to but he wouldn't.'

'Pity.'

'Martin,' she asked in a trembling voice, 'do you think he's the person who killed Howard?'

'He isn't, I can assure you of that. We traced that earlier call he made to you. It was from Thailand. We made some enquiries and we know Manning was there on the day your husband was shot.' He paused. 'It's unlikely he'll return straight away, but would you like me to come over, Karen?'

'No,' she said after a moment's hesitation. 'Thank you but I'm going out in a minute. I have to take some stuff to the rubbish tip, and then...' she made a sudden decision, '... I'm going to get a dog.'

It was only after the call had ended that she realised she had forgotten to ask him about the helplines.

\* \* \*

When Karen arrived at the local recycling centre, she unloaded the bags containing Howard's clothes and shoes from the car and, with a sense of vindictive pleasure, carried them in turn up to the area used for general waste. She considered this the most appropriate resting place for articles that had touched Howard's body. She even relished the putrid smell emanating from the huge and festering pile of household rubbish.

As she was emptying the bags, a man in a fluorescent yellow jacket materialised by her side and watched open-mouthed as one of Howard's immaculate suits landed on top of an oily mess of ordure. 'Oi!' he shouted. 'Don't throw them things there. Clothes and shoes go in them bins.' He pointed towards a line of large green containers.

Karen emptied the last bag on to the refuse pile. 'Don't touch them!' she warned the man, in case he was taken with an urge to salvage the suits. 'My husband had a nasty disease.'

The man stared at her in alarm but before he could say anything, she hastened back to the car and drove to the animal rescue centre.

The noise assailed her ears as soon as she arrived: a deafening cacophony of barks, yelps and howls. Inside the building she was led through a central aisle, on either side of which dogs of all shapes, sizes and colours, occupied wired enclosures. Some were pacing frantically up and down; others were lying with their heads slumped forlornly over their paws, gazing mournfully through the wire. Two young women were moving busily around the kennels, distributing bowls of food. Others were bringing dogs back after their morning exercise.

Karen peered closely at each animal as she passed along the aisle. Some watched her warily; others bounded hopefully up to their kennel door to greet her. She was instantly captivated by Rufus, a young, rust-coloured mongrel with floppy spaniel ears but the body of a much larger dog. He looked at her with sad eyes and when she spoke gently to him through the wire, he lifted a paw, as though pleading with her. That was the clincher. 'I want this one!' she told the young man who had accompanied her thorough the dogs' enclosure.

The man told her that Rufus had been found abandoned on the common outside Moxton during a cold snap in January. 'Probably another unwanted Christmas gift,' he said with a sigh. 'It happens every year.'

Karen was disappointed to learn that she couldn't take Rufus home straight away. 'We have to carry out a home check first,' the woman in the office informed her. She asked Karen a surprising number of questions: how many people lived in the house; whether there were other pets; where Rufus would be kept and whether there would be anyone at home during the day.

Karen was relieved that the woman didn't seem to recognise her name when she wrote down her personal details. After agreeing a date for the home visit, she drove home, looking forward to giving the children a welcome surprise.

'We're going to have a dog!' she announced at tea-time.

Poppy, still in her pirate's costume, squealed with delight.

Simon dropped his fork on the table. 'Wicked! What kind of dog?'

Erica continued to chew steadily, maintaining a cool indifference which Karen knew was contrived.

'He's about a year old and quite big. A sort of reddish brown, with floppy ears. His name's Rufus.'

Poppy jumped up from her chair, her amber eyes shining with excitement.

'Where is he?'

'He's not here yet, darling.'

'Why not?'

'The people running the rescue centre have to visit us to make sure this is a good home for a dog. Someone's coming next week to see what the house is like and where he'll sleep.'

'Oh.' Poppy drooped with disappointment.

Simon pulled worriedly on his earlobe. 'What if they won't let us have him?'

Karen laughed. 'I'm sure they'll let us have him. There are so many abandoned dogs, they'll be only too pleased to let him come and live with us.'

'Can we go and see him?' Simon asked eagerly

'Yes, on Saturday, if you like.'

'Wicked!'

'Mummy?' Poppy tugged at Karen's arm. 'When he comes, can I take him for walks?'

'Of course. You all can.'

Poppy's face broke into a wide smile. 'Can we buy a bed for him, and some dog biscuits and a lead?'

'Yes, as soon as it's agreed that he can come and live with us.'

Poppy picked up her cardboard sword and waved it in the air, singing, 'we're going to get a dog! We're going to get a dog!'

Erica gave her a disdainful look. She left the table and sauntered out of the kitchen without a word.

Karen sighed. Would her daughter's sulk ever come to an end?

Martin rang while she was clearing up the tea things. 'The SIO has agreed to send an unmarked car to keep a watch on the house.'

'That's great. Thank you.'

'It needn't be for long. If Manning's going to come back, we reckon it'll be fairly soon.'

'Oh dear.' In the excitement over the dog, Karen had lost some of her apprehension about the man's return.

Martin seemed to sense her alarm. 'I could call by tomorrow morning, if you like, after the kids have gone to school?'

'Thank you, but I won't be here. I'm going to have coffee with a friend.'

'It's good to hear you're resuming normal activities.' He sounded pleased.

*Normal?* she thought. *What's normal?*

Joan rang later that evening. 'Are you feeling better, Karen?'

'Yes, I'm fine.'

'Really? Last night you were pretty upset.'

'Yes I was, but I'm fine now.'

'Are you sure? It must have been a terrible shock hearing that Howard was a --'

Karen interrupted her, 'Joanie, do you remember that song from a Hollywood musical, *I'm going to wash that man right out of my hair?*

'Yes,' Joan said dubiously. 'What about it?'

'Well, that's just what I've been doing.'

'You've been washing your hair?'

'No. I was speaking metaphorically, if that's the right word. I mean I'm getting rid of Howard. I've taken all his clothes to the rubbish tip and I'm getting a dog. He wouldn't let the children have one, remember? And the next thing I'm going to do is change that horrid car of his.

I want to get something smaller and more economical.'

'Oh.' There was a short silence. 'I suppose that makes sense, but don't act too hastily, Karen. You need time to come to terms with what's happened.'

'I know exactly what I'm doing and it's making me feel better.' Karen wondered if Joan understood how important it was for her to perform these ritual acts to cleanse herself of Howard.

'Take things slowly, Karen,' Joan urged her. 'You may be feeling better at the moment, but after all you've been through, you could come crashing down. And it would be better if you didn't hit the bottle so much, especially when the children are in the house.'

Karen smiled to herself. She was deriving considerable pleasure from drinking Howard's expensive wines, the ones he kept for the "special occasions" that never seemed to arrive. Seeking to change the subject, she remembered that she hadn't told Joan about her unwelcome visitor. 'That awful man Gerald Manning called here this morning.'

'Gerald who?'

'Manning. Didn't I tell you about him? He's one of Howard's associates. Martin says he's a member of the paedophile ring--' She heard Joan gasp. 'He came to the house?'

'Yes, but I didn't let him in. He said he needed Howard's laptop, but I pretended I didn't know what he was talking about. He said Howard kept the accounts on it, for a charity helping children. *Helping* children!' She started to laugh hysterically. 'Can you believe it?'

'Calm down, Karen,' Joan said worriedly. 'Did you call the police?'

'Of course I did. As soon as he'd gone.'

'Did they get him?'

'No, but he said he's going to come back again. He's ghastly, Joan. He's got a nasty little ponytail and an earring in one ear. He was quite aggressive when I wouldn't let him in.'

Joan expelled a loud breath. 'I think you and the children should come and stay with us, Karen. He might be dangerous.'

'There's no need for that. Martin said they're sending an unmarked police car. It'll be stationed near the house.'

'Even so, you'll be much safer with us. You and the girls can stay in the spare room and Simon--'

'No,' Karen said firmly. 'It's really kind of you, Joanie, but I don't want the children to have any more disruption. Anyway, Manning's not after *us*. He just wants that laptop.'

'But you don't know what lengths he'll go to, to get it.'

'Well as long as he thinks it's still here, the police will have a better chance of catching him.'

'Karen, that's putting the children and yourself at risk.'

'Not if the police are watching the house.'

Joan clicked her tongue disapprovingly. 'Well I don't like it, Karen; I don't like the sound of it at all. I think you're being foolhardy.'

Later that evening, Karen received an unexpected call from Geoff Murray. 'The police have been to my home,' he announced angrily. 'They've taken my iPad and personal computer away for examination.'

'Oh Geoff, have they?' She could hear Celia's shrill voice in the background.

'What do you think they're looking for?'

'I've no idea,' she lied.

'Surely they can't think I was involved in Howard's murder.'

'Of course they don't.'

'Then why did they come to my home? Has it got something to do with that offshore account Howard opened?'

'I don't know, Geoff. The police don't tell me how they're conducting the investigation.'

'I can't be doing with all this, Karen,' he barked. 'I've got the business to run and a reputation to maintain, both personal and professional. Whatever Howard got up to outside *Armstrong and Murray* is nothing to do with me.'

'It's nothing to do with me either,' Karen responded with some asperity. 'Howard never confided in me about his work or about any financial dealings he was involved in. As far as I'm concerned, this is all a total nightmare.'

His voice softened. 'I'm sorry to take it out on you, Karen. But having the police here again has been a shock. I just wondered if you had any information; whether they've told you anything.'

'I'm afraid not,' she said tremulously.

'Just a moment.' Geoff's voice receded and she could hear him talking to Celia. 'Karen...' he started hesitantly when he resumed the call. 'I know it was Howard who started the business, but under the terms of the partnership, you do realise it will now revert to my name alone?' He coughed. 'After all the...um...adverse publicity, I think it advisable that this should happen as soon as possible. Obviously, as Howard's widow, you'll be entitled to a share of the profits accruing at the time of his death. Our lawyers will make sure everything is handled properly. I assume you have no objection?'

'None at all.'

Karen found herself quivering with resentment after the call ended. Once again Howard's actions had rebounded on her. Thanks to him, her small circle of local acquaintances had shrunk considerably. She had always liked Geoff but it was clear that their friendship was coming to an end. She had lost Mo, and the few other people she had been on close terms with now either avoided her or regarded her as an object of pity. She was grateful that she had met someone who might become a new friend.

# Chapter 11

Juliet Morgan's front garden was exactly as she had described it: a mess. Children's bicycles and scooters were strewn across the path leading to the front door. Weeds, abandoned toys and grubby footballs fought for space on the untended flower beds.

Juliet herself was a vision in purple jeans and an orange, Indian-style tunic. A string of black beads as big as marbles was looped around her neck, and gold earrings fashioned into the shape of small skulls, dangled from her ears.

Dressed in her customary monochrome clothes, Karen felt extremely drab by contrast.

Juliet greeted her warmly and ushered her into the house. The interior was as chaotic as the outside. As they passed through the hall, Karen was obliged to step carefully over shoes, toys and pieces of garden equipment. In the large, sunlit kitchen, the cooker and worktops were covered with unwashed pans and dishes.

Juliet grinned on noticing Karen's surprised expression. 'Sorry about the mess. I never seem to get on top of it. When I do have a clean-up, it's just as bad a few hours later. So what's the point? Life's too short.'

Karen was inclined to agree. After years of failing to live up to the Everest standard of tidiness imposed by Howard, she felt nothing but admiration for someone who had no compunction about allowing her home to display all the signs of being lived in.

Juliet swept plastic bags and articles of clothing off two kitchen chairs. 'Sit down while I make the coffee. I bought some blueberry muffins on the way back from school. I hope you'll have one.'

'Yes, thank you. That would be lovely.'

Juliet put the muffins on a plate and filled a coffee pot with ground coffee and boiling water. She sat down opposite Karen while it brewed. 'How are you? Are you feeling any better? '

'I'm fine ...I'm...' Karen tried to smile but the bravado of the previous day had ebbed away and with a suddenness that surprised herself, she started to weep uncontrollably.

Juliet slid a box of tissues across the table and waited silently until the paroxysm had subsided.

When the sobs had given way to hiccups, Karen pressed a tissue to her eyes and blew her nose. 'I'm so sorry,' she stammered, 'I didn't mean to do that.'

Juliet shook her head sympathetically. 'No need to apologise. Anyone would feel distraught after losing their husband in such a terrible fashion.'

'No, it's not because of that.' Karen stifled a hiccup. 'I mean, it was terrible, but since he died, I've found out that Howard wasn't a good person. In fact he did some dreadful things.'

'Did he? Oh dear.' Although Juliet sounded surprised she didn't ask Karen to elaborate. She poured the coffee into two mugs and pushed one of them and the plate of muffins, across the table. 'Help yourself to milk and sugar.'

Karen inhaled deeply to try and suppress another

hiccup. She wondered how much information about Howard she could safely divulge. She had no intention of mentioning what was on his laptop but felt that what she had just blurted out required some explanation. 'He was involved in some dodgy financial dealings, you see. The police told me he'd invented a bogus charity and opened a secret offshore account. They say he was money laundering.'

Juliet's eyes widened. 'Wow!'

'There's more. I discovered he'd been having an affair for over a year... with Mo, my closest friend.'

Juliet whistled. 'Jesus!'

'She's Poppy's godmother. I went to see her. She admitted it but had the nerve to say I was exaggerating, making too much of it.'

'Yipes! What a cow!'

Karen sniffed and dabbed at her nose with a tissue. 'She's been really helpful to me in the past. She had the children for a few days after Howard died, when I wasn't in a fit state to do anything.'

Juliet snorted. 'That doesn't give her *carte blanche* to fuck your husband.'

'No, but the children keep asking me why we don't see her anymore and Erica, my eldest, won't speak to me because Gemma, Mo's daughter, is, or rather, *was*, one of her best friends. I can't tell her Mo and her dad were having an affair, can I?'

'I suppose not.' Juliet gazed at her sympathetically. 'Poor you. What a ghastly time you're having.'

Karen hiccupped. 'I've begun to dread the police coming round in case they tell me something else I didn't know about Howard.' She gave a tremulous smile. 'I took all his clothes to the recycling centre yesterday and threw them on top of the rubbish.'

'Atta girl!' Juliet exclaimed, admiringly. 'That's exactly what I would have done in your shoes!'

'And the other night I got rather pissed and flushed his ashes down the loo!'

'You didn't!' Juliet gave a peal of laughter. 'That's bloody wonderful!'

Karen started to laugh too. 'My sister Joan was with me at the time. I think she disapproved.' Feeling somewhat better, she took a bite of her muffin and glanced round the kitchen. 'This is a lovely bright room.'

Juliet smiled. 'Yes, it's south-facing.' She sipped her coffee. 'Do the police know who shot your husband? Or would you prefer not to talk about it?'

'No, it's OK. I don't think they have a suspect yet but to be honest, now that I know what Howard was really like, I don't really care who did it.' She paused. 'Oh dear, I shouldn't have said that, should I? It's been a dreadful shock for the children, losing their father so suddenly.'

Juliet looked at her shrewdly. '*You* don't miss him, then?' Karen hesitated. 'No, I don't.'

'Did you love him?'

'I don't know. I wasn't *in* love with him if that's what you mean, but I admired him, looked up to him. He was generous, a good provider.' Karen chewed on a mouthful of muffin then, aware that the conversation had been all about herself, asked quickly, 'what about you, Juliet? Do you have a good relationship with your husband?'

Juliet grinned. 'Happily divorced! We were seventeen when we met and eighteen when we got married. Big mistake! But it lasted ten years and we have two lovely kids. It was quite amicable when we broke up, and Andy's been a good dad to Joe and Miranda. He lives in Hereford now and has them once a month.'

'Have you met anyone else?'

'It's not easy when you've got two young kids. Anyway, I prefer it like this for the moment, just me and them.'

Karen swallowed the rest of her coffee. 'I don't think I could live with another man. Howard was terribly...fastidious. He'd have a heart attack if he so much as found a kid's sock on the floor!'

'Well it sounds to me that you're well rid of him.'

'You can say that again!'

Juliet stared at her for a moment. 'Do you always wear grey or black?'

Karen blushed. 'Well, I am supposed to be in mourning.' She didn't mention that she invariably wore drab colours so as not to draw attention to herself.

'From what you've told me, you don't have a lot to mourn. I'd say it's time to move on. Ditch the widow's weeds! If you ask me, you need to make a new start.'

'How do I do that?' Karen wished she could be a free spirit like Juliet.

'The first thing is to get a new image. You need colour!' Juliet stood up, plucked a green scarf from a pile of clothes in a laundry basket and held it up against Karen's face. 'There... that really brings out the colour of your eyes.' She dropped the scarf and stared at Karen again. 'You've got nice hair but it's a bit...faded. If you had it cut and lightened, it would look gorgeous.'

Karen laughed self-consciously. 'You sound like one of those women's magazine beauty columnists. To tell you the truth, I've always felt very unattractive.'

Juliet wagged a disapproving finger at her. 'That's cobblers! You're tall and slim, and you've got cheekbones to die for. With a bit of TLC, you could look like a model. Tell you what, why don't the two of us go shopping one day, get you some new clothes?'

'That would be lovely.' It was ages since Karen had bought herself anything. She had always felt guilty about spending any of the money Howard gave her on herself, especially as the children always needed new things. 'But I can't really buy much yet, not until Howard's Will has been sorted.'

In truth, she was finding it difficult to manage after years of not having to worry about money. The savings she had accumulated from her monthly allowance were being rapidly depleted, although she still had Child Benefit and some other allowances that Martin's information sheets had alerted her to.

Juliet didn't appear to have heard. 'It would have to be a Tuesday or a Friday. I work on the other days.'

'What do you do?'

'I'm a home help for housebound elderly.'

'Gosh, that must be difficult.'

'The work isn't; the bureaucracy is. Some of those poor souls are really lonely, but we're only allowed to spend about fifteen minutes with each of them, then we have to rush off to the next person. But I enjoy helping. Most of the people I see are very appreciative. One old lady calls me her visiting angel. Me, an angel? What a joke! More coffee?'

Please.' Karen gazed at her in admiration. 'I think it's fantastic, to be able to help people like that.'

Juliet shrugged. 'It's just a job, one that fits in with

childcare. And there's nothing else I'm qualified to do.' She refilled Karen's mug and handed it to her.

'Well you're a lot more qualified than I am,' Karen commented ruefully. 'I haven't got any qualifications, not academic ones anyway. Before I was married, I worked in a carpet store in Cheltenham. That's where I met Howard. He came in to choose floor coverings for the house in Moxton, the one I live in now. He came back several times afterwards and sought me out. I couldn't understand why.'

'He obviously found you very attractive.'

'I'm not sure about that. Anyway, I haven't had another job since then. I don't know what I'm going to do next.'

'Early days, Karen,' Juliet said gently. 'One step at a time.'

'Well, I've already taken a few steps and there's one more thing I want to do.'

'What's that?

Karen removed the wedding and engagement rings from her left hand. She put the engagement ring - an expensive cluster of diamonds and opals - into her bag. 'I'm going to sell that one, but I want to throw this one away.' She held up the thick band of gold. 'I want to bury my married life forever.'

'That's my girl!' Juliet jumped up enthusiastically. 'Let's go and bury it somewhere. I'll get a spade.'

'No, I want to drop it somewhere really grotty, like in a muddy field.'

Juliet grinned. 'I've got a better idea. How about down a drain? Then it can fall into the sewer and catch up with your husband's ashes! There's a nasty one at the end of the street that keeps getting blocked.'

'Yes!' Karen jumped up in her turn. 'Let's do it!'

The two of them left the house and proceeded together to the end of the road. The drain Juliet had mentioned was filthy and surrounded by litter as well as mud and debris from where it had overflowed after a heavy shower.

While Juliet hummed the Funeral March, Karen ceremoniously tossed her wedding ring through the grills. It made a tiny but satisfying plop as it dropped into the scummy water.

# Chapter 12

As the next day was a Saturday and the children stayed in bed longer than usual, Karen decided to rearrange her room before getting breakfast. First she moved some of her own clothes into Howard's empty wardrobe and chest of drawers. Next she dragged his ugly trouser-press on to the landing and added it to the pile of his remaining belongings that were destined for a charity shop. Afterwards she turned her attention to the double bed she and Howard had shared for fifteen years. As it didn't hold particularly happy memories, she thought she would replace it with one of the divans she had seen on special offer in the local paper.

'Mummy?' Poppy came trotting into the room. She was dressed and was carrying two of her favourite dolls. 'Can I go outside and play in the Wendy house?

'It's a bit early, darling. Hadn't you better wait till after breakfast?'

'I want to go now.'

'Just for a short while, then. I'll call you when breakfast's ready.'

Karen accompanied Poppy downstairs and unbolted the back door. After Poppy had run down to the Wendy house, she lingered on the doorstep for a moment. It was a lovely autumn morning. The leaves had just begun to turn a rich shade of bronze and only a few flecks of wispy cloud spotted the otherwise flawless blue sky. On such a day it was hard to believe that the murder and subsequent revelations about Howard had actually happened. She sometimes felt she was living in two parallel universes: in one she was caught up in a nightmarish sequence of horrors of a kind she had formerly associated with crime series on the television; in the other, she was leading an uneventful domestic existence much the same as the one she had led before Howard had died. For the sake of the family and her own sanity, she felt it was vital to keep the two worlds apart. She had to ensure that the children's lives remained as normal as possible.

She closed the back door and went to the kitchen. As she prepared the breakfast, she planned how she and the children would spend the day. Later that morning she would take them to the animal rescue centre to meet Rufus. In the afternoon, they would go to the local leisure centre where there was a swimming pool. Afterwards she would drive Erica to her friend Lisa's birthday party. She wondered whether such invitations would still be forthcoming if Howard's secret activities were ever made public.

She was cutting slices of bread when a movement outside the window caught her eye. She looked up and gave a stifled scream on seeing Gerald Manning in a light-coloured suit and dark glasses, standing on the path with Poppy. He was holding her hand.

Dropping the bread knife, she rushed frantically through the back door and ran down the garden to intercept them.

'Look, Mummy!' Poppy held up a tube of sweets. 'The man gave me these.'

Karen grabbed her by the arm. 'Come inside, Poppy! Come back indoors with me.' With a sickening feeling she remembered that her mobile was in her handbag upstairs.

Poppy gazed at her, wide-eyed. 'What's the matter, Mummy?'

Manning continued to hold tightly on to the little girl's hand. He grinned, revealing his absurdly white teeth. 'Poppy's been showing me her Wendy house, haven't you, sweetheart? Pretty little thing, isn't she? A credit to you, Mrs A.'

Karen felt a wave of revulsion. 'Let go of her!' she shouted.

He shook his head. 'You should take better care of her, Mrs A,' he murmured. 'Pity if she came to any harm.'

Karen froze. 'Don't you dare make threats against my daughter!'

'Not a threat, Mrs A. Just a friendly observation.' With his eyes hidden behind reflective sunglasses, Manning's expression was sinister.

Karen prised Poppy away from him and hauled her, complaining, back up the path to the back door. 'Give me the sweets,' she ordered.

'But Mummy--'

'Give them to me!'

Poppy's face crumpled as she handed over the tube of sweets.

Karen thrust them into her pocket. 'Now, go and get my handbag for me, Poppy. It's on my dressing-table. Quick.'

'But--'

'Now!'

Poppy burst into tears and ran upstairs.

Manning had followed them to the door and stood on

the threshold, intimidatingly close to Karen. 'So, did you find that laptop, Mrs A?'

Karen backed inside, her heart thumping with panic. 'Yes I did find one,' she replied, endeavouring to keep her voice steady. 'It was in the shed. I handed it to the police.' She thought it wise to hide the fact that she knew what was *on* the laptop.

His lips curved in a kind of snarl. 'You wouldn't be lying to me by any chance?'

She stared at him defiantly. 'You can ring our police liaison officer and ask him, if you like. I'll give you his number... As a matter of fact he's coming here this morning,' she added as an afterthought, 'so you can ask him in person.'

'What's going on? Why were you shouting, Mum?' Simon, still in his pyjamas, appeared at the door beside her. He stared curiously at Manning.

Manning leered at him. 'I'm an old friend of your dad's, young man. I heard the sad news and I've come to pay my respects.'

Simon blinked at him, mystified.

'At nine thirty in the morning?' Karen snapped. 'Why didn't you come to the front door?' she asked for Simon's benefit.

He gave her a quizzical look. 'I believe in taking short cuts, Mrs A. I promised you I'd come back and I always keep my promises. Pity you didn't give me that laptop,' he added in a menacing undertone. 'I hope you won't regret it.' He glanced at his watch. 'Must get going. Plane to catch. Sorry for your loss, young man.' He hastened back down the garden and disappeared into the back alley.

Poppy came running down the stairs and thrust Karen's

bag into her hand. 'Can I have my sweets now?'

'No!' Karen tossed the tube of sweets into the dustbin and shut the back door with a bang. 'There are some sweets in the kitchen drawer. You can have them after breakfast.'

Poppy's eyes filled with tears again. 'But I want the ones the man gave me,' she wailed. 'They're mine.'

'You can't have those. They're not very nice.'

This provoked another tearful outburst.

'Who was that man?' Simon asked.

Karen hesitated. 'Just someone your dad used to...work with. Go and wake Erica, will you, darling? Tell her breakfast will be ready soon. And Poppy, could you put the plates on the table? Don't forget we're going to see Rufus after breakfast.'

Poppy quickly forgot her grievance and squealed with excitement.

After the two children had moved away, Karen rummaged in her bag for her mobile and called Martin. There was no answer. She left him a message, telling him what had happened.

He rang back about half an hour later. 'Back already? How did he manage to get past Surveillance?'

'He came through the alley at the back of the house, so whoever was in the police car wouldn't have seen him. He scares me, Martin. He was making veiled threats about harming Poppy.'

She heard him give a sharp intake of breath. 'Do you know where he went?'

'No. After I told him I'd given the laptop to the police, he said he had a plane to catch. Was it OK to tell him you've got it?'

'Yes, absolutely. The last thing you need is that scumbag coming to the house, especially when the children are there. Unless he was lying about catching a plane, this was probably a last-ditch attempt to find the laptop before he leaves. We'll try to intercept him at one of the airports.'

\* \* \*

After the shock of Manning's visit, Karen was relieved that the rest of the day proceeded as planned. The children loved Rufus on sight and the outing to the leisure centre was highly successful. The evening, however, brought another worry.

At eight o'clock, Erica came home from her friend's birthday party. Her expression was mutinous as she hung up her jacket.

Karen steeled herself. 'Did you have a nice time, darling?'

Erica scowled. 'No.' She glared at Karen accusingly. 'Gemma was there. She told me Auntie Mo and Uncle Tony are getting divorced.'

'Divorced?'

'Yes, and she said it's *your* fault!'

'*My* fault!' Karen was flabbergasted. 'Why is it *my* fault?'

'Because of that row you had with her.'

'Don't be silly, Erica, I'm not to blame for whatever's going on between Mo and Tony.'

'Well Gemma thinks you are.'

'That's absolute nonsense.'

'Well because of you, Gemma said she'll never be my friend again. I hate you!' Erica ran upstairs and slammed her bedroom door. When Karen went up a little later, she could hear her daughter sobbing. She went quietly into the room and found Erica lying face down on the bed. She sat down beside her and gently stroked her hair. 'Tell me what's wrong, darling. This isn't just about Gemma, is it?'

After a few moments the sobs subsided and Erica rolled over. Her face was red and puffy and smeared with tears.

Karen handed her a tissue.

Erica sat up and mopped her eyes. 'I miss Dad,' she whispered. 'I really miss him, Mum.'

'Of course you do, darling.' Karen put her arms round her and kissed the top of her head. She experienced a renewed wave of fury against Howard. He didn't deserve such filial devotion.

# Chapter 13

Martin arrived unexpectedly on Monday morning. 'The SIO is going to make another appeal for witnesses on Wednesday,' he announced while Karen was making him coffee in the kitchen. 'He wonders if you would be prepared to say a few words. Hearing about the impact of a crime on the family of the victim sometimes prompts people to come forward.' He fixed her with his unsettling blue eyes. 'It's completely up to you, of course, so don't hesitate to refuse if the idea doesn't appeal.'

Karen tugged at a strand of her hair. 'I couldn't possibly, Martin. I'd feel a fraud.'

'I thought not, but I had to ask. You can nominate someone to speak for the family if you like. Your sister perhaps?'

She shook her head. 'I don't think Joan will do it either, not now she knows what was on Howard's laptop.'

Martin frowned. 'You told her about it? We warned you not to mention it to anyone.'

Karen flushed. 'I had to tell someone or I would have gone mad. Don't worry. Joan won't breathe a word.'

'I very much hope she won't. Any loose talk could compromise the investigation into *Pied Piper*. Did you stress how important it is that this shouldn't get out?'

'Yes of course I did. Believe me, *I* don't want any of this to get out either.'

'Well I'd better have a word with your sister, just in case.'

'If you like. You've got her number.' She passed him a cup of coffee.

'Thanks. Would you object if *I* spoke on your behalf?' he asked, returning to the subject of the call for witnesses.

She looked at him in surprise. 'No, not if you think it will help the investigation.'

'Good. You can't leave any stone unturned in a murder enquiry. But I'd better warn you, the appeal could generate more publicity so you may have reporters hanging round again.'

She sat down opposite him. 'Does this mean you haven't made any progress in finding the person who shot Howard?'

'The investigation's moved on.' Martin stirred his coffee and took a sip. 'We're pretty sure that the perpetrator had something to do with your husband's... extracurricular activities. That's the main focus at the moment.'

Karen gave a nervous laugh. 'To be honest, Martin, after what you told me the other day, I don't really care who killed him.'

He nodded sympathetically. 'In the circumstances I can understand that.'

'What about Manning? Did you catch up with him?' She shuddered as she remembered him standing in the garden with Poppy.

'He caught a plane from Bristol to Bangkok on Saturday afternoon, using a passport in the name of Phillip Henderson. Interpol was alerted and it's our understanding there was a reception committee waiting for him when he arrived. Manning's a key figure in the child porn ring your husband was involved in.'

Karen winced.

'I'm sorry, it must be very hard to accept that you were married to someone who ...' Martin's voice tailed off.

She was touched by his embarrassment. 'It is. I keep telling myself this is just a terrible nightmare and one day I'll wake up and it will all be over.'

'If only things were that simple.' He gazed at her admiringly.

'But you appear to be dealing with all this remarkably well, Karen.'

'You think so?' She turned her head away so he wouldn't see the tears that started to well up. 'You can't imagine how dreadful I really feel but I mustn't give way or I'll fall apart. I have to pretend I'm OK for the children's sake.' She didn't tell him that most evenings, after the children had gone to bed, she drank nearly a whole bottle of wine to try and erase the horror from her mind.

'Oh, I nearly forgot.' He took a leaflet out of his pocket and handed it to her. 'Here are the details of child protection agencies and helplines, just in case you wanted some advice or support.'

'Thank you.' She placed the leaflet on the kitchen table. 'After you told me what was on the laptop, I asked Erica and Simon whether their father had ever...touched them in an inappropriate way. From the way they reacted I'm pretty sure Howard didn't do anything to them. I haven't said anything to Poppy yet, but she's generally such a happy child, I'm sure I would have noticed something in her behaviour if he had interfered with her.'

Martin nodded thoughtfully. 'I hope you're right. But we don't know yet whether your husband molested *any* children. He might not have gone beyond just looking at images of abuse.'

'Even so, he was aware that children were being abused and made money out of it. That's just as bad as being an abuser himself.' She paused. 'And there was that trip he took to Indonesia-- '

'What trip?' Martin asked sharply.

'Didn't I tell you?'

'No. I don't recall you mentioning a trip to Indonesia.'

'You knew that Howard worked for several charities on a voluntary basis; did their accounts?'

'Yes.'

'They all have something to do with children in the Third World.'

'I know,' he said. 'We've already discovered that.'

'Oh? I only realised it myself after you told me what was on the laptop. A few years ago, Howard visited an orphanage sponsored by one of the charities in Indonesia. I think it's called something like *Crisis Aid*. He went during his annual leave.' She recalled how resentful she was at the time as it was during the long school holiday and she felt he should have spent his leave with her and the children.

Martin frowned. 'Can you remember when that was?' She reflected for a moment. 'It was in 2010, in August.'

He nodded thoughtfully. 'We'll look into it. Now, you're sure you don't want to say anything when the SIO appeals for more witnesses to come forward?'

'Absolutely sure. I can't act the grieving widow now, Martin. It would feel too hypocritical.'

'Fair enough.' He put down his coffee cup and rose to

his feet.

'Martin,' she said as she accompanied him to the front door. 'Who else knows about the porn ring apart from us?'

'Just those of us working on the murder enquiry and the special investigating team looking into *Pied Piper*. Why?'

'What about Geoff Murray? Does he need to know?'

'Not necessarily. We've checked and nothing's come up to suggest he's connected. At the moment the fewer people who know about it, the better.' He turned to leave.

She sighed with relief. 'Before you go, there's a favour I'd like to ask.'

'Oh? What's that?'

'I need to change the car. I don't like driving Howard's Volvo. I want to exchange it for something smaller and more economical, but I've never bought a second-hand car before. My brother-in-law doesn't know anything about cars and I don't know who else to ask.'

'Yes,' he said after a moment's thought. 'I know a good local dealer who could do a part exchange. I'll have a word with him if you like, ask him to show you some decent small cars.'

'That would be kind. Thank you.'

After Martin had left, Karen plucked up the courage to ring one of the child protection numbers in the leaflet. Haltingly, she told the friendly woman who answered the phone that she wanted to make sure her daughter hadn't been abused by a man who was under police investigation. The woman suggested she brought Poppy along to a special clinic and added that there was a cancellation on the following Monday afternoon.

* * *

'How about indulging in a spot of retail therapy after dropping the kids off tomorrow?' Juliet suggested when they met at the school gates that afternoon. 'We can get you some new clobber. You need to inject some colour into your life, girl!'

'Yes, why not?' Karen felt she could afford to buy some clothes as she had received an excellent price for her engagement ring. The jeweller had goggled at the ring when she went to have it valued. 'Are you *sure* you want to sell it?' he had asked. 'It's a very expensive piece.'

'Absolutely sure,' she had declared.

'And shall I make a hairdressing appointment for you?' Juliet continued. 'I spoke to my hairdresser and she can fit you in on Wednesday morning?'

Karen hesitated. She couldn't remember the last time she had had her hair done. 'I don't know. I wouldn't want to overdo it.'

'New life, new image, my girl! You need to take the bull by the balls ...sorry, mixed metaphor, but you know what I mean.'

Karen put a hand up to her hair. It felt lank and floppy. 'OK, I'll give it a go, but I don't want to end up looking like an old boiler dressed up as lamb, to use another mixed metaphor.'

'Trust me!'

\* \* \*

On Wednesday afternoon, she made her way self-consciously to school to pick up Poppy. She was wearing the burgundy jacket and skinny blue jeans she had bought at Moxton's only decent-sized department store. Juliet had gently nudged her away from the black or navy items she instinctively veered towards, and had also persuaded her to buy several brightly coloured tops and some high- heeled ankle boots.

That morning, an enthusiastic young hairdresser had lightened her hair to a warm blond, then cut and styled it so that it softly framed her face. She was surprised at the difference it made to her appearance. She thought she looked younger and almost pretty. A man had even whistled at her when she walked past a building site.

As she walked along the High Street, she saw an unmistakable figure coming towards her, her massive bosom wobbling alarmingly: Celia Murray. Karen stopped abruptly and peered into the nearest shop window - it was a butcher's shop - hoping that Geoff's unpleasant wife would pass by without noticing her. It was a forlorn hope. While she was pretending to scrutinise the cuts of meat, Celia came to a halt beside her.

'Karen?'

She turned, feigning surprise. 'Hello, Celia.'

'Good lord!' Celia looked her up and down with a shocked expression. 'Aren't you still in mourning?'

'I--'

'Your husband was murdered just a short while ago!'

Karen's cheeks started to burn. 'Do you suppose I'm not aware of that, Celia?'

Celia's voice was cold. 'Well, I wouldn't have thought...I wouldn't have expected you to --'

'To what, Celia?'

Celia pursed her lips. 'To get yourself all glammed up, quite so soon.'

Karen took a deep breath and drew on her burgeoning

sense of assertiveness. 'Maybe you don't realise what it's like to lose someone in such terrible circumstances, Celia. The last two months have been an absolute nightmare for me and my children. But we're not living in Victorian times. I don't have to wear black for the rest of my life. If it offends you that I've had my hair done and bought some new clothes, tough! But it has helped *me*; it's made *me* feel better, and that's exactly what *I* need at the moment.'

'If you say so.' Celia's features had become pinched. 'I suppose it takes all sorts. Goodbye, Karen.' After a final disapproving glare, she stomped heavily away.

Karen watched her departing back with intense dislike before continuing on her way to the junior school.

When Poppy spotted her, she stopped, stared, then ran up to her, beaming. 'Mummy! You look just like a princess!'

Karen smiled self-consciously but felt gratified. 'I don't think so, darling.'

'Yes you do! I like your hair. It's all fluffy and yellow.'

Karen laughed. 'You make me sound like a baby duckling!' She was aware that other mothers were staring at her and whispering, but she didn't care.

'Wow, Mum,' Simon exclaimed when he returned from school. 'I nearly didn't recognise you. You look beautiful.' He reached up and shyly touched her hair. 'Your hair's all soft!'

Erica's reaction was less agreeable. 'Women of your age shouldn't bleach their hair!' she snapped. 'And *I'd* like some new clothes. Why did you buy stuff for yourself and not us?'

Karen's fragile euphoria evaporated immediately. Had she been terribly selfish spending money on herself instead of on the children? 'As soon as your dad's affairs are sorted, we'll all go shopping,' she said quickly.

But Erica wasn't mollified. 'You're so selfish. You only think of yourself!' she yelled before pounding upstairs and, as had become a daily occurrence, slamming her bedroom door.

* * *

'Goodness, Karen. Whatever have you done to yourself?' Joan gazed at her amazement when she called round that evening so that they could watch the appeal for witnesses on TV together.

Karen ran a hand through her cropped hair. It still felt unfamiliar. 'Juliet, the woman I met at Poppy's school, arranged an appointment for me with her hairdresser. I wasn't sure about having it lightened. Do you think it looks OK?'

Joan took off her glasses and peered closely at her before replacing them. 'More than OK. You look great, ten years younger.' She laughed. 'Maybe I should go to that hairdresser myself.'

'You don't think it's too soon to change my appearance?' Karen asked anxiously. She was aware that her new appearance had raised eyebrows and was probably prompting gossip among her neighbours.

Joan hesitated. 'No,' she said finally, 'though I suppose some might think so.'

'I bumped into Celia Murray in town and from the way she reacted you'd have thought I was the Whore of Babylon.'

Joan snorted. 'Celia Murray would disapprove of Mother Theresa! Why shouldn't you have your hair done if you want to?'

Karen heaved a sigh of relief. 'Did Martin Harrison ring you? He wasn't pleased that I told you about Howard's laptop.'

'Yes, he called on Monday. I assured him I wouldn't spill any beans.'

'Good. I promised him you wouldn't tell anyone.'

Joan looked shamefaced. 'Well, I did tell Greg. He was absolutely appalled.'

Karen's heart sank. 'You didn't! Oh, Joan. Does Martin know?'

'I'm afraid not. I didn't tell your nice policeman in case he arrested me on the spot. Don't worry. Greg won't say anything.'

'Are you sure?' Karen was doubtful. Greg, Joan's affable husband, lived up to his name by being extremely gregarious, especially after a few pints in his local.

'Yes,' Joan said grimly. 'I said I'd divorce him if I ever find out that he's he mentioned it to anyone.'

After the children had gone to bed, Karen told her about Manning's second visit.

Joan reacted with shock. 'I said you should have come to stay with us. That man sounds dangerous. What if he had hurt Poppy?'

'Well he didn't, thank God. Anyway, Martin said he's in Thailand now and the police have caught up with him.' She poured herself a glass of red wine and took a gulp.

Joan shook her head despairingly. 'Karen, I do wish you'd listen to me sometimes. You're drinking far too much.'

Karen shrugged. 'It helps.' She took the glass and the bottle with her when they went to the sitting room to watch the appeal for witnesses.

Senior Investigating Officer DCI Evans was flanked by a characteristically severe-looking DI Parker. Martin Harrison, immediately recognisable by his distinctive white hair, stood behind them. Camera bulbs flashed as DCI Evans appealed for new witnesses to come forward. He was peppered with questions from the assembled reporters: *how is the investigation going? Do you have any suspects yet? Have you discovered a motive for the murder?*

Evans parried the questions as evasively as he had done on the first occasion, again emphasising that it was a complex enquiry. 'At the moment we're following up a very important new lead,' he added tantalisingly. 'I'm afraid I can't reveal any details at this moment in time.'

Karen was relieved that he didn't elucidate, but she nearly choked when Martin stepped forward and spoke stirringly about the plight of the family Howard had left behind. 'Mr Armstrong's widow and his three children are struggling to cope with the loss of a loving husband and father. His widow is still far too distressed to speak in public.'

Karen drained her glass and refilled it under Joan's disapproving gaze.

\* \* \*

As Martin had predicted, the renewed appeal for witnesses brought an immediate and unwelcome spotlight back on to Karen and the family. The following morning, reporters again hovered in the street outside, hoping to pick up some morsels of information to pad out the slim body of detail supplied by the police. When Karen and the children left the house, they crowded round them, shouting questions.

As a result, she decided to drive the three children to and from school for the next few days to prevent them from being pestered. She hoped that the fresh publicity wouldn't prompt any further bullying or harassment by other pupils. Although she believed Erica was capable of standing up for herself, she worried about Simon, and warned him that he might be the object of renewed attention from other boys. 'Ignore them,' she advised him. 'Don't answer any questions about your dad or rise to any taunts.'

He gazed at her miserably without answering.

Karen prayed that the flurry of renewed interest would soon fade away and in the event, her fears for the children proved groundless. Neither Erica nor Simon reported any problems when she picked them up in the afternoons and, to her relief, the reporters had disappeared by the weekend.

'Wow!' Martin exclaimed admiringly when he called at the house the following Monday.

Karen patted her hair nervously. 'You don't think it's a bit premature?'

He hesitated for a fraction of a second. 'No, you look great.'

'But I'm not living up to the image of the distressed widow you described?'

'Different people react to traumatic events in different ways. I knew a woman who shaved off all her hair after a family tragedy.' He gave one of his rare smiles. 'I think what you've had done is infinitely preferable. Now...' He produced a large brown envelope from a briefcase, extracted a number of photos, and handed them to her. 'I'd like you to look at these. Do you recognise any of these people, Karen? Can you remember if any of them ever visited your husband?'

She peered at the photos. They were all of men of different ages; some white, some of Asian appearance. 'No I've never seen any of them. Who are they?'

'They're members of the *Pied Piper* ring. They're on an international wanted list as part of a coordinated attempt to stamp down on child porn. We've had a tip-off that some of them may be in England.'

Karen stiffened in alarm. 'You don't think they'll come to the house, looking for Howard's laptop?'

'Don't worry. It's likely they'll know by now that the police have got it. Manning may have contacted them before he was arrested.'

She frowned. 'If the investigating team have already identified so many people in the ring, does that mean they already knew about Howard?'

'It's possible, though he could have been operating under a false name, like Manning.'

'In that case --'

'In that case?'

'This will sound terrible, but it's just as well Howard died when he did.'

'Before the shit hit the fan, you mean?'

'Yes.' She gazed at him beseechingly. 'I don't suppose there's any way of keeping his involvement in the ring out of the spotlight, is there?'

He shook his head. 'I'm afraid it's not up to me, Karen. As you know there are two investigations going on at the moment, the murder enquiry and the child porn enquiry. The second one is still pretty hush hush, but assuming the two *are* connected as we strongly suspect, your husband's activities are bound to come up as the murder investigation progresses.'

She sighed. 'I suppose it was a silly question.'

'It was a perfectly natural one in the circumstances. But your husband's relationship with *Pied Piper* will come out sooner or later, though later would be preferable. At the moment we don't want to muddy the waters. If the tabloids get wind of something like this, they'll be like a dog with a bone.'

\* \* \*

That afternoon, pretending it was a routine health check, Karen took Poppy to a special clinic to keep the appointment she had arranged through the child protection agency. The visit was far less stressful than she had feared. After a motherly woman had taken Poppy into a brightly painted room full of toys and pictures, she had a private interview with a sympathetic health professional and, without going into all the details, explained as briefly as possible what her fears were. She felt almost faint with anxiety but Martin had assured her that anything she said about Howard would be in complete confidence. He also told her that the agency would be made aware that the information was highly sensitive as it was under police investigation.

After the interview, Karen waited in a state of feverish anxiety in the reception area. About half an hour later, Poppy emerged from the side room with the motherly woman. She was relaxed and laughing. 'We played some games, Mummy.'

The woman smiled at Karen. 'Nothing,' she murmured. 'No signs.'

Karen felt such a profound sense of relief, she could have kissed her.

# Chapter 14

The next morning Karen drove to the car dealers Martin had recommended. When she arrived, she discovered that he had already rung the owner and asked him to sort out a good deal for her. The man offered her a fair price for Howard's Volvo in part exchange for a three-year-old hatchback just big enough to accommodate the family as well as a dog. Joan and Greg had offered to lend her the money to pay the balance. She arranged to return the following week to complete the paperwork and pick up the car.

Driving home, she felt a small glow of satisfaction at having taken yet another step to remove the remaining traces of Howard from her life.

That afternoon, when Erica returned from school, she banged the door so hard that the house vibrated. She stalked into the hall, scowling at the screen of her phone.

Karen sighed inwardly, anticipating yet another scene. 'Is something the matter, darling?'

Erica raised her eyes from her mobile for a fraction of a second. 'They're saying things about us.'

Karen was startled. 'Who's saying things about us?'

'People.'

'What people?'

'People on *Facebook* and *Instagram*.'

Karen knew very little about these social networking sites. Aware that Poppy and Simon were listening, she drew Erica into the living room. 'What are people saying? Tell me.'

'They're saying things like...Dad was a psycho and that was why he was shot and that you're a slag and --'

'That's enough!' Karen was rigid with shock. 'I don't want to hear any more. How dare people say things like that? Do you know who they are?'

'No.' Erica tapped rapidly at the screen of her mobile.

'Don't you have to use your name on network sites?'

'Not always.' Erica glowered at her. 'And I've been getting a bunch of nasty texts.'

'Oh, darling,' Karen said, dismayed. 'Who from?'

'Mostly kids at school.'

'Why didn't you tell me?'

Erica flushed pink. 'I didn't want to. They were too...gross.'

'Abusive online messages and texts are against the law.' Karen didn't know whether this was true, but she thought it might be. 'I told you after Dad died that this might happen. I'll ring Martin Harrison and he --'

'Not *him* again!' Erica retorted. She tossed her head and her glossy dark hair swung from side to side.

'What do you mean "not *him* again"?'

'He's *always* here.'

'He's *not* always here, Erica. He calls round occasionally because he's been appointed our family liaison officer and he has to keep in touch during the murder enquiry.'

Erica smirked. 'He only comes because he fancies you.'

Karen felt the blood rise to her face. 'That's rubbish. It's his job. Listen, why don't you switch your mobile off and leave it at home tomorrow?'

'Switch it *off*?' Erica gaped at her. 'I can't do that. *Nobody* goes to school without their phone.'

'If you give it to me,' Karen suggested patiently, 'I'll ask Martin to have the messages investigated and he can find out who's sending them.'

'No way!' Erica clutched her phone protectively to her chest. 'You're *not* giving it to *him*!'

'In that case I'll ring the head and tell her about it. Maybe she can put a stop to the texts you're getting.'

'No!' Erica shouted angrily. 'Leave it, Mum! Don't interfere. I wish I'd never mentioned it.' She marched upstairs and didn't say another word to Karen for the rest of the evening.

Karen felt deeply uneasy. Who was leaving the abusive messages? Was it just spiteful children or were there adults involved? The renewed appeal for witnesses must have reignited salacious interest in Howard's murder. She didn't tell Erica that she had received offensive calls and texts herself and had changed her mobile and landline numbers on Martin's advice.

* * *

The following afternoon, Simon came home from school alone.

'Where's Erica?' Karen asked. She was peeling potatoes in the kitchen while Poppy watched a children's television programme in the living room.

He dropped his schoolbag on the floor. 'She wasn't on the bus. What's for tea?'

Karen stared at him. 'Why wasn't she on the bus?'

'Dunno,' Simon answered indifferently. 'She probably had something after school.'

'That's unusual. She doesn't usually stay after school.' Karen felt a prickle of anxiety. Erica had recently decided that extracurricular activities such as sports, music or drama weren't "cool".

Simon yawned. 'She probably went to someone's house and forgot to tell you. What's for tea?'

'Shepherd's Pie.'

'Cool.'

Karen rang Erica's mobile. As there was no reply, she left a message. 'It's Mum, Erica. Where are you? Call me *asap*.'

She waited half an hour then rang the school only to learn that Erica hadn't been seen on the premises since classes had finished. She called Lisa and Caroline, Erica's closest friends, but they said they hadn't seen her since the end of afternoon school either.

By now Karen was on the verge of panic. Could one of Gerald Manning's associates have travelled to Moxton, bent on revenge because she had given the laptop to the police? She imagined her daughter being dragged screaming into a car. In desperation, she rang Martin.

'It's too early to report her missing,' he told her. 'She's probably just gone somewhere with a school friend.'

'Then why isn't she answering her phone? What if a member of the paedophile ring has taken her?'

'That's very unlikely, Karen. Have you called her friends?'

'Only the two she usually goes around with.'

'Are you sure she didn't say anything about coming home late this morning?'

'Absolutely sure. But she was very upset yesterday.' Karen told him about the text and internet taunts.

He frowned. 'I'm afraid cyber bullying is a fact of life nowadays. If the messages are extremely abusive, we can follow them up. These days we check social network sites as a matter of course in murder cases. They could reveal people with a grudge against your husband or clues to the motive for the shooting. Give it another hour or so. If Erica hasn't come home or contacted you by then, let me know.'

Karen continued to call Erica's mobile at frequent intervals, but each time it went into answer mode. She cooked the evening meal mechanically, attempting to hide her mounting terror from Simon and Poppy. Finally, when she could bear the suspense no longer, she called Martin again.

'OK,' he responded. 'Try not to worry. We'll see if we can find her.'

By now Karen was almost prostrate with anxiety. While Simon and Poppy were eating their meal, she stood in the hall staring at the phone, willing it to ring.

At twenty past seven it did.

'We've found her,' Martin announced triumphantly. 'She was in the market square.'

'Thank God.' Weak with relief, Karen sank on to the hall chair.

'What was she doing there?'

'She was with a group of teenage boys. They were larking about near the fountain. Uniform's picked her up. They're bringing her home. She should be back any minute.'

'Thank God,' Karen repeated. She replaced the phone and went to wait by the front door.

When the police car arrived, the driver, a female officer, got out and opened the back passenger door. Erica emerged, scowling ferociously.

Karen ran down the path and threw her arms round her. 'Thank goodness! I've been out of my mind with worry.'

Erica shook her off impatiently. 'I only went into town. What's the big deal?'

'Why didn't you answer your phone? I've been ringing you for ages.'

Erica shrugged. 'Probably didn't hear it.' She pushed past Karen, stalked up the path and entered the house.

After thanking the policewoman, Karen hastened after her. 'Don't walk away when I'm speaking to you, young lady.'

Erica turned round with a look of fury disturbingly similar to an expression Karen had often seen on Howard's face. 'You showed me up in front of my mates, sending a police car. It was *so* embarrassing!'

'Of course I called the police,' Karen snapped. 'You disappeared after school and nobody knew where you were. Can't you understand how worried I've been? The police said you were in the market square with a group of boys.'

Erica shrugged again. 'Yeah, so what?'

Karen felt like slapping her. 'For goodness sake, Erica, you're only thirteen.'

'So? That's old enough.'

'Old enough? Old enough for what?'

'Old enough to go into town with some mates, without you sending a fucking police car after me.'

Karen attempted to control her anger. 'Don't you dare use that kind of language with me, Erica. You can't just go off like that, with a group of boys.'

'Why not? We were only hanging out. What's your problem?'

Karen gazed at her. She could foresee trouble ahead. Erica was growing up fast. Her body was filling out and with her creamy skin and the dark good looks she had inherited from her father, she was becoming very attractive; *too* attractive.

'I'll tell you what my problem is,' Karen said slowly. 'There are some very...unpleasant people around; men who go round looking for young girls like you.'

Erica snorted incredulously. 'That is so OTT. I was with my mates from school, not with some dirty old man!'

Karen gripped her arm. 'Erica, don't you realise that the man who shot your dad is still out there somewhere? What's more, every reporter in the county is watching us, just waiting for the chance to find some gossip to fill the newspaper columns.'

'If you don't want people to watch us,' Erica retorted, 'you shouldn't have bleached your hair and bought those stupid boots.'

Karen could no longer contain herself. 'This isn't about *me*, Erica, it's about *you*!' she yelled. 'Listen to me, young lady. Don't you *ever* do that again, do you hear? From now on, I want you to come home on that school bus, do you understand? You're grounded for the next two weeks!' She only realised she had been shouting when she noticed Simon and Poppy standing at the foot of the stairs. They looked frightened.

Erica appeared stunned by her outburst. 'That's so not fair,' she muttered after a brief silence. 'I think you're horrible. I don't want any tea so don't bother to give me any.' She ran upstairs and slammed her bedroom door.

It took Karen some time to recover her equilibrium and calm the anxieties of the younger children. After they had gone to bed, she rang Joan and told her what had happened. 'Erica's really gone off the rails,' she complained.

'She's just a teenager, Karen.'

'I'm not sure what being a teenager is. I don't remember what I was like at that age.'

'Very shy and far too timid to be a tearaway,' Joan said gently. 'Don't forget Erica's still grieving. She loved her dad. You have to make allowances.'

Karen dissolved in tears. 'I'm sick of making allowances. She seems to blame me for everything.'

'It's just a phase she's going through, Karen. But you're right to put your foot down. She can't go wandering off after school at her age, especially after all that's happened.'

'That's what I told her.' Karen blew her nose before adding, 'by the way, I'll be collecting Rufus soon.'

'Who's Rufus?'

'The dog I mentioned, the one at the animal rescue centre. I had to wait for us to be checked out before they'd let me have him.'

'What do you mean, "checked out"?'

'The animal rescue centre had to make sure that we'll be responsible dog-owners and that we're giving him a good home.'

'Good lord,' Joan snorted derisively. 'What a lot of fuss. You'd think they'd be only too pleased to have someone take a dog off their hands.'

# Chapter 15

Rufus whined and lurched nervously from side to side on the back seat, forcing Karen to drive carefully on the way home from the rescue centre. She had forgotten how large he was and hoped the new car would turn out to be big enough to carry him as well as a family of four.

When they arrived home, she let him prowl freely around the house, sniffing at the furniture. After he had investigated the rooms, she gave him some water and dog biscuits, then clipped a lead on to his collar and led him outside for a walk.

She headed towards the woods north of Moxton. By now, autumn had really taken hold and windblown leaves lay in untidy brown and yellow piles in the gutters. The intermittent rain of recent weeks had imparted rich tints to the formerly parched gardens and hedgerows. An earthy smell of damp soil hung in the air, laced with an elusive scent of wood smoke. Karen had always loved this time of the year. She felt more at ease when the evenings started to get dark again.

Although he had been regularly exercised at the rescue centre, Rufus didn't seem accustomed to a lead. He persisted in running from one side of her to the other, wrapping the lead round her shins and ankles. When she stooped to disentangle it for the umpteenth time, a small black poodle bounded up to them. He and Rufus leapt at each other in a frenzy of excited barking.

'Albert!' called a voice Karen recognised. Looking up, she saw Mo advancing rapidly towards her. She was thinner and paler than when Karen had seen her last, and there were dark circles under her eyes. Her hair was rather unbecomingly scraped back behind her ears.

'Karen?' Mo exclaimed with surprise. 'I hardly recognised you. You look amazing.'

'Thanks,' Karen said coldly. She attempted to pull Rufus away from Albert and walk away, but Mo seemed intent upon engaging her in conversation. 'I didn't know you had a dog.'

'I've only just got him.'

'Down, Albert!' Mo hauled Albert off Rufus by his collar. 'I like your hair,' she said as she straightened up, 'it suits you like that.' Before Karen could reply, she added abruptly, 'Tony wants a divorce.'

'Yes, Erica mentioned it.' Karen had no desire to discuss Mo's marital problems.

'The police questioned him about where he was on the day Howard was killed and then it all came out. He's absolutely furious. The atmosphere at home is terrible.'

Karen resisted saying "I told you so". She again tried to move away, but Mo seemed bent on continuing her unwelcome confidences.

'Tony and me...we'd got bored with each other. The marriage had gone stale. I suppose we only stayed together because of Gemma, and Howard said he loved me --'

Karen gave a sarcastic laugh. 'And you believed him?'

She wondered how Mo would react if she ever discovered Howard's involvement in child pornography. Would she feel as degraded and sickened as she did herself?

'Yes.' Mo seemed near to tears.

He used to say he loved **me**, Karen thought, jerking the lead in another vain attempt to pull Rufus away from Albert, but that was a long time ago and now she knew he must have been lying.

Mo was staring at her curiously. 'Are you OK, Karen?'

'No,' she snapped, 'I'm far from OK. This has been the worst period of my life. Come on, Rufus!' She yanked the lead again, took a step past Mo then impulsively turned back. 'When you were seeing Howard, did he ever mention any business dealings he was involved in, abroad?'

'Abroad?' Mo seemed surprised. 'Whereabouts, abroad?'

'Somewhere like Thailand or Indonesia.'

'Oh.' Mo flushed pink. 'Fetch it, Albie!' She hurled a ball into the distance and the poodle scampered after it. When she turned back to Karen, her expression was nervous. 'Look Karen, I don't want another row.'

'Neither do I. I just need to know.'

Mo avoided meeting her eye. 'He did ask me to join him in Thailand for the second week of his trip.'

Karen stared at her. 'What trip?'

'The trip he was going to take after the end of July. Good boy, Albie!' Mo picked up the sodden ball that the puppy had deposited at her feet and launched it into the bushes. Albert scampered after it again while Rufus whined and strained at his lead, anxious to join in the fun. 'He said it was a business trip.'

'A business trip?'

'You didn't know?' Mo appeared genuinely astonished.

'He didn't mention it?'

'No,' Karen said grimly. 'He didn't. What exactly did he say?' Just when she thought there was nothing more she could learn about Howard, another potential bombshell seemed about to explode.

Mo threw the ball again for Albert. 'You're *sure* you want to hear?'

Karen swallowed. 'Yes, go on.'

'He said he had business to attend to in Indonesia the first week, and asked me to join him in Thailand the second week so we could have a holiday together.'

Karen went hot with anger. Howard had told her he was too busy to take her and the children on holiday during the summer. She had protested volubly, provoking a furious argument. She took a deep breath before she spoke. 'How could you have managed that without Tony knowing?'

Mo had the grace to look shamefaced. 'It would have been when Gemma was away at adventure camp. I was going to pretend I was having a week's holiday with a friend. But it was too complicated to arrange, so I told Howard I couldn't go.'

'Did he say what kind of business trip it was?'

'He said it was to do with some charity or other he did the accounts for. Good boy!' Mo stooped, picked up the ball again and hurled it into the distance. As Albert sped off, Rufus tried to follow. It took all of Karen's strength to restrain him.

'Can you remember anything else about it?' she asked when she had regained her breath.

Mo reflected for a second. 'Well, he did ask me to bring something for him in my luggage.'

Karen stared at her. 'Oh? What?'

'Some work stuff.'

Karen felt a prickle of apprehension. 'What sort of work stuff? Did he ask you to take a laptop?'

'No, just some files.'

'What kind of files?' she asked casually. 'Paper files? Computer files?'

'They were on some of those little things, what are they called?

Memory sticks. Anyway, what does it matter now?'

'But why did he want *you* to carry them?'

'He said he was only taking hand luggage.'

Karen found this extremely odd. Howard, always so fastidious about his clothes, invariably took a huge suitcase with him when he was travelling. 'If it was a work trip, wouldn't he have needed the files in Indonesia?'

Mo shrugged. 'Maybe. I never asked.'

'But memory sticks are absolutely tiny,' Karen said, thinking of the ones Erica had used to download photographs from her laptop. 'Surely Howard could have carried them himself.'

'I suppose so. I think he said...' Mo screwed up her face as she tried to remember. 'Yes, I'm sure he said something like he didn't want them to fall into the wrong hands.'

Karen suppressed a gasp. 'What did he mean by that?'

Mo looked blank. 'Dunno. I didn't ask. He never talked to me about his work. He didn't tell me what he was going to do over there.'

'Did he ever mention someone called Gerald Manning to you? Someone he knew in Indonesia or Thailand?'

Mo looked puzzled. 'I don't think so. It was ages ago when he suggested the holiday and we only talked about it a few times. He was pretty upset when I said I couldn't go. He tried to persuade me but I said it was too difficult. Why are you asking me all these questions?'

'I'm trying to sort out Howard's finances,' Karen said cautiously. 'He had some overseas business dealings I'm not clear about. Did you tell the police that he asked you to meet him in Thailand and carry memory sticks for him?'

'No, I didn't think it was important as he cancelled the trip.' Mo gazed at her imploringly. 'Please don't tell them about it, Karen. I don't want Tony to know I was thinking of going on holiday with Howard. . Things are bad enough at home as it is.'

'I'm afraid I'm going to have to. It could help the enquiry. Goodbye Mo.' Karen moved away, dragging Rufus on the lead behind her. As she followed the muddy path out of the woods, she realised that her anger towards Mo had largely dissipated. Her betrayal now seemed a slight offence compared with the quagmire of evil and deception in which Howard had been immersed.

She shortened the lead to keep Rufus trotting by her side and set off briskly for home, intending to ring Martin as soon as she arrived. However this proved unnecessary as he called at the house not long after she had shut the front door.

'This your new mutt?' he asked, gazing down at Rufus who had scampered into the hall at the sound of the bell.

'Yes, this is Rufus.'

'Hello, boy.' He reached down and stroked Rufus's soft, droopy ears. 'I've got some news.'

'So have I. Coffee?'

'No thanks. What's your news?'

'Tell me yours first.' She led him into the living room.

Martin beamed triumphantly as he lowered himself on to an armchair. 'Gerald Manning's been charged with child abuse and trafficking. He's in custody in Bangkok. Now what's yours?'

Karen described her conversation with Mo.

He listened with keen interest. 'Well, this *is* a turn up! You had no idea he was contemplating going to Indonesia and Thailand in the summer?'

'None at all. He told me he was far too busy to go away during the long school holiday. He didn't mention any work trips. He must have decided not to go after Mo said she couldn't join him.'

Martin frowned. 'He could have been planning a return visit to that orphanage in Jakarta, though there were no references to it on his computers or in the diary. You say he asked Maureen Field to carry some flash drives for him, but not a laptop?'

'Yes, he told her he would only be taking hand luggage, though that was weird if he was planning to go for two weeks. He used to take a vast number of clothes with him when he travelled anywhere.'

Martin gazed thoughtfully into the distance. 'It's probably safe to assume that your husband was intending to download some of the files from the laptop on to USB sticks. Maybe he'd already done that before he mentioned them to Mrs Field. But why couldn't he have carried them to Thailand himself? They're small enough, tiny! He could easily have concealed them in his bag or his clothes.'

'I asked Mo that. She said he told her he didn't want them "falling into the wrong hands".'

'Well I suppose that makes sense. Maybe he knew that the police were closing in on the people at the Asian end of the *Pied Piper* operation so he was reluctant to carry any incriminating material in his luggage or on his person. Asking Mrs Field to take the stuff could have been a security measure in case he was searched on arrival. Or...,' Martin's blue eyes narrowed as he speculated aloud, '...perhaps he was afraid his associates in Thailand were so desperate to get hold of the files that they might try and take them off him by force. They're a dangerous bunch, that lowlife he was involved with. For some reason, he needed to keep them safe, maybe as a bartering tool. If he was the only person who knew where the files were, he may have thought he wouldn't come to any harm.'

Karen shuddered. 'So why did Gerald Manning come here?'

'Manning may have been expecting your husband to visit Thailand as planned, and when he failed to arrive, decided to come and get the laptop himself. I'm not surprised he was desperate to find it. There's some very incriminating stuff on it, not just the porn images but details of the money your husband was ripping off from the sales and transferring to his personal overseas account. He also had a list of the key *Pied Piper* members in Europe which has proved very useful to the investigating team.' Martin leaned forward and patted Rufus's head that had suddenly inserted itself between his knees. 'Friendly chap, isn't he?'

Karen smiled down at Rufus. 'But if Howard *had* given Mo the memory sticks, couldn't she have looked to see what was on them?'

'She might have done, but your husband would have made sure the contents were locked.' He rose from his chair. 'I'll have to report this to the SIO. We're going to have to interview your friend Maureen Field again. Your husband was obviously prepared to use her even if it meant putting her in danger.'

'She's *not* my friend,' Karen retorted.

# Chapter 16

Karen took Rufus with her when she walked to school that afternoon. When Poppy spotted him, she ran across the playground, squealing with delight. She crouched down and stroked him. 'His ears are all soft,' she declared. 'They're like brown mittens. If his name wasn't Rufus, we could call him Mitten.'

Rufus nuzzled her hand.

When Erica and Simon came home from school, it was another case of mutual enchantment. Rufus ran round them in circles, barking excitedly. Simon beamed with delight and even Erica emerged from her epic sulk long enough to enthuse about the new arrival. 'He's red brown, Mum, just like the autumn leaves.'

Karen was relieved. These were the first civil words Erica had addressed to her in twenty four hours.

'Can he sleep in my room, Mum?' Simon pleaded.

'I don't see why not.'

Joan was less impressed when she called round that evening. She backed away when Rufus approached her. 'What kind of a dog is it?'

'Of mixed parentage I suppose you could say.'

Joan eyed him warily. 'Do you think he'll be a good guard dog?' Karen laughed. 'He'd probably lick a burglar to death.'

'Mum's going to put a sign saying "Beware of the Dog" on the front gate,' Simon told Joan.

She chortled. 'I'm sure that'll be a *very* effective deterrent.'

After the children had gone to bed, Karen made Joan a cup of herbal tea and poured herself a generous glass of wine before describing her encounter with Mo. 'I couldn't get away from her. She told me that Tony wants a divorce.'

'I'm not surprised,' Joan grunted. 'Serve her right.'

'She said Howard invited her to spend a week with him in Thailand in the summer.'

Joan nearly spilled her tea. 'In the summer? After he told you he was too busy to take you and the kids on holiday?'

'Yes,' Karen said bitterly. 'And Mo agreed, but in the end she couldn't go and he wasn't too pleased. Apparently he'd asked her to carry stuff for him.'

'What kind of stuff?'

'Work files he'd put on memory sticks. They could have been downloaded from the laptop I found, though I don't know that for sure.'

'Did she tell the police?'

'No, but I did, this morning. I rang Martin and he said they're going to interview Mo again.'

Joan gave an angry snort. 'It's a wonder you didn't slap her face.'

Karen took a long draught of her wine. 'I don't care about Mo any more. I think Howard was just using her.'

Joan raised her hands in a despairing gesture. 'What else are you going to find out about him? Where is all this going to end?'

Karen sighed. 'I wish I knew, Joanie.'

\* \* \*

The next morning Karen received a phone call from Martin. His tone was apologetic. 'Are you going to be in this morning? I'm afraid the SIO wants the house searched. As the children will be at school, he thought it might be a good time.'

Karen's heart sank. 'Again? It's already been searched once.'

'Not thoroughly enough. He thinks it could be of use to both enquiries in view of the new information about your husband's proposed trip to Indonesia and Thailand. The memory sticks may be somewhere in the house.'

'But what about the neighbours? There'll be gossip if they see police coming here again.'

'Don't worry, Karen,' he assured her, 'they won't be in uniform, and I assure you they'll put everything back as they found it.'

Three officers turned up about an hour later, two men and one woman. They were polite but taciturn. Karen unlocked cupboards and drawers, then left them to get on with the search. They worked from room to room, concentrating mainly on Howard's study. She could hear banging upstairs as she waited anxiously in the living room. She was beginning to get the impression that the focus of the enquiry had shifted from the search for Howard's murderer to an investigation of his own misdeeds.

When the police had finished going through the house, they asked her for the keys to the shed, the garage and the car. It was another hour before they finished their work and when they left the house, they didn't tell Karen whether or not they had found anything of interest.

She checked each room and was relieved to find that they didn't look disturbed. She herself, however, felt extremely disturbed by the invasion of her home. Too agitated to settle to anything, she rang Juliet, remembering that Tuesday was one of her days off. 'Can I come round?'

'Sure.' Juliet sounded surprised. 'Has something happened? Are you OK?

'No. Do you mind if I bring the dog? I've only just got him and don't want to leave him on his own.'

'Yes that's fine.'

When Juliet opened the door she was wearing a man's shirt spattered with bright pink paint. 'Sorry about the mess,' she said cheerfully. 'I've decided to brighten up the living room. Come and see.'

The floor at one end of Juliet's living room was covered in newspaper. A stepladder stood in front of the window, a paint tray and roller perched precariously on its top rung. The walls next to the window had certainly been brightened up. They had been painted a vivid shade of fuchsia.

Karen felt awkward. 'I'm sorry. You should have told me you were busy.'

'Nonsense.' Juliet smiled reassuringly at her. 'I need a break. I'm famished. Like to join me for a gourmet lunch? A tin of chicken soup?'

'Thank you, yes, if you're sure.'

Juliet led the way to the kitchen which was even untidier than the last time Karen had visited. She pushed aside toys, children's shoes and an overflowing laundry basket and opened the back door. 'Why don't you let the dog out? It's totally enclosed so he can't run away.'

Karen removed Rufus's lead and he bounded into the overgrown garden.

Juliet poured the contents of the tin of soup into a saucepan and lit a gas ring. 'Sit down; it'll only take a moment.'

Karen removed a pair of child's pyjamas from a kitchen chair and obediently sat down.

A few minutes later Juliet placed two steaming bowls of soup and some bread on the table and sat down opposite her. 'OK, what's up?'

Karen hesitated before she answered. 'I'm not supposed to mention this,' she murmured hesitantly, toying with a piece of bread. 'Only the police and my sister know, but I can't keep it to myself any longer.' She looked across the table at Juliet. 'Can I trust you not to say anything?'

'Of course you can.'

Juliet listened in silence as Karen told her about Howard's hidden laptop and the child porn investigation, her face registering varying degrees of shock as the story unfolded. After Karen had finished, she gave a long low whistle. 'Oh my God!'

Karen fidgeted nervously. 'You don't think *I'm* involved in any of this, do you? You don't think I knew what Howard was doing?'

'Good God, of course not!' Juliet reached across the table and squeezed her hand. 'This is unbelievable. What a bastard your husband was! As though you hadn't been through enough. How on earth are you coping with all this?'

Karen put down her spoon. 'I have to keep going for the kids' sake.' Her eyes began to smart. 'And I suppose it's rage; *rage* is getting me through it. I'm not going to let Howard destroy me.' To hide her tears, she rose and stood with her back to the table, facing the window.

Juliet rose from her chair and tactfully placed a box of tissues on the window sill. 'You're a very strong woman, Karen Armstrong. Much stronger than you think.'

'You've got to be joking,' Karen dabbed at her eyes and gazed distractedly through the window at Rufus nosing round the back garden. 'I'm not strong at all. I'm a total coward.'

'No you are not!' Juliet put a hand on her shoulder. 'That's the last thing you are. How many women could cope with all the terrible things you've had to put up with? I think you're amazing.'

Karen gave a self-deprecating laugh. 'No, Juliet, I'm not amazing either!'

'Take it from me, you are!' Juliet said firmly. 'You've got amazing reserves of resilience, otherwise you couldn't have survived all this. But you do need to take care of yourself. You're getting far too thin. Come and finish your soup.'

Karen obediently followed her back to the table. She realised she was feeling quite hungry.

'You had no inkling that your husband was ...that way inclined?' Juliet asked after they both had eaten in silence for a few minutes.

'Absolutely none.' Karen reached for a piece of bread and crumpled it in her hand. 'I don't understand it. Why did he marry me if he was really interested in children?'

Juliet grimaced. 'Some men hide their perverse inclinations behind a normal family life. It makes their actions easier to get away with.'

'In other words,' Karen said miserably, 'marriage was just a charade, a convenience for him. But then, I suppose it was for me as well,' she added after a short pause. 'I wasn't really in love with Howard when I agreed to marry him. I was desperate for security.' She felt ashamed of her cowardly use of marriage to avoid leading an independent life.

'You're not the first woman to marry for security,' Juliet gently observed, picking at a splash of paint that had hardened on the back of her hand. 'And certainly not the last.'

At the sound of scratching at the back door, she rose to her feet. 'I think your dog wants to come in.' She opened the back door and Rufus lolloped inside, ears bouncing. 'He seems happy. Has he settled in?' She placed a bowl of water on the floor.

'Yes.' Karen gazed fondly down at Rufus as he noisily slurped the water. 'It only took a day. He's already part of the family.'

Juliet resumed her seat at the table. 'Do you think whoever shot your husband is connected to the child porn ring?'

'The police seem to think so and I suppose it makes sense. But that means Howard's own involvement is bound to come out sooner or later and I can't bear the thought of that.' Karen gazed at her despairingly. 'How will the children cope when they find out their dad was a...' she could barely bring herself to say the word, '... *paedophile*? What are people going to think?'

'Bugger what people think!' Juliet snorted. 'Look, I think you need something to take your mind off this. You could make yourself ill by brooding on your bastard of a husband and what he got up to.'

Karen stared at her incredulously. 'What could possibly take my mind off this?'

Juliet reflected. 'Is there anything you like doing? A hobby? Something for *you*, not for the children; something that isn't involved with housework and looking after kids. Was there any particular activity you enjoyed before you were married?'

Karen gazed round the kitchen and her eyes alighted on the old- fashioned dresser, its shelves piled with pieces of mismatched crockery. 'I liked pottery. I used to do it, you know, years ago.'

'Then number one, you sign up for a pottery course and pick it up again.'

Karen gave a wan smile. 'Maybe I will one day, but not yet. It's much too soon. What's number two?' She finished her soup and mopped up the last drops with a piece of bread.

'Why don't you plan a holiday for yourself and the children, somewhere away from Moxton? You deserve a break after what you've all been through.'

Karen reached down and stroked Rufus who had flopped down beside her chair and was gazing up at her imploringly. 'We can't do anything like that until the Will is sorted out, and that could take months. I sent the life insurance company a copy of the death certificate, but they said they can't process my claim till the circumstances around Howard's death have been fully investigated.'

Juliet carried the empty soup bowls to the sink and added them to the pile of dirty dishes already covering the draining board. 'Well, half term's coming up. Why don't you try and take the children somewhere then, even if it's only for a few days?'

'It's a nice idea, but going away in a school holiday period would be much too expensive.'

Juliet nodded sympathetically. 'Yeah. Prices always go up during school holidays, don't they? Bloody marvellous how the travel industry fleeces parents.'

'Would you like to bring Joe and Miranda over one afternoon during half term?' Karen asked shyly, the thought having just occurred to her.

'Yes, we'd love to!'

Karen was pleased. She hadn't invited any children to the house since Howard had died. Even while he was alive, she had been reluctant to host "play dates", fearing his reaction to any resulting disturbance to the house or garden.

Juliet put the kettle on. 'I'll make us a cup of tea, then, if you don't mind, I'd better get on with my wall painting before it's time to pick up the kids.'

# Chapter 17

On Friday morning, Karen went to collect her Toyota. She drove it home cautiously. A nervous driver, she found it easier to manoeuvre than the Volvo which Howard had only allowed her to use for shopping and trips to the children's schools.

On her return, she found a phone message from Martin asking her to ring him back as soon as possible.

'Does the name Baxter mean anything to you?' he asked when she did.

'No.'

'Your husband never mentioned anyone called Alan Baxter?'

'No, why?'

'A man by that name has been picked up for questioning in connection with your husband's murder. His name hasn't been released yet so please don't mention it to anyone, but DCI Evans wanted to know if you knew him.'

'Do you think he did it?' she asked anxiously.

'I'm afraid I can't give you any details at the moment as he hasn't been charged.'

'But there must be a reason why the police picked him up. Is there anything to suggest that he was the one who shot Howard?'

'I can't tell you that, Karen. It only happened this morning. I wanted to let you know in case you heard about it from another source…'

As soon as the call ended, Karen switched on a TV news channel She didn't have long to wait. After reading reports of recent national and international events, the newsreader declared, 'A thirty-six-year- old man is helping police with their enquiry into the murder of accountant, Howard Armstrong.'

Martin called again in the early afternoon. 'I thought you ought to know. Baxter is on the Sex Offenders' Register. He's been charged with molesting children and we think he has had some connection with *Pied Piper.*'

This was the scenario Karen had been dreading. After speaking to Martin she called Joan. 'Have you heard the news?'

'No. What's happened?'

'The police are questioning a man about Howard's murder.'

'About time. Who is it?'

'They haven't released his name yet.'

'Do they think he did it?'

'I don't know, but it's already been on the news and…' Karen's voice trembled… 'Martin said he's on the Sex Offenders' Register. He has a record of molesting children.' She heard Joan gasp. 'What if people put two and two together and assume Howard was also a paedophile?'

'There's no reason for anyone to think that. Why should they?'

'But it's possible, isn't it?'

'Not necessarily.' Joan spoke soothingly. 'Try not to worry, Karen. For all you know, this man may have had nothing to do with Howard's murder.'

But Karen wasn't listening. 'It's half term next week,' she wailed. 'If reporters start hanging around the house again, I'll have to keep the children indoors.'

'Surely that won't be necessary.'

'If that man's charged, there's bound to be a lot of publicity and I don't want them to be harassed or photographed. They'll have to stay in the house.'

Joan was silent for a second, then, 'I've got a better idea,' she said. 'You know that old cottage on the Welsh coast Greg inherited from his aunt? We've been intending to do it up and sell it but just haven't had the time. It's still exactly as it was when she was alive. Why don't you take the kids there for half term? It's a bit old-fashioned but it's fully furnished and probably got everything you'd need.'

'Are you sure?' Karen dimly recalled going to Wales once when she was five or six. Her father was still alive then and she had been very excited about sleeping in a caravan. She remembered seeing some big ruined castles and fields studded with sheep.

'Of course. It will be good for you all to get away.'

'What about Greg? Will he mind? It's his cottage.'

'I'm sure he won't mind. The place could probably do with an airing. Nobody's been there since the old lady died. The woman next door has a spare key. I'll ring and ask her to sort out some bed linen for you. You'll probably need a sleeping bag for the sofa.'

'How would we get there?'

'You'd have to drive. Would that be OK?'

Karen had a moment of terror at the thought of driving to Wales in the unfamiliar car, but she decided anything would be better than running the gauntlet of media reporters. 'Yes, I've just picked up the new car. We could go early tomorrow.'

'In that case,' Joan said briskly, 'I'll bring the keys and a map after work, and explain how everything works.'

Karen hardly heard. She was thinking furiously ahead. If they set off very early the next morning, they should miss the reporters. Rufus would have to go in the back with Simon and Poppy (who still had to use a booster seat). They would need food supplies of course, but she could pack what she already had in the kitchen and buy anything else they needed there. She felt almost exhilarated at the thought of taking the children so far on her own.

After the call to Joan had ended, she sent a text to Juliet: *taking ur advice and going away for half term will call on return*.

That afternoon she decided to pick the three children up from school herself. As she backed the car out on to the road, some men with cameras rushed up and called to her. 'Mrs Armstrong! Mrs Armstrong! What do you think about ...?'

Ignoring them, she accelerated away.

Erica and Simon were surprised to find her waiting for them at the school bus stop. She told them quietly that the police were questioning a man in relation to their father's death and that reporters had arrived at the house.

Simon looked distressed.

Erica frowned. 'Is it the man who shot Dad?'

'The police don't know yet, darling. Please don't mention it in front of Poppy. I left her in the car with Rufus so I could tell you without her hearing.'

The two of them were subdued as she drove home.

When they reached the house, Karen avoided the

reporters by driving straight into the garage. She waited until the children were having their tea then made the announcement. 'I have a surprise! As it's half term, we're going to have a trip away, a holiday.'

Poppy squealed with delight and Simon shouted, 'wicked!'

Erica looked shocked. 'A holiday? Where?'

'Wales.'

'*Wales?*' Erica couldn't have sounded more outraged if Karen had said they were going to the moon.

'Where will we stay?' Simon asked.

'In the cottage Uncle Greg's aunt left him. Auntie Joan said we could use it. It's by the sea.'

Simon crowed with delight and Poppy danced around her excitedly 'Can we go swimming?'

'It'll be too cold to swim at this time of year, darling, but of course we can go to the beach. Now, I want to get ready tonight because we need to leave very early tomorrow morning. It's a long drive. Auntie Joan is coming over this evening to help us get ready.'

'*Tomorrow?*' Erica exclaimed in astonishment. 'Why are we going tomorrow?'

Karen gestured at the window. 'To get away from the people out there.'

Erica scowled ferociously. 'But Lisa's invited me to her house on Sunday.'

'Then you must arrange to see her another time.'

Erica banged her fork down on the table. 'I don't *want* to go to Wales! Why do we have to?'

'I've just told you why. We'll need to pack enough for about eight days. It often rains in Wales, so you'll need boots and raincoats and some games and books. If you've finished eating I want you to start packing now. No more arguments, Erica!'

'It's not fair!' Erica pushed her plate away and angrily rose to her feet. 'I don't *want* to go.'

Karen sighed as she heard her stomping up the stairs.

'Is Rufus coming?' Simon asked worriedly.

'Of course he is. We can't leave him behind.'

When Joan arrived, she helped Karen put provisions into boxes and pack the car. Before she left, she gave Karen the keys and a list of instructions relating to the cottage. 'Drive carefully and call me as soon as you get there.'

# Chapter 18

Karen roused the children with difficulty at six the next morning and bundled them into the car. She had never driven so far before. Unused to motorways and busy A roads, she felt nervous and tense. Erica sat in sullen silence in the front passenger seat, tapping furiously on her mobile. Simon and Poppy were squashed in the back of the car with Rufus. After less than an hour, they began to quarrel and Karen snapped at them to keep quiet.

Just after eight o'clock, she drew up at a service station. They took Rufus for a short walk on the grass verge then went inside for breakfast. While they were in the café, Karen realised that she had forgotten to tell Martin that she would be away for a week. Leaving the children at the table, she went outside and called him. 'We're on our way to Wales, the Gower Peninsula. My brother-in-law has a cottage there. There were reporters outside the house and --'

'I quite understand,' he interjected. 'I'm pleased you're having a break. It will do you all good.'

'Has that man been charged?'

'Not yet. And if he isn't by tonight, DCI Evans is going to apply for an extension to continue questioning him. I'll let you know if there are any developments.'

After they left the service station, it was a

straightforward run to Swansea. The short drive from there along the Gower Peninsula took them through some of the loveliest scenery Karen had ever seen - a dramatic combination of moor and woodland and vertical limestone cliffs descending to breathtaking sweeps of sandy beaches.

The village they were heading for nestled between two small hills overlooking the coast. Greg's cottage was situated at the end of a line of other buildings which, grouped around a church, consisted of a pub, a village shop, and a scattering of small houses. As they all tumbled out of the car, Karen stopped to gaze at the glorious view that stretched out in front of them. In the distance she could see the sea. Above it, the pearl-coloured sky seemed to extend forever.

The cottage itself was picturesque but, despite the efforts of the kindly neighbour next door, still smelt damp. The woman had put out a pile of slightly musty bed linen with which Karen made up a double bed in one room for herself and Poppy, and a single one in a smaller room for Erica. Simon, who adored camping, was allocated a sleeping bag to put on the sofa in the living room.

After Karen had improvised lunch from the tinned and packaged food she had brought with them, they descended the cliff path to the shore. Birds soared and wheeled above their heads as they crossed a line of tall sand dunes. Beyond them, Karen could see people strolling along the beach. The brisk wind had whipped the sea into large foaming waves. On them in the distance, a group of surfers bobbed up and down like miniature toys.

Simon and Poppy ran excitedly down towards the water's edge, while Erica sauntered slowly behind them, peering intently at the screen of her phone.

Noticing a sign proclaiming the beach to be "dog-friendly", Karen let Rufus off the lead. He immediately bounded off and shortly afterwards the air was rent with ferocious barks and snarls. She tried to hurry in the direction of the noise but her progress was slowed by the soft, yielding sand. When she reached the source of the disturbance, she found a tall man with glasses and thinning grey hair, attempting to pull Rufus and an angry alsatian apart.

'I'm sorry,' she said breathlessly, hastily clipping on Rufus's lead and hauling him away from the larger animal. 'He was just trying to be friendly.'

'No harm done. Elvis believes he owns this beach!' The man had a pleasant deep voice with a strong Welsh accent. 'He's letting your dog know that he's Top Dog around here.'

She straightened up. 'I'm afraid Rufus doesn't know the pecking order yet. We've only just arrived.'

'Oh? On holiday are you?'

'Yes, just for half term.' She tightened her grip on the lead as Rufus strained to reach Elvis. 'Those are my children down there, heading towards the sea.'

He glanced in the direction of her finger. 'You'll be staying at the Bed and Breakfast then?'

'No, we're at the cottage up there.' She indicated the hills behind them. 'The one right at the end.'

'Mrs Jones' cottage?' He sounded surprised. 'Has it been sold then?'

'No, she left it to her nephew, my brother-in-law. He's letting us stay for the week.' She gazed at the view in front of her. 'It's lovely here.'

He smiled. 'Well I think so of course. It was the first designated Area of Outstanding National Beauty.' He held out his hand. 'Melvyn Jenkins. Most people call me Mel.' He had a firm, dry handshake.

'Karen Armstrong.' She waited for a horrified reaction but none came. Instead he smiled again. 'I live in the house behind the church. If you need any help or information while you're here, don't hesitate to knock on the door and ask.'

'Thank you.' Karen watched him stride away with his dog trotting at his heels. A nice man.

She let Rufus off the lead and he bounded in front of her as she went to join the children further down the beach.

Erica was sitting on a rock, gazing moodily into space. Poppy had taken off her shoes and socks and was splashing in the foam at the water's edge. 'Ooh,' she squealed. 'It's cold!'

Simon was throwing pebbles into the sea. 'Who was that man you were talking to?' he asked.

'Someone who lives here. Rufus tried to attack his dog or vice versa.'

'Rufus wouldn't attack anyone. Fetch, Rufus!' Simon hurled a piece of driftwood into the sea. Rufus stood hesitantly on the water's edge then splashed into the waves after it. When he emerged, he shook himself vigorously, spraying them with drops of cold water.

Poppy tugged at her sleeve. 'Mummy, I'm still hungry.'

Karen had had the foresight to put a packet of crisps in her bag. She took it out and gave it to her daughter. 'Offer some to Simon and Erica.'

A pale sun had appeared in a break in the clouds and was creating a shimmer on the surface of the water. Gazing at it, Karen felt calmer than she had in a long time. Away from the whispering and inquisitive stares she had experienced in Moxton, her anxiety about the man being questioned by police began to recede. The champagne air and invigorating wind seemed to be having a cleansing effect, washing away some of the stress and tension of the last three months.

\* \* \*

When they left the cottage after breakfast the following morning, they again bumped into Mel Jenkins and Elvis. The two dogs barked at each other, but after some preliminary skirmishes, Rufus seemed to accept his subordinate position in the canine hierarchy.

Mel offered to accompany them on their walk and as they strolled along the coast path, he gave them the names of the exquisite bays they passed. 'You might like to visit Rhossili Beach one day while you're here,' he suggested. 'You'll love it! If you walk to Burry Holmes at the north end, there's a glorious view to Worm's Head. But make sure you check the tides if you go down to the beach? They're pretty lethal. You wouldn't want to be cut off.'

As they walked, he chatted amiably to the children, entertaining them with local tales of smuggling and pirates. When Erica and Simon decided to have a race and ran on ahead, he told Karen he was a lecturer at the University of Wales in Swansea and was currently on a three- month sabbatical, writing a book on British imperial history. 'It's very peaceful here as you can see. I write for three hours early in the morning, then another three late in the afternoon. At ten o'clock Elvis and I usually go for a long constitutional.'

'Are you here on your own then?' Karen wondered if there was a Mrs Jenkins.

'Yes, just me and Elvis. He's good company. What about you?'

She realised he was expecting reciprocal information. 'I'm a widow,' she volunteered hesitantly. 'My husband died a few months ago.'

'Oh, I'm very sorry.'

'A bad man shot my daddy,' blurted Poppy who was walking alongside Karen, holding her hand.

Mel's eyes widened with astonishment.

Overcome with embarrassment, Karen hurriedly extracted a tennis ball from her pocket. 'Poppy, why don't you throw the ball for Rufus and Elvis?'

'My husband was murdered,' she informed Mel quietly after Poppy had trotted ahead. 'A few months ago. Someone shot him as he came out of his office in Moxton. Maybe you heard about it on the news?'

'Good God!' he exclaimed coming to an abrupt halt on the path. 'No, I didn't know. I don't watch TV or listen to the radio much when I'm working on a book. How dreadful. I'm so sorry.'

Karen stood motionless beside him. 'We don't know who did it yet. The police are questioning a suspect but...' Her voice tailed off. She didn't want to destroy her new sense of wellbeing by thinking about Alan Baxter.

'I'm so sorry,' he repeated. 'What a terrible thing to happen.'

Karen felt tears pricking her eyelids.

'I can understand a little of what you must be going through,' he continued. 'I lost my wife to cancer five years ago.'

'I'm sorry. That must have been awful.'

'It *was*, terrible, but a murder...that must be so much worse.'

*If he only knew.* She turned her head away so he couldn't see her brimming eyes. 'Do you think...could we talk about something else?'

'Of course.'

As they resumed their walk, he told her about his two sons, both grown up, one of whom worked in Leeds, the other in Brussels.

'Do you see much of them?' Karen asked when she had composed herself.

'Not a great deal. They do come to see me occasionally, but both have demanding jobs, and even more demanding girlfriends. I try to visit them whenever I can, though that's not often. Come on, kids!' he called to the children who were waiting for them at the next bend. 'Let's have a race. Last one to reach that bush is a chicken!' He loped along the path on his long legs, followed by the children and the two dogs.

After a few days, it seemed perfectly natural to meet up with Mel when he was walking Elvis on the cliff or on the beach, and for him to join them on some of their outings. Using his own car, a four-wheel drive that was big enough to carry all of them and the two dogs, he drove them to exquisite coves, archaeological sites and ruined castles they might not otherwise have found. Karen appreciated the fact that he never pestered her with questions about Howard's murder. She also appreciated how much the children enjoyed his company. Poppy loved the way he teased her and Erica, after her initial standoffishness, was won over by his affable charm. But Karen observed with a pang how

Simon, who had never succeeded in gaining the love of his father, watched out for Mel, walked by his side and hung on his every word.

The three of them seemed generally happier, she noticed approvingly. Liberated from the routine of school, they were obviously enjoying the spontaneous outings and improvised meals. Erica had stopped grumbling and joined in games on the beach, explorations of rock pools and walks along the coastal path. She and Simon appeared to have forgotten that a suspect was being questioned about their father's murder.

For Karen herself, the sojourn on the Gower acted like a protective bubble insulating her from the outside world. The wildness of the place exhilarated her and she didn't mind the frequent rain or the strong winds that often howled across the cliff tops. Her sole contact with Moxton during the week was Joan who rang a few times to see how they were getting on.

She watched the news only once, on the small, old-fashioned television set in the living room, and learned that the police had been granted an extension to question Alan Baxter. She didn't switch it on again. Instead, she made a supreme effort to avoid dwelling on recent happenings and to concentrate on *being in the moment*, which was what most of the self-help books she had read, advised. They also recommended talking to children about a parent who had recently died, but this was something she couldn't bring herself to do. Perhaps taking their cue from her, Erica, Simon and Poppy rarely mentioned their father in her presence. Whether they talked about him among themselves, she didn't know.

# Chapter 19

The short idyll soon came to an end and on their last day, Karen plucked up courage to ask Mel to join them for a meal at the cottage in the evening. 'It'll be very simple,' she warned him.

He beamed with pleasure. 'It's the company that counts. Of course I'd be delighted.'

She tidied the kitchen and concocted a meal of pasta, salad and fruit from the limited provisions available at the local shop. In the evening she put on the only dress she had brought with her, a plain, knee-length, navy one.

When Mel arrived carrying a box of chocolates and a bottle of wine, he gazed at her admiringly. 'You look very nice.'

She blushed. 'It makes a change from boots and an anorak.'

'You would look lovely in anything,' he said chivalrously.

'You look nice yourself,' she countered rapidly to hide her embarrassment. Instead of his usual jeans and rainproof jacket, he was wearing a fawn sweater and smart grey trousers. When he sat down at the table, he took off his glasses which had misted up in the heat of the kitchen. Karen thought he looked a lot younger without them.

It was a jolly and convivial meal, and the children were in the best of spirits despite their regret that the week had come to an end. After they had finished eating, Erica and Simon went to the living room to play Scrabble and Karen took Poppy up to bed. When she came downstairs, she and Mel sat at the kitchen table finishing the wine, with the two dogs curled up at their feet.

'Thank you for your help while we've been here,' she said shyly. 'You know the area so well. We never would have found all those places on our own.'

He poured a generous measure of wine into her glass. 'Oh I think you would. They're all marked on the maps. I just short-circuited the process for you. And I've enjoyed the company. I'm quite used to being here on my own, but it can be a bit lonely, just Elvis and me.'

She sighed. 'I don't want to go home, none of us do, but the children have school on Monday.'

'It's a shame you can't stay for longer.' He smiled at her. 'Perhaps you'll come again one day?'

'We'd love to, when the investigation's over.'

He nodded. 'It must be extremely difficult for you, not knowing who killed your husband. I didn't like to ask before, but how have the children coped with losing their father so suddenly?'

She swallowed some of her wine. 'It's been awful for them. Erica was devastated, she adored her father, and Simon had terrible nightmares at first. Poppy was very upset too of course, but she seems more puzzled than anything. It's been harder for the other two, particularly at school with kids whispering about them and asking spiteful questions. Simon was bullied for a while. We all needed this break.'

'I'm sure you did. Well I hope they find the culprit soon. Didn't you say that someone was in custody?'

Karen nodded. 'Yes. A man was being questioned by the police but I don't know if he's been charged with murder yet. I haven't been listening to the news. To tell you the truth, it's been a huge relief to get away from it all, especially as...' She hesitated, wondering how much she could confide in him. 'You see, since my husband died, I've discovered things about him. Not very nice things.'

He frowned. 'Oh dear, that must have been very distressing.'

'It was a shock. The police found out that he was involved in some illegal financial dealings and--'

'It's OK, Karen, you don't need to go into details.' He patted her gently on the hand. 'But I do understand that something like that must have made the whole situation even more painful and difficult for you.'

'It did, especially as certain people seem to think I *knew* what Howard was up to, but I didn't. It was terrible, coming on top of his being killed.'

He topped up her glass. 'Were you and your husband happy together, or is that an indiscreet question?'

'Not very, at least not in the last few years,' she admitted. 'What about you and your wife?'

'We were very happy. We met at university, Sophie and I, and got married straight after. We had a good number of years together until she became sick, then it was hospitals, chemotherapy, all the usual stuff, and a long and difficult decline.' He coughed and turned his head away. 'Luckily the boys had left home by then, so at least she wasn't leaving young children behind.'

Before she could think of anything to say, Simon burst

into the kitchen. 'Mum, is "bunkum" a proper word? Erica says it isn't.'

'Yes it is, darling, but please finish your game quickly. We have to pack everything up tonight.'

Simon scurried away.

Mel drained his glass and rose to his feet. 'I'd better leave you in peace. Thank you for a lovely evening.'

She followed him into the living room where he gave Erica and Simon a goodbye hug.

Simon was tearful. 'Will you come and see us in Moxton, Mel?'

Mel glanced at Karen. 'Maybe. If your mum can put up with a visit, that is.'

Karen muttered something non-committal. She was sure there was no way he would want to visit them once news broke about Howard's activities. But at his request, she wrote her address and home phone number on a scrap of paper and gave it to him.

When she accompanied him to the front door, Mel kissed her on the cheek. 'It's been lovely meeting you, Karen. Send me an email some time and let me know how you all are.'

'I'm afraid I don't do emails,' she said awkwardly.

'Well send a letter then, or, better still, give me a call. You've got my mobile number.'

Watching him stride into the night with Elvis at his heels, she felt suddenly bereft.

\* \* \*

'We couldn't find any solid evidence to connect Baxter with your husband's murder,' Martin informed Karen when he called at the house a few days after their return from Wales. 'But he is going to be prosecuted for possession of indecent images of children.'

Karen felt a sense of relief although she realised this was only a temporary reprieve before the inevitable revelations about Howard's own involvement in child pornography. 'Where does that leave the enquiry?' she asked.

'Moving on,' Martin assured her. 'Baxter admitted belonging to the *Pied Piper* network and gave us some names of other members who are in this country.'

'So he knew Howard?'

'Yes. He told us Manning suspected that your husband was creaming off some of the profits from the sale of child abuse images. That's why he was summoned to a meeting with leading members of *Pied Piper* in Bangkok.'

Karen winced.

'We re-interviewed Maureen Field and it sounds as though your husband got cold feet and decided not to go. Hence Manning's arrival in this country. He wanted to get his hands on the accounts your husband kept, and find out where the money had gone. Are you OK, Karen?'

Karen made an attempt to appear more alert. 'Not really. I've been feeling a bit under the weather since we got back.'

Martin looked concerned. 'That's not surprising after everything that's happened. Pity you couldn't have had a longer break.'

'Yes, it *is* a pity.' She thought longingly of the little cottage on the cliff from where you could hear the rhythmic crashing of the waves and the gusting of the wind as it skimmed the top of the dunes. She wondered if they would get another opportunity to stay there before Greg sold the property.

'Look after yourself,' Martin told her as he left the house. 'You've coped magnificently up to now.'

In truth, readjusting to life in Moxton was proving far harder than Karen had expected. Whereas the children had settled back at home and school with little apparent difficulty, she found resuming a normal life almost impossible. The short break had liberated her temporarily from the gloom and sense of oppression that had weighed on her since the day Howard had died. Now those feelings had returned, closing in on her with redoubled force. The little self- assurance she had gained before going to Wales had completely ebbed away. She had no appetite and slept little, finding herself still awake at four every morning, obsessively seeking answers to the same unanswerable questions that had assailed her before they went to Wales: how had Howard managed to conceal his clandestine activities from her for so many years? How could he have been complicit in the abuse of children when he was a father himself? Had their marriage been a complete sham from the start?

Much of the time she was consumed by a visceral hatred for Howard. She had nothing but contempt for those wives she had seen on the news, arriving at law courts loyally clutching the hands of husbands who had been charged with a string of indecent assaults on children. If Howard's secret life had come to light while he was still alive, she would have found it impossible to stand by him.

In her calmer moments, however, she remembered that he had displayed affection for her in the early years. He had been a good father to Erica, albeit less affectionate towards the other two. And he had made financial provision for her and the children. So he couldn't have been a *complete* monster, could he? Maybe he had been belatedly drawn into child porn, influenced or coerced by evil men such as Gerald Manning. Maybe it was something he had always been attracted to, but had struggled against before succumbing.

Worn out by sleeplessness and depression, she dragged herself through the days, barely managing to perform essential domestic tasks. Unable to muster the energy to cook, she got into the habit of buying convenience foods and ready meals. Dreading the endless, wakeful nights, she stayed up late in the evenings, drinking glass after glass of Howard's expensive wine.

She was short with the children, snapping at them when they quarrelled or when their boisterousness set her nerves on edge. Sometimes she caught Simon watching her anxiously and felt overwhelmed with guilt. But this only exacerbated her misery. If it hadn't been for the necessity to buy food, convey Poppy to and from school and take Rufus for walks, she probably wouldn't have left the house at all. When she did venture outside, she kept her head down and avoided encounters with anyone she knew.

Joan, who occasionally called round after work, was worried. 'You can't go on like this, Karen. It's wearing you down and having a bad effect on the children. They must know you're depressed. You should go and see your doctor.'

Unable to withstand her nagging, Karen reluctantly visited the surgery.

Her GP prescribed antidepressants but they only made her feel worse. 'You must persevere,' he told her when she returned and complained about nausea and dizziness. 'The side effects are only temporary. It can take up to three weeks for your body to accommodate to the new medication.'

She stopped taking the pills.

# Chapter 20

Juliet rang at ten one Friday morning, catching Karen off guard. 'Hi there,' she greeted her cheerily. 'You've been very elusive recently. Is something the matter?'

'I'm sorry,' Karen stammered. 'I haven't been feeling too good lately.'

'Oh? Shall I come over?'

'No,' Karen said quickly. 'I wouldn't be good company.'

'I'll be the judge of that! I'll see you shortly.'

Juliet arrived bearing a flowering plant and a bag of Danish pastries. She was wearing a multi-coloured woollen cape and her glossy hair was secured on top of her head with a plethora of gleaming combs. Karen thought she looked like an exotic bird.

Juliet put the plant on the hall table and scrutinised her with a shocked expression. 'Christ! You look awful.'

'Thanks! I haven't been sleeping well.' Karen led the way to the kitchen.

'And you're wearing grey again! Has all my good work gone to waste already?'

'Grey reflects my mood,' Karen muttered sullenly.

'Well, if that's what having a few days away does for you,' Juliet retorted, 'you'd be better off staying in Moxton for the rest of your life.'

Karen felt the tears well up and brushed them quickly away. 'That's just it. Getting away was so good, I can't handle being back here again. I've been feeling terrible, even worse than before. The GP prescribed antidepressants but they had such awful side effects, I stopped taking them.'

'Poor you. Sit down. I'll make coffee.' Juliet pushed her gently on to a chair then bustled about the kitchen as though she owned it. She made a pot of coffee, put the Danish pastries on a plate and placed them on the table. 'So you had a good time in Wales?' she asked, sitting down opposite Karen. 'Tell me about it.'

Karen described the cottage and its view of the sea. She described the rugged cliffs, the dunes and the sandy bays. She described the exhilaration she had experienced walking along the beach and cliff path. 'And we met this man--'

'A man?' Juliet exclaimed with interest.

'Just someone who lives near the cottage. He has a dog called Elvis. He showed us lots of places we wouldn't have found by ourselves. He was really good with the kids.'

'What was his name?'

'Melvyn, Mel.'

'How old is he?'

'Oh Juliet, I don't know. Fiftyish maybe.'

Juliet grinned. 'I knew you'd pull after you'd had your hair done! Has he been in touch since you got back?'

'No.' Karen felt irritated. 'I didn't "pull". He was just being a good neighbour, that's all.'

'If you say so.' Juliet poured the coffee into two mugs and pushed the plate of pastries towards Karen. 'Have one of these. You need fattening up, my girl.'

Karen took a sip of coffee and picked listlessly at a

Danish pastry.

Juliet eyed her thoughtfully. 'I heard that the man the police were questioning wasn't charged,' she commented.

Karen shrugged. 'They didn't have enough evidence to charge him. I'm beginning to believe they'll never catch the person who shot Howard.'

'Well it's only been a few months.' Juliet patted Rufus who had placed himself in front of her knees, hoping to catch some crumbs. 'It can take years to solve a murder.'

'I don't mind if it does take years.' Karen felt the tears coming again and dabbed hastily at her eyes. 'I don't care if they never find the person who did it.'

Juliet frowned. 'You *are* in a bad way, aren't you? Tell me if I'm interfering, but I can suggest something that might help. There's an emotional therapy group that meets once a week in Moxton. Why don't you try it? It'll be better than antidepressants.'

'Emotional therapy?' Karen snorted sceptically. 'Not likely!' She had a horror of anything that involved self-exposure. Several people, including Joan and her doctor, had recommended bereavement counselling, but she had resisted.

'Why not?' Juliet secured a fugitive strand of her hair with one of the metal combs. 'Don't dismiss it out of hand. The group's run by an experienced psychotherapist. It gives people an opportunity to express their feelings in a small, supportive group rather than bottling them up.' Noticing Karen's appalled expression she added quickly, 'it only involves a few people, three at the most. Honestly, Karen, it would be much better than sitting at home with everything going round and round in your head.'

'No!' Karen said emphatically. 'I couldn't. There's no

way I'm going to tell complete strangers about Howard and what he was doing.'

'You wouldn't need to mention all the stuff you've found out about him. You could just say that your husband died suddenly and you're having trouble coping with your emotions.'

Karen took a gulp of her coffee and pushed her plate with the uneaten pastry away. 'I know you mean well, Juliet,' she said finally, 'but I'm not interested. Anyway, what if did go to something like that and someone recognised my name? That's the last thing I need.'

'They only use Christian names in the group and you could always use a different one if you wanted to.'

'How come you know so much about it?' Karen asked suspiciously.

Juliet looked embarrassed. 'My marriage break-up was amicable, but it was a pretty emotional time and I went to pieces for a while. A friend suggested the group to me and it really helped. Why don't you give it a try? It would only involve a couple of hours once a week. I'll give you the number of the woman who runs it. She's very good. There's a small fee per session, unless you get referred by a GP.'

'I'll think about it.' Karen had no intention of doing so, but hoped this would deter Juliet from trying to persuade her.

\* \* \*

After the children came home that afternoon, she put food on the table for them - a shop-bought pizza - then, as had become a habit, escaped upstairs to her bedroom.

She was lying on the bed when Simon crept hesitantly into the room.

'Mum, are you OK?' he whispered.

She rolled over and forced a reassuring smile. 'I've got a bit of a headache that's all.'

He stood at the end of the bed, tugging at his earlobe. 'Mum?'

'Yes?'

'Why don't you …?'

'Why don't I what?'

'Talk to us anymore, spend time with us?'

Karen hauled herself up into a sitting position. 'I'm sorry, darling, but I haven't been feeling very well lately.'

'Are you feeling sad?' Simon was gazing at her anxiously. 'Is it because of Dad?'

'Yes. It is because of Dad.' That at least was true.

'I've been feeling sad too.'

'Of course you have, darling, that's understandable.'

Simon's grey eyes were shiny with tears. 'I don't want you to be sad. You were happier when we were away. When you're unhappy it makes me unhappy too.'

Karen was overwhelmed with guilt. She hadn't realised how closely he had been monitoring her moods. Swinging her legs off the bed, she stood up and hugged him. 'You really mustn't worry about me, Simon. I'll be fine. I'm coming downstairs now.'

She followed him down to the kitchen and made an effort to communicate with the three of them while they finished their pizza. Poppy babbled about what had happened at school that day, but Erica, who was listening to pop music on her headphones, ignored her. Since their return from Wales, Karen had abandoned the attempt to stop her listening to music at meal-times. She couldn't bear the aggro.

As Simon continued to watch her anxiously throughout the weekend, she decided she must take action to shake off her depression. She couldn't go on feeling sorry for herself at the expense of the children's wellbeing.

On Monday she rang the number Juliet had given her.

A brusque female voice answered. 'Helen Ford. Can I help you?'

Karen took a deep breath. 'My name's Kay. A friend told me about the emotional therapy group and gave me your number. She thought it might help me.'

'I see. Why do you think you need to join the group?'

'Because...' Karen hesitated, '...because my husband died very suddenly recently and I've been having some ... emotional problems.'

There was a pause before the woman responded. 'I have a new session starting next week, on Monday morning. There are three people at the moment. I usually keep the number to three but I could take a fourth. Can you come and have a chat with me first? I always meet people who want to join the group beforehand to make sure it's the right thing for them.'

Karen arranged to meet Helen at her home the following afternoon.

\* \* \*

Helen was tiny and grey-haired with sharp hazel eyes.

'Can you give me some personal details?' she asked when they were seated in her small living-room. 'It's Kay what? This is just for me, by the way. We only use Christian names in the group.'

'Kay Armitage.' Karen amazed herself at the ease with which she lied. She gave Joan's address.

After Helen had written down the information, she spent a few minutes describing to Karen how the sessions worked.

'Through my work as a psychotherapist, I came to the conclusion that talking therapies and antidepressants aren't enough for some people who are suffering from severe stress and emotional problems. They need other techniques as well. The groups I run are for individuals who have tried other methods but haven't been helped by them. I devised the sessions to give them a range of tools to help them through difficult periods in their lives. The sessions provide a safe space for individuals to express emotions that they can't, or daren't, express to their families or other people they're close to.'

Helen looked searchingly at Karen who tried to smile back. 'Nothing is taboo,' she continued. 'Every person who attends the group is at liberty to say anything they feel they need to. They can reveal as much or as little as they want about their personal problems. It's meant to be a sharing, listening process, and hopefully, one of mutual support. It's all explained here.' She handed Karen a leaflet and fell silent while she scanned it.

'Do you think something like this would help you?' she asked when Karen had finished reading.

Karen nodded, 'I hope so.'

'Tell me again why you think you need it.'

Karen repeated that she was experiencing difficulty coming to terms with the sudden death of her husband. Then, as Helen seemed to be waiting for her to elaborate, she added hurriedly, 'I've been feeling really depressed lately and I'm worried about the effect it's having on my children.'

Helen made some notes on her pad. 'How old are they?'

Karen told her.

'Do they talk about their father?'

'No, at least not to me.'

'Is that because you don't talk about him to them?' Helen asked gently.

'Probably. I find it really difficult.'

'Suppressing feelings can be harmful, Kay.' Helen gazed at her thoughtfully for a long moment and Karen wondered whether she had deduced that Kay wasn't her real name. 'I'm assuming you've tried other things for your depression?' she asked eventually.

'I was prescribed antidepressants but I couldn't tolerate them.'

'Have you tried any form of personal counselling?'

'No.'

'Not bereavement counselling?'

Karen blushed. 'It was suggested to me, but I didn't want to. It would feel hypocritical. It wasn't a particularly happy marriage, you see. We had …problems.'

'I understand.' Helen wrote some more notes on her pad. 'Before you decide, I must stress that whatever people reveal in the sessions has to be completely confidential.' She peered intently at Karen. 'Everything that is said in the group *must* remain in the group. Each person has to commit to this before joining. Respect for other members is key. Those who come to the sessions are extremely vulnerable and they need to be able to trust each other. Betrayal of that trust could seriously exacerbate a person's emotional problems.' She gazed at Karen again. 'Are you able to commit to this, and are you absolutely sure this is the kind of process that can help you?'

Karen nodded. 'Yes, if you'll have me.'

Helen smiled. 'This isn't a selection process, Kay. Not everyone is ready to expose their innermost thoughts and emotions to others. It's useful to find that out before any commitment is made.'

'Well I'd like to try.'

Helen nodded approvingly. 'Then come along to the clinic in Marlborough Street next Monday morning at ten thirty. There is a small fee but you could ask your doctor for a referral.'

'No.' Karen said quickly, 'that might take too long. I'd rather pay.'

'Fine.' Helen named a sum and made a final note on her pad. 'Once you've started, you must attend a set number of sessions. Establishing and keeping to a routine is part of the healing process.'

# Chapter 21

The following Monday morning, Karen stood nervously at the door of the building in Marlborough Street where Helen held her sessions. The labels on the double line of buzzers indicated that the establishment housed a number of other clinics offering therapies such as homeopathy, acupuncture, reiki and aromatherapy massage.

She found Helen's buzzer alongside one for *Nature's Nutrition*. She pressed it and waited. Nothing happened. She was contemplating flight when she heard Helen's muffled voice through the intercom. 'Who is it?'

'It's Kay.'

'Come up to the second floor.'

The front door swung open and Karen ascended the stairs. Her legs were shaking.

Helen was waiting on the landing

'Come in Kay. The others are already here.'

She led Karen into a room where three people were standing by a small window through which the grey autumn light barely penetrated. Shelves piled with folders and box files covered two of the walls, a third had a whiteboard attached to it. A large desk was pushed into a corner. On it stood a vase of flowers, an electric kettle, and a tray holding tea cups and a jug. Four chairs were arranged in the middle of the room.

'This is Kay,' Helen announced. She introduced Karen to Charles, a haggard-faced man with an unnerving facial twitch; Lucy, a tall, thin young woman with severely cropped brown hair and a number of facial studs and piercings, and an older woman, Stella, whose greying dark hair was pulled back in a skimpy ponytail.

After a brief introductory preamble, Helen led the four of them through some gentle relaxation exercises that involved stretching and deep breathing. Afterwards, she invited them to sit on the chairs provided. When they were seated in a semi-circle, she pulled out the desk chair and sat facing them. She regarded them each in turn.

'Who wants to kick off? You, Charles? Tell us a little about yourself and how you're feeling today. Don't hold back. There's nothing to be afraid of.'

In a low, stuttering voice, Charles told them that after he had returned from active service in Afghanistan, he couldn't get over the horrors he had witnessed there. 'Since I got back, I haven't been able to settle to anything. I've been given antidepressants but they don't help. I can't talk about it to my wife. I feel desperate.' His left eyelid started twitching uncontrollably. 'I've come here as a last resort. I've been drinking heavily and sometimes that makes me violent. I don't mean to be. My wife has threatened to leave me.' Tears started rolling down his cheeks and Karen felt a rush of sympathy for him.

Helen stood up and wrote the words *despair* and *hope-lessness* on the whiteboard with a black marker pen.

Stella, the older of the two women, wept as she told them how, after a series of miscarriages, she had given birth to a baby boy who had died at the age of three weeks. 'It was a cot death. I've been to courses on handling grief but I still can't, I can't...' her voice gave way and she hung her head.

Tears smarted in Karen's own eyes as she listened. Sitting next to Stella, she reached out and gently touched her arm. Stella turned and gave her a grateful look. Close up, Karen could see she was younger than she had thought, probably only in her mid thirties. Helen wrote the words *grief* and *anguish* on the whiteboard.

When it was her turn, the young woman called Lucy muttered that something had happened to her that she didn't want to talk about. She tugged nervously at her sleeves and Karen noticed a skull and crossbones tattoo on her left wrist.

'That's OK, Lucy, just tell us how you feel about it,' Helen prompted.

Lucy mumbled incoherently for a while then announced in a gruff voice, 'sometimes I want to scream.'

'You *can* scream if you like,' Helen told her.

Lucy uttered several startling, ear-splitting screams then collapsed back on her chair sobbing loudly. Stella whispered some words of comfort in her ear.

Helen wrote the words *pain*, *suffering* and *desperation* on the whiteboard, after which she looked expectantly at Karen. 'What about you, Kay? Tell us something about yourself and why you're here.'

For a moment Karen was tongue-tied and when she did manage to speak, her voice trembled. 'Several months ago, my husband died. It was very... sudden,' she informed the others, then relapsed into nervous silence.

'Can you tell us how you feel about that?' Helen urged encouragingly.

'Angry,' Karen blurted, '*terribly* angry.'

Helen nodded and wrote the word *anger* on the board. 'People often feel angry with the deceased for leaving them,' she told Karen gently. 'Anger is a common component of grief after a bereavement.'

Karen shook her head. 'I don't feel grief, not any more that is. After my husband died, I discovered he'd been having an affair with my closest friend for a year.' She had decided that she would use Howard's affair with Mo as a convenient proxy for all his unsavoury activities.

There was a murmur of sympathy from Stella.

'Ah.' Helen nodded thoughtfully. 'And how did you feel about that?'

'Shocked, sickened, disgusted.' Karen's voice strengthened as she went on to express the violent emotions Howard's more serious misdemeanors had aroused in her. 'Now I *hate* him,' she concluded, 'and I'm *glad* he's dead.' There, she'd said it! And having vented her feelings, she felt vaguely cleansed. She imagined this was how Roman Catholics must feel after they had been to confession.

Helen gazed at her for a moment then wrote *shock*, *disgust* and *hatred* on the whiteboard.

'What about your friend?' Stella asked. 'How do you feel about her?'

'I hated her at first too. Now I think she's not important. My husband was the one who instigated it. But I'm worried about my children. They like her and they can't understand why I don't want to see her anymore. I don't want them to know what their father was doing because they're still grieving for him. I feel I can't tell them.'

Helen added the word *anxiety* to her list on the board.

'Of course you can't,' Stella murmured reassuringly, but her voice was drowned by Lucy. 'If your husband was an arsehole,' she shouted, 'then your children should know about it. You should tell them!'

'No, Lucy,' Helen reprimanded her gently. 'Kay's children are still very young and they've only recently lost their father. It wouldn't be fair to burden them with that kind of information.'

Lucy scowled.

During the rest of the session, Helen encouraged them to discuss the emotions she had written on the whiteboard, pointing out that whereas one could expect to experience most of them over the course of a lifetime, some, such as anger, hatred and desperation, could be damaging. She suggested techniques for dealing with such emotions when they threatened to become overwhelming, and concluded the session by reminding them about the importance of complete confidentiality. She also warned them not to expect an immediate improvement to their depression. 'You may think you're feeling better but it will only be temporary. It takes a long time to work through powerful emotions.'

Before they left, she made tea for them all. Everyone except Lucy appeared visibly more relaxed.

\* \* \*

The sense of relief Karen experienced during the session quickly wore off and by the next morning her spirits had plummeted again. She was beginning to feel very lonely, particularly when the children were at school. She regretted having so few friends and the extent to which she had sequestered herself within the family for so many years. Martin's visits had tailed off and he didn't contact her quite so often these days. She was surprised at how much she missed his visits.

She rang Joan when she knew it was time for her coffee break and, in the course of the conversation, casually mentioned that she had attended an emotional therapy session.

'Emotional therapy?' Joan sounded surprised. 'What on earth is that?'

'It's something that helps people manage their feelings.'

'What did you do there?' Joan asked dubiously.

'First we did some relaxation exercises --'

'We? You mean there were other people there?'

'There were four of us and the psychotherapist who runs it. She encouraged us to talk about our emotional problems.'

'Karen, you didn't tell them about Howard--'

'No, of course not. I only said that my husband had died and that I'd found out he'd been having an affair with my closest friend. That allowed me to let rip on what I thought about him. It was quite therapeutic, but...' Karen hesitated before admitting, '...I gave a false name - Kay Armitage.'

'Why on earth did you do that?'

'In case anyone there recognised my real name. And I'm afraid I gave Helen, the psychotherapist, your address.'

'You gave her *our* address?'

'Yes, just in case--'

'Just in case what?' Joan exclaimed in exasperation. 'You're becoming paranoid, Karen.'

'I don't want anyone there to know who I really am,' Karen mumbled. 'It won't make any difference. Helen's not likely to contact me at your address.'

Joan gave an audible sigh. 'I hope not. I'm not going to pretend to be you. Are you going there again?'

'Yes, I've signed up for a group of sessions.'

'Is that wise? You could be letting yourself in for a load of useless psycho-babble.'

'I don't think so. I believe it's going to be helpful.'

Karen was tempted to return to bed after speaking to Joan, but instead she forced herself to put on her raincoat and take Rufus for a walk.

It was now November, a month which had brought gloomy wet days and heavy, slate-coloured skies. She did a few quick turns round the block before taking the dog home, then reluctantly left the house again. Geoff Murray had asked her to call at the office to sign some papers relating to his assuming sole ownership of *Armstrong and Murray Accountancy Services*. It would be the first time she had visited Bartholomew Court since Howard had died, and she wasn't looking forward to it.

When she arrived, she noticed that the name Armstrong had already been removed from the main doors as well as from the signs in the foyer. These now informed visitors that *Geoffrey Murray Accountants* was on the third floor of the building.

She took the lift.

'Mr Murray is expecting you, Mrs. Armstrong,' the youthful receptionist greeted her,' adding with obvious embarrassment, 'we're all so sorry…'

As Karen passed through the open plan area, the office workers looked up from their desks and watched her curiously. Some of them seemed surprised. Several awkwardly mumbled greetings. She glanced briefly at the door of what had been Howard's office and noticed that his name had disappeared. It hadn't yet been replaced by another.

Jennifer, Howard's erstwhile secretary, rose from her desk and asked how she and the children were. 'It must be so difficult--'

Karen cut her off hurriedly. 'Thank you, Jennifer, we're fine.' The last thing she wanted was to hear yet more expressions of sympathy. She wondered how Jennifer, who had worked loyally for Howard for over a decade, would react if she knew about his connection with child porn. Had the police questioned her about his offshore account? She assumed they had.

Geoff's eyebrows rose a little when he opened the door of his office and saw her. Although they had spoken on the phone, it was the first time they had met since Howard's funeral. She wondered if it was her hair that caused his surprise, though she assumed Celia would have mentioned her changed appearance.

'Thank you for coming, Karen.' He gave her a quick peck on the cheek and ushered her inside. He shut the door and motioned her to a chair. Resuming his seat behind the desk, he gazed at her with an expression of concern. 'How are you? You look as though you've lost weight.'

'Do I?'

'Are you taking proper care of yourself?'

'Yes,' she assured him. 'But I've been rather unwell lately.'

'I'm sorry to hear that. Would you like some coffee?'

'No, I'm fine, thanks.'

'Children OK?'

'As well as can be expected.' She wished he would get on

with the business he had asked her to come about.

As though sensing her thoughts, Geoff started shuffling papers on his desk and pushed some towards her. 'My solicitors have drawn up these documents. Everything's been looked into thoroughly, and I'm pleased to say the books are quite in order.' He coughed and a fleeting expression of embarrassment crossed his broad face. 'That's um… that is to say, we found nothing untoward. So, as Howard's widow, you are of course entitled to a share of the profits accruing at the time of his death. That can go ahead immediately.'

Karen breathed a silent sigh of relief and signed the papers on the lines he had indicated with a cross. The money would come in really useful.

'The police don't seem to have made much headway,' he remarked casually, stuffing the signed papers into a large brown envelope.

'I don't really know. They don't tell me much.'

'They let that fellow they were questioning go, I hear.'

'Yes.'

'The investigation seems to be taking rather a long time.' He looked at her questioningly. 'Did you ever find out what that offshore account business was all about, or the initials you mentioned that were in Howard's diary - PP?'

Karen was startled. 'Um, no, yes…that is, I'm not really at liberty to say. The police are still looking into it as part of the murder enquiry.'

Geoff frowned. 'That woman detective, Parker, has been round here again. Nosey Parker I call her. There's nothing else I can tell them. The police have been over the accounts and files with a fine- tooth comb.'

'I suppose they have to do that, Geoff.'

'I'll be mightily relieved when the investigation is over. So will you, I've no doubt.'

She nodded.

He smiled. 'When things have calmed down, you must come over and have a meal with us. I'm sure Celia would love to see you.'

'Thank you.' *I'm sure she would not!*

\* \* \*

When Karen arrived home, she peered closely at herself in the bathroom mirror, something she hadn't done for a while. She was shocked. No wonder people in the office had been staring at her. Her eyes were hollow and her face was haggard and the colour of parchment. She looked truly dreadful. She was half-heartedly dabbing some moisturiser on her cheeks when her mobile rang. Answering it, she was startled to hear Melvyn Jenkins' voice.

'I'm going to Leeds next Saturday.' His Welsh accent seemed much stronger on the phone. 'I'm giving a seminar at the university on Monday and taking the opportunity to visit my youngest son. If it's not too much of an intrusion, I thought I might break the journey and call in to see how you all are. It's not far out of my way.'

'Oh.' She felt alarmed at the prospect. 'What about Elvis?'

She heard him laugh. 'I won't be bringing him. My neighbours always look after him when I'm away. If I do divert to Moxton, it would probably be around late morning. Would that suit you?'

'Yes,' she stammered. 'I think so. The children will be pleased to see you.'

'And yourself?'

She feared she must have sounded rude. 'I will too, of course.'

'Are you *sure* it won't be an intrusion?'

'Of course it won't. We'd love to see you.'

'Splendid. I'll call you nearer the time.'

Karen felt panic-stricken. It was one thing accompanying someone she hardly knew on cliff walks in Wales; quite another to have him visiting her in her own home. She wondered how she had found the courage to invite him for a meal at the cottage. But that was different, she told herself. She hadn't been on her own territory. This time she would feel exposed. Would he expect lunch? What would she give him? Would he notice how awful she looked? How long would he want to stay? Should she ring him back and put him off?

She was preoccupied with these questions when she collected Poppy from school that afternoon. As they walked home together they passed Lucy. She was wearing a very long trench coat and heavy hiking boots. She acknowledged Karen with a slightly sardonic smile.

Karen muttered a greeting and hurried on. Helen had urged them not to have any communication with each other outside the group while they were still attending the sessions.

'Who was that man?' Poppy asked.

'It wasn't a man, darling, it was a lady.'

Poppy looked puzzled. 'Why has she got hair like a man?'

'Because some ladies like to have their hair cut very short.' It occurred to Karen that Lucy might have been treated with chemotherapy. 'And sometimes it's because they've been ill.'

'Well I think it's silly,' Poppy declared decisively. 'And what are all those things on her face?'

'They're studs and piercings, a bit like earrings.'

Poppy grimaced. 'Don't they hurt?'

'I expect they did when they were put in.'

Poppy considered this for a moment. 'I'm never going to have those things put in my face!'

'I think that would be very wise, darling.'

# Chapter 22

Helen employed a different format in the second session. After the relaxation exercises, she gave each of them a specific form of role- play designed to help them express their respective emotional problems. Karen's task was to confront Howard with the discoveries she had made about him since he had died. This presented her with a problem as it obliged her to restrict the language she used to make it sound relevant only to his having had an affair. Stuttering self- consciously, she told Charles, who was standing in for Howard, how shocked she had been on discovering his relationship with Mo and how resentful and betrayed she felt after the way he had treated her during the last years of their marriage. She was careful not to mention Howard's actual name.

'Come on, Kay, use your voice!' Helen urged. 'Tell him exactly what you think of him, loudly. Let it all go!'

Karen took a deep breath and yelled, 'I *hate* you! You're a bastard, a bloody liar and a hypocrite...*and a pervert and a monster,*' she added silently to herself.

Charles flinched at the onslaught.

'I think it's missing the point of the therapy,' Karen confided to Juliet when she bumped into her at the junior school that afternoon. 'I can't express how I really feel about Howard without telling everyone exactly what he did.'

'Are you sure you can't tell them?' Juliet asked. 'After all, anything you say in the group is supposed to be completely confidential.'

Karen was appalled at the idea. 'I can't possibly mention that Howard was involved with a child pornography ring. I'm not sure yet how much I can trust the others in the group.' She thought of Stella, almost totally immobilised by grief; Charles, a jittery bag of nerves, and Lucy, slightly unhinged, full of explosive and unexplained rage.

Juliet nodded understandingly. 'Well at least you've started to do something about your depression. It's a step in the right direction. You're looking better already, and you're not wearing grey, thank God!'

Karen was relieved. Since scrutinising her face in the mirror, she had been taking a little more care over her appearance and had even started to eat more at mealtimes instead of merely picking at her food. She felt she was gradually, albeit slowly, emerging from the abyss of despair she had plunged into after the half-term week away.

'Do you remember that man I told you about, the one in Wales?' she asked Juliet. 'He wants to call on us next Saturday when he's on his way to Leeds.'

'Aha!' Juliet clapped her hands. 'I thought there must be something between you!'

'There isn't anything between us,' Karen protested. 'He's only coming to see how we all are. He got on really well with the children and wants to see them again.'

'Don't tell me that!' Juliet wagged a finger at her. 'He's coming to see *you* of course. Men don't go out of their way to call on a woman unless they're interested in her.'

Karen felt herself blush. She wasn't used to male interest and didn't want to read more into Mel's visit than he intended. She had noticed a certain old-fashioned gallantry in his manner whenever he spoke to any woman, not just herself. 'No,' she said firmly. 'I don't think he is interested in me, not in the way that you mean. Anyway, I'm not ready for anything like that, not yet.'

Juliet merely smiled. 'Well you can tell me all about it next Tuesday. Come over for coffee after you bring Poppy to school.'

Joan was less thrilled about the impending visit when Karen mentioned it casually over the phone. 'What's he coming for?' she asked suspiciously.

'To see how we are, he said.'

Joan snorted derisively. 'Has he got designs on you?'

'Good heavens no! I hardly know him. He's just being friendly. He knew Greg's aunt. She was one of his neighbours.'

'Well you'd better be careful. It's far too early for--'

'For what?'

'You know what I mean. You can't get entangled with another man so soon after Howard died, particularly while the investigation's still ongoing.'

'I'm not getting "entangled" with any man,' Karen retorted with exasperation. 'I didn't *ask* him to come, he suggested it himself.'

'Well I'm telling you again, be careful. You're still in a very vulnerable state.'

* * *

That Friday, Martin paid her a brief visit. Although they

had spoken on the phone, it was the first time Karen had seen him since shortly after her return from Wales.

'I thought I'd pop by and let you know how things are going.' He eyed her. 'How are you doing, Karen? You look--'

She cut him off. 'I know I've lost weight. People keep telling me.'

'No. I was going to say you seem... a tad more rested than when I saw you last.'

'I feel a bit better now.'

'I'm pleased to hear it.' He smiled. 'You'll feel better still when I tell you--'

'Tell me what?'

'Do you remember that Baxter gave us the names of some other members of *Pied Piper* in this country? Two of them have been picked up. They're being charged with possession of indecent images of children as well as illegal possession of firearms. Their homes are still being searched. They've been questioned about their whereabouts on the afternoon your husband was killed. We think one of them may have been the perpetrator.'

Karen felt a rush of apprehension.

'He has a motorbike similar to the one the guy who shot your husband was riding, a Honda Rebel. Forensics have examined it although there's no evidence so far that it's the right one. I thought you'd like to know.'

'It sounds promising,' she said with an effort.

'The SIO's pulling out all the stops. He wants to arrange a reconstruction of the crime on *Crimewatch*, the TV programme. How do you feel about that?'

'I'm not sure.' The idea appalled her.

'It could be useful. The programme has a good record of

jogging people's memories. Someone may have seen this guy.' He glanced at his watch. 'Sorry, must go. We're rushed off our feet at the moment.'

After he had left, Karen sank on to a chair. Her improved sense of wellbeing had drained away.

The following morning she dragged herself round the house in a nervous dither. After some perfunctory cleaning and dusting - chores she had neglected for several weeks - she made a casserole in case Mel was expecting to stay for lunch, then took a pizza out of the freezer in case it didn't cook in time.

She changed her clothes several times. She didn't want to appear dowdy but was afraid of looking too smart in case he assumed she had dressed up for his benefit. She couldn't understand why she found the visit so intimidating. The children, on the other hand, were delighted that he was coming and took the prospect completely in their stride.

When she opened the front door, however, and saw Mel standing there, she was surprised at how pleased she was to see him again. She had forgotten how tall he was and that he had such a nice smile.

'You look as lovely as ever,' he commented gallantly, though from the way he scrutinised her, she was sure he had noticed her loss of weight.

He had brought flowers and a bottle of wine for her, small gifts for the children and a squeaky toy for Rufus. He chatted to the three children, communicating with each of them at their own level. He talked knowledgeably to Erica about her favourite boy band and even sang a few lines of their songs in a pleasant tenor voice. He listened to Poppy's reading (she had a new library book about a talking cat), and accompanied Simon to his room to admire his school project on dinosaurs.

Within half an hour of Mel's arrival, Karen felt totally relaxed and wondered why she had been so anxious about the visit before. The meal turned out to be just as convivial as the one they had shared in Wales. The casserole had turned out well, Erica didn't put her headphones on, and they all remained seated at the table long after their plates were empty.

When the children took Rufus into the garden to play with his new toy, Karen and Mel were left alone in the kitchen.

He gazed at her across the table. 'You're looking a little pale, Karen. Have you been unwell?'

'I was for a while,' she admitted. 'I felt rather depressed after we came back from Wales, but I'm feeling better now.'

'That's good. Have there been any developments in the investigation?'

She swallowed. 'The family liaison officer told me yesterday that two men are in custody. Their homes are still being searched.'

'Well I'm sure you'll be pleased when someone's behind bars.'

'No!' she exclaimed vehemently.

He looked surprised. 'No?'

She felt her cheeks go hot. 'No. If someone's charged with Howard's murder, that stuff I've found out about him will be made public.'

'You mean the illicit financial dealings you mentioned?'

'Not just that.'

He looked even more surprised. 'Not just that?'

Karen cursed herself. The wine must have loosened her tongue. As Mel was driving, she had drunk most of it herself. 'No,' she said hesitantly, 'there's more. I discovered that he was having an affair, with my closest friend.'

'Ah.' An expression of sympathy crossed Mel's face. 'No wonder you--'

'I've started going to a support group,' she rushed on, 'for people with stress and emotional problems.'

'And is it helping?'

'I think so, a bit anyway.'

He reached across the table and touched her hand. 'Well I think you're doing remarkably well, considering what you've been through.'

Before she could respond, the children rushed noisily through the back door.

'Mummy,' Poppy shouted, 'Rufus has found a dead bird. Should we bury it?'

'Yes, if you like.' Karen rose to her feet and started stacking the plates.

Mel stood up and checked his watch. 'Goodness, it's nearly three o'clock. I must get going. I've got a long drive ahead.' He smiled at her warmly. 'Thank you for your hospitality. It's been a pleasure seeing you all again.'

They accompanied him to the front door and waved him off.

Simon looked sad as the car disappeared down the road. 'I really like Mel,' he told Karen. 'He knows all about dinosaurs.'

Karen put her arm round him. She couldn't remember Howard ever expressing an interest in Simon's school projects.

She mused on the visit while she was clearing up the

lunch things. Perhaps Juliet was right. Maybe Mel was "interested" in her, but did she actually *want* that? Before she was married, she had both desired and dreaded male interest in equal measure. Now she just felt confused. Nevertheless she was sure that once Mel got to hear about Howard's involvement in child pornography, any interest he had in her would quickly evaporate.

She decided she must forget about him and concentrate wholly on the children.

\* \* \*

Sunday turned out to be an unusually sunny day and as Erica was spending the afternoon with her friend Lisa, Karen took Simon and Poppy to the local park. There was a playground there and a hard surface where Simon could practise on the skateboard Joan had given him for his last birthday. So far, he had only tried it out on the garden path as Karen was afraid he might hurt himself using it in a larger, more public space.

At the park, she watched him attempting jumps and turns in the area sometimes used for basketball. When she felt that he was sufficiently skilled to avoid breaking his neck, she took Poppy into the playground, first tying Rufus to the railings, as dogs weren't allowed in the children's enclosure. From here she could still keep an eye on Simon on the basket ball court.

While she was pushing Poppy on a swing, she was startled to hear the little girl shout, 'Look, Mummy, there's the ladyman!'

'What "ladyman"?'

'The man with short hair you said was a lady.'

Karen looked in the direction Poppy was pointing and was surprised to see Lucy. Dressed in her long trench coat and heavy boots, she was standing in front of the small kiosk that sold snacks outside the playground, drinking something from a polystyrene cup. When she noticed Karen and Poppy staring at her, she scowled but gave no sign of recognition. After a few seconds she tossed the cup into a bin and abruptly strode away.

Karen shook her head in mystification. Lucy was a very strange young woman, she decided.

When Poppy became bored with the facilities offered by the playground, Karen untied Rufus and called Simon to join them. She bought ice creams at the kiosk and they ate them walking along the river path. It was an idyllic afternoon and Karen was overcome with guilt when she realised that the reason she was enjoying it so much was because Erica hadn't accompanied them. Just like Howard had done in the past, Erica filled the house and clouded family outings, with tension.

* * *

'Well, how did it go?' Juliet asked when Karen turned up at her house for coffee on Tuesday morning.

Karen pretended not to know what she was talking about. 'How did what go?' She busied herself removing Rufus's lead and letting him out into the back garden.

Juliet sniggered. 'Your visit from the mysterious Welshman of course.'

'Oh that! It was very pleasant. And he's not at all mysterious, quite the opposite in fact.' Karen wondered how Juliet always managed to look so exotic. Today she was wearing a crimson sweater that reached almost to her knees, dangly gold earrings, and diamond-patterned black tights.

Juliet studied her quizzically. 'Just pleasant?'

'Yes. He came to lunch, played with the children, made polite conversation, then went on his way.'

'How was it left? Did he suggest visiting you again or you visiting him?'

'We didn't make plans, Juliet. He's only a casual acquaintance.'

'Casual? Are you sure?' Juliet eyed her appraisingly. 'You certainly seem to have perked up since he came. You should wear blue more often. It suits you. If you wore that jumper on Saturday, I'm not surprised he fancies you.'

Karen felt herself blushing. 'No, I didn't wear it and I'm sure he doesn't "fancy" me.'

Juliet grinned. 'Methinks she doth protest too much! It's great that you've met someone so soon after--'

Karen uttered an exasperated groan. 'Juliet, after everything's that's happened, there's no way I want to get involved with another man. Not yet. Maybe not ever. Can we change the subject?'

'OK.' Juliet handed her a steaming mug of coffee. 'Your hair needs touching up again.'

'Does it? I'll make an appointment.'

There was a short silence while they both sipped their coffee.

'Have you heard how the investigation's going?' Juliet asked after a while. 'Any developments?'

'Yes. Our liaison officer told me that two men are being questioned. He said they're both members of that... ring Howard belonged to.' Even though Juliet was sympathetic,

Karen still found it difficult to utter the word "paedo-phile". 'Apparently one of them has a motorbike similar to the one the murderer was riding.'

'That's good news, isn't it? Maybe they've found the right guy at last.'

Karen shook her head. 'I don't think it *is* good news. If he *is* the right guy, Howard's connection with *Pied Piper* is bound to come out, and when that happens, people will be pointing and whispering at us.' She felt tears prick her eye-lids. 'I can't bear the thought of the children being picked on at school because of what their father was.'

Juliet put down her mug and squeezed her arm. 'It's much too early to be worrying about that. Even if one of them *is* charged, it could be ages before a trial takes place.'

Karen blinked away the tears. 'It doesn't matter how long it takes. Once people know that Howard was part of a child porn ring, I'm certain to be guilty by association. We'll have to move away.'

'That's nonsense,' Juliet declared. 'You can't let spiteful people force you out of your own home. Anyway, would you be in a position to move? Is the house yours?'

'I hope it will be. Howard left everything to me and the children, but because of that sham business and money laundering, I'm not sure whether we'll be entitled to it.'

Juliet fingered one of her dangly earrings as she consid-ered this. 'Have you got a good solicitor?'

'The company dealing with Howard's Will is *Jackson and Jackson*. They're doing the tax and legal work, but I haven't spoken to them yet. Howard's partner Geoff is the executor and he's in touch with them.'

'Hadn't you better speak to them yourself? Find out what your position is?'

'No,' Karen replied vehemently. How could she possibly reveal Howard's misdeeds to complete strangers? 'If I told them what the police have found out, they'd have to mention it to Geoff.' Her eyes filled with tears again.

'How's it going with Helen?' Juliet asked gently. 'Is she helping?'

'I think so, a bit anyway.'

'What are the other people in the group like?'

'Just people with problems, like me.' Not wanting to say any more, Karen sought to change the subject. 'By the way, Juliet, I haven't forgotten that I asked you over at half term--'

'Yes, but then you skedaddled off to Wales.'

'But I didn't mean --'

Juliet laughed. 'I'm only teasing. It did you good to get away, especially as you met a... Oops! I'm not supposed to mention him, am I?'

Karen tried to smile. 'How about next weekend? Would you like to bring the children over for tea on Saturday? I promise I won't disappear to Wales this time.'

'You're on! Joe and Miranda will be pleased.'

Karen wondered whether any other children would be allowed to visit the house once Howard's activities became public knowledge.

# Chapter 23

After the relaxation exercises, Helen said she was going to introduce them to meditation. 'You'll find it enormously helpful at times of emotional stress. It will calm you.' She pulled down the window blind, plunging the room into semi-darkness.

Lucy elected to sit cross-legged on the floor but Karen, Stella and Charles preferred to sit on the chairs.

'I want you to start by taking some very deep breaths,' Helen instructed them. 'Close your eyes and try to empty your minds. I know you'll find it difficult at first but I promise it will come with practice.'

She led them through some deep breathing exercises which sent Charles into a paroxysm of coughing. She waited until he had recovered. 'Sometimes it's easier if you chant to yourself, like this,' She closed her eyes and intoned, '*om... om...om.*'

After a few seconds she opened her eyes and smiled at them. 'The repetition becomes almost hypnotic and helps you to stay relaxed. We'll start now. We'll do it for about ten to fifteen minutes.'

Karen took some deep breaths and tried to relax but the ten minutes seemed interminable. Aware of Charles breathing heavily on the chair next to her and Lucy murmuring '*om*' on her other side, she found it almost impossible to empty her mind. However hard she tried, it refused to be stilled. Without the numbing effect of alcohol and sleeping pills, her usual prophylactics, her thoughts seemed sharper and clearer than usual. They roamed unfettered from one subject to another - Mel's visit and Juliet's conviction that he was interested in her; her inability to deal with Erica's teenage tantrums; the possibility that someone might soon be charged with Howard's murder and the probable resulting revelations about Howard's involvement in child porn. She imagined lurid news headlines: *Murdered Accountant Member of Paedophile Ring... Murdered Father Was Child Abuser.*

By the time Helen gently roused them, Karen was in a state of intense agitation. This must have shown on her face for Helen said gently, 'don't worry, Kay. Lots of people find meditation very difficult to begin with. You should try it at home for a few minutes at first, then gradually increase the time on successive days. I promise you it will get easier with practice. What about the rest of you. How did you get on?'

She announced that from then on, she would be incorporating a period of meditation into each session.

\* \* \*

As Karen stepped outside, she was dismayed to see Celia Murray walking along the pavement towards her. Before she could escape, the rotund little woman waved and came to a halt beside her at the clinic door. Her cold eyes rapidly scanned the labels on the buzzers, each of them announcing a different form of alternative treatment. 'Oh dear,' she murmured with exaggerated concern. 'Are you unwell, Karen?'

'I'm perfectly well, thank you.' Karen had no intention of explaining the reason for her visit to the Poison Dwarf. That would be tantamount to shouting it through a megaphone in the middle of the town square.

'Hm.' Celia scrutinised Karen's face as though searching for some sign of physical or mental malaise. 'By the way, I saw your Erica on Sunday afternoon.'

'Did you? She was at her friend Lisa's house on Sunday afternoon.'

Celia's eyes narrowed. 'Are you sure?'

'Of course I am, why?'

Celia gave a faint smile. 'When I saw her, she was in the High Street...with a boy.'

'A boy?'

'Yes. They were holding hands. She's a bit young for that kind of thing, don't you think?'

Karen felt her face go hot.

An expression of spiteful pleasure flitted across Celia's podgy face. 'You need to keep a careful watch on girls that age, Karen. You wouldn't want Erica to get a bad reputation or...make a mistake, would you, especially at such a sensitive time?'

'Erica's getting on for fourteen,' Karen retorted furiously. 'Times have changed since we were young, Celia. It's common for girls to have friends of both sexes these days.'

Celia smirked. 'If you say so.'

'I do.' Karen turned and strode away, unsure who she felt most angry with: Erica for the deceit or Celia for the evident pleasure she took in revealing it.

By the time Erica returned from school that afternoon,

Karen was ready to do battle. She waited until Simon and Poppy were out of earshot before accosting her eldest daughter in the hall.

'Erica, why did you tell me you were going to Lisa's on Sunday.'

Erica's face went slightly pink. 'Because I *did* go to Lisa's.'

Karen picked up the telephone receiver. 'I'll ring Lisa's mother, shall I, and ask her if you were there all afternoon?'

'I did go to Lisa's,' Erica muttered hastily, 'but it was only for a few minutes.'

Karen replaced the receiver. 'A few minutes? Was that to ask Lisa to cover for you by any chance? Where did you go after the few minutes were up?'

Erica gazed at her defiantly. 'Nowhere in particular.'

'Someone saw you in the High Street.'

'So?'

'Who were you with?'

Erica was silent and her face assumed a tight, shut-in expression that reminded Karen painfully of Howard.

'Who were you with, Erica?' she repeated.

The girl's face turned dark red. 'Jamie Markham,' she muttered sullenly.

'Who's Jamie Markham?'

'A boy who used to be at Moxton High. He's really cool.'

'I don't care whether he's cool or not. Why did you tell me you were going to Lisa's? Why did you lie to me?'

'Because I knew you wouldn't let me go out with him.'

'You bet I wouldn't. You're only thirteen. You're too young to be going out with boys.'

'No I'm not,' Erica retorted. 'I'm nearly fourteen. All the girls in my class have boyfriends.'

Karen made an effort to keep her voice calm. 'I doubt that. How old is this Jamie Markham?'

'Sixteen, nearly seventeen. He just started college. He's training to be a plumber.'

'How long have you been seeing him?'

Erica's face resumed its habitual mutinous expression. 'Not very long.'

'*How* long?'

'I only started hanging out with him two or three weeks ago, at weekends.'

'And on those occasions did you tell me you were going to see Lisa?'

'Yes,' Erica muttered, fixing her eyes on the floor. 'I knew you wouldn't let me see him if I asked you.'

'Too right.' Karen reflected for a moment. 'Perhaps I'd better meet Jamie Markham.'

Erica stared at her, astounded. '*Meet* him?'

'Yes, bring him round and introduce him to me.'

'You mean bring him *here*? To the house?'

'Yes, why not?'

'You've got to be joking.' Erica's dark eyes flashed indignantly. 'I'm not going to ask him to come to meet my *mother*. This isn't, like, Victorian times when parents ask what a boy's intentions are. Anyway, he wouldn't *want* to come here. He'd *hate* it. It would put him off me.'

'That wouldn't be a bad thing. And because you lied to me, you're grounded for the next two weeks. After that, you're not going out after school or at the weekends unless you tell me the truth about *exactly* where you're going and *who* with, and believe me, I shall check every time.'

'That's so not fair,' Erica shouted furiously. 'Dad would have let me go out with a boy.'

Karen restrained her anger with difficulty. 'Oh no he wouldn't. And now that your dad's no longer here, it's me who sets the rules, young lady.'

Erica burst into a storm of crying. 'I hate you,' she yelled. 'I wish it had been *you* who died instead of Dad!' She ran upstairs and slammed her bedroom door so hard the house shook.

Before Karen could react, the phone rang. It was Martin.

'I promised I'd keep you in the loop,' he told her. 'Those two guys I told you about, the ones that were being questioned, unfortunately time ran out and we don't have enough evidence to charge either of them in connection with your husband's murder.'

'Oh.' Still shaking from the exchange with Erica, Karen barely registered what he was saying.

'But they're being remanded in custody for other offences - illegal possession of firearms and indecent images of children.'

She felt a glimmer of hope. 'Does that mean they're no longer suspects?'

'No, we just need more evidence. But we're getting closer. The net's closing in on the British members of the *Pied Piper* network. They could all have borne a grudge against your husband for creaming off the profits from the sale of child porn images. All we have to do is find the weak link; someone who'll talk and tell us who ordered the shooting.'

\* \* \*

'You can't keep a girl that age wrapped up in cotton wool,' Joan advised when Karen rang her after the children had gone to bed. 'Teenagers are much savvier than we were. It's quite common for them to have early relationships with members of the opposite sex these days. We see it at the youth centre all the time.'

'Relationships?' Karen repeated faintly. 'Erica's far too young to have a relationship with a boy.' She ran a distracted hand through her hair and had the irrelevant thought that she must remember to get the colour touched up.

'Does she know about safe sex and contraception?' Joan asked.

'Good God, Joan, you don't think she--'

'You've got to be realistic, Karen. This is the Twenty-First Century. Haven't you discussed these things with her yet?'

'Not really.' Karen felt ashamed. She was obviously a terrible mother. 'I did talk to her when she started her periods, but I didn't go into detail. I thought they were given that kind of information at school. She probably knows more about it than I do.'

'That's exactly my point,' Joan declared. 'Youngsters today are far more knowledgeable about these matters than we were at that age. I suggest you bring the subject up with her. She may need advice. Better to be safe than sorry, that's all I'm saying. Talk to her, Karen.'

'She won't listen to anything I say, Joan. She says she hates me.'

'Of course she doesn't hate you. That's just normal teenage stuff, raging hormones and all that, and don't forget she's still grieving for her father. You're bound to be first in line whenever she lets off steam. Would you like me to have a quiet word with her?'

'Oh Joan, would you? She's far more likely to listen to you.'

'Her birthday's coming up in December. Why don't I offer to take her clothes shopping as a present, then we can have lunch or tea somewhere, and I'll tactfully work it into the conversation.'

Karen breathed a sigh of relief. 'Thanks Joanie, you're a star!'

'In the meantime my advice is, cut her a bit of slack.' Joan laughed. 'And you never know when you might need a plumber!'

After the call had ended, Karen collapsed on to an arm-chair in the living room. She was still trying to come to terms with her husband's perverted sexuality. Now she had a teenage daughter's raging hormones to deal with as well. It was all far too much.

* * *

Erica was still sulking and wouldn't come out of her room when Juliet brought Joe and Miranda to the house on Saturday afternoon.

'I suppose I've got all this to come,' Juliet murmured sympathetically when they adjourned to the living room after tea. 'Miranda will be a teenager in a couple of years.'

'You may be lucky.' Karen glanced at Miranda who was sitting on the sofa with Simon, politely admiring his collection of dinosaur pictures. She was a soft-spoken, fair-haired girl, not at all like Erica with her flashing dark eyes, heavy brows and mercurial temperament. 'Miranda seems very gentle and sweet-natured. I'm afraid Erica's inherited her father's disposition. If she doesn't get her own way, she goes into a sulk that lasts for days. Poppy's totally different, she's always been as chirpy as a skylark.' She gazed fondly down at Poppy who was lying on the floor next to Joe, creating a complicated structure with pieces of Lego.

'So Erica's been seeing a boy?'

'Yes, she pretended she was going to her friend Lisa's on Sunday afternoon, but someone saw her hand-in-hand with him in town.'

Juliet grinned. 'Oh dear, naughty Erica. What did you do?'

'Hit the roof, read her the riot act, and told her she was grounded.'

'You've stopped her seeing him?'

'I wanted to, but Joan thinks I'm overreacting, so I've decided she can see him occasionally, but not in the evenings, and only after the two weeks are up.'

'You shouldn't worry too much,' Juliet assured her. 'It'll probably fizzle out. I remember having a boy friend at that age. I thought I was madly in love with him and it lasted all of five days.'

'You may be right. Erica's so intense, she'll probably scare him off anyway.'

Juliet stroked Rufus who had put his head on her knee. 'What was it you were telling me about Crimewatch?'

Karen gave her a warning glance and rose from her armchair. 'Come back to the kitchen for a minute.'

Juliet followed her out of the room.

'I don't want the children to hear about it,' Karen explained, shutting the kitchen door behind them. 'The police are staging a reconstruction of Howard's murder. It'll be on next Tuesday evening.'

'How do you feel about that?'

Karen shrugged. 'It doesn't bother me, but I'm worried some of the kids at school might see it and start picking on Simon and Erica.'

Juliet patted her on the hand. 'You shouldn't worry about that. Kids don't watch TV much these days. They're far too busy playing computer games or going on social networking sites. Are you going to watch the programme yourself?'

'I don't know. My first instinct was not to, but I might, just out of curiosity.'

Juliet looked surprised. 'I know your husband was a right bastard, but don't you think seeing a reconstruction of what happened to him will upset you?'

Karen shrugged again. 'Maybe. I don't know how I'll feel. It'll be weird. Anyway Joan said she'll come and watch it with me.'

'And your brother-in-law?'

'Greg?' Karen laughed. 'That's very unlikely. He spends most evenings in the pub. That's why my sister's so disapproving of alcohol. He drinks enough for both of them. Speaking of which, would you like a glass of wine before you go?'

'Love one, but only a small one as I'm driving.'

As they sat chatting companionably together, Karen realised how much she missed entertaining friends. She couldn't remember the last time another mother had brought her children round for tea.

# Chapter 24

Helen asked them to sit in a comfortable position then pulled down the window blind and switched off the light.

'Think of a place you love,' she urged them in a low, melodious voice. 'Somewhere tranquil and beautiful. It could be a garden or woods; a beach maybe, a lake or a mountain. Wherever it is, transport yourself there in your mind. Visualise the place and *feel* it; listen to the waves rolling in, the sound of the branches waving in the wind. Smell the earth, the scent of the flowers, the tang of the sea. Imagine you can feel the breeze and the warm air on your skin...' Her tone changed abruptly. 'Is something the matter, Lucy?'

Karen looked down at Lucy. Seated on the floor, her long, trousered legs folded in the Lotus position, she appeared agitated. 'Can't we get rid of the bad places first?' she muttered.

Helen frowned. 'The idea, Lucy, is that immersing yourself spiritually in a good place can help to neutralise the memory of the negative experiences you've had somewhere else. Once you've found a place you can retreat to in meditation, it will become a healing tool you can utilise at will.'

Lucy scowled.

'I think Lucy's right, Helen,' Stella interjected shyly.

'Don't we need to …um…I mean, like Charles had all those awful experiences in Afghanistan, didn't he? That was a really bad place for him. Doesn't he need to, um…?' She hesitated, fumbling for the right word.

Karen surprised herself as she supplied it. 'Exorcise it?'

Helen reflected for a moment. 'Thank you, Kay. *Exorcise* could be the right expression. And thank you, Lucy, for suggesting this. I think it's important to follow the wishes and instincts of the group. So, before we start our "good place" meditation, let's do a preliminary exercise.'

She went to the desk, picked up a small candle in a glass holder, then opened a drawer and took out a box of matches. 'I keep these in case there's a power cut, but they'll be useful for what we're going to do now.' She struck a match and lit the candle. 'Just for a few moments, I want you to think of a place that holds particularly bad memories for you. Afterwards I'm going to ask each of you in turn to say out loud, "I'm leaving…" wherever it is you're thinking of. I want you to repeat the phrase three times, then blow out the candle; snuff it out. It will be a symbolic way of stopping that place having power over you.'

In the silence that followed, Karen was acutely aware of Charles twitching on the chair next to hers. She felt per-plexed. She had been at home on those terrible days when she had learnt that Howard had been shot and when she had discovered his clandestine activities, but she didn't want to leave or "exorcise" her home, even if it was only in the form of a declaration. She needed to think of another "bad place". Her thoughts started floating back in time and, before she could stop them, they entered the mine-littered no man's land she had striven to erase from her memory: the time when she was ten years old; the year her mother had died. Plunged back into that period, she felt a rush of anguish and despair.

'Time's up,' Helen announced. She stood in front of Charles holding the candle. 'We'll start with you, Charles. I want you to say three times, "I'm leaving..." wherever it is, then blow out the flame.'

Charles leaned shakily towards the candle and murmured, 'I'm leaving Helmand Province.'

'Again, Charles, but don't whisper. Say it like you mean it.'

'I'm leaving Helmand Province,' Charles repeated in a stronger voice. He paused, then bellowed, 'I'M LEAVING HELMAND PROVINCE,' making Karen jump. He blew out the candle and collapsed back on his chair with an expression of relief on his haggard face.

'Well done, Charles!' Helen relit the candle. 'Stella, what about you?'

Stella took a deep breath and repeated in a loud but quavering voice, 'I'm leaving St Catherine's,' three times before blowing out the flame.

'Good, Stella!' Helen struck a match and lit the candle again. 'Now you, Lucy.'

Lucy gazed at the flame for a second, then, her face distorted with fury, muttered twice through gritted teeth. 'I'm leaving Sherwood Drive!' She shrieked the phrase a third time then blew the candle out so violently that Karen could see spittle flying through the air.

'Excellent, Lucy. And finally you, Kay.'

Karen stared at the candle, visualising the cold and comfortless house she and Joan had lived in after their mother had died. 'I'm leaving Wilton Avenue,' she declared in a firm voice. 'I'm leaving Wilton Avenue.' She paused then shouted as loud as she could, 'I'm leaving Wilton Avenue!' Blowing out the candle, she felt an immediate sense of release. Was this what the word "catharsis" meant?

Helen regarded the four of them approvingly. 'Very good, all of you. And now that you've left your bad place, I want you to concentrate on a good one; one you'll be able to return to in your mind every time you feel overcome by sadness or despair. Visualise it; feel it…' In a low voice she began to repeat the hypnotic phrases with which she had started the session.

Karen's thoughts drifted effortlessly to the coastal path along the Gower Peninsula. Traversing it in her mind, she entered a pleasurable state of peace and calm.

\* \* \*

'Are you sure you want to watch it?' Joan asked when they were seated in front of the television in the living room on Tuesday evening. 'We don't have to if you think it's going to upset you.'

'Yes, I want to watch it.' Ignoring Joan's disapproving gaze, Karen took a gulp of her red wine. She had drunk enough before her sister arrived to achieve a state of insouciance. 'But we'll have to change the channel quickly if any of the children come down.'

The reconstruction of Howard's last moments on *Crimewatch* was a strange affair. After the presenter had briefly outlined the facts of the case, Karen watched an actor playing Howard, but who looked nothing like him, pick up a briefcase, descend some stairs and open an outer door. As he stepped on to the pavement, a motorbike roared up the street then slowed down a few yards away from him. The tall, leather-clad rider, whose face was hidden by a visor, aimed a gun at him, pulled the trigger and fired twice. The pretend Howard fell to the ground and lay there, motionless. Blood seeped on to the pavement. The motorbike sped away.

After the reconstruction, DCI Evans appeared on the screen. He was standing in front of a huge photograph of Howard, an enlarged copy of one Karen had given the police to assist their investigation. 'On the afternoon of Friday, the thirty-first of July,' he said gravely, 'the Honda Rebel motorbike was picked up by CCTV cameras, travelling at speed along Vale Road and Cedars Avenue. We're not sure what route it took beforehand. If anyone saw the motorbike or can identify the person riding it, please ring this number as soon as possible. It's essential that we catch this cold-blooded killer as soon as possible.'

A phone number appeared on the screen and the programme presenter moved swiftly on to the next featured crime.

Joan turned to her with a concerned expression. 'Are you OK, Karen?'

'I'm fine.' Karen realised that when the actor playing Howard was shot, she had felt absolutely nothing.

However, she found it difficult to sleep that night. Whether this was due to the reconstruction or to her overindulgence in wine, she couldn't tell. But as she rolled restlessly from side to side of the bed, she was aware of something nagging at her; something lingering provocatively at the periphery of her mind. What was it? Something that had happened? Something she had forgotten to do? She went over the events of the last few days but failed to find anything to nudge whatever it was into full consciousness. Finally abandoning the attempt, she took several deep, relaxing breaths then willed herself to enter the "good place" she had chosen to be her calm retreat: the coastal path on the Gower Peninsula. She saw herself striding along it with Rufus trotting happily at her heels. In her imagination, she heard another dog barking. Elvis scampered into view and a tall man fell into step beside her. It felt perfectly natural for them to continue along the path together. They walked companionably without speaking, just listening to the sound of the wind and waves...the wind and the waves...the wind and the waves...the imagined sounds lulled her and finally she fell asleep.

'Mum!' Simon was shaking her. 'Get up. Me and Erica have had our breakfast. Poppy's still in bed. She'll be late for school.'

'Oh God.' Karen leapt out of bed and scrambled into her clothes. She dashed into Poppy's room, woke her up, then ran downstairs where she found Simon tying his shoelaces in the hall and Erica finishing a bowl of cereal in the kitchen.

Ignoring her, Erica stood up and leaving her empty bowl on the table, stalked into the hall to join Simon.

'Bye, Mum,' he shouted as the two of them left the house to catch the school bus.

Three quarters of an hour later, as Karen was hurrying Poppy through the school gates, she spotted Juliet waiting on the pavement nearby. As usual, she was hard to miss. She was wearing a Russian- style, fake fur hat below which dangled huge earrings that resembled miniature chandeliers.

'Bye, darling.' Karen waved as Poppy ran across the

playground. Juliet joined her at the gates. 'Did you watch the programme?'

'Yes.'

Juliet regarded her with a concerned expression similar to the one that had been on Joan's face the previous evening. 'And? How did you feel?'

'I didn't feel anything. The actor didn't look at all like Howard.'

'Even so, it was pretty gruesome, wasn't it? Didn't it shock you?'

Karen reflected. 'No. It didn't shock me. It seemed totally unreal, like an episode in a film or TV drama. I didn't feel it had anything to do with me.'

'I'm relieved.' Juliet hugged her and one of her enormous earrings brushed with a tinkling sound against the side of Karen's face. 'I thought it might have knocked you for six, whatever you felt about your husband.' She released Karen and smiled. 'Fancy a coffee? I've got the day off.'

Karen glanced at her watch. 'Can I take a rain cheque? I'm going to the hairdressers, on your advice.' Since the funds from Howard's share of the partnership had come through, she didn't feel so guilty about spending money on herself.

Juliet smiled approvingly. 'Good for you. You're looking a lot better. I think you've put some weight on at last.'

'That's probably the wine. I'm afraid I've been overdoing it lately.'

\* \* \*

Karen felt revived after having her hair cut and the colour touched up. Eyeing herself approvingly in the hairdresser's mirror, she cocked an imaginary snook at Celia Murray.

That afternoon she received a call from Martin asking her whether she had watched the televised version of Howard's last moments.

'Yes I did.'

'I hope it didn't distress you too much.'

She was touched by the note of concern in his voice. 'No, it didn't seem real to me.'

'A number of people contacted us after the programme,' he told her. 'Some of them said they saw the motorbike before it entered Vale Road, so now we know what direction it came from.'

'Has anyone identified the rider?' Karen asked with trepidation.

'One or two names have been suggested. We're checking on them now. I'll let you know when there's any news.' He ended the call.

Karen felt a frisson of anxiety but she was instantly distracted by Rufus who was barking and frantically pawing at the front door. She realised guiltily that she hadn't taken him out for his usual long walk. She hurriedly clipped on his lead, left the house and headed towards the river. It was a fine day and the cold air was bracing.

As she crossed the market square with Rufus, she was dismayed to see Mo and her poodle approaching from the opposite direction. Mo waved and hurried towards her.

Karen decided to walk past with a cursory nod, but as on the previous occasion when she had bumped into Mo, the two dogs leapt at each other, barking excitedly.

'Come *here*, Albert.' Mo stooped to catch hold of the poodle's collar. 'Your hair looks really nice,' she commented admiringly as she straightened up.

'Thank you,' Karen muttered curtly, tugging at Rufus's lead.

'Did you watch *Crimewatch* last night?'

'Yes.'

'Wasn't it awful?'

Karen didn't answer.

'Whatever you think of me, Karen,' Mo blurted, 'I really did care for Howard, you know.'

'Huh!' Karen wondered whether she would admit this if she knew the truth about Howard.

'Did the police receive any calls after the programme?' Mo continued. 'Shut up, Albie!' She rummaged in her bag and found a dog treat which she gave the puppy to chew.

'I don't know,' Karen replied coldly. She turned to move away but Mo stepped quickly in front of her. 'Karen, was Howard ...was he up to something before he died?'

Karen stared at her, alarmed. 'What do you mean?'

'Two detectives came to the house and questioned me for ages about that time Howard asked me to meet him in Thailand. You told them about that?'

'Yes, I had to. It could have been important.'

'They wanted me to tell them who he was meeting there and why he wanted me to carry memory sticks for him. They kept asking me exactly what he said and whether he'd ever given me anything else to look after for him. I told them I couldn't remember what Howard said about Thailand and I didn't know anything about the memory sticks. I thought it was just a holiday and he wanted to spend time with me.' Her voice tailed off. 'Why did they want to know? *Was* Howard involved in something, Karen, something illegal?'

'The police think he was,' Karen said guardedly.

'Do they think I'm implicated?' Mo's face was furrowed with anxiety. 'Is that why they asked me all those questions?'

Karen shrugged. 'I shouldn't think so, but they don't tell me everything about the investigation. They're obviously investigating all of Howard's *affairs*...' she couldn't resist using the word '...as part of the murder enquiry.'

Mo's little-girl face crumpled. 'I don't want to be involved, Karen. Tony and I aren't getting a divorce any more. We've decided to make another go of it, for Gemma's sake.'

Mo looked so miserable that Karen felt almost sorry for her. She was genuinely relieved that, in addition to all his other misdeeds, Howard hadn't managed to destroy another couple's marriage. 'Listen, Mo,' she said in a friendlier tone, 'whatever Howard was involved in before he was killed, I'm sure it wasn't anything to do with you. The police probably won't need to bother you again.' She was about to step past Mo, when out of the corner of her eye she glimpsed a familiar figure.

Wearing her ankle-length trench coat and with a very long knitted scarf wound several times round her neck, Lucy was standing on the corner of the square, watching them. She ignored Karen and was staring fixedly at Mo.

Mo started as she followed Karen's gaze. 'Do you know that woman?'

Karen hesitated then answered vaguely, 'I've seen her around now and again.'

Mo appeared uncomfortable under Lucy's hard, unblinking gaze. 'I wonder who she is. I've noticed her hanging around at the end of our road. There's something really strange about her. Why is she staring at me like that?'

Karen shrugged. 'I don't know. Maybe she's got problems. Come on, Rufus.' She turned and walked on towards the river. Once she reached the tow path, she let Rufus off the lead and allowed him to run ahead of her. Following at a brisk pace, she pondered on Lucy's odd behaviour. What did the young woman did all day? She didn't appear to have a job. How had she found her way to Helen's group? Had she been referred by a doctor? Maybe she was on medication or even drugs. If she was, that might account for...

She came to a sudden halt. The elusive thing that had been nagging at her during the night had suddenly flashed into her mind.

# Chapter 25

She had no time to pursue the matter that afternoon but while the children were having their tea, she went upstairs to Howard's study. She rarely ventured into the room these days, partly out of habit, it having been Howard's exclusive domain; partly out of a superstitious feeling that it was still pervaded by his forbidding presence. Although she had reorganised the living room and main bedroom, she had left the study exactly as it was before he had died.

Pulling out the top drawer of the filing cabinet, she started hunting feverishly through the documents the police hadn't considered necessary for their enquiry.

'Mum?'

Startled and irritated at being interrupted, she turned and saw Simon standing at the door.

'What are you looking for?'

'Just some papers. Have you finished your homework?'

'Yes.' He continued to linger by the door.

She shut the drawer and straightened up. 'What's the matter, Simon?'

His face went slightly pink. 'A boy at school said that there was something about Dad on TV. His mum saw it.' His voice dropped to a whisper. 'She told him she saw Dad being shot. I didn't believe him. How can that be on TV?'

Karen tried to hide her dismay. 'It's nothing to worry about, darling. The police are still searching for the person who shot Dad, so they were trying to jog people's memories by presenting a staged version of what happened, using actors. It was what they call a reconstruction. They were hoping it might persuade more witnesses to come forward.'

He looked relieved. 'Oh. Did anyone come forward?'

'Martin said the police had a few phone calls after the programme. He'll let us know if there are any developments.'

Simon pulled at his earlobe. 'They *will* catch him, won't they, Mum?'

'I'm sure they will. But it's taking time because the police have to be very careful that they find the right person.'

'I suppose so.' He took a step on to the landing then turned back again. 'Mum, it's going to be Erica's birthday soon. Are you planning anything?'

Karen felt a rush of guilt. She had forgotten about the birthday.

'Why didn't Erica ask me herself?'

'She wanted me to because she thinks you're still angry with her.'

She sighed. 'I'm not the one who's angry, Simon. Your sister's angry with *me*. She's been sulking because she's been grounded.'

'Does that mean we're *not* going to do anything for her birthday?' he asked, sounding almost tearful.

She gazed at him tenderly. It was so like Simon to be upset on someone else's behalf. 'Of course we'll do something, darling. I'll come down and we can talk about it.'

As she descended the stairs, she tried to think of an

appropriate way of celebrating Erica's fourteenth birthday. Throwing a party at the house for a group of noisy teenagers was out of the question in current circumstances, but at the very least they could have a traditional birthday tea with Joan and Greg. Joan always made wonderful birthday cakes for the children. But she knew this wouldn't be enough to satisfy Erica.

As she had predicted, Erica was unimpressed by the idea of a birthday tea (an idea that delighted Poppy), but she perked up when Karen made a further suggestion. 'We could have the tea here on the actual day, then at the weekend, you could take some of your girlfriends to that pizza restaurant you like and afterwards you could all go to the cinema.'

Erica considered this for a moment. 'How many friends?'

Karen thought rapidly about the potential cost. 'Three maybe?'

Erica dropped her customary sullen manner. 'Instead of the cinema, could we go tenpin bowling at the leisure centre?'

It crossed Karen's mind that this might be a ruse to meet up with Jamie Markham but she decided not to mention it. 'I don't see why not.'

Erica's face lit up.

'And Auntie Joan is going to take you clothes shopping one weekend as a birthday treat.'

Erica beamed. 'Ace!' It was the most animated Karen had seen her for some time. Maybe the epic sulk was finally over.

After the children had finished their meal, she resumed her search through Howard's papers in the study. She removed several bundles of folders and neatly-stapled documents from the filing cabinet and started rifling through them. But she couldn't find what she was looking for - documentation relating to the flat Howard had owned before he moved to Moxton. Eventually, in the lowest drawer of the cabinet, she discovered a box file labelled *Property Sale*. She extracted some of the papers inside and gave a grunt of satisfaction on finding a letter from a solicitor dated May 1997. It was addressed to *Mr. Howard Armstrong, 9 Sherwood Drive*.

Karen's stomach lurched. After spotting Lucy in the market square, she had suddenly remembered that the troubled young woman had declared that the "bad place" she wanted to leave was *Sherwood Drive*. She had been too caught up in her own emotional turmoil to register it at the time, but the street name had obviously resonated somewhere in her consciousness. Was it just a coincidence? There might be other roads with the same name in different parts of the country. But what if it *was* the same Sherwood Drive? She replaced the letter in the box file and sat down heavily on the desk chair.

How long had Howard lived in Sherwood Drive? She thought it might have been four or five years, while he was working as an accountant in the area. Could Howard have known Lucy then?

Lucy was twenty something, twenty five or six at the most. That meant she would have been seven or eight when Howard had sold his flat and bought the house in Moxton. Could the traumatic event Lucy had alluded to in Helen's sessions have happened while she and Howard were both living in the same road; in the same building even? It was a thought almost too appalling to contemplate, but could Howard have molested or abused Lucy when she was only a little girl? The idea made her feel nauseous. She preferred to believe that child porn was a perversion Howard had got into in recent years, perhaps under the influence of evil people like Gerald Manning. It made his behaviour seem marginally less culpable. But what if he had engaged in paedophile activity before they were married, before they had even met? Had she married someone, shared a bed with someone, who had previously been interfering with little girls? It was as if an icy hand had gripped her heart. Rising shakily from the chair, her eye fell on the framed photo of the three children on Howard's desk. How had he maintained the pretence of being a normal family man for so long?

She stood up and paced agitatedly around the room, wondering how she could find out whether Lucy had known Howard when she was a child. Should she try to initiate a discreet conversation with her at the end of the next session when they all had tea? She realised that would be difficult as Helen discouraged them from asking each other personal questions. And how could she bring the subject up without revealing who she was and why she was asking?

She wondered whether she should tell Martin about Sherwood Drive. She had given her word that she would keep everything she heard in the group strictly confidential. In view of this, she decided not to mention it, persuading herself that telling him wouldn't make any difference. The police were already aware of Howard's inclinations and even if he *had* done something awful to Lucy, he couldn't be charged with anything now that he was dead.

When she finally forced herself to go to bed, sleep again

eluded her.

\* \* \*

After Karen returned from taking Poppy to school the next morning, she found Martin waiting in a car outside the house.

As soon as he saw her, he opened the driver door and clambered out. 'I've got some news.'

Her heart sank. 'Have you? What is it?'

'May I come in?'

'Of course.' She led him quickly into the living room. 'Has something happened?'

He lowered himself on to an armchair. 'Does the name Bellamy mean anything to you? Patrick Bellamy? Ring any bells?'

'No, why?'

'He never came to the house? Your husband never mentioned him?'

'No,' she repeated, perplexed.

'Well we're now pretty sure it's him.'

She felt a stab of apprehension. 'You mean—'

'Yes.' Martin beamed triumphantly. 'I didn't want you to hear about it on the news. I wanted to tell you in person.'

'Why do you think it's him?' she asked faintly.

'He's one of the two we were questioning, the one with the motorbike. We did another search of the property he's renting. It's about ten miles from here, a cottage on farmland. He moved to the area about eight months ago. I told you we'd already found firearms at the property? Well, this time we examined the surrounding farmland as well and we found another gun in a dew pond. The bullets your husband was shot with, match it.'

'How can you tell?'

'It's a bit technical.' Martin ran a hand through his white hair. 'When a gun's fired, the rifling or grooves on the interior of the barrel make impressions on the surface of the bullet. These and any other marks inside the barrel are imprinted on the bullet's surface. This means it's possible to identify the specific gun any bullet has come from.'

She felt panic rising. 'What happens now?'

'We're still questioning Bellamy. His name hasn't been released just yet, so I'd be grateful if you wouldn't mention it to anyone. He's denied any involvement in the shooting of course, but we believe we've got a very strong case so it's only a matter of time before he'll be charged with the murder.' He glanced at her. 'Won't it be a relief to have the case cleared up at last?'

She clasped her fingers together so tightly that they hurt. 'Only if Howard's…proclivities can be kept quiet.'

He shook his head. 'I'm afraid I can't promise you that. Both your husband and Bellamy have been members of *Pied Piper*. The connection will obviously be a strong element in any evidence.'

'Should I tell the children someone's going to be charged?' she whispered.

'That's entirely up to you, Karen, but they're bound to find out once the media hear about it.' He gazed at her thoughtfully. 'There'll be a preliminary hearing to determine whether there's enough evidence for Bellamy to go to trial, but hopefully his affiliation to *Pied Piper* won't emerge until a full trial takes place. We can't afford any leaks at this stage.'

'That's a relief.' Although she attempted to sound calm,

Karen was quaking inside. Was there any way she could prepare the children for the inevitable revelations about their father that a murder trial might bring?

Martin seemed to have guessed her thoughts. 'When the time comes, I think you should contact one of those support agencies I brought to your attention. They'll be able to advise you on the best way of helping your children come to terms with what they going to find out about their dad. You shouldn't try to deal with this on your own. In cases like this, children need counselling from appropriate experts.'

He rose to his feet. 'I must go.' He touched her gently on her shoulder. 'Try not to worry, Karen. Whatever happens, people have short memories.'

She shut the door behind him and went to the kitchen. Overwhelmed with despair, she sank on to a chair and covered her face with her hands. How long would it be before Howard's involvement in paedophilia would be spread across the front pages of the tabloids?

Rufus padded up to her and laid his head on her lap. It felt comforting.

After a few minutes she went into the hall and rang Joan. 'Can you talk?'

'Just for a moment. What's up?'

'Martin came round. He said a man's about to be charged with Howard's murder.'

She heard Joan give a sharp intake of breath. 'Who is it?'

'I'm not supposed to mention his name because it hasn't been released yet.'

'Do you know him?'

'No, I've never heard of him.'

'Has he confessed?'

'No, but Martin reckons they have a really good case. He's got a motorbike like the one the killer used and the police found a gun on farmland near where he lives. It's the one that was used to shoot Howard.'

'Well, that sounds pretty foolproof, doesn't it?'

'I'm scared, Joan. Martin says he's a member of the *Pied Piper* ring—'

'So you think Howard's own involvement in the ring will be made public. That's understandable. But it'll take a while for anything to get to court, won't it?'

'I suppose so, but once the man's name is released, the press will start digging and when they find out…' Karen's voice started to rise hysterically, '…who knows what effect it will have on the children.'

'Try to keep calm, Karen,' Joan murmured soothingly. 'Whatever happens, you know Greg and I will help as much as we can. You won't be on your own. I've got to go now. I'll ring you tonight.'

As Karen replaced the phone, she noticed an envelope lying on the doormat. She bent to pick it up and saw that it was addressed to her in unfamiliar handwriting. When she opened the envelope, she was surprised and pleased to find that it contained a postcard with a view of Rhossili Bay and a letter from Mel.

*My dear Karen,*

*I know you don't do emails so I'm resorting to an old-fashioned form of epistolary communication to thank you for your recent hospitality and to say how much I enjoyed meeting up with you and your children again. The brief time I spent with you at your lovely home turned an otherwise long and tedious drive into a pleasure rather than a chore.*

*Karen, I am very aware of the difficulties you have been experiencing and I want you to know that I have the greatest admiration for the stalwart way in which you are dealing with circumstances that would have caused frailer human beings such as myself to fall apart. I fervently hope that the police will soon solve the case so that you can begin picking up the threads of a normal life again, (that is if life can ever return to normal after what has happened to you).*

*Should you wish to escape to this beautiful part of the country again, I would be only too delighted to reprise my role as friend and guide whenever my duties at the university permit. My sabbatical ends after Christmas but academic terms are fairly short. To entice you back, I enclose a picture of a view I know you particularly liked when you visited the Gower last month.*

*Remember me to Erica, Simon and Poppy. I'm sending Simon a book I've found on dinosaurs that he might find useful for his project.*

*Do keep in touch and if there is any possible way I can be of assistance to you, don't hesitate to write or ring.*

*Yours affectionately, Mel Jenkins*
*PS Elvis sends grrrreetings to Rufus*

Karen was touched. She gazed longingly at the picture on the postcard for a moment. Turning it over, she saw that Mel had written *come and visit us again soon* on the back.

\* \* \*

The announcement she had been dreading was made on

Friday evening. It was on the six o'clock news.

*A forty-year-old man has been charged with the murder of accountant Howard Armstrong.*

Karen received several phone calls that night asking for her reaction. Some callers were sympathetic, others merely curious.

As it was wet on Saturday, she and the children remained indoors. While Poppy was playing in her room in the morning, she told Erica and Simon quietly what had happened and warned them to be prepared for comments when they returned to school on Monday.

Simon looked distressed. 'Who is he? What's his name?'

'His name hasn't been released yet, darling. Maybe it's someone your dad knew from his work.'

Erica had turned crimson with anger. 'I hope they hang him!'

'We don't execute people in this country any more, Erica, and the man hasn't been found guilty yet. He may be completely innocent. There will have to be a trial but that could take a long time.'

'Why is everything taking so long? ' Erica demanded furiously. 'Why didn't they catch him ages ago?'

Karen sighed. 'I don't know, darling. But I'm sure the police have been doing their best.'

'Well I don't think much of their best and I hope he gets sent to prison for a hundred years!' Erica burst into sobs and ran upstairs.

Karen turned anxiously to Simon. 'Are you OK, darling?'

'I'm glad someone's been caught,' he said, 'aren't you, Mum?'

'Yes of course,' she lied.

Worried about Erica, she rang Joan later to enlist her help, knowing that she could be relied upon to calm her eldest daughter.

When Joan arrived she went up to Erica's room and came down about half an hour later. She smiled reassuringly at Karen. 'Don't worry. Hearing about this was bound to reinforce her grief about her dad. I let her pour it all out. She's still very upset of course, but I mentioned the birthday shopping expedition, and that distracted her.'

# Chapter 26

The mystery of Lucy and Howard's similar address, which Bellamy's arrest had driven temporarily from Karen's mind, now returned to obsess her. She needed to find an explanation. When she took Poppy to school, she watched out for Juliet - always easy to spot in her flamboyant multi-coloured cape - and accosted her as soon as she saw her leave Joe in the playground. 'Can I ask your advice about something?'

'Sure.' Juliet glanced at her watch, 'but I haven't got long before my first appointment. Walk with me to the car.'

'Thanks.' Karen accompanied her up the road. 'It's about--'

'The man who's been arrested?'

'No, something else.'

'Oh?'

'There's a strange young woman who comes to Helen's sessions. I don't know anything about her but she always seems very agitated. She apparently had some kind of traumatic experience long ago, but hasn't said what it was. I've just discovered that when she was a little girl, she and Howard both lived in a road with the same name. It may even have been in the same building, and I'm wondering…' her voice tailed off.

'Crikey!' Juliet came to an abrupt halt. 'You're wondering whether the traumatic experience was something to do with your husband?'

Karen came to a standstill beside her. 'Yes, but I don't know how to find out.'

Juliet stared at her. 'Are you sure you *want* to find out?'

'Yes, it seems important. But I haven't got a clue how to bring the subject up.'

'Are you sure it was the same road?' Juliet set off again and Karen fell into step beside her. 'What's it called?'

'Sherwood Drive.'

'Well, there could be other Sherwood Drives, couldn't there? Do you know whether they lived in the same town or area?'

'No, but it seems such a coincidence. Sherwood Drive isn't a particularly common name for a road. How can I find out if it was the same one and whether she and Howard knew each other?'

'Why don't you instigate a conversation with her?' Juliet suggested. 'Mention your husband's name and see how she reacts.'

'I don't know how to bring it up. She doesn't know who I am. They know me as Kay. I told Helen my name's Kay Armitage.'

Juliet gave a peal of laughter. 'Karen, you're priceless!' She rummaged in her bag and extracted her car keys. 'Here's a suggestion. After the next session, have a chat with her about any old thing, then ask in passing if she watched *Crimewatch*. She doesn't need to know why you're asking. Your husband's murder is the most dramatic thing that's ever happened in Moxton. It would be quite natural to mention it. Then you could see how she reacts to his name.'

'I don't know,' Karen said dubiously. 'Anyway, she always rushes off straight after the session.'

'Then go after her and engage her in conversation.' A car nearby beeped as Juliet pressed the remote key.

'I'm not sure. You know we're not supposed to have contact with each other outside of the sessions.'

'It's up to you, girl. That's what I'd do. Gotta go or I'll be late. Give me a bell later and tell me what happened.' Juliet climbed into the car, blew her a kiss, and drove away.

\* \* \*

Karen observed Lucy closely during the following session, but the young woman seemed oblivious to her gaze and continued to fidget and mutter to herself in her customary manner. Charles, on the other hand, seemed calmer than on previous occasions and Stella also appeared more relaxed. Karen herself was beginning to find it easier to block unpleasant thoughts and retreat to her "good place" during meditation.

After the ten-minute quiet time, Helen produced scissors and a reel of black ribbon. 'Today we're going to cut the ties,' she announced.

They gazed at her uncomprehendingly.

'There may be people in your life,' she explained, 'individuals or groups, to whom you are strongly emotionally attached either by love, or by negative and draining emotions such as guilt, fear or hatred. These ties may be stopping you from going forward. Even if the individuals concerned have died, they may still have power over you. They may still demand such powerful reserves of love, grief or remembered pain that they constantly pull you back into situations that caused you distress. If that is the case, they will be exerting an unnecessarily stultifying effect on your life.' She gazed at them for a moment to gauge their reaction.

Karen noticed that Lucy had stopped fidgeting and was listening intently.

'What I want each of you to do,' Helen resumed, 'is to take a few minutes to identify which individuals may be holding you back. Put yourself in a calm and peaceful state and visualise them. You don't have to tell us who they are. When you have done that, I want each of you in turn to take the scissors and cut the ribbon. As you do it, say to yourself - quietly or aloud - *I am cutting the ties that bind me to you.* Make it a very strong affirmation. If it was a person you loved who has passed, wish them peace then say a final goodbye and tell them you are moving on. If it was someone you disliked or feared, or someone who harmed you in any way, tell them firmly, *you no longer have any power over me. I will no longer be held back by you* - and mean it!'

What Helen was saying made sense to Karen whose thoughts inevitably fastened on Howard.

After they had spent some moments in silent thought, Helen handed each of them in turn the scissors then stood in front of them, holding a horizontal length of black ribbon tautly in both hands, ready for them to cut.

Karen watched as the other three performed the ritual.

Charles stood up stiffly and his lips moved silently as he cut the ribbon.

Stella trembled with emotion as she made what Karen

guessed was a final tearful farewell to her dead child.

When it was Lucy's turn, she leapt to her feet, her face contorted with fury. Jerking violently, she uttered a stream of incomprehensible words as she cut the ribbon, then collapsed back on to a chair. Karen wondered whether it was Howard she had been addressing. When Helen handed *her* the scissors, she shut her eyes for a second and visualised his face. Opening them, she cut the ribbon and silently informed him, 'you no longer have any power over me! I will no longer be held back by you!' She felt an immediate sense of release.

There was no opportunity to strike up a conversation with Lucy at the end of the session as Helen was constantly within earshot and Lucy, as was her wont, hurriedly left the room as soon as she had swallowed her tea. As luck would have it, however, she dropped her woolly hat as she went out of the door. Impulsively Karen picked it up and rushed downstairs after her, but by the time she reached the street, Lucy was already more than a hundred yards ahead of her.

Karen hastened in pursuit, waving the hat and calling her name, but Lucy appeared not to hear. Striding swiftly on her long legs, she turned into River Road. Karen followed and saw her heading rapidly down the hill. Half way down, Lucy stopped, removed her backpack and disappeared into a large and forbidding-looking building that Karen had never noticed before. When she reached it a few minutes later, she found the stout double doors locked. A peeling sign above them informed her that this was St. Dominic's Refuge. It appeared to be some kind of hostel.

She tugged the old-fashioned bell pull. Nothing happened. She pulled it again. Eventually the door opened and a stout middle-aged man appeared.

'Yes?' he enquired curtly.

Karen held out the hat. 'The young woman who just came in here dropped this.'

'What young woman?' The man turned and peered down the passage behind him.

'Her name's Lucy, she's got very short hair.'

'You mean Lucy Bellamy?'

Karen stared at him, astounded. 'I don't know her surname.'

'Well that's the only Lucy we've got staying here. I'll give it to her.' The man took the hat and shut the door.

Karen stood motionless for a moment, trying to make sense of what she had just heard. Lucy *Bellamy*? What could it mean? Was it just another weird coincidence or was Lucy connected not only to Howard, but also to the person suspected of being his murderer? Mystified, she set off for home where Rufus was waiting impatiently for a walk.

The mystery of the double coincidence preoccupied her until late that afternoon, when Erica burst through the front door, hurled her bag and coat on to the floor, and stormed up to her room sobbing loudly.

Karen looked questioningly at Simon who trailed in behind his sister.

'I don't know,' he said before she had even asked the question. 'She was crying on the bus. She didn't say anything to me.'

Loud wails came from upstairs.

Poppy ran out of the living room. 'What's the matter with Erica? Why's she crying?'

'I don't know,' Karen said worriedly. 'I'd better go

upstairs and see.'

She found Erica lying on her side on the bed, sobbing pitifully. She sat on the bed beside her and stroked her hair. 'Can you tell me what the matter is, darling? Is it because a man's been arrested? You knew it was only a matter of time.'

'No.' Erica rolled over and sat up. 'It's Jamie, Mum,' she wailed. 'He's *dumped* me!'

'Oh dear.'

'And...' Erica's face crumpled, '...he's going out with *Gemma*!' She burst into a renewed paroxysm of sobbing.

Karen folded her in her arms. 'Oh dear,' she said again, keenly aware of the inadequacy of this response but anxious to avoid meaningless clichés such as *plenty more fish in the sea*. 'How did you find out?'

Erica answered after her sobs had subsided. 'I've been texting him but he hasn't answered. Then Gemma told me on the bus that *she's* going out with him now. She was gloating!'

'You poor love.' Karen understood what a calamity this was for Erica. Being dumped was bad enough, but to discover that Jamie was seeing her erstwhile best friend must make the blow doubly hard to bear.

Erica abruptly extricated herself from her embrace. 'What do you care?' she yelled. 'You didn't want me to go out with Jamie in the first place. If you hadn't grounded me, this wouldn't have happened.'

Karen felt helpless. She understood that Erica needed to vent her feelings and wondered how she could help her recover from her first heartbreak. 'It's true,' she admitted. 'I didn't want you to start going out with boys yet. I thought you were too young, but I did agree you could start seeing Jamie again and I certainly didn't want you to get hurt.'

Erica was silent.

'What you must do,' Karen continued, feeling her way carefully through the minefield of teenage sensitivities, 'is to show Jamie and Gemma that you don't care. It's your birthday next week. When Joan takes you shopping, you can get some lovely new clothes. That will make you feel better and Jamie will see what he's missing. You're heaps prettier than Gemma anyway.'

*Oh dear.* She heard herself sounding like a cross between an agony aunt and one of Erica's school friends. She handed Erica a tissue.

'Do you think so?' Erica blew her nose loudly.

'I know so,' Karen declared firmly. In her opinion, Gemma, though petite and blonde like her mother, couldn't hold a candle to Erica, with her cascade of shining dark hair, creamy complexion and flashing dark eyes. But she also realised that Gemma would be a less challenging girlfriend for the young man than her intense and mercurial eldest daughter. 'Wash your face then come down for tea. You don't want puffy eyes tomorrow or Gemma will think she's won.'

She left Erica gazing into a hand-mirror and dabbing at her eyes.

While the children were eating their meal, Karen went to the living room, shut the door and rang Juliet from her mobile.

'Did you speak to her?' Juliet asked immediately. 'The young woman you told me about?'

'No, but she dropped her hat so I followed her after the session and I found she's staying at a place called St.

Dominic's on River Road. '

'I know it. It's a hostel for homeless people.'

'When I called at the door to give her the hat, a man answered. He told me Lucy's surname is *Bellamy*. I was flabbergasted.'

'Why?' Juliet sounded puzzled.

'Because ...You know that someone's been charged with Howard's murder?'

'Yes, what about it?'

'*His* name's Bellamy.'

Juliet whistled. 'You mean she may have lived in the same street as your husband *and* she has the same name as the guy who shot him?'

'Yes. They can't both be coincidences, can they? Sherwood Drive isn't a common street name and I don't think Bellamy's a particularly common surname either.'

Juliet gave an incredulous laugh. 'Crikey, what a turn-up!'

'I don't think she's his wife,' Karen mused. 'Or if she is, they're not living together and she doesn't wear a wedding ring.' She had noticed that Lucy wore plenty of other rings, on her thumbs as well as on her fingers. 'What do you think?'

'How old is the guy? The one they're questioning?'

'Forty they said on the news.'

'Older than her, then?'

'Yes, by about fifteen years. Lucy's probably in her mid twenties.'

'Well she could be related to him, a sister or a cousin, even a niece.'

'It's possible, but if so, why would she be living in a refuge for homeless people? Martin said Bellamy's been renting a house for the last eight months. It's on a farm, about ten miles away.'

'Family members don't always live together,' Juliet observed.

'I suppose not.' Karen felt a sudden rush of anxiety. 'I haven't mentioned any of this to the police yet. Do you think I should?'

'Of course you should,' Juliet replied without hesitation. 'It could be important. If Lucy *is* related to that guy and if your husband *did* abuse her when she was a kid, maybe Bellamy shot him in revenge.'

This idea had already occurred to Karen but she was painfully aware that if it turned out to be an accurate version of events, it was bound to bring Howard's perversions under a glaring public spotlight. She knew she must steel herself for such an eventuality.

'You're right,' she said. 'I'll ring Martin tomorrow.'

# Chapter 27

Erica was still subdued when she came downstairs in the morning, but Karen noticed that she had taken special pains over her appearance. She had brushed her hair till it gleamed, slightly accentuated her eyes and lips (with what Karen suspected must have been her make-up), and had arranged her clothes with far more care than usual. She left the house to catch the school bus with her head held high.

Karen was proud of her daughter's evident determination to present a brave face to her peers. She knew there was no way Erica would allow Gemma to retain the upper hand.

She herself remained apprehensive about where her discoveries about Lucy might lead. She decided it would be better to speak to Martin face to face as she couldn't convey the complexity of her feelings about what had happened over the phone. Before taking Poppy to school, she rang him and left a message asking him to call round later that morning.

When he arrived, she noticed that his hair had been cut very short and now stood up from his head like a coarse white brush. She thought it made him look considerably younger.

Noticing her surprised glance, he gave a self-conscious

grin. 'My wife thought it was getting too long. She tries to keep me looking smart but it's an uphill task.'

Karen felt envious of what she imagined was a mutually affectionate relationship. 'Come and have some coffee.' She led him into the kitchen.

'I have some news for you,' he announced, sitting down at the table and patting Rufus who had padded up to greet him.

She winced in anticipation.

'No,' he said quickly, 'this time it's good news, about your husband's finances. My colleagues have gone through them with a fine-tooth comb and you'll be pleased to hear that all the funds he had here, in his accounts in this country, are above board, perfectly legit. He obviously kept his illicit dosh rigorously separate.'

She gazed at him. 'Does that mean...?'

He smiled. 'Yes. It means that the provisions in your husband's Will can go ahead without a hitch and the life insurance policy can be processed. The company will be informed. There'll be a few formalities, but there shouldn't be any more difficulties or delay.'

A huge feeling of relief washed over her. 'That's wonderful.'

He leaned back in his chair. 'So, what did you want to speak to me about?'

She poured the coffee into mugs and placed them on the table. 'Has Bellamy admitted to Howard's murder yet?'

'No,' Martin shook his head in exasperation. 'Although he's been charged, he still insists he didn't do it.'

She handed him his coffee and sat down opposite him. 'I thought you said you were sure it was him.'

'We *are*, pretty sure anyway. The problem is there are no

prints on the weapon or the motorbike, so all the evidence is circumstantial and might not stand up in court.' He looked across at her apologetically. 'I'm sorry if that's not what you wanted to hear.'

'Actually, that wasn't what I wanted to talk to you about.'

'Oh?' He stirred his coffee and took a sip.

'There's a young woman, Lucy. She comes to the same group as me, the emotional therapy one I told you about. She seems to have suffered some kind of traumatic experience in the past but has never said what it was. She's always very agitated, angry. I think she's rather unstable.'

'And?'

'Well,' Karen took a deep breath. 'I'm not sure but I think she may have lived in the same road as Howard, years ago, when she was a child.'

He stared at her. 'The same road? That would be a coincidence. You think it was the same road or you know it was?'

'I think it was. We were doing an exercise at the therapy group. We had to think of a place that had bad memories for us and when it was Lucy's turn, she said Sherwood Drive. The penny didn't drop at the time but afterwards I remembered that before Howard moved here, he lived in a place called Sherwood something near Cheltenham. And when I looked through his papers, I found his address was also Sherwood Drive.'

Martin's eyebrows lifted a fraction. 'That's interesting. Your husband called his bogus business *Sherwood Enterprise.*'

'Yes, you told me.'

He frowned. 'It's a coincidence, I grant you, and it's not

a common name, but there may be other Sherwood Drives in other parts of the country.'

'Yes, I know and I don't want to jump to conclusions but-- '

'You think the "traumatic experience" this young woman mentioned may have happened during a time when she and your husband were possibly living in the same road?'

'Yes.'

'And you're afraid your husband may have had something to do with it?'

'The idea that Howard might have abused Lucy when she was a child has been torturing me.' Karen clasped her hands tightly over her chest. 'I *need* to know whether Howard was ... doing things to children before we were married, but at the same time I'm terrified of finding out that he was. Can you understand that?'

He gazed at her thoughtfully. 'Yes, I do understand, but you have no proof that your husband and this young woman lived in the same road.'

'No.'

'How old is this Lucy?'

'Twenty something.' Karen swallowed. 'But there's more, Martin. I've discovered that her surname is Bellamy!'

'Bellamy?' Martin put his mug down so heavily that a few drops of coffee spilled on to the table. He leaned towards her eagerly. 'Are you sure?'

'Yes.'

'Why didn't you tell me this before?'

'I only heard her surname for the first time yesterday.'

'This could be significant,' he said excitedly. '*Very* significant.

Where does she live now?'

'At St. Dominic's.'

'The hostel for homeless people? How long has she been there?'

'I don't know. I only found out that she was staying there yesterday.'

Martin stood up and paced round the kitchen for a few minutes.

'Has she ever mentioned your husband?' he asked when he resumed his seat.

'No. Not in my hearing.'

'Have you asked her if she knew him?'

'No. I didn't know how to bring it up. We're not supposed to ask each other personal questions in the group therapy session. And she doesn't know my name.'

He raised his eyebrows. 'She doesn't?'

'No, we only use Christian names in the group.'

'So how did you find out her surname was Bellamy?'

'She dropped her hat after the session yesterday. I ran after her with it and a man at St Dominic's told me.'

Martin took his phone out of his pocket. 'We need to bring her in for questioning. I'd better call the chief.'

Karen was panic-stricken. 'Wait! If you question Lucy, please don't mention me. We're not supposed to tell anyone what happens in the sessions. We have to keep everything that's said there completely confidential. I promised.'

'In this instance I'm afraid that the murder investigation must take precedence,' Martin said gently. 'But I'll see what I can do. If we discover that Lucy *is* related to Patrick Bellamy, we'll have a perfectly legitimate reason to question her without bringing you into it. In the meantime, please don't tell anyone else what you've found out, not yet.'

Karen blushed. 'I'm afraid I've already mentioned it to a friend, Juliet Morgan.'

He frowned. 'Pity. Is she discreet?'

'Yes, I'm sure she is, totally.'

'I hope so. If the young woman is as unstable as you say, she'll have to be approached very carefully. I don't want her frightened off before we speak to her.' He rose to his feet. 'I'll call DCI Evans from the car. This could be an important missing part of the jigsaw, the piece we've been looking for; the motive for your husband's murder.'

She saw him out.

The conversation with Martin heightened Karen's preoccupation with the question that had been haunting her ever since she discovered that Howard and Lucy had lived in a road with the same name. If Howard had been responsible for the trauma Lucy had suffered in her past, had she herself spent fifteen years with a man who had been sexually abusing children even before they were married? She had an agonising presentiment that the answer to the question would turn out to be yes.

To distract herself, she decided to go shopping in preparation for Erica's birthday. As Martin had reassured her that Howard's domestic finances were in order, she felt she would be justified in splashing out for the occasion, especially as Erica was going through such a hard time. No sooner had she left the house, however, than it started to rain heavily. Stoically, she pulled the hood of her raincoat over her head and made her way to the town centre where, although it was only midday, the shops already had their lights on.

Alerted by Erica's unsubtle hints about what would be a

suitable gift, she visited a digital centre. There, guided by a young male assistant, she purchased a new smartphone, one she would never understand how to use herself. Afterwards, she went to a supermarket and bought an array of sweet and savoury items for the birthday tea. She was intending to go straight home with her purchases, but as she emerged from the shop into even heavier rain, she spotted Lucy, striding along on the other side of the road. Clad in her long trench coat and endless knitted scarf, she was clutching a huge black umbrella that bloomed over her head like a giant mushroom.

Normally Karen would have walked straight past with just a slight nod of recognition. This time, however, she impulsively called Lucy's name and hastened across the road to intercept her.

Lucy came to a halt and looked startled then alarmed as Karen splashed her way towards her.

On reaching Lucy, Karen couldn't immediately think of how to start a conversation. She put her bulging carrier bags down on the pavement, glanced up at the leaden sky in hope of seeking inspiration, then asked lamely, 'did you get your hat? You dropped it at the clinic.'

Lucy stared at her blankly. Rivulets of rainwater were pouring down the curve of her umbrella and falling on to the pavement.

'I ran after you and left it for you, at St Dominic's '

Lucy frowned. She appeared ill at ease and anxious to get away.

'How long have you been at St Dominic's?' Karen continued, uncomfortably aware of how ridiculous her attempt to make conversation must seem in such conditions. Whereas other pedestrians had taken refuge from the rain in shop doorways, she and Lucy were standing alone together on the wet pavement, like two castaways on an island. As if to emphasise the absurdity of the situation, the wheels of a passing car sent a wave of cold puddle-water over her ankles and shoes.

'Too long,' Lucy replied gruffly.

She started to move away but Karen swiftly stepped in front of her and posed the question she had intended to ask after the last therapy session. 'Did you watch *Crimewatch* the other night?'

Lucy appeared taken aback by the question. 'What's that?'

'It's a TV programme; one that encourages members of the public to help the police solve crimes.' Karen wiped the rain from her eyes and pulled her hood, which had slipped down, back over her hair.

Lucy looked blank. 'I don't watch television. There's only one at St Dom's and everyone there watches crap.'

Karen took a deep breath. It was now or never. 'The last programme had a reconstruction of a local murder; a murder that happened here, in Moxton. Do you remember? A man called Howard Armstrong was shot.'

Lucy recoiled as though she had been shot herself, and started to back away, swinging her open umbrella in front of her body like a shield.

'You didn't hear about it?' Karen persisted, stepping after her. 'It happened in July. There was an awful lot of publicity. You can't have missed it.'

'No,' Lucy mumbled. 'Didn't miss...' She tried to push past Karen, then stopped abruptly. 'I saw you with his wife!'

'Whose wife?' Karen asked, bewildered. '*His* wife.

Armstrong's wife.'

Karen was almost speechless. 'You saw *me* with Howard Armstrong's *wife?*'

A sly, almost triumphant grin crossed Lucy's face. 'The other day, near the river. You were with her. You had dogs.'

Karen thought back to the day she had walked to the river with Rufus. It was the afternoon when she had bumped into Mo. She remembered that when they spotted Lucy, she had been staring disconcertingly at Mo, and Mo said she had seen her loitering in the road where she lived. But *why* would Lucy think Mo was Howard's wife?

Lucy had started to babble incoherently. 'Had to stop… his wife…the girl…saw them… at the house…'

Karen was confused. 'What girl?'

'She's got a girl.'

'Who's got a girl? What girl are you talking about?'

'It had to stop!' Lucy shouted. She shook her open umbrella so violently that Karen was obliged to step into the flooded gutter to avoid being speared by its spokes.

'What had to stop? Tell me what you mean, Lucy.'

'Some people deserve to die,' Lucy hissed, almost spitting out the words. This time she succeeded in pushing past Karen, almost knocking her down in the process, and disappeared rapidly down the road.

Karen stared after her, stunned. It was clear that Lucy *had* known Howard and when she said some people deserved to die, she must have been referring to him. It was beginning to make sense. If Howard had abused Lucy and if Lucy believed Mo was his wife, she may have feared that he was also abusing Gemma. If that was the case, had she persuaded a male relative, Patrick, to kill Howard in order

275

to put a stop to it?

With these thoughts buzzing in her head, Karen decided she must ring Martin at once. Oblivious to her wet feet and soaked clothes, she picked up her carrier bags and rapidly squelched her way home through the puddles.

Martin listened to the details of her encounter with Lucy with excitement. He assured her that the investigating team intended to question the young woman as soon as they had caught up with her. Karen felt guilty about putting Lucy in this position but realised she had no choice. She made an attempt to put aside her concerns. The next day would be Erica's birthday and she wanted to make it as happy and harmonious an occasion as possible.

# Chapter 28

Erica was delighted with her gift when she unwrapped it in the morning, and kissed Karen for the first time in months. She also graciously thanked Simon for the DVD he had bought with his pocket money, and Poppy for the birthday card she had created with ribbon and pieces of coloured paper.

While the children were at school, Karen busied herself preparing the celebration tea. Determined to dissipate the gloom and melancholy that had pervaded the house for so long, she tried to make it look festive by displaying Erica's birthday cards on the living room mantelpiece and hanging blue and gold balloons emblazoned with the figure 14 in the hall. In the kitchen she arranged an assortment of sandwiches and cakes on her best plates. After leaving the room for a few seconds, she was dismayed to find that Rufus had demolished a whole bowl of crisps. She shut him in the back garden to reflect on his sins.

When Erica returned from school that afternoon, she proudly showed them the cards and gifts she had received from friends. Her face was flushed and she was visibly excited at the prospect of her birthday outing on Saturday. Karen hoped that it would lessen the pain she felt at losing Jamie to Gemma.

Joan and Greg arrived promptly at five o'clock. Greg, a carpenter by trade, brought a carved wooden box for Erica to store her DVDs in, while Joan had made a magnificent iced birthday cake, on the top of which she had created a group of sugar swans and ballerinas. The theme had been prompted by Erica's love of Swan Lake which Joan had taken her to see on her previous birthday. Erica was thrilled with the cake and Poppy even more so. Her eyes widened when she saw it. 'Can *I* have a cake with birds and ladies on it when it's my birthday?'

Joan beamed with pleasure. 'You can have whatever you like on your cake, my darling.'

Erica appeared happier than she had done for weeks. She even joined in a game of charades after tea, something she would have scorned a few weeks earlier.

Although Karen put on a show of enjoying the occasion, she couldn't stop worrying about what Lucy might reveal to the police when they got round to questioning her. To calm her anxiety, she slipped into the kitchen at every opportunity and took surreptitious sips of red wine from a bottle she had hidden in a cupboard. She realised she hadn't yet told Joan her suspicions about Howard and Lucy but didn't want to spoil the family party by mentioning anything unpleasant.

After Joan and Greg had gone home and the children had gone to bed, she went to the kitchen and took the bottle out of the cupboard. It was nearly empty. She poured the remaining wine into a glass and swallowed it in one go. It slid pleasurably down her throat, leaving a satisfying warm sensation.

She looked at the kitchen clock. It was after half past nine and there had been no word from Martin about Lucy.

In one sense this was a relief, but it was also prolonging the agony. All she could do was wait. Since Howard had died, she seemed to have spent much of her time waiting: waiting for his attacker to be identified; waiting to be told how the investigation was going; waiting for information about her financial position - all situations over which she had no control. Now she felt that the denouement was imminent: Howard's killer was in custody, a trial would soon take place and Howard's secret life would be revealed to the world. Was she ready for this? A day or so ago, she believed she was, but *now*? Tears stung her eyelids as she opened another bottle and poured another glass of wine.

Her mobile rang, startling her. She made her way rather unsteadily to the dresser to retrieve it. It was Juliet, inviting her for coffee on Friday morning.

'Are you OK?' Juliet asked when she responded.

'Fine.' Karen only just managed to get the word out. 'Been celebrating Erica's birthday.'

Juliet sounded amused. 'Hey up! Your voice is slurred. Have you been hitting the bottle, lady?'

'Afraid I have.'

'Well take it easy! I'll see you on Friday morning.'

As she replaced her mobile on the dresser, Karen caught sight of something on the top shelf. It was the postcard of Rhossili Bay that Mel had sent her. Tucked behind it was his note. Unfolding it, she read it again. When she reached the last sentence, *if there is any possible way I can be of assistance to you, don't hesitate to write or ring*, she impulsively picked up the phone again, found his name in her contact list and pressed *call*.

After a few seconds, his pleasant baritone voice answered, 'Melvyn Jenkins.'

'It's me, Mel, Karen.'

'Karen?' He sounded astonished. 'Are you alright?'

'I …I…' She relapsed into miserable silence, uncertain of what to say.

'Has something happened?'

'No…yes…' She dissolved in helpless tears.

'Karen, my dear, take a deep breath and tell me what's happened.'

The words came out in a confused and staccato burst. 'The young woman called Lucy…not supposed to tell anyone …Howard may have abused her when she was a child… the police are going to question her … waiting to hear…'

'What do you mean, *abused*, Karen?' Mel asked sharply. 'What are you waiting to hear?'

The dam burst, and punctuated by sobs and hiccups, the story of Howard's complicity in child pornography, her dread of public disclosure of his activities, her discovery of the shared address, and her fears for the children, poured out in an incoherent flood. 'It's Erica's birthday and I've been drinking,' she added unnecessarily.

Mel was momentarily silent. When he finally spoke, he sounded incredulous. 'Let me get this straight. Are you telling me your husband was a paedophile?'

'Y…yes,' she hiccupped.

'When did you find out?'

'Not long after he was shot.'

'And you've kept it to yourself all this time?'

'My sister knows.'

'And you say he may have abused a young woman of your acquaintance when she was a child?'

Through the thick, alcohol-induced fog that had

enveloped her brain, Karen tried to organise her thoughts and speak in proper sentences. 'I think he did. He had disgusting images on a laptop. I didn't see them. He was selling them.'

Mel reacted with outrage. 'That's appalling! You poor, poor girl. No wonder you've been in such a state.'

The sympathy in his voice turned the tap of tears on again and she began to weep uncontrollably. Through her sobs she faintly heard Mel speaking gently to her. 'Karen my dear, listen to me, I can tell you're not in a fit state to talk any more. I want you to put the phone down now, drink lots of water, then go to bed. Try to get some sleep. Will you do that? Are you listening to me, Karen? Put the phone down now, drink some water and go to bed. Do you hear me? I'll ring you tomorrow.'

Meekly she obeyed.

\* \* \*

When she rose the next day her head was spinning painfully, her eyes were scratchy and there was an unpleasant taste in her mouth. She tottered out of the bedroom and was about to go downstairs to make the children's breakfast when the terrible truth hit her. She froze as she remembered: the previous night she had called Mel and told him about Howard being a paedophile. Her stomach clenched. How *could* she have told him? What would he think of her? He would probably never speak to her again.

'Mum? Are you alright?' She turned to find Simon on the landing behind her. He was watching her anxiously.

She made an effort to smile at him. 'I'm fine, darling, I've just remembered something, that's all.'

Returning rapidly to her bedroom, she stood trembling in front of the door, appalled at what she had done. She caught sight of herself in the dressing-table mirror. Her face was puffy and there were dark rings under her eyes. She bitterly regretted having drunk so much the evening before. If she hadn't been so inebriated she would never have dreamt of calling Mel. As she strove to remember his reactions to her disclosures, she thought she recalled him saying he would ring her back, but maybe her alcohol-befuddled brain had imagined it. She uttered a groan of despair. She was certain he would never contact her again.

With difficulty she dragged herself downstairs where, in contrast to her own mood, she found the children unusually chirpy. From their conversation it was clear they had all enjoyed Erica's birthday tea and the games they played afterwards. It saddened her to remember how few cheerful family celebrations they had experienced, even before Howard had died.

After dropping Poppy off at school, she took Rufus for a long walk in an attempt to shake off her hangover. It was a damp and gloomy day. The gutters were still overflowing from the recent rain and the pavements were littered with dirty piles of sodden leaves into which Rufus kept poking his nose. The leaden skies intensified her despondent mood as she turned into the tow-path along the river. The last time she had come this way was when she had bumped into Mo then had noticed Lucy standing nearby, watching them.

The further she walked, the angrier with herself she became for ringing Mel and being such a blabbermouth. To think she had even started to half believe Juliet's contention that he was interested in her, more than just as a friend. How delusional that now seemed.

Shortly after she returned home, her mobile rang. *Could it be?* Her hand shook as she took it out of her bag and her heart leapt when she saw that it *was* him.

'Karen? I just wanted to check that you're feeling better.'

'I'm really sorry about last night,' she stuttered, overcome with relief and embarrassment. 'I didn't mean to disturb you --'

'I was pleased that you did,' he assured her. 'You obviously needed to talk. How are you feeling today?'

'Ghastly, but it's my own fault. I drank far too much yesterday.' She trembled as she broached the dangerous subject. 'Look, Mel, what I told you last night, about Howard--'

'It's an appalling story,' he interjected. 'You told me your husband was a cheat and a crook and that was bad enough. But this...You poor girl. You must have been through an unbelievably awful time, far worse than I could have imagined.'

As she made no comment, he added, 'you could have confided in me before, you know.'

'No,' Karen replied emphatically. 'I couldn't. How could I tell you or anyone that my husband was a paedophile? And the police asked me not to say anything while the child porn ring was being investigated.'

'Not even to your friends?'

'I don't have many friends. Howard didn't like ...' her voice tailed away. She didn't want to tell him how controlling Howard was. It would make her sound too weak, too cowardly. 'No-one knows apart from my sister and someone I met at Poppy's school. I haven't dared mention it to anyone else. People might think I knew about Howard and what he was doing, but didn't say anything.'

'Why would anyone think that?'

'Because people always believe the worst....' Karen was aware that her voice had become shrill. '...but I honestly had no idea Howard was like that.'

'Of course you didn't.'

'When the police found that awful stuff on his computer, I vomited.'

'I'm not surprised.'

She tried to speak more calmly. 'I don't know how we can go on living here once people know --'

'What your husband did was nothing to do with you, Karen,' Mel told her firmly. 'You can't be held responsible. Your true friends will know that. Anyone who thinks otherwise isn't worth giving the time of day to.'

Tears of gratitude started to flow down Karen's cheeks. She made an effort to suppress them. 'I'm so worried about the children, Mel.'

'Ah.' There was a brief silence before he said hesitantly. 'You mean your husband might have --'

'Interfered with them? I'm sure he didn't. I've spoken to Erica and Simon. I didn't tell them why of course, but I'm fairly certain he never touched them, not in *that* way. I took Poppy to a children's clinic and they said they were sure he hadn't abused her either. He never had much to do with Poppy anyway, or Simon come to that. No, my biggest fear is how they're going to react when they find out what their father did, what he *was*. I can't stop worrying about that, Mel. It haunts me. The man who's been charged with Howard's murder is a member of the same child porn ring. When he stands trial, Howard's own involvement will come out. When that happens, there'll be loads of ghastly publicity and the children are bound to hear about it.'

'I can understand how worrying that must be for you.' Mel cleared his throat. 'Karen, when this chap goes to court, you will all need to get away, for a while at least. So why don't you come and stay here until it all blows over?'

'*If* it blows over,' she said bitterly.

'People have short memories, Karen. Listen, your brother-in-law's cottage hasn't been sold yet?'

'No, not yet.'

'Then you could all come and stay in it for a while, couldn't you?'

She sighed. 'It's a tempting idea. But what about the children's schools?'

'Surely their head teachers would understand that these are exceptional circumstances and let them have time off on compassionate grounds? You wouldn't want other kids picking on them because of what they'd heard on the grapevine, would you?'

'No, of course not.'

'And the children liked it here, didn't they?'

'They loved it.'

'Well there's your answer. And it's quite possible that you could get them into schools in this area, on a temporary basis at least.'

'Yes, maybe.' She didn't think the idea was very realistic but was willing to entertain it as a pleasant fantasy.

'Now, Karen,' Mel's voice was gentle, soothing. 'I want you to promise me something. Whenever you're feeling like you did yesterday, whenever you want to let off steam, confide or just talk, about anything at all, just pick up a phone and ring me. You've got my mobile number. If I don't answer immediately, leave a message and I'll get back to you as soon as I can. Will you promise me that?'

'Yes,' she said, 'I promise.'

After the call ended, Karen felt as though a huge weight had been removed from her shoulders. If Mel knew about Howard and hadn't judged her after such short acquaintance, maybe others wouldn't judge her either.

# Chapter 29

After taking Poppy to school the following morning, Karen made her way to Juliet's house in Shaftesbury Road.

'How did Erica's birthday go?' Juliet asked as soon as she arrived with Rufus. 'From the way your voice sounded on the phone, I got the impression *you* were certainly enjoying it!'

'It was very successful. It's the first time Erica's looked happy for weeks. She even kissed me.' Karen gazed at Juliet enviously. Her hair was tied in a casual knot on top of her head and she was wearing a huge yellow sweater and imitation leopardskin leggings. How did she manage to be so effortlessly glamorous?

'That's good. She's been giving you a hard time lately.'

Juliet led her into the kitchen which was overflowing as usual with unwashed dishes, toys and mountains of laundry. 'Off you go, boy.' She opened the back door and Rufus bounded into the back garden. 'And what about that mysterious young woman you think may have lived at the same address as your husband?'

'The police were going to question her but I haven't heard anything yet. By the way, I shouldn't have said anything about it to you.'

Juliet put two mugs on the table. 'Don't worry.

Discretion's my middle name.' She scrutinised Karen's face. 'I hope you're not worrying about it too much.'

'I can't help it. I'm terrified of what she might tell the police. After Erica's birthday tea, I rang Mel, you know, the man in Wales?'

'You didn't!' Juliet held the coffee pot suspended in the air. 'You dark horse! And you pretended you weren't interested!'

Karen blushed. 'I didn't intend to call him. I'd been tippling away all evening because I was so anxious about what Lucy might say to the police, and I just did it.'

'Well done you!' Juliet poured the coffee and sat down. 'What did you say to him?'

'That's the awful thing...I ended up telling him about Howard and the child abuse stuff. I didn't mean to tell him. It just came flooding out.'

'How did he react?'

'He was incredibly sympathetic. But when I woke up yesterday and remembered what I'd done, I thought he'd never speak to me again.'

'Why wouldn't he?'

'Because I thought he might think what Howard did reflected on me. But he didn't. He rang to see how I was.'

Juliet grinned. 'There, what did I tell you? He's smitten.'

Karen blushed again. 'Oh, I don't know about that.'

'And it sounds as though you are too.'

'No,' she said with embarrassment. 'It was only when I read his letter--'

'Letter? What letter?' Juliet wagged a finger at her. 'Karen Armstrong, you never said he'd written to you! Why didn't you tell me?'

'I've had other things on my mind lately. It was only a

short thank-you letter, after that time he visited us and stayed for lunch. But he sounded so kind, I suppose that's why I rang him.'

Juliet looked at her archly. 'You're just being coy, my friend.'

'And you, my friend, have been reading too many *Mills and Boons*! Can we change the subject now?'

\* \* \*

On her way home from Juliet's, Karen took Rufus on a detour through the park. It was a pleasant morning, almost warm in the low November sun. Gazing at the yellow and mahogany leaves that remained on the semi-denuded trees, she felt an unaccustomed sense of peace. But her mood was swiftly destroyed by the jangling ring tone of her mobile.

Her heart thumped when she heard Martin's voice. 'Are you at home?'

She was seized with apprehension. 'I'm out with the dog. What's happened?'

'It's better if I come round. When will you get home?'

'In about twenty minutes.'

Dragging Rufus, who strenuously resisted leaving the park, behind her, she hurried back, steeling herself for what Martin had to say.

He looked grave when he arrived and declined her offer of coffee.

Her hands trembled as she conducted him into the living room.

'Patrick and Lucy Bellamy have been interviewed separately,' he announced as soon as he sat down. 'And we've done extensive background checks on both of them.'

She perched tensely on the arm of the armchair facing him. 'Are they related?'

'Yes, they're first cousins. Patrick's father was Lucy's mother's elder brother. He's quite a bit older than Lucy. He was already an adult when she was living in Sherwood Drive.'

'Was it the same address as Howard's?' Karen was sure she already knew the answer.

'I'm afraid so. They lived in the same building in the 1990s. There were three flats. Your husband rented the top one and Lucy and her mother occupied the basement.'

'What about Patrick Bellamy? Did he live there too?'

'No, he lived about three miles away, near to a farm where he had a labouring job, but he occasionally went to visit them.'

'So both he and Lucy would have known Howard?'

'Yes.' He looked at her with a worried expression. 'You won't want to hear this.'

Karen clasped her hands together tightly. 'I think I can guess what you're going to say.'

Martin coughed and cleared his throat. 'Bellamy and your husband belonged to a group of local paedophiles who were operating in the area at the time. They were grooming vulnerable children and supplying them to members of the group.'

She shuddered. 'And that included Lucy?'

'I'm afraid so. She was passed around all the men in the gang.'

Karen gasped. Although she had been expecting something like this, hearing it acted like a blow to the solar plexus. She rose unsteadily from the armchair, walked over to the window and stood with her back to Martin while she attempted to compose herself.

Martin waited in silence until she sat down again. 'I'm sorry, Karen, it's not a pleasant story.'

'What about Lucy's parents?' she asked in a trembling voice. 'Did they know? Did she tell them what was happening?'

'She never knew who her father was and her mother was a drug- addict, totally incapable of protecting her. It sounds as though it was a hopeless situation.'

Tears pricked Karen's eyelids. 'Couldn't Social Services have helped her?'

He frowned and the strongly etched lines leading from his nose to his mouth deepened. 'I'm not sure whether they knew about it, but if they did, nothing was done to rescue her at the time. That seems to have happened a lot in those days.'

She swallowed. 'How long did the abuse last?'

'Several years I'm afraid. After her mother overdosed on heroin, Lucy was taken into Care, so she did manage to escape from the cartel in the end.'

'Did she?' Karen said dubiously. From what she had heard on the news, a child's safety wasn't guaranteed even in a children's home. 'What happened to her after that?'

'She had a series of foster homes, but none of them lasted long because the foster parents found her too challenging. After she left school and the children's home, she drifted for a few years doing a series of dead-end jobs in shops, cafés and bars. She worked as a courier for a while, delivering documents and packages for a firm in Cheltenham. But I imagine she was far too unstable to keep any job for any length of time. Last year she was treated for heroin addiction and mental health issues.'

Karen felt an overwhelming surge of sympathy for Lucy whose life had been blighted at such an early age. 'Poor girl. What a terrible life she's had. No wonder she's so damaged.'

Martin nodded. 'That's true enough. She's obviously in a very fragile emotional state.'

'How did she end up here, in Moxton?'

'About six months ago, after she was discharged from the clinic where she was being treated, she decided to track Bellamy down and confront him with what he and the other members of the group had done to her. When she discovered he'd moved to this area, she came here looking for him. She lived rough for a while, until a homeless charity picked her up and arranged for her to have a room at St Dominic's. She's been staying there for the last few months. The warden said they found her rather disruptive so he persuaded the doctor who visits the hostel to refer her to a psychotherapist.'

'Helen? The woman who runs the group we go to?'

'Maybe, I don't remember the name.'

'What about Patrick Bellamy? How did he react when Lucy confronted him?'

'She said he claimed what had happened to her as a child was entirely your husband's doing as he was the leader of the paedophile group. She seems to have believed him. Unfortunately, Patrick also told her where the *Armstrong and Murray* offices were. After that, she started hanging round outside Bartholomew Court watching for your husband. She said he often left the building at half past four on the dot.'

Karen gave a wry smile. 'That doesn't surprise me. Howard was obsessive about time-keeping.' She remembered his glowering disapproval if anyone was even just a few minutes late.

An expression of embarrassment flickered across Martin's face and he busied himself removing a piece of fluff from his sleeve. 'She said she sometimes followed him when he left work in the afternoons. She said he often went to a house in Gladstone Avenue - Maureen Field's house. She believed that was where he lived.'

'Oh,' Karen breathed. 'That must be why she thought Mo was Howard's wife.'

'I imagine so. She started watching the house. Mr Field always leaves for work at seven in the morning and doesn't get back till late in the evening, so Lucy never saw him. But she did see the daughter a few times. She seemed upset about her. She thought your husband might be abusing her.'

'That's not surprising after what had happened to her.' Karen reflected for a moment. 'It's beginning to make sense. Lucy must have told Bellamy what time Howard left work. She must have persuaded him to drive past Bartholomew Court at exactly four thirty one day and shoot him as he came out of the building.'

'No, she didn't.'

'She didn't?'

'I'm afraid not.' Martin gazed at her silently for a second. 'She talked him into lending her a gun and teaching her how to use it. Then she borrowed his motorbike and gear, she already knew how to ride a motorbike as she'd been a courier, and --'

'No!' Karen put a hand to her mouth. 'You mean it was Lucy--?'

'Yes, it was Lucy who shot your husband.'

She stared at him, speechless with astonishment.

'Fortunately we found this out just before Bellamy was due in court for the preliminary hearing.'

'Has she admitted doing it?' Karen stuttered as soon as she had regained her voice.

'In so many words, yes. Apparently she was extremely incoherent, but the detectives who interviewed her have managed to piece the story together.'

Karen continued to stare at him, stunned. 'I always thought the person who did it was a man.'

'Everybody made that assumption, including the witnesses, and I suppose *we* did too, from what we saw on the CCTV footage. Lucy's a very tall girl and she was wearing men's leathers. The perpetrator has usually been referred to as "he". To any casual observer, she would have looked like a man.'

'I can understand that.' Karen pictured Lucy with her closely cropped hair and oversized men's clothes. 'Poppy saw her a couple of times and was convinced she was a man. But if Patrick Bellamy knew what she intended to do, why didn't he try to stop her?'

'Basically, she blackmailed him. She threatened to go to the police about his involvement in child abuse and she also discovered that he had a stash of illegal firearms. But it sounds like he didn't need much persuasion. He knew that your husband had been creaming off some of the profits from the sale of child porn images, so he was happy to let her get on with it.'

Karen remained puzzled. 'But when *he* was arrested for Howard's murder, why didn't he shop Lucy to get himself off the hook?'

'Because he was an accessory to the crime. He'd lent her

the gun, the motorbike and all the gear, fully aware of what she was going to do. He knew that the evidence against him was mainly circumstantial so it was easier for him to deny everything and hope we never caught up with Lucy. After all, nobody was looking for a woman, especially not her. Mind you, if he was eventually convicted in court, I've no doubt that he would shop her in order to get a lesser sentence. By the way, the leathers, crash helmet and gloves have been found in an unused outhouse at the farm and there's no doubt that it was Lucy.'

Karen was silent for a while. 'What will happen to her?' she asked.

'I can't say, but as she's so obviously disturbed, she could be declared unfit to plead and sent for psychiatric tests or treatment. Even if she does go to trial, it's possible that the judge will order her to be detained under the Mental Health Act. As for Bellamy, I hope he gets the long sentence he deserves.'

'I don't blame Lucy for shooting Howard,' Karen declared fiercely. 'In her place I would have been tempted to do the same thing. Why the hell did he get married if he was only interested in young children?'

'It's not uncommon, Karen. Lots of paedos hide their inclinations by masquerading as respectable family men.'

She swallowed. 'You think Howard was using marriage and fatherhood to camouflage his real leanings?'

'Not necessarily. There's nothing to suggest that your husband wasn't genuinely fond of you and the children, Karen. But like many paedophiles, he was extremely clever at leading a double life and keeping them both strictly separate. And he was clearly still attracted to women, otherwise --'

'He wouldn't have had an affair with my closest friend,' she muttered bitterly.

'Perhaps not.' Martin rose to his feet. 'Anyway, thanks to you, the case is virtually wrapped up. If you hadn't come across Lucy and discovered that she used to live in Sherwood Drive, we wouldn't have put two and two together. Lucy Bellamy wasn't exactly on our radar. We probably would have worn Patrick down eventually, but that might have taken a while.'

'When will the press hear about this?' Karen asked tremulously as she accompanied him to the front door.

'There will be a press release or briefing, but not all of the information I've just told you will be given out just yet. We certainly won't divulge all the facts associated with the case at this point. The investigation into *Pied Piper* is at a sensitive stage. And given Lucy's mental state, her name probably won't be released yet either. The press will try to find out who she is of course. If they succeed, we'll probably neither confirm nor deny.'

\* \* \*

When Joan called to take Erica on her birthday shopping trip on Saturday morning, Karen motioned her into the kitchen, shutting the door carefully behind them, and told her that a woman had been charged with Howard's murder.

'A woman?' Joan exclaimed in astonishment. 'I thought a man had been arrested.'

'Yes, Patrick Bellamy. But he wasn't the one who shot Howard. It was someone Howard had abused years ago, when she was a small girl.'

'No!' Joan recoiled in shock. 'That's horrible. Who is she?'

'Her name's Lucy Bellamy, she's Patrick Bellamy's cousin. The police interviewed her after I found out that she used to live at the same address as Howard before he moved to Moxton.'

Joan stared at her open-mouthed. '*You* found out where she lived? How? Do you know her?'

Karen explained how she had met Lucy at the therapy sessions, heard her mention Sherwood Drive, then discovered her surname was the same as that of the man arrested for Howard's murder. 'The police managed to piece together the whole story after they questioned them both. They're going to provide a press statement but Lucy's name won't be released.'

Joan was stunned. 'Why didn't you tell me this before?'

'It only happened earlier this week and I felt bad about telling anybody, even the police. We're not supposed to say anything about what goes on in the emotional therapy sessions.' She heard Erica clattering down the stairs ready for her outing. 'The children don't know anything about this, Joan, so please don't say anything to Erica, or to anyone for that matter.'

# Chapter 30

*25-year-old Woman Charged with Accountant's Murder.*

Karen's heart pounded painfully when she spotted the headline as she passed a newsagents on her way to the therapy session on Monday morning. She didn't stop to read the details.

It was the last of the group sessions but this time there were only three of them attending. If Helen knew what had happened to Lucy, she gave no sign of it.

'As today is the final session,' she announced when they had finished the relaxation exercises and meditation, 'I want to consolidate what we've done so far. You have described and examined the emotions you have all been feeling. You have learned how to relax and how to take yourself to a "good place" in meditation. You have expressed your feelings to people who have passed or to those who have done you harm, and you have cut your ties with people and situations that have been holding you back. Today I'd like you to go a step further.'

Karen found it hard to concentrate on what Helen was saying. Her thoughts kept drifting back to the headline about Lucy's arrest.

'A drawback to being a psychotherapist,' Helen confided, 'is that you're not supposed to give advice. One of the reasons I started these sessions is because I found this too constraining. Sometimes vulnerable people actually want advice though they may not accept or follow it.' She picked up a black marker pen from her desk and went to the whiteboard attached to the wall in front of them.

'These are some of the emotions you told me you have been feeling.' She wrote a list of words in descending order on the board - *suffering, misery, grief, anger, hopelessness, desperation, anxiety, bitterness, hatred* - then turned to face them.

'These are common human feelings and as I said in our first session, we all experience some if not all of them during our lifetime. But if we allow them to consume us, they can do us physical as well as mental harm. For this reason, it's important to find a way of replacing or *dis*placing these emotions with more positive states of mind.' She pointed at the words on the whiteboard. 'What are the opposites of these feelings?'

'Hope?' ventured Stella timidly.

'Good, Stella, that's an extremely important one.' Helen wrote the word next to *hopelessness*. 'What else?'

'Contentment?' Karen suggested.

'Yes.' Helen wrote the word next to *suffering* and *misery*. 'Any other ideas? Charles?'

Charles fingered his chin reflectively. 'er...being calm, serene?'

'Yes. Calmness and serenity are states of mind that are the direct opposite of the effect of some of the emotions I've written here, like desperation, anger, fear and anxiety, all of which *disturb* rather than soothe the psyche.' Helen wrote the words on the board.

'Love?' suggested Stella.

'Of course, Stella.' Helen wrote the word then sat down facing them. 'I'm not saying we can experience positive feelings and states of mind just by wanting to. But we can try to achieve some of them.'

'How do we do that?' Stella asked. 'How do we achieve hope?'

'By no longer seeing yourselves as victims of events, circumstances or other people.'

Helen paused and regarded each of them steadily in turn.

Karen's ears pricked up and she started to listen attentively as she felt Helen's sharp hazel eyes on her.

'By beginning to see yourselves as valuable, worthwhile individuals in control of your own lives and your own destiny,' Helen continued. 'Of course we will always feel sorrow or grief when bad and painful things happen to us,' she continued. 'That's perfectly natural and we can't deny these emotions. We should accept them, but not allow them to control us. If we do, they will feed off us and become our *raison d'être*. If that happens, our lives will be diminished. Think of Queen Victoria and all those gloomy decades of mourning; think of Miss Havisham in her tattered wedding dress, stopping all the clocks.'

'Who's Miss Havisham?' asked Charles, puzzled.

'A character from a Dickens novel,' whispered Stella.

Helen smiled at Charles indulgently. 'Of course painful or negative emotions won't disappear overnight. But they can be displaced.'

'How?' he muttered.

'They can be displaced when we have something to aim for; something that takes our attention away from them.' Helen stood up, went to the desk and took some sheets of paper from a drawer. 'I suggest you set yourselves goals, just small ones to begin with, like, tomorrow I'm going to start reading a new book. Tomorrow I'm going to smile at people when I pass them. Tomorrow I'm going to contact a friend I haven't seen for a while. When you've achieved the first goal, set yourself another one, and so on. Make it incremental.'

'How will that help?' Stella asked.

'Having a goal or purpose creates hope, Stella; achievement of a goal brings satisfaction, and satisfaction can block negative feelings.'

Karen thought of her own small steps to shake off misery and depression - getting rid of Howard's ashes and his clothes, changing the furniture, buying a car, getting a dog. She saw these now as achievements of small goals which had indeed temporarily distracted her from the negative emotions aroused by Howard's actions.

After handing each of them a sheet of paper, Helen put a pot of pens and pencils on the desk. 'For today's exercise, I want each of you to imagine, then try to express in a drawing, something positive that you would like to happen in the future - something you would like to do, something you'd like to change, *anything*, so long as it's positive. Just draw whatever comes to mind, but don't make it something that would be impossible to achieve, like winning the Lottery, as this will only reinforce negative feelings.' She laughed when she saw their alarmed expressions. 'Don't worry, I'm not expecting Picasso! You can write rather than draw if you want, but expressing something graphically can sometimes be more intuitive or revealing than putting it into words.'

The three of them sat motionless with indecision for a

few minutes. Then Charles took a pencil from the pot and held it uncertainly over his sheet before starting to make tentative marks.

Stella picked a pen and after a moment's thought, began to scribble on the paper.

Karen stared at her blank sheet for a long moment before grasping a handful of coloured pencils. She found herself drawing a crude picture of the sea, a wide sandy beach and a cliff. On top of the cliff she sketched a small house. In front of it she drew four two-legged figures and a four-legged one.

\* \* \*

'It's been mentioned on the news,' Joan said breathlessly, when she called at the house after finishing work. 'It's been announced that a woman's been arrested for shooting Howard.'

'I know.' Karen led her into the kitchen and shut the door. 'I'm glad you've come, Joanie. I want to ask you something.'

'Oh yes?'

'Now that the press knows about Lucy, what Howard did to her is bound to come out sooner or later and there'll be gossip, especially in a small place like this. When it happens, could we go and stay in the cottage again as it hasn't been sold yet?'

'Of course you can.' Joan backed away as Rufus snuffled round her legs. 'Though it will be cold there in winter.'

'I don't mind that.' Karen pulled Rufus away from her and he settled back on his blanket, emitting a deep rumbling sound.

'When do you think you'll need to go there?'

'It depends on the preliminary hearing.' Karen surprised herself by speaking about it so calmly. 'If Lucy's considered fit to plea, the case will be sent to Crown Court, though that probably won't happen till early next year. But if the media discover her connection with Howard before then, I'd rather we were in a place where people don't know us.' She smiled uncertainly at Joan. 'It might mean going to the cottage before Christmas though I hope it won't come to that.'

Joan looked crestfallen. 'But you always spend Christmas with us.'

'I know, but if people find out about Howard's connection to Lucy beforehand, we'd have to go then. Simon's already been bullied because of what happened to his father and Erica's had abusive messages from kids at school. I keep warning her not to go on social media sites but she won't listen. If it happens again, I'll take them out of school before the end of term.'

'Would that be a good idea?' Joan asked doubtfully. 'They won't want to miss Christmas here, will they? Erica's really excited about the school party and disco. She bought a dress specially for it when we went shopping on Saturday. She'll be dreadfully disappointed if she can't go.' Karen felt her resolve slipping. 'It probably won't come to that, but we'll definitely have to get away sooner or later. And when we're in Wales, I'm going to start looking at properties.'

'Properties?' Joan exclaimed in surprise. 'Why?'

'I'm going to put the house on the market as soon as the deeds are in my name. I've made up my mind.'

Joan gazed at her, dumbfounded. 'That's a bit over the

top, isn't it? Whatever happens, things are bound to blow over eventually.'

'Maybe, but I don't want to be here before they do.'

'But what about the children? Have you discussed moving to Wales with them?'

'Not yet, but they all loved it there.'

'That was in the autumn, Karen. It will be different there in winter. The weather can be really bad in the west. How can you make such a decision when you spent such a short time there? How will the children feel about leaving their schools and their friends?'

Karen had anticipated this argument. 'There'll be other schools, other friends - people who won't know that Howard was their father. In the first instance I'll just tell them that a woman has confessed to their father's murder and that we need to go away for a while to escape the publicity. I won't raise the subject of a permanent move until we're there and only when I think it's the right moment. I don't want them to have to deal with too many new situations at once. I think Simon and Poppy will be OK with the idea, though Erica will probably make a fuss. But even she may accept the change when she knows the reason for it.'

Joan's eyes widened. 'You mean you're going to tell them about Howard?'

Karen shuddered. 'I'll probably have to, before they hear the sordid details from someone else. I need to figure out the best way of doing it. I may ring the child protection helpline again and ask for advice. I won't say anything to Poppy, of course.'

Joan's eyes had started to brim with tears. 'I don't want you to leave Moxton, Karen. You and the children are the only family I've got apart from Greg. I'll miss you all so much.'

Karen's own eyes started to smart. 'And I'll miss you, Joanie. You've been a wonderful sister and friend. But don't worry. Nothing's going to happen overnight. It could take ages to sell this place and find somewhere to move to near the Gower.'

Joan removed her glasses and mopped her eyes. 'Has this got something to do with that man you met, the one who visited you?' she asked suspiciously.

Karen reflected before she answered. 'No, it's nothing to do with him, though it's good to know that I'll have at least one friend there.'

Joan regarded her gravely. 'This is a very big decision, Karen, not one to be made on the spur of the moment. There are four of you to consider. Are you sure you've given it enough thought?'

Karen knew she hadn't, but she was convinced that it was the right decision. It had come to her in a light-bulb moment when she had drawn that picture during Helen's last session. 'My mind's made up, Joan. All my life I've tried to do what other people wanted or expected of me, but now I have to stand on my own feet and do what feels best for me, for all of us. And moving to Wales feels right.'

'Then you'd better start preparing the children.'

Karen didn't have any choice in the matter because, at that moment, Erica and Simon hurtled noisily into the kitchen.

'Is it true?' Erica shrieked. 'Was it a *woman* who shot Dad? We just heard someone say it on the TV.'

Karen quickly shut the door behind them.

'Is it true, Mum?' Simon asked anxiously.

'Yes it is true.'

'What woman? Who is she?' Erica's face had turned crimson with emotion.

'She's a ... very disturbed young woman.'

'*Why* did she shoot Dad?' Erica shouted. 'What was the reason?'

Karen exchanged a quick glance with Joan. 'That's something the police have to find out before a trial.'

'Sometimes the people who do this kind of thing aren't very well, my darling,' Joan said gently. 'They're ill.'

'Do you mean she's mad?'

Joan shook her head. 'That's not the right word, Erica. She may be mentally ill, in which case she wouldn't have been in her right mind when she did it.'

Erica clenched and unclenched her fists. 'I don't care if she was in her right mind or not. I *hate* her! I hope they send her to prison for the rest of her life.'

'Calm down, Erica.' Karen put an arm round her. 'I've just been asking Auntie Joan whether we could use the cottage in the Gower again.' She picked her words carefully. 'There's bound to be a lot of media attention on the case and the press may try to dig up unpleasant stuff about Dad.'

'What stuff?' Erica impatiently shook off her arm. Her eyes blazed. 'Why would they? Dad didn't do anything. It wasn't his fault he got shot.'

'It's what the tabloids do. They like to sensationalise every story, look for gruesome details.'

'Even when they're not true?'

'I'm afraid so. So in case that happens, we have to go away for a while. And Auntie Joan says we can use the cottage again.'

Simon beamed. 'Wicked! We can see Mel.'

Joan frowned. 'Is he the man you met there?'

'Yes,' Simon turned to her eagerly. 'He's really nice, Auntie Joan. He sent me a book on dinosaurs for my project.'

Joan didn't seem impressed.

Erica's expression was thunderous. 'I don't want to go.'

'I didn't mean we're going to the cottage right now,' Karen said reassuringly. 'But there's a small chance we might have to spend Christmas there, though it's more likely to be the New Year.'

Erica rounded on her furiously. 'Christmas? Are you serious? I'm *not* going to miss Lisa's Christmas party and the school disco.'

'You probably won't miss either of them. I just wanted to warn you it could be on the cards if things get unpleasant for us here. We'd still have a proper Christmas.'

'Maybe Greg and I could come too,' Joan suggested. 'We could book into a hotel nearby, so we could all be together.'

Karen felt embarrassed. 'What about Greg? He might not like the idea.'

'Greg will do what I tell him!'

# Chapter 31

Christmas approached. Although Karen forced herself to start the usual preparations, her thoughts were elsewhere and anything but festive. Martin had told her that Lucy was being kept in a secure facility pending the preparation of a report on her mental state. Her name hadn't been released and although reporters had been trying to find out who she was, no-one had yet succeeded.

Karen wasn't reassured. She was convinced that once Lucy's story was revealed, the children would hear about Howard's role in her abuse. In desperation she rang the child protection helpline she had contacted earlier.

'After my husband died earlier this year,' she told the woman who answered the phone (a different voice this time), 'I found out that he had been involved in child pornography.'

'Oh dear. I'm so sorry.'

Karen's voice trembled. 'I have three children and --'

'We can help,' the woman said quickly. 'There are people here who are trained to provide help and support for children who have been sexually abused.'

'No, he didn't abuse *them*. But he did abuse other children. The police know about it and I'm afraid my own children are eventually going to find out about it. When they do, how can I explain it to them?' Karen heard her voice rising hysterically. 'How will they cope with knowing that their father did such dreadful things?'

'I do understand your problem,' the woman murmured sympathetically. 'How old are your children?'

'Fourteen, eleven and six.'

'The little one could be too young to understand, so I wouldn't recommend saying anything to him or her just yet, but for the other two, there are specially trained counsellors and therapists they can talk to on an individual basis. There are also numbers they can ring any time of the day or night. I can give you all the details.'

'Thank you,' Karen said quickly. 'I don't want to give them that information until it's absolutely necessary. But what can I say to them myself if I need to, before they hear about it from someone else?'

'There's no easy way to tell them, I'm afraid. I can only give you some very simple advice.'

'Yes?'

'I would suggest that you sit down with them and have the conversation in a calm atmosphere. Make sure there are no distractions. Explain that their father did some very bad things and you want to help them deal with it. Try to make what you tell them age-appropriate. The language and kind of detail you use will depend on how mature the two eldest children are. You needn't be totally explicit, but do tell them the basic truth: that their father did unacceptable things to other children; that he touched them in a bad, indeed a criminal way.'

Karen shuddered. 'It will be so hard to tell them that.'

'I know, and that's why it would be better for them to speak to an expert as your own emotions could get in the way.'

'I understand,' Karen whispered. 'But I still need to know the best way to deal with their reaction when they learn about their father.'

'There are a few basic things I can suggest. It's very important for your children to understand that what their father did wasn't anything to do with *them*. It wasn't their fault. They didn't cause him to abuse others. You must make that clear.'

'Yes, I know how important that is.'

'Let them express how they feel about what you've told them and be prepared for them to take their anger and pain out on you. You'll be telling them the last thing they'll ever want to hear. They'll feel loyal to their father and very resentful that you're telling them stuff that will taint his memory.'

Karen sighed. 'Yes, I'd expect that.'

'However explosively they react, try to stay calm. Assure them they can speak to you about what has happened at any time, and if they don't feel comfortable talking to you, tell them you can arrange for them to speak to a specially trained person either in person or on the phone. If you give me your postal or email address, I'll send you all the details.'

'Thank you, that's very helpful.' Karen felt slightly better armed with this information although she dreaded having to use it.

\* \* \*

At the beginning of the third week in December, her worst fears were realised. She was standing in a queue at the local post office when she spotted a headline on the front page of a tabloid in the newspaper rack: *Was Murder Victim Armstrong a Paedophile?* Underneath it, written in smaller typeface, she read, *Homeless Woman held on Murder Charge.*

She froze in horror for a second then hurriedly left the shop. As she stooped to untie Rufus from the lamp post where she had left him, she heard a familiar voice hailing her. Looking up, her heart sank as she saw Celia Murray hastening across the road towards her. She was wearing a light-coloured, belted coat that accentuated her rotund form.

'Have you seen what the papers are saying?' Celia began without any greeting, 'they're saying that Howard was a *paedophile*? A *paedophile*!' Her features formed a grimace of disgust. 'Is it true?'

Karen made no response. It was uncanny how Celia Murray always seemed to turn up at the most inopportune moments.

'It's absolutely shocking. Though it could explain a lot of thing Geoff is devastated.' Celia's protruding eyes glittered malevolently behind her glasses. 'Is it true?' she repeated. 'Did you know, Karen? What do you make of it?'

'Nothing,' Karen muttered angrily, fumbling with the lead. 'Rumours and innuendo, that's all. You shouldn't believe everything you read in the tabloids, Celia.'

'Well, the story must have come from somewhere. No smoke without fire. Are you sure you--?'

'I don't know anything about it,' Karen snapped. After she had succeeded in releasing Rufus from the lamp post, he leapt up at Celia and tried to lick her face. Standing on his hind legs he was nearly as tall as she was.

Celia stumbled backwards, yelling, 'get *off*.'

'He's only being friendly.' Karen pretended to pull Rufus away from her but deliberately kept the lead slack. 'I think he likes you.'

'Get off!' Celia shrieked again, pushing at Rufus with both hands. 'Get your dirty paws off my coat.'

'Down, Rufus!' Karen tightened the lead and pulled Rufus away from her.

'That dog's a menace!' Celia dabbed frantically at the front of her coat. 'You should keep it under better control. Look at the filthy marks it's made. I'll have to take my coat to the dry cleaners.'

Karen didn't bother to respond. 'Good boy, Rufus!' she murmured as she walked rapidly away from Celia with him trotting along beside her. But the moment of satisfaction was brief and quickly replaced by a sense of desperation. She and the children must get away as soon as possible.

She rushed home and rang Joan.

Her sister reacted with dismay when she heard about the headline. 'I didn't expect it to happen so quickly. Of course you must go to the cottage. I'll ring Mrs Lewis. She's still got a spare key. I'll ask her to put the heating on and air some sheets. Don't worry about anything. I'll check on the house while you're away. And if I can find a suitable hotel in the area, we'll come and join you for Christmas.'

Next, Karen rang Martin. He said he had been expecting her call.

'How did they find out?' she asked.

'There's a limit to what can be reported about a preliminary hearing for indictable offences, but I'm afraid a local reporter did a bit of snooping and found out about Lucy and her relationship to Patrick Bellamy. After that, others picked up the story.'

Karen groaned. 'But how do they know about Howard?'

'They probably don't. But they must have discovered that Bellamy is on the Sex Offenders' Register and a member of a notorious paedophile ring. So they're assuming your husband might also have been involved, especially as there's a much younger woman involved. It's sheer speculation, Karen. That's why the headline you saw is a question rather than a statement.'

Karen's hand shook as she held the phone. 'We'll have to get away, Martin. I'm going to take the children to my brother-in-law's cottage in Wales as soon as possible to protect them from any fall- out. If I can make the necessary arrangements, we'll probably go tomorrow.'

'I don't blame you. If there are any developments I'll let you know.'

After finishing the call, Karen sent a quick text to Juliet explaining what had happened, then started to pack. She filled bags with supplies from the kitchen and put the Christmas presents she had already bought for the children into a box. She went upstairs and packed cases for herself and Poppy. Simon and Erica could sort out their own things when they returned from school. Hopefully the rumours wouldn't have reached there yet. She was relieved that Erica hadn't missed Lisa's party and the school disco, but judging from the dreamy expression that had recently appeared on her daughter's face, Karen had a strong suspicion that she might have acquired a new boyfriend to replace the faithless Jamie. She anticipated resistance.

Poppy's eyes widened when Karen brought her home from school and she saw the suitcases and boxes in the hall. 'What's happening, Mummy?'

'It's a surprise! We're going to Wales tomorrow, to the cottage where we went before.'

'Yeh!' Poppy shouted with delight. 'Does that mean I don't have to go to school tomorrow?'

'Yes, you're having the last days off. I want you to pack the toys and books you want to take with you in your wheelie bag, not too many, or they won't all fit in.'

Poppy ran eagerly upstairs.

Karen's phone vibrated. It was an answering text from Juliet: *dont let the wnkrs get you down good luck keep in touch J xx*

When Erica and Simon returned from school, they too stared in amazement at the pile of luggage in the hall.

'What's all this?' Erica asked suspiciously.

'We're going to Wales tomorrow. We'll be spending Christmas there.'

'Cool!' Simon exclaimed, but Erica looked thunder-struck.

'Tomorrow? School hasn't finished yet.'

'I'm going to ring the head this afternoon and tell her you'll have to miss the last three days.'

'Why?' Erica demanded. '*Why* do we have to go so soon?'

'Because the press has found out the name of the woman who shot your dad.'

'So? What difference does that make?'

'It might get unpleasant for us here, Erica.'

'Why? Why might it get unpleasant?'

'Because reporters will be hanging around again, trying to find out information.'

'What information? We don't know anything.'

Remembering the advice of the woman on the helpline,

Karen knew now wasn't the time to reveal the truth. 'We'll be leaving in the morning,' she said firmly, 'so I want you and Simon to pack tonight. You'll need warm clothes and boots. We'll take all the Christmas things.'

'But--'

'No buts, Erica. We're going and that's that.'

'I don't *want* to go!' Erica yelled. Her dark eyes flashed with rage. 'I'll stay with Auntie Joan.'

'You can't. They'll be coming to join us.'

Simon ran excitedly upstairs and eventually, discovering that her furious protests were in vain, Erica reluctantly followed him. When Karen went up later, she heard her muttering furiously to someone on her phone. 'Mum says we've got to go tomorrow. I *hate* her! She's *so* unreasonable. It means I won't be able to come on Saturday.'

# Chapter 32

The drive to Wales was an ordeal. Erica sat hunched in the front passenger seat and remained mutinously silent throughout the entire journey. Sitting in the back, Simon and Poppy grumbled incessantly about being cramped on either side of Rufus, with their feet propped on boxes and bags.

Karen, still a nervous driver, felt tense and her spirits didn't rise when they finally got to the Gower only to find the breathtaking views obscured by low cloud and heavy rain. The cottage, however, was warm as Mrs Lewis, the kindly next-door neighbour, had switched on the antiquated central heating. She had also left milk and bread for them in the kitchen, together with a written invitation to call by for a cup of tea when they arrived. After Karen had rung Joan to reassure her that they had reached their destination without mishap, they gratefully took advantage of the offer, which turned out to include freshly baked scones with cream and jam.

By the time they left Mrs Lewis's house, there was just enough daylight to take Rufus for a quick walk. Karen left the children unpacking and set off with him along the coastal path. As the rain battered her umbrella and the wind did its best to prise it from her grasp, she wondered if she had made a terrible mistake coming to Wales in December. On returning to the cottage, she plucked up the courage to ring Mel and announce their arrival, but there was no reply. She left him a message.

After an improvised meal, she and the children spent the rest of the evening in the small living room. Dominated by an oversized sofa bed and two matching armchairs, it felt crowded and slightly claustrophobic when the curtains were drawn. She hadn't been aware of this when they had visited in October.

Simon found some ancient board games in a cupboard and persuaded Karen and Poppy to play Monopoly. Erica, however, loftily refused to join in, claiming it was boring. She slouched on the sofa, scowling and uttering long drawn-out sighs before beginning to text furiously on her phone.

As soon as the game had finished, Karen accompanied Poppy up to the bedroom they were sharing and was helping her prepare for bed when she heard Erica utter a loud cry. Seconds later, Simon pounded up the rickety stairs.

She rushed to the bedroom door. 'What's the matter, Simon?' His face was flushed. 'There was something about Dad on TV.'

Karen's heart missed a beat. She stepped on to the landing and gave Simon a warning look when Poppy joined them, looking puzzled. 'Why was Erica shouting?' she asked Simon.

'It's nothing, darling,' Karen said quickly. 'She...can't find the TV remote, that's all.' She turned to Simon. 'I'll come down and look for it in a minute.'

Simon nodded and retreated downstairs.

Karen waited anxiously for Poppy to fall asleep before

following him. When she entered the living room, she found Simon hovering by the door and Erica crouched in front of the old-fashioned television set in the corner. 'What's happened?' she asked, although she already knew the answer.

Erica switched off the television and rose shakily to her feet. Her face was white. 'They're saying they think Dad was...that he could have been... a *paedo*!'

Karen's heart started to beat so fast that she put a hand to her chest in a vain attempt to slow it down. 'Who's saying?'

'It was on the news. We heard it when I was changing channels.'

'Are you sure? What exactly did the newsreader say?'

Erica's voice was husky with emotion. 'She said...she said the police are investigating the possibility that Dad was shot because he was a paedophile and may have been part of a network of people involved in child pornography.'

'It's not true is it, Mum?' Simon, his thin face creased with anxiety, tugged frantically at her sleeve. 'Paedophiles are people who hurt children aren't they?'

'Yes, darling, they are.'

'But Dad didn't hurt us,' he said tremulously.

Karen's legs gave way beneath her and she collapsed on to one of the worn armchairs. 'Sit down both of you. I need to talk to you.'

Simon sank on to the armchair facing her and Erica perched reluctantly on the edge of the faded sofa, nervously clasping and unclasping her fingers on her lap. 'Why are they saying things like that?' she demanded fiercely, 'it's not true.'

Karen took a deep breath. 'This is exactly what I wanted to avoid,' she began, 'I didn't want you to hear it from--'

'What?' Erica leapt to her feet. 'You mean you already *knew* what they're saying?'

Karen made a supreme effort to keep her voice steady. This was the most difficult thing she had ever had to do in her life and she was desperate to remain calm. 'Please keep your voice down, Erica. I don't want Poppy to wake up. And whatever you do, don't mention anything about this to her.' She paused, seeking the necessary courage. 'I'm really sorry to have to tell you this, but after your dad died, the police discovered that he had done some very bad things.'

Erica and Simon stared at her, stupefied.

'I'm afraid it *is* true what they're saying.' She swallowed. 'Your father *was* a member of a paedophile ring and he was involved in selling child pornography.'

'No!' Erica almost screamed. 'You're *lying*. I don't believe you.'

'The police have the evidence, Erica. They found ...' she swallowed hard, '...they found hundreds of indecent images of children on his computer. I'm so sorry.'

'They're lying.' Erica's voice had become hoarse with emotion and her face had turned from white to crimson.

Simon's gazed at Karen beseechingly. '*Are* the police lying, Mum?'

Karen gulped. 'I'm afraid they're not lying, darling. They think the young woman who shot your father did it because he... abused her, years ago, when she was a little girl.'

'No!' Erica uttered an agonised cry. 'You told us that woman's mad, crazy. She must have made it up. Dad wouldn't...he couldn't...' She collapsed back on to the sofa and burst into a storm of anguished crying.

Simon had also started to sob.

Karen felt as though her heart would break. She went and sat down beside Erica and put an arm round her shoulders, trying with difficulty to control her own emotion. 'I wish it wasn't true, darling. I'm so sorry you had to hear about it like this. I would have done anything in my power to spare you finding out because I knew how much it would hurt you.'

Erica violently shook off her arm. 'The police have got it wrong. Why do you believe them? You're just as bad as they are. Dad wouldn't hurt *anyone*.'

Karen gazed at her helplessly. 'I'm afraid everything the police have found out about your father is true, darling. I know how hard it's going to be, but we're all going to have to try to deal with it.' She felt she was floundering.

Erica rounded on her in fury. 'What do you mean, *deal* with it? How *can* we deal with the police telling lies about Dad?'

Although she was trembling, Karen tried to appear calm. 'There are people you can talk to, trained counsellors, who know how you feel and what you're going through. They'll be able to help. I have the phone numbers. You can ring them any time.'

'I'm not going to speak to *strangers* about *this*,' Erica was almost screaming. 'It's disgusting, it's *gross*. And it's not *true*, any of it.'

Karen put a restraining hand on her arm. 'Keep your voice down, Erica, or you'll wake Poppy.'

Simon rose from his chair. He was trembling. 'Why did Dad hurt children, Mum? Who were they?'

'I don't know, Simon. I really don't know.' She stood up and put her arms round him, feeling powerless to comfort him. After a few seconds she released him and addressed the two of them in as steady a voice as she could muster. 'I want both of you to understand that whatever your father did - and I don't know the extent of it - had absolutely nothing to do with you. You're not responsible. But we need to be prepared. Now that the press has got hold of this, there's bound to be unpleasant publicity; people will start whispering and some may say hurtful things about us. They'll assume we knew what your dad was doing. That's why we had to leave home so suddenly. I wanted to come to a place where hardly anyone knows us. But even while we're here, unkind people may say things or send us nasty messages.'

She turned to Erica and said softly, 'I don't think you should go on social media sites for a while, darling.'

'*What*? If you think I'm going to…' Erica stopped midsentence and her expression abruptly changed to one of consternation. 'What are my friends going to think when they hear about this? *They* won't know it's not true. If they believe Dad was a…a paedo, they won't speak to me anymore.' She burst into anguished tears.

Karen tried to take her hand but was rebuffed. 'In that case, they're *not* your friends, Erica. Real friends would support you in a situation like this.'

Erica's sobs redoubled. 'What about Ryan? What will he think?'

'Who's Ryan?' Karen asked, perplexed.

'A boy I know. This is the worst thing that has ever happened to me.' Erica ran out of the room and pounded upstairs. A few seconds later Karen heard her footsteps in the room above. She turned her attention to Simon. 'You should go to bed, darling, we're all tired after the journey, and you've had a terrible shock.'

He blinked unhappily at her and tugged at his earlobe. 'Is it really true, Mum? *Did* Dad do awful things?'

Karen sighed and stroked his hair. 'I'm afraid so, darling. There's no denying it. The police have the evidence. But I promise you, we *will* get over this. As long as we all have each other, we'll be OK.' She realised she was saying this to reassure herself as much as him. 'Now where's your sleeping bag?'

She helped Simon open the sofa and make up a bed, then sat with him till he fell asleep. When she went upstairs, she could hear muffled crying coming from Erica's room. She knocked gently on the door and went in.

Erica was lying on her side in a foetal position.

Karen sat on the side of the bed. 'I'm so sorry, darling,' she murmured to Erica's back. 'It was terrible for you to have to hear about it like that.'

Erica rolled over, her face swollen and tear-stained. 'Why?' she sobbed, '*why* do you believe the lies they're telling about Dad? You should be defending him, not agreeing with them. You're as bad as they are.'

Karen smoothed Erica's hair away from her forehead. 'We can't ignore the evidence, darling. I was just as shocked and devastated as you are when I found out.'

'Go away!' Erica hissed. 'I hate you!' She rolled back and faced the wall.

Karen got up and left the room, overcome with fury towards Howard for causing his own children so much misery.

She tiptoed into the bedroom she was sharing with

Poppy. The little girl was lying peacefully asleep in the double bed with her arms round a toy penguin. Karen gazed down at her with a heavy heart. Would there ever be a right time for her to hear the awful truth about her father? She couldn't bear the thought of Poppy's childhood innocence being abruptly destroyed.

Before getting into bed beside her, she checked her phone. There was still no reply from Mel. She wondered if he had also heard the news and, despite his earlier declarations of sympathy and support, had decided to have nothing more to do with her.

# Chapter 33

The next morning Karen was woken by a bird singing. As she struggled into full wakefulness, she realised it wasn't a bird. It was a child's high treble voice. Poppy was sitting up in bed beside her, singing *Away in a Manger* to her penguin.

Glancing at her watch, Karen saw that it was just after eight. Within seconds, the memory of the previous evening came flooding back and she was immediately plunged into despair. As there was no noise from the other bedroom or from downstairs, she assumed Erica and Simon were still asleep. She dreaded witnessing their distress again.

'Mummy,' Poppy chirped, 'is it going to be Christmas soon?'

'Yes,' she responded with false cheerfulness. 'Very soon, darling. Stay in bed while I go and put the heating on.'

Swinging her legs over the side of the bed, she got up and pulled on some clothes, then opened the faded curtains. It was another dreary wet day. She sighed, feeling more miserable than at any time since Howard had died. Leaving Poppy in bed, she went downstairs, switched on the heating and filled the kettle. While waiting for it to boil, she fed Rufus then went to the back door - the best place in the cottage to get a signal - and rang Joan's home number.

'Karen?' Joan sounded surprised at the early call. 'Is everything OK?'

'No, everything's not OK. Howard was mentioned on the TV news yesterday evening. Apparently the newsreader said there's speculation that he could have been a member of a child porn ring.'

She heard Joan take a sharp inhalation of breath. 'You didn't hear it then?'

'No, we were out last night. I hope the children didn't--'

'They did. I'm afraid Erica and Simon heard it.'

'Oh no!' Joan gasped in dismay.

'They're absolutely distraught, especially Erica. She refuses to believe what they're saying and thinks I'm the Wicked Witch of the West because I had to tell them it was true. It was one of the worst evenings of my life, Joan. Erica's in a terrible state.'

'I'm not surprised,' Joan said grimly. 'Poor girl must be devastated.'

'Would *you* speak to her,' Karen pleaded. 'Call her on her mobile. She listens to you. Try and convince her that I'm not colluding with the police in telling lies about her father.'

'Of course. I'll try, though I'm not sure that anything I say will help. It's a terrible thing for any child to find out about their dad. What about Simon, how has he reacted?'

'He's absolutely devastated too, but I think he believes it. Poppy doesn't know anything.'

'When would be a good time to ring?'

'A bit later if you can. Erica's not up yet. If there's *any-thing* you can think of that might soften the blow…Just a minute, Joan, I think I can hear Simon coming down.

Speak later.' Karen quickly ended the call.

Simon wandered into the kitchen. He looked sleepy and was shivering in his thin pyjamas. 'It's cold. Who were you speaking to?'

'Auntie Joan. I've put the heating on so it should warm up soon. Use the bathroom before Erica gets up. You know how long she takes in there.'

Simon lingered by the kitchen door, his face puckered with anxiety. 'Mum,' he murmured uncertainly.

'Yes?'

'That bad stuff they say Dad's done, does everyone know about it?'

'Who's everyone?'

'People at home, in Moxton.'

Karen chose her words carefully, 'I suppose *some* of them may have heard it on the news, but not everybody.'

He pulled at his earlobe. 'But if some people know, it'll get round school and those boys will start picking on me again.'

'No they won't,' Karen said fiercely. 'That is *not* going to happen, Simon. I'll make sure it doesn't.'

'How? You won't be there. How can you stop them?'

'If necessary, we'll change your school.' She thought it was time to start preparing the ground for the idea of a permanent move.

'Change school?' He looked bewildered.

'It's just a thought, Simon.'

At that moment Poppy entered the kitchen clutching her penguin.

'How many days left till Christmas, Mummy?'

'Just a few.' Christmas with its obligatory festivities was the last thing on Karen's mind, but now she thought it might turn out to be a welcome distraction.

'Can we put the decorations up?'

'Yes, they're still in the box. You can put them up after breakfast. You can be in charge, Poppy.'

Poppy's face glowed with a happiness that was in stark contrast to how the rest of the family were feeling. 'Will we get a Christmas tree?'

Karen hadn't thought about a tree. 'Yes, we'll have to see if we can find one here. Go and get dressed quickly, darling, I don't want you to catch cold; you too, Simon.'

Poppy trotted back upstairs followed, more slowly, by Simon.

Karen had just put a packet of cereal and some bowls on the table when Erica came down. Her eyes were red and puffy. She stood at the kitchen door and fixed Karen with a hostile stare.

Karen thought it best to act normally. 'Would you like some cereal, Erica?'

'No, I'm not hungry.'

'Well have some tea then. I'm just making it.'

Erica marched out of the kitchen without answering. Seconds later, Karen heard the living room door bang. Almost immediately, Rufus started to bark. He was pawing at the back door. She waited until Simon and Poppy had come down for breakfast, then put on his lead. She took him to the living room where she found Erica lying on the sofa with her eyes shut, listening to something on her iPod. Tinny sounds of pop music leaked from her headphones.

'Erica,' Karen said loudly, 'could you take Rufus for a quick walk while Simon and Poppy are having their breakfast?'

Erica ignored her.

Karen repeated the question with the same result. She sighed. 'In that case, I'll take him myself. I'm leaving you in charge. There's tea in the pot if you want it. I'll be about ten minutes.'

There was still no reply.

Karen pulled on her raincoat and left the cottage with the dog. It was a raw, damp day. A bitter wind was blowing and the sky was black with menacing rainclouds. She walked about a hundred yards then let Rufus off the lead. He sped off and disappeared round a bend in the path. Shortly afterwards, she heard him barking in the distance. 'Rufus!' she called, hastening to follow him, 'come here!'

When she rounded the bend she spotted him running round in circles with another dog - a dog that looked familiar. The tall man walking towards her, also looked familiar.

As he drew closer, he stopped and regarded her in amazement. 'Karen? What a lovely surprise. I thought that dog was like Rufus. Why didn't you tell me you were coming? When did you arrive?'

'Yesterday. I rang you. Didn't you get my message?'

'What message?' Puzzled, he took his phone out of his pocket and tapped into it. 'Ah...no wonder, it needs charging.' He beamed at her. 'Where are the children?'

'Having breakfast. I had to leave them for a few minutes. Rufus needed to go out.'

'Are you staying at the cottage?'

'Yes. Just for a while.'

'Well it's wonderful to see you. How are you?'

To her shame and humiliation, she burst into tears.

'Karen, my dear.' He reached awkwardly for her hand. 'What's happened?'

'It's…it's…' but she was crying too hard to finish the sentence.

'Tell me.' He put his arms around her and for a moment she pressed her head against his chest, then quickly, with acute embarrassment, extricated herself from his embrace. Mopping her eyes, she stutteringly told him what Erica and Simon had heard on the news.

'Oh dear.' His pleasant face was a picture of concern. 'I'm so sorry. That's extremely regrettable. They will have taken it very badly, I assume.'

'Yes, especially Erica. I knew the press had got hold of the story, that's why I brought them here, to prevent them hearing about it. They're absolutely distraught and I don't know how to comfort them.' She shivered in the cold wind. 'I'd better get back. I don't like leaving them on their own. I said I'd only be a few minutes.'

Mel accompanied her as far as the cottage gate. 'Why don't you all come round for tea this afternoon,' he suggested before they separated. 'You know where I live. I'll get some cakes or something from the village shop. It'll take a bit of the pressure off you if Simon and Erica have someone else to talk to. I won't mention what's happened, of course.'

'Thank you, we'd love to.'

'About three?'

'Perfect.' Karen prised Rufus away from Elvis and hurried inside.

The living room was empty but Simon and Poppy were still sitting at the table in the kitchen.

'I just bumped into Mel and Elvis,' she told them breathlessly. 'We're going to his house for tea this afternoon.'

Simon perked up. 'Cool!'

Poppy scrutinised her face. 'Have you been crying, Mummy?'

'No darling, it's just the wind. It made my eyes water. Where's

Erica?'

'She had a phone call.' Simon pushed his empty cereal bowl away. 'I don't think she wanted us to hear. She went out the back to answer it.'

Glancing through the kitchen window, Karen spotted Erica standing tensely by the back door with her mobile clamped to her ear. She hoped the call was from Joan.

After about ten minutes, Erica came indoors. She passed silently through the kitchen and went straight upstairs. Karen thought it advisable to leave her to her own devices for a while. 'Come on Poppy,' she said with feigned cheerfulness. 'If you've finished your breakfast, you can put the Christmas decorations up now.'

Squealing with delight, Poppy jumped up from the table.

'You can help too, Simon.'

Simon rose unenthusiastically and slowly followed Poppy into the living room.

Karen fetched the box from the back of the car and watched as the two of them hung shiny baubles from the lamps and shelves and draped tinsel across every available surface. After years of suffering Howard's disapproval of "gaudy clutter" at Christmas time, she was pleased to see the brightness the decorations imparted to the drab room.

\* \* \*

Mel's living room, unlike the one in their cottage, was spacious and had a comfortable, lived-in look that made Karen feel instantly at home. Ceiling-high bookcases overflowed with books and scholarly journals. Those that couldn't be accommodated on the shelves lay in untidy piles on the floor. The furniture was defiantly old-fashioned. A magnificent mahogany grandfather clock with a swinging pendulum, ticked loudly in a corner. Opposite it stood an antique glass cabinet in which three exquisitely-crafted model ships complete with masts and sails, were prominently displayed. The only concessions to modernity were a wide-screen television and a matching chrome DVD player.

Karen was pleased to see a log fire burning in a huge open hearth. The leaping flames and the mellow light emanating from several fringed lamps, made the room feel cosy in the darkening afternoon. Mel had arranged chairs around the fire and was frequently obliged to push Elvis and Rufus off the rug in front of it so that they could all feel the benefit of the warmth.

Karen watched the children anxiously. Poppy was intrigued by the massive pendulum swinging from side to side inside the clock and Simon appeared mesmerised by the model ships. She was relieved to see that he looked slightly less distressed. Erica, however, was very subdued. She hadn't wanted to come but Karen had insisted. Now she sat silently by the fire, gazing blankly into the flames.

Mel glanced at Erica worriedly as he served them tea and passed round biscuits and small iced cakes. He apologised for the absence of Christmas decorations. 'I wasn't expecting visitors and as there's only myself and Elvis here, I don't bother with such things these days.'

'Are you staying here for Christmas then?' Karen asked politely. She experienced a slight jolt of disappointment when he announced that he would be spending the festival with his sister and her family in Carnarvon. 'My sons and their girlfriends will be joining us. That's what we usually do these days. My sister's cooking is a vast improvement on mine. But I shall be back for the New Year.' He glanced at Karen. 'Will you still be here then?'

'Yes.' She noticed that Erica had stopped gazing into the fire and seemed to be listening intently.

'Well I hope it won't be too dull for you. This is a rather quiet place at this time of year, though it gets extremely busy in the summer of course. We're a peace-loving community.'

A quiet and peaceful place was exactly what Karen had been hoping for. 'It'll be just fine,' she assured him. 'My sister and brother-in-law are coming to join us, if they can find a hotel in the area at such short notice.'

'Oh?' He picked up the teapot and refilled her cup. 'Maybe I can help with that. Some friends of mine have a small hotel about three miles from here. It's not luxurious but it's quite comfortable and I can recommend it. They're always busy in the summer months, but at this time of year there are sometimes rooms available.'

'Thank you. Can you give me the details?'

He wrote the information on a piece of paper and hand-ed it to her. This provided Karen with an excuse to call Joan and find out whether it was she who had rung Erica. 'Do you mind if I ring my sister to tell her about it?' she asked him. 'It'll save her wasting time searching for some-where else.'

'Not at all.' Mel accompanied her to the back door

which, as at the cottage, was the best place to get a signal, then left her to make the call.

'Did you speak to Erica this morning?' she asked as soon as Joan answered.

'Yes I did.'

'And?'

'I think I've convinced her that you and the police have been telling the truth. She's absolutely devastated of course; nothing's going to change that. I don't know whether children can ever fully recover from hearing this kind of thing, but I said she could call me any time she wants to talk about it or let off steam. I also told her she shouldn't take her distress out on you.'

Karen felt a strong sense of relief. 'Thanks, Joan you're a star. By the way, Mel's given me the name of a hotel not far from here. If you haven't found anywhere, he says they may still have a room.' She passed on the information about the hotel.

'Karen …' Joan sounded hesitant. 'I think it would be best if you all stay at the cottage for a while. Don't come back straight after Christmas.'

Something in her voice made Karen wary. 'Why do you say that? What's happened?'

'Well, it's um…' Joan was uncharacteristically stammering. 'It's nothing really.'

Karen felt a tug of nervousness. 'It obviously isn't nothing or you wouldn't have mentioned it. Tell me.'

'I'm afraid you won't want to hear it.'

'Go on. You've got to tell me now.'

'When I went to round to check on your house at lunchtime today, I found someone had daubed something… unpleasant on the gateposts in red paint, I won't bother to tell you what it was.'

'Oh God.' This was exactly what Karen had been afraid of. A wave of panic surged through her. She sat down heavily on a kitchen chair. 'Anything else?'

'Nothing else so far as I could see. I've informed the police of course, and they said they're going to investigate. Greg will go round after work and see if he can get the paint off. But it's probably best if you stay where you are while this kind of nastiness is happening.'

'I intend to,' Karen said forcefully. 'It's exactly what I was expecting. That's why we've come here.'

'It probably won't go on for long.' Joan had recovered her normal brisk tone. 'Most people will be far too preoccupied with Christmas to bother harassing you. I expect they'll have forgotten all about it by the New Year.'

'Until Lucy's trial, then it will start all over again,' Karen found herself hoping that Lucy wouldn't be considered fit to go to trial.

'Is everything OK?' Mel asked when she returned to the living room.

'Fine,' she lied. 'I've passed on the hotel details and Joan's going to follow it up.' She was pleased to see that Erica had joined the other two in a noisy game of cards. 'We should get back soon,' she commented, although she was reluctant to leave the cosy warmth of Mel's home

'May I offer you a glass of wine first?'

When she accepted, they went together to the kitchen where he opened a bottle of prosecco. He poured the wine into two glasses and looked at her shrewdly as he handed her one. 'You seem preoccupied. Has something else happened?'

Karen told him about the writing on the gateposts.

He looked grave. 'I suppose it was predictable, but the children shouldn't be exposed to that kind of nastiness and neither should you, Karen. Have you considered my suggestion?'

'What suggestion?'

'That you move away from Moxton.'

'Yes I have considered it, and that's what I've decided to do.' She noticed that his face brightened as she said this. 'I'm going to sell the house as soon as Howard's Will is finalised. I'll ask the solicitor to try and speed up probate so that it can be put in my name. While we're here, I thought I'd look around to see what properties are available in this area. I'll need to check on local schools too, of course.'

Mel beamed. 'That's very good news. Given what's happened, I think moving will be for the best, for all of you.' He went slightly pink. 'Though I must admit to an ulterior motive. I'll be selfishly pleased if you do move here, for my own sake as well as yours.' He raised his glass. 'Your very good health!'

They clinked glasses.

Karen took a sip of the prosecco and savoured its clean, sparkling taste. 'I haven't said anything about moving to the children yet,' she told him. 'They've got more than enough on their plate at the moment. And I'm sure Erica will react badly to the idea of a permanent move. She really misses her friends. She's at an age when she wants to be out and about with other teenagers.'

'Then what about Swansea?' Mel suggested. 'It's a great place, a university town, full of young people, much livelier than Moxton. She'd love it there. You should spend a day or two in Swansea while you're here. Give them a taste of it. There's Christmas markets, ice- skating, plenty for young people to do.'

At that moment, Simon and Erica exploded into the kitchen.

'Mum, he's been cheating,' Erica yelled angrily.

'No I haven't, Poppy gave me the wrong card.'

'No she didn't. Don't blame Poppy. You're a dirty cheat!'

Karen was pleased to see that Erica had reverted, if only temporarily, to her usual stroppy self. 'Finish your game now, we have to get back.'

'Shall we meet on the cliff for a dog walk tomorrow morning?' Mel suggested as they were preparing to leave. 'It'll be like old times.'

An indignant small voice interrupted when Karen agreed. 'Mummy, you said we could go and buy a Christmas tree tomorrow!'

Karen laughed. 'I think we can manage to do both. It can't be a big tree, mind. The cottage is too small. We've got to do a food shop as well.'

'I'll help you find a decent tree,' Mel volunteered. 'But we have to keep the dogs happy. Let's meet on the cliff path at around ten thirty, for their constitutional.'

# Chapter 34

Karen's spirits rose when she opened the curtains the following morning and saw blue rather than leaden skies. They lifted even further when Joan called to say that she had booked a room at the hotel Mel had recommended and that she and Greg would be arriving on the twenty third of December. 'Don't bother trying to get food for Christmas meals,' she told Karen. 'I'll bring all that's necessary.'

Karen went downstairs and put the breakfast things on the table before calling the children. Erica, however, failed to appear. She served the other two then went apprehensively up to her daughter's room. She found Erica sitting, fully dressed, on her bed, gazing at her phone.

'Are you OK, darling?'

Erica looked up with a tragic expression. 'None of them have answered.'

'None of who?'

'None of my friends. I texted them all the day we got here. Ryan hasn't answered either,' she added miserably.

'You haven't heard from Lisa, Melanie or Caroline?'

'No.' Erica's dark eyes glistened with tears.

Karen was dismayed. Erica's three friends had accompanied her on her birthday outing only a few weeks earlier. 'It could be something to do with the bad signal,' she suggested without conviction.

'It's not because of that,' Erica said bitterly. 'Because I did get this.' She handed the phone to Karen.

Karen held the screen at a distance from her eyes (she didn't want to admit that she needed reading glasses) and squinted at the text. It read, *ur dad was a fcking pedo.* Her heart sank. 'Who sent this?'

Erica gave a hollow laugh. 'Gemma, who do you think?'

'Gemma? That's so uncalled for.' Karen's indignation at the spite directed at Erica was nevertheless tinged with satisfaction that Mo might now be aware of Howard's true nature.

'Mum,' Erica wailed, 'it means they've heard what people are saying about Dad. That's why no-one's answered my texts.'

Karen noticed that she was no longer querying the veracity of the claims about Howard. 'You can't be sure that's the case, darling.' She sat down beside Erica on the bed and put an arm round her shoulders.

Erica burst into tears. 'Caroline and Lisa *always* text back immediately and so does Ryan. He seemed so keen, and I really like him, Mum.'

Tears of sympathy pricked Karen's own eyes. Once again she found herself struggling to find appropriate words to comfort her daughter. How many more blows would she have to suffer because of the actions of the father she had adored? 'I'm afraid people often react in hurtful and small-minded ways to this kind of situation,' she murmured for want of anything more helpful to say. 'That's why we're better off staying here, at least for the moment.' She wondered when would be the best time to drop the bombshell about a permanent move.

'It's so hard, Mum,' Erica sobbed against her shoulder.

Karen stroked her thick dark hair. 'I know it is, darling; it's terribly painful and there's no way I would have wished this on you. But we're going to have to be strong. We're *not* going to let ignorant, insensitive people bring us down, do you hear? We *are* going to get over this.'

'How?' Erica hiccupped.

'I promise you there will be other friends, *and* boy-friends, who won't blame you for what your father did. And *they* will be the friends worth having. Oh, and by the way, Auntie Joan and Uncle Greg are arriving in a few days' time.'

Her daughter's face brightened immediately.

'Now,' Karen rose to her feet. 'I want you to come down for breakfast then we're all going for a walk with Mel and Elvis. The fresh air will make you feel better.'

Erica sniffed unenthusiastically, but after a minute she rose from the bed and slowly followed Karen downstairs.

When they met up with Mel, they found he was accompanied by a young girl with an unruly mop of curly ginger hair. 'This is Bryony, my neighbour's daughter,' he told them. 'She's going to join us.'

Fifteen-year-old Bryony was chatty and friendly and she soon engaged Erica in serious discussion about the things that matter to teenage girls. Deep in conversation, the two of them fell rapidly behind as they strolled along the coastal path.

Karen was touched by Mel's thoughtfulness. 'Thank you. That was such a good idea.'

Mel took a ball from his pocket and handed it to Simon. 'Why don't you throw this for Rufus and Elvis? See which of them can catch it first.' He waited until Simon and Poppy had scampered ahead of them, then turned back to Karen. 'I thought Bryony might cheer Erica up. She's a lovely young woman.'

'You didn't tell her about--?'

'About your husband? No, of course not. I thought that while you're here, she could introduce Erica to some of her friends. '

'That would be a godsend.' Karen told him about the text Erica had received from Gemma. 'It's going to be so difficult for them to go back to this kind of nastiness. That text is probably only the start. I haven't told them about the graffiti Joan saw on the gateposts. We may have to stay here longer than I anticipated after Christmas. The sooner we can leave Moxton for good, the better.'

He nodded. 'I think you're right. You haven't mentioned it to them yet?'

'I haven't had the courage. It'll be so hard for them to be uprooted from their home, their friends, everything they've always known. I'm not sure how they're going to take it, especially Erica. She's in a bad enough state as it is.'

Mel fingered his chin. 'Maybe you should familiarise them with the wider area before you say anything. Take them into Swansea for a day; let them see the city sights. It might make the idea more palatable. I could take you all there, if you like, show you what's what. It would be easier than the four of you traipsing round on your own, not knowing where to go.' He paused with a look of embarrassment. 'But I wouldn't want to intrude. You might prefer to go on your own.'

'No,' Karen said quickly. 'We'd appreciate your company. But are you sure you have the time?'

'I don't go to Carmarthen till Christmas Eve, so would tomorrow suit?'

'Tomorrow would be perfect. My sister and brother-in-law are coming the following day.'

He beamed. 'That's settled then.'

'Mel!' Poppy trotted back to them. 'Elvis keeps getting the ball before Rufus.'

Mel laughed. 'That's because it's *his* ball! Is Rufus trying to take it away from him?'

'Yes they're having pretend fights.' Poppy ran off again.

The interruption reminded Karen of an obstacle to the proposed day out. 'Oh, I didn't think. What about Rufus? I can't leave him in the cottage on his own all day.'

'No problem,' Mel assured her. 'You can bring him over to my house beforehand. I have a long-standing arrangement with Bryony and her brother to feed Elvis and take him out whenever I can't be at home. As he and Rufus are such good friends, I'm sure they wouldn't mind looking after the two of them.'

Karen continued the walk in good spirits. It was a bright, crisp winter's day and their shadows created diagonal stripes across the path in front of them. For the first time since they had arrived, the view over Three Cliffs Bay was revealed in all its glory. The horizon was clear and under the low winter sun, the sea appeared to be threaded with strips of glittering tinsel. Other groups of morning strollers called out friendly greetings as they passed.

Before they returned to the cottage, Erica ran breathlessly up to Karen. 'Mum, Bryony's asked me back to hers for lunch. She's meeting some of her friends this afternoon and said I could join them. Can I?'

'Of course you can, as long as you're back before it gets

dark.'

Erica ran to rejoin Bryony.

Poppy pulled on Karen's arm. 'Mummy, you said--'

'Don't worry, Poppy, we'll go and find a Christmas tree as soon as we've had some lunch.'

\* \* \*

The day in Swansea was a resounding success. Mel drove them slowly around the city, pointing out places of interest, then shepherded them on foot through streets and indoor arcades, crowded with Christmas shoppers. He showed them the Grand Theatre, the shops and the large indoor market, and walked them round the Waterfront and Marina. When they were all tired, he took them for a seafood lunch which he insisted on paying for. 'My Christmas treat,' he replied when Karen tried to press money on him.

The restaurant was situated on the top floor of the tallest building in Wales and had magnificent views over Swansea Bay.

'Well, how do you like Swansea?' Mel asked while they were eating their meal.

'Wicked!' declared Simon, his eyes glowing. He was excited by Mel's suggestion that they could go skating on one of the temporary ice rinks before driving back to the cottage.

'It's bigger than Moxton,' Poppy observed, pushing a chip round her plate with a fork.

'Of course it is,' Erica said loftily. 'And it's got much better shops.' She appeared more animated than at any time since their arrival on the Gower. The afternoon she had spent with Bryony and her friends seemed to have taken some of the edge off her distress.

Karen was relieved that they were so taken with the city. She decided she would announce the decision to move to Wales after Joan and Greg arrived, hoping that with Joan's assistance, she would be able to persuade the children of the necessity for it. Worrying about their reaction nonetheless kept her awake for a long period that night. She still anticipated strong resistance from Erica even though she might now appreciate the reason for such a move. She expected Simon to feel anxious about the change but hoped he would accept it without protest. Poppy would probably view the prospect as a treat, without understanding the implications of leaving her familiar home environment for good.

# Chapter 35

Unlike the day before, the twenty third of December was grey and gloomy, and Karen felt sick with nervousness about making her announcement. She rehearsed what she was going to say while clearing up the breakfast things, choosing her words with care to try and minimise the blow. She was almost word-perfect when Erica and Simon came into the kitchen and shut the door behind them.

'Mum,' Simon started hesitantly, 'we've got something to tell you.'

'Oh?' She felt a stab of apprehension. 'What is it?'

'Well, we think, that is, Erica and I think...' He shuffled his feet.

'We think we should stay here,' Erica declared in a loud voice, 'in Wales.'

Karen stared at them in stupefaction. 'You what?'

'We think it would be better if we moved here,' Erica repeated. 'Well, not exactly here, but maybe somewhere nearer to Swansea or in Swansea itself. We don't want to go back to Moxton.' She stared at Karen defiantly. 'And we definitely don't want to go back to Moxton High.'

'What do you think, Mum?' Simon asked worriedly. 'We can't go back to school because--'

Erica finished the sentence for him. 'Because of Dad,

because of what he did.' Her eyes filled with tears.

Karen felt such a rush of relief that at first she couldn't speak. 'But what about your home, your friends?' she stuttered eventually. 'Wouldn't you miss them?'

'*What* friends?' Erica muttered bitterly. 'They're *not* my friends if they've dropped me because of what Dad did.'

'Erica,' Karen said slowly. 'I know you're very upset about your friends not getting in touch, but this isn't a decision to be made lightly on the spur of the moment. It has to be properly considered, thought through.' She remembered that these were almost the same words Joan had used when she had broached the subject. 'You've spent all your life in Moxton. It would be a massive change to move here.'

'I don't care,' Erica snapped. 'I don't want to go back. I want to stay here, where nobody knows us and where nobody knows about Dad.'

Before she could check them, tears began to roll down Karen's cheeks.

Simon clutched her hand. 'Don't be sad, Mum. We don't have to move if you don't want to.'

Karen put an arm around each of them. 'I'm not sad,' she said tremulously. 'I'm relieved. I think you're absolutely right.'

His eyes widened. 'You mean--?'

'Yes, I think moving somewhere in this area would be an excellent idea.'

They gazed at her in astonishment.

'You mean we *can*?' Erica asked incredulously. 'We can leave Moxton?'

'Yes, we can and we will.'

'Wicked!' Simon jumped up and down with excitement.

'When?'

'I'm afraid it may take a while,' Karen warned. 'You must understand that moving here won't be quick or easy. I have to get the Moxton house transferred into my name before putting it on the market. Then we'll need to see what properties are available here and decide where would be the best area to live. We'll have to find a suitable house to buy and work out how to get all our stuff here. We'll also have to find suitable schools--'

'Bryony said her school's brilliant,' Erica interrupted impatiently, clearly bored with the list of complications.

'Yes, well, we can look into that, but--'

'Mel would help,' Simon interjected. 'He knows all about schools and stuff.'

'I know he does, but I don't want you to think that moving here will solve all the problems. We have to face the fact that even here, people could eventually find out about your dad, so we could still face unpleasantness.'

Erica's face fell.

'But that's not going to stop us,' Karen added quickly. 'Remember, you are *not* responsible for what your father did. That has to be your answer if anybody says anything about him to you.'

Simon was trembling with excitement. 'Can I go and tell Poppy?'

'Yes, of course you can.'

Poppy was mystified at the prospect of a permanent move. 'Will we get a new house, Mummy?'

'Yes, but not until we sell the one in Moxton.'

'And can we bring my bed?'

'Yes, we'll bring everything, but it might take a while.'

'Will there be room for my Wendy house?'

'Yes, darling, I'll make that a priority.'

The little girl appeared satisfied with these assurances.

Overcome with emotion, Karen left the three of them together and slipped out of the front door to have a quiet moment on her own. She didn't underestimate the magnitude of the practical and emotional difficulties that lay ahead and didn't discount the possibility, if not probability, that Erica would just as abruptly change her mind about where she wanted to be. And maybe Simon and Poppy would too. For the time being, however, she was overwhelmed with gratitude at being relieved of the burden of unilaterally imposing a life-changing decision on the three of them. It was like a miracle.

As if to order, the clouds abruptly parted and a watery sun illuminated the view spread out before her in all its rugged splendour.

'Are you OK, Mum?' Simon suddenly appeared beside her.

She put an arm round his shoulders. 'Yes, Simon. I am OK. I'm very OK.'